BLACK MOON OVER MALVERN

Rob Kail-Dyke

Copyright © 2021 Rob Kail-Dyke

This book is a work of fiction. Names, characters, businesses, organisations, places and events are either the product of the author's imagination or used fictitiously. Any resemblance to actual persons, living or dead, is entirely coincidental.

All rights reserved. No part of this book may be reproduced, or stored in a retrieval system, or transmitted in any form or by any means, electronic, mechanical, photocopying, recording, or otherwise, without express written permission of the publisher.

ISBN: 9798663417273

CONTENTS

Title Page
Copyright
Prologue
Chapter 1   1
Chapter 2   16
Chapter 3   27
Chapter 4   41
Chapter 5   59
Chapter 6   75
Chapter 7   89
Chapter 8   106
Chapter 9   125
Chapter 10   143
Chapter 11   159
Chapter 12   173
Chapter 13   186
Chapter 14   201
Chapter 15   220
Chapter 16   234
Chapter 17   246
Chapter 18   258

Chapter 19	275
Chapter 20	288
Chapter 21	305
Chapter 22	319
Chapter 23	335
Chapter 24	346
Chapter 25	361
Chapter 26	380
Chapter 27	398
Chapter 28	414
Chapter 29	432
Chapter 30	449
Chapter 31	468
Chapter 32	484
Chapter 33	498
Epilogue	514
For further information...	521

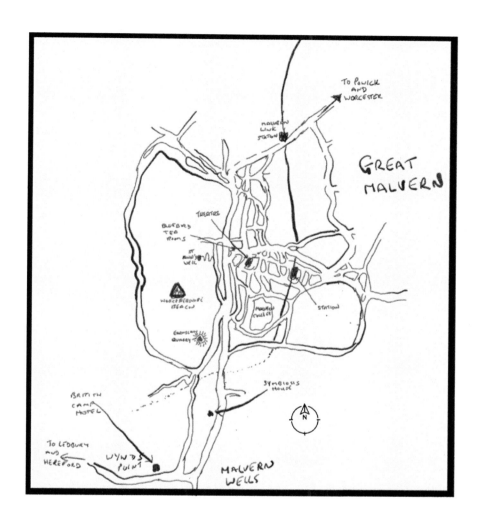

Map of the Malvern Area

PROLOGUE

Tuesday 30th November 1948

11.00 p.m.

It is a moonless night; a pulse of breeze vibrates the leaves of the laurel bushes in the garden. To the rear of Symbiosis House, the hills rise precipitously, forming a backdrop of such intense blackness that the human eye instinctively looks upwards, seeking reassurance from the sky's faint luminescence, above the undulating Malvern ridge. Somewhere, far-off on the Severn plain, a church clock strikes eleven.

After a while, another sound can be heard; just a low hum at first but growing louder as a car approaches, from the direction of Great Malvern, along Wells Road. Then, with a squeal of tyres and a scattering of stones, it sweeps through the gateway and climbs the steep drive, its headlamps raking the pinnacles, crenelations and mullioned windows of the empty house as it crests the hill.

It comes to rest on a gravel concourse in front of the house, the engine falls silent and four men get out. A fifth man: bound, hooded, with his head lolling forward, as if he were sedated, is pulled from the rear of the car. He is half dragged, half carried over the gravel, across a lawn and finally through a narrow gap in the hedge, into a section of the garden, completely encircled by dense evergreens and lit by a single paraffin lamp. There is a deep pit at the centre of the enclosure and a heap of freshly excavated earth beside it.

Foliage shivers in the breeze.

After a few seconds' agitated whispering at the edge of the pit, one of the captors pulls a revolver from his belt and positions its barrel against the side of the prisoner's head. There is a single muffled shot and then the body flops, jelly-like, into the void.

The pit is refilled, and the paraffin lamp is extinguished. The car returns down the steep drive, the glow from its taillights staining the laurel bushes red. The whine of the engine gradually fades to a hum and then it is gone completely.

A solitary dog barks somewhere out on the Severn plain. In the enclosed area the breeze scatters a flurry of dead leaves across freshly turned earth.

CHAPTER 1
Powick Mental Hospital

Wednesday 27th March 1957

7.00 a.m.

'Morning Mr Powell,' said Stanley the gatekeeper; bright and breezy as usual, despite the early hour. He slid the visitors' book under the grille. 'I signed Dr G. in at six-thirty as per usual so he should have a nice brew on the go by now.'

'I need to get a move on,' said Dennis, signing his name in the designated space. 'My motorbike didn't want to start this morning so I'm running a bit late.'

'The old Triumph Tiger? I bet that's got a good few miles on it by now.'

'Yes, and it'll need to do a good few more yet, I can tell you.'

'No plans to replace it then?'

'Not on my wages I'm afraid.'

'The Tiger's not a bad machine though, is it?'

'It's all right once it's bothered to start I suppose.' He slid the book back under the grille.

'By the way,' said Stanley, 'I really enjoyed your last

"Wells and Springs of Old Malvern" column in the Gazette: the one about that underground spring you've been trying to track down.'

'Oh yes, the elusive Chamber Spout. As you could probably tell, it's been the bane of my life for years now.'

Stanley nodded. 'I could tell you were pretty fired up when you wrote it.'

'Frustrated more like. There was I thinking I'd tracked the wretched thing down at last, only to find it was just another red herring.'

'Anyway, it was gripping stuff. By the end, I was getting quite excited about the Chamber Spout myself. I'm sure a lot of other readers felt the same.'

'I doubt it. Jeff Stephenson, my editor, is always threatening to stop printing the "Wells and Springs" column because he doesn't think enough people are interested in it.'

'Well you can tell him from me; he'd be making a big mistake if he did that. It's the first column I turn to every Friday; it's one of the things that makes the Gazette a proper local paper.'

'Well I'm glad to know someone appreciates it,' said Dennis, looking pointedly at his watch. 'Actually, it really is time I was getting along. Dr Gajak will be wondering what's keeping me. He's a proper stickler for punctuality as you know.'

'Oh, don't worry about the time,' said Stanley. 'The tower clock's three minutes slow and the Doc always sets his pocket watch by it as he comes through the gate. If you get a move on, he'll think you've arrived on the dot. Hang on a sec and I'll shift the barrier for you.'

He came out of his kiosk, jangling a bunch of keys. He used one of them to unlock the expandable metal trellis that blocked the arched gateway. It squeaked and rattled as he pulled it back, and then he stood to one side, waving Dennis through with a sweep of his hand.

'I'm pleased to see you're running a tight ship as usual,' said Dennis.

'You can't be too careful in this place. Not that the inmates are a problem; it's the reprobates we keep letting in that bother me,' said Stanley, with a big wink.

Dennis laughed obligingly at the well-worn joke before hurrying away across the courtyard.

Dr Gajak was pouring himself a cup of tea as Dennis entered his consulting room. 'Ah Dennis,' he said, looking up. 'You're a little late.'

'Am I?'

'You are indeed. That clock in the courtyard isn't to be relied on at all. I prefer to synchronise with the pips on the wireless at six o' clock.'

'Old Stanley's under the impression you swear by the tower clock.'

'Is he now?' said Gajak, smiling. 'But then I suppose it's only natural he'd think I stop to set my watch when, in fact, I'm just checking how far adrift of Greenwich Mean Time it is. Do you know; it was seven minutes slow a month ago but oddly, over the last few days, it's started to catch up again?' He took a sip from his china cup. 'I expect that makes me sound rather compulsive, doesn't it?'

'It does a bit. What would Sigmund Freud say about that sort of thing?'

'Oh, Freud has some extremely interesting things to say about clocks.' He chuckled to himself as he leaned forward to pour a cup of tea for Dennis. 'In one of his lectures on neuroses, he described the clock as a symbol of female genitalia, which puts an interesting slant on my little obsession, doesn't it?

'I'm sure it does,' said Dennis, blushing.

'Sorry, it's probably not an appropriate topic for so early in the morning. Anyway, it's time we got down to business - you said, on the phone, that you'd made a significant discovery.'

'Well it seemed significant yesterday but now I'm not so sure.'

Gajak placed his cup back on its saucer and scrutinised Dennis through small gold-rimmed spectacles. He sported a neat white beard that made him look a lot like Sigmund Freud and, as if to stress the resemblance, a framed print of the great man hung on the wall, directly behind him. Alongside it was a matching picture of Carl Gustav Jung who appeared to have spurned the archetypal psychiatrist's beard in favour of a discreet moustache.

'But you were full of it when you phoned so why the sudden doubts?'

'I'm worried I'm wasting your time. You must have far more important things to do than listening to me go on about my latest bit of research.'

'That's nonsense Dennis and you know it. If you recall, *I* was the one who initiated these chats of ours, after reading one of your excellent articles in the Malvern Gazette, and you were kind enough to indulge me by agreeing to give up an hour of your valuable time, every week. It's no exaggeration to say that, without these sessions, I would probably have gone as mad as some of the poor devils I'm paid to treat. The world of wells and springs is a perfect antidote to the tribulations of my work and I'm deeply grateful that you continue to indulge me - especially as it always requires you to get up so early in the morning.' In his vehemence, a faint Polish accent had crept into his otherwise impeccable English tones.

'Sorry.'

'There's no need to apologise; I just want you to appreciate how much your visits mean to me that's all. Now, could this sudden twinge of self-doubt have anything to do with that irascible father of yours?'

'Possibly.'

'Have you been arguing again?'

Dennis nodded.

'So, what was it about this time?'

'Nothing very dramatic; not on the face of it anyway. I'd just discovered a family connection with Malvern's spa town history, and I thought I'd see if he could tell me any more about it.'

'A new discovery eh? I'm surprised; I thought you'd exhausted that line of enquiry years ago.'

'You can never know everything about a subject though, can you? Anyway, most of my previous research has focused on the mid-nineteenth century period - the Wilson and Gully era. Recently though, I've been concentrating on a lesser-known period: the late 1880s and early 1890s, when hydropathy went through a brief revival.'

'Of course, the famous Malvern water cure had gone out of fashion before that, hadn't it?'

'Yes, Dr Wilson died in 1867 and Dr Gully retired at about the same time. They'd been its main exponents so there was no-one left to drive it forward anymore.'

'But you're saying business picked up again at the end of the 1880s?'

'Yes and, amazingly, it seems that the man responsible

for this brief resurgence was my grandfather, Henry Powell.'

'Really? How fascinating. So how did all this come to light then?'

'I was looking in the newspaper archives. I vaguely knew that one or two new establishments had popped up at the end of the 1880s but, until this week, I hadn't got around to checking it any further. A few of the local histories mention the revival in passing but I'm not aware of any detailed research into it. I've only managed to scratch the surface myself so far.'

'But you've gleaned enough to prove that your grandfather was involved?'

'Oh yes, I can prove that all right. The first reference I came across was an advertisement for The St Werstan Spa Hotel in an edition of the Malvern Gazette from October 1888. It described the various hydropathy treatments on offer there, including wet packing, the Sitz Bath and the Douche; you know the sort of thing. It claimed the establishment had received glowing testimonials from many satisfied patients, not least those sent by eminent visitors from the birthplace of hydropathy itself; Gräfenberg in Austria. The thing that leapt out at me though was the name underneath, "Henry Powell, Proprietor".'

'It's not a particularly unusual name though, is it? There could easily have been other Henry Powells living in Malvern at that time, so how could you be sure it was your grandfather?'

'I couldn't, that's why I went through the rest of the newspaper to see if I could find anything else. I didn't have much time because I was doing it between reports and I knew that Jeff, my editor, would start asking questions if I didn't get back to my desk soon. Fortunately, something interesting caught my eye almost straightaway; a headline that said,

"Owner of successful spa hotel elected as new chairman of Malvern Chamber of Commerce." Reading on, I found that this was Henry Powell again and there was even a mention of his address; Santa Rosa, Foley Terrace. That's the house my father eventually inherited and where my parents now live.'

'Was that where you lived as well?'

'No, we lived in Graham Road while I was growing up. Henry died in 1921 but my grandmother Rosamund carried on living at the house in Foley Terrace for another twenty odd years after that. My parents moved there a few months after she died in 1945.'

'So, having confirmed it *was* your grandfather who'd owned the St Werstan Spa Hotel, you decided to pick your father's brains about it?'

'That's right. I knew it was going to cause trouble but who else was I going to ask? The thing is, he'll pick an argument with you about anything: the colour of your tie; the way you just cleared your throat; some innocuous remark you made five years ago. He seems to thrive on conflict so nothing's too petty for him. He's the same with everyone: me; my brother Nigel who's a detective inspector; Nigel's wife Judith. Even Susan, my sister, gets a tongue-lashing from him on the rare occasions he sees her. Worst of all, he's like it with my mother too and she's forced to live with him all the time. How she puts up with it I honestly don't know. It's obvious now that I should just have avoided the subject, but unfortunately curiosity got the better of me and yesterday evening, when I called round on one of my dutiful visits, I asked him what he knew about Henry's time at the St Werstan Spa Hotel.'

'And I take it the question didn't go down too well?'

'Not at all, in fact it made him as angry as I've ever seen him – worse possibly.'

'Even though you were only asking him about your family history.'

'I know; it's ridiculous, isn't it?'

'So, what did he say?'

'Nothing at first. He just went red in the face and looked at me aghast as if I'd said the most awful thing imaginable. The silence didn't last long though; after a few seconds, he launched into a furious tirade, laden with expletives.'

'Goodness me, I hope your mother wasn't around.'

'No, she'd gone out to see one of the neighbours. Not that she'd have been particularly bothered by the swearing though, because, as I said before, we've all been on the receiving end of his outbursts at one time or another; it was his tone of voice and the venomous glint in his eye that would really have shocked her.'

'You still haven't told me what he actually said.'

'Well, sparing you the colourful language, it went along the lines of: "How dare you ask me about that. You make me sick. I won't have you dredging up my family's past, just so that you can spew it out in that filthy rag of yours, for all and sundry to see. Why don't you crawl back into the sewer with all the other members of your so-called profession, and leave me alone?"'

'Nasty.'

'It certainly was, and if you'd been there and seen the look on his face, you'd have found it even nastier, I can assure you.'

'What did you say?'

'Nothing at all because, at that very moment, we heard my mother turning her key in the front door. By the time she'd come in, he'd picked up his book and started to read as if nothing had happened. I'm sure she knew something was wrong though because it must have been written all over my face.'

'But she didn't comment?'

'No, she simply announced that she was going to put the kettle on and went out into the kitchen. Anything for a quiet life I suppose.'

'Why do you think the question upset him so much?'

'I haven't got a clue but something about it obviously touched a raw nerve.'

'How old would your grandfather have been when he died?'

'In his mid-fifties I think. The circumstances of his death were pretty dramatic actually: Henry fell into Gullet Quarry while he was out walking on the hills. The coroner gave a verdict of Accidental Death.'

'That must have been traumatic for everyone.'

'I'm sure it was but, to be honest, I didn't really take it in at the time.'

'You were still quite young I suppose.'

'Yes, I was ten, Nigel was seven and Susan was just three.'

'But I daresay your father was pretty shaken up by it?'

'I don't actually recall him being particularly upset but he was suddenly desperate for us to move away from Malvern, I do remember that much.'

'To escape from its unhappy associations, presumably.'

'I'm sure you're right. He kept saying he was going to find a job in another town, the further away the better. He just wanted to sell our house and move on.'

'Remind me what your father did for a living.'

'He's still working actually, even though he's well past retirement age. He's manager of a wine and spirits merchants, Thomas Radford and Sons in Church Street.'

'So, he was confident he could get a job doing that somewhere else?'

'With good cause, I think. Remember, it was only three years after the end of the Great War so men of working age - especially those with his experience – were in short supply.'

'But presumably you didn't move in the end.'

'No.'

But why not, if he was so keen?'

'Because of me, or, to be precise, because of my poor health. I've had chronic bronchial problems since I was small. I'm a lot better now but, when I was very young, I'd often be hunched over, gasping for every breath. It was terrifying because I always thought I was going to suffocate and die. I saw lots of doctors but none of them were any good. They took the view that it was all in my mind and if I could only learn to relax a bit more, the symptoms would go away.'

'A psychosomatic condition. Sadly, that's how asthma tended to be regarded back then; it still is, to some extent, even now.'

'But when I turned eight, I started seeing a Dr Patterson who was quite young and more inclined to treat it as a physical condition rather than a mental one. My asthma attacks were less frequent after that, and a lot less severe. He completely changed my life.'

'And if you'd moved away, you wouldn't have been able to see him anymore.'

'That's right. My mother regarded Dr Patterson as our saviour. She'd been at her wits' end about me until then but now; at last, she could relax and not worry that my next attack would be the one that carried me off. She was adamant she wasn't going to risk a move that might jeopardise my improved health.'

'And so, she stood her ground with your father?'

'Yes, and it must have been really hard for her. They had blazing rows about it all the time.'

'Did he focus any of that anger on you?'

'No, not immediately, I think the anger came much later. To start with, he was just more remote. He hadn't had much time for any of us before, but now we saw even less of him. He always seemed to be at work: we were usually still asleep when he left, and in bed again by the time he came back in the evening.'

'So how did you feel during that time?'

'Relieved at first but then I started to feel guilty because I knew I was preventing him from doing what he wanted.'

'Even though your illness was the real culprit, not you?'

'I see that now but, as a ten-year-old child, I wasn't capable of making the distinction. I just blamed myself.'

'And is that still the case?'

'I expect so but...'

'But what?'

'Are you sure you really want to continue this?' said Dennis hesitantly.

'Of course, why do you ask?'

'Because, you once told me to stop you, if you ever lapsed into professional mode?'

Gajak smiled. 'Ah yes, so I did. And, suddenly, here I am, sounding just like the typical psychiatrist.'

'It doesn't matter to me,' said Dennis, 'but you were so insistent about it, when we started having these meetings, that I thought I'd better remind you.'

'Quite right too. As I said at the time: normal conversation is such a blessed relief to me after hours of listening to patients or discussing cases with colleagues, that the last thing I want is for our precious meetings to become just a continuation of that.'

'So, do you still want me to answer your question?'

'Why not?' said Gajak with a shrug. 'After all, rules were made to be broken, weren't they?'

'In which case, the answer is yes, I *do* still feel guilty. What's more, my father knows that very well and he never fails to take full advantage of it.'

'So, give me an example.'

'All right, this is a good one I think: during the war my brother Nigel served with the 7th Battalion of the Worcestershire Regiment. I'd been declared unfit for military service because of my respiratory problems so I spent the entire war, here, in Malvern. While he was away fighting, the rest of us used to gather at my parents' house for a family tea every Sunday. There'd be me, Nigel's wife Judith and my parents of course. My sister Susan was part of it as well at the beginning but after her husband James was invalided back from the Far East, she didn't come any more. I think these teas were supposed to engender a spirit of family solidarity, but I always hated them because gatherings like that are anathema to me. They obviously meant a lot to Judith and my mother though, so I gritted my teeth and went along with it for their sake. Every few weeks I'd arrive to find my parents in a state of high excitement, and I'd know straightaway that it was because they'd just received one of Nigel's' letters from the front. When we'd finished eating our tea, my father would make a big point of reading it out to us.

'Nigel wrote back from the front as often as he could to describe what was going on. He's got a good way with words and I wouldn't have minded listening if it hadn't started to become obvious that my father was using the letters to get at me.'

'Get at you how?'

'It was subtle in a way I suppose but it hit its mark all the same: whenever he'd read out a section referring to casualties they'd suffered or to the harsh conditions they were enduring, he'd make a point of pausing for a few seconds to fix me with one of his gimlet-eyed stares.'

'Presumably, to make you feel bad about the fact that you weren't having to endure those things as well.'

'Exactly.

'And, furthermore, reminding you that that your illness had been, and still was, a real irritation to him because it had once prevented him from moving away from Malvern.'

'I'm sure that's right.'

'He sounds like a proper bully, and, going by what you said earlier, an indiscriminate one.'

'That's right, over the years we've all been subjected to it, one way or another. He's got a different excuse for each member of the family: He regularly gets nasty with Judith because he's convinced she's trying to turn Nigel against him, which is complete rubbish because Judith's not like that at all. Then he starts haranguing Nigel for being too weak to stand up to her. My mother's constantly getting it in the neck because he thinks she's got divided loyalties and fails to give him the support he thinks he's entitled to. The way she sided with me over my illness all those years ago is probably just one of many instances he throws back at her. And last, but not least, Susan blotted her copybook because she married a man he inherently disliked and distanced herself from her family in the process.'

'He's incorrigible, isn't he?'

'He certainly is. That's why I should have known better than to ask him about my grandfather and the St Werstan Spa Hotel. It was bound to cause more problems than it was worth.'

'Oh, I don't know,' said Gajak, distractedly checking his pocket watch and then glancing at the clock on the wall.

'Sorry,' said Dennis 'I've kept you longer than I should have done, haven't I?'

'Not at all. I'd be more than happy to talk about this for another hour if I could but unfortunately duty calls and I have to get along to my next appointment.'

He got up; stretched as if to ease his back and then walked stiffly over to his desk.

'For what it's worth,' he said, as he gathered up papers and slid them into a brown leather briefcase. 'I don't think you were mistaken at all in raising the subject with your father; I think your instincts are leading you towards an inevitable, and very necessary, catharsis.'

'What sort of catharsis?'

'The *only* sort,' said Gajak, peering down him. 'A purging process that draws out the truth. It won't happen without a fair bit of kicking and screaming but, in asking your father about the St Werstan Spa Hotel, I'm sure that's the course on which you're now set.'

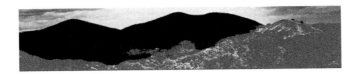

CHAPTER 2
Relics of Sabrina

Wednesday 27th March 1957

8.30 a.m.

As he parked his motorbike in Pierrepoint Terrace, Dennis weighed up whether to do battle with the jammed side door to his first-floor flat, or simply go in through Relics of Sabrina, the antiquarian book and map shop below. In the end, he decided to go through the shop. Mr Winstanley, his landlord and the proprietor of Relics of Sabrina, was in early as usual and the shop bell clanged as Dennis pushed open the door and entered the dark and musty space inside. Through the gloom, he could just make out Mr Winstanley, sitting behind a trestle table towards the rear of the shop, sorting through teetering piles of old books. He looked up as Dennis approached. His eyes were rheumy and the glow from a single overhead bulb cast a jaundiced sheen over his grizzled features.

'You must have been up with the lark this morning,' he said. 'I was just coming out of the newsagents at around six forty-five and I saw you riding off down Church Street like a bat out of hell.' He had the husky voice of a twenty-a-day man, though Dennis had never actually seen him smoke. He thought it probably had more to do with all those years inhaling dust; an occupational hazard for anyone in the antique maps and books trade.

'I had to be over in Powick for seven,'

'The early bird catches the worm eh?'

'Something like that.'

'What were you doing over there then?'

'Oh, just work. The usual sort of thing really.'

'Is it going to make the next front page of the Gazette?'

'More like page twenty I should think; somewhere between the obituaries and the WI reports.'

'Still, it's not a bad way to earn a crust, is it?'

'It's all right but I wouldn't mind doing what you do either: I always think selling old books and maps must be a first-rate way to make a living.'

'Make a living? That's a joke. If it wasn't for the rent you pay me for that flat of yours, I'd have gone under years ago.'

'That reminds me,' said Dennis. 'I don't suppose you've had a chance to look at my side door yet have you? The last time I went in that way I had to shunt it three times with my shoulder before it would budge. I'm afraid I'll knock it off its hinges if I carry on like that.'

Winstanley shook his head. 'Sorry, I've been busy. I'm not sure if I told you but I was at that big antiquarian book, cartographic and ephemera fair in Cheltenham last week and I came back with a van full.' He extended his arm to indicate the overflowing crates and cardboard boxes lined up along one side of the shop. 'I've hardly made a dent in it yet. I'll try and look at the door later.'

'I'd be glad if you would. The door might survive a bit

longer but I'm not sure my shoulder will.'

'Point taken. By the way, talking of that antiquarian fair: I picked up a few items there that might be of interest to you. Now where did I put them?'

He got up, opened the doors of a tall, wardrobe-like cupboard behind him and scanned the haphazard piles of books and papers inside.

'Did you hear about the body that's been found?' he said as he climbed onto a chair to survey the cupboard's upper shelves.

'Found where?'

'Up in Malvern Wells, at Symbiosis House; the place where that psychiatrist, Mathias Friedman used to live.'

'A body?' said Dennis as he absorbed the full significance of what he'd just heard. 'You mean a *dead* body?'

'Of course, is there any other kind? I found out about it as I was coming down through the Priory churchyard earlier on. I heard a police car going along Wells Road like the clappers with its bell ringing. I asked this bloke who was sweeping up by the church door what was going on and he told me what I just told you, that a body had been found at Symbiosis House.'

'How did he know that if the police were only just on their way?'

'Don't ask me, I'm just telling you what happened. He could have been making it up I suppose but, seeing as he was wearing an ecclesiastical robe, I assumed he was a religious type, so I took him to be telling the truth… ah, here it is.' He reached into the depths of the cupboard, making the chair he was standing on lurch forward precariously on two legs. Then, clutching a bundle of items close to his chest and with an agility that belied his decrepit appearance, he jumped down onto the floor.

'Symbiosis House is empty now isn't it?' said Dennis as Winstanley placed his finds on the table and sat down again.

'It has been for years, ever since the army gave it up after the war.'

'I didn't know the army was ever there.'

'Oh yes, they requisitioned it as a military training centre around 1943, a few years after Friedman disappeared. There were a load of boffins there for a while, training soldiers how to use new-fangled wireless equipment. After they went, in forty-seven, the place was closed up.'

'What happened to Friedman exactly? Didn't things turn a bit nasty for him?'

'That's putting it mildly. The war had just started, and he was German, wasn't he? Well Austrian anyway; back then, people thought it amounted to the same thing. Of course, the crazy thing is that everyone thought the sun shone out of his arse before that: famous psychiatrist doing good everywhere; holding all those fancy parties up at Symbiosis House and his smiling mug all over the newspapers. Then Germany went and invaded Poland and it all went sour for him. You were still in Malvern at the time, weren't you? You must remember what happened?'

'My mind's a bit blank about that period,' said Dennis.

'Well you can take it from me, it all got pretty ugly: a big mob went on the rampage up there, brandishing pitch forks, pick-axe handles, and goodness knows what else. The police were called but, from what I hear, they didn't go out of their way to put a stop to it. Friedman was never seen again after that and I've never met anyone who knows what happened to him or, at least, is prepared to say. It could be his body they've just found up there for all I know and there'll be quite a few others round here, thinking the same.'

'I expect I'll find out more when I get into the office. Someone from the Gazette's bound to be onto it.'

'Probably that skinny reporter you work with, what do they call him? The Whippet isn't it?'

'Brian Fairclough you mean? Yes, I'm sure it will.'

'You chose the wrong place to be this morning, over in Powick. Not much use being the early bird if the worm's popped up somewhere else is it?'

'Not really,' said Dennis, keen to change the subject. 'Anyway, what about this stuff you've got for me?'

'Oh yes,' said Winstanley, looking down at the pile in front of him, 'I don't know how useful any of it actually is but there might be a couple of items that interest you.'

He lifted a book from the top of the pile and handed it to Dennis. 'This is a copy of "Fotheringham's Survey of Malvern's Water Features" published in 1846. I don't know if you've got it already; I shouldn't think so, it's quite rare.'

Dennis pulled up a chair and sat down opposite him. He flicked through the yellowing pages, releasing yet another cloud of dust in the process. 'No I haven't. I've seen extracts from it quoted in later works, but I've never set eyes on the original before. It's marvellous, thanks very much.'

Winstanley passed him the next volume. 'And this is "The Hydropathic Gazetteer" for 1843. I think I found you one from 1847 before but this looks as if it might have some different material in it.'

Nodding enthusiastically as he opened it at random pages, Dennis said, 'Again, it's just what I've been after. It covers the early period, not long after Gully and Wilson opened their first water cure clinics in Malvern, so I can see it providing some really useful background information for my column in the Gazette.'

'That's good then. Now this one is probably the crème de la crème, that's why I've saved it 'til last.' He passed a slim, leather-bound volume across the table. He waited a few seconds while Dennis perused its contents and then he said, 'I bet you've never seen this before, have you?'

Dennis looked up, slowly shaking his head, partly in answer to the question and partly in sheer astonishment. 'I had no idea this even existed.'

'I know,' said Winstanley, plainly delighted with the reaction he'd elicited, 'but it's just the sort of thing you'd have written if you'd been around then isn't it. I think you must have a nineteenth century doppelganger.'

'Dennis turned back to the title page, running his fingers over the gothic script as he read it aloud,

'Hidden Realms of Rock and Water

Malvern's Subterranean Hydro Chambers:
Myth or Reality?

By

Nathanial Byng-Hawley

1837

Byng–Hawley - I've never come across him before.'

'He's new to me as well and, as far as I could see, there's no biographical information about him in there at all.'

'Fascinating,' said Dennis. 'And you're right, this *is* the sort of thing I might have written back then; in fact, a few months ago, I wrote an article on much the same subject; it was about a particular underground chamber spring - I tend to refer to it as the Chamber Spout - that's rumoured to exist somewhere in Malvern Wells.'

'It might be time for an update then.'

'Possibly, but it all depends on how close Byng–Hawley actually comes to answering the myth or reality question.' He turned the brittle pages again as he spoke. 'I won't know that until I get a chance to read it properly later.'

'Interesting though isn't it?'

'*Very* interesting. Thanks very much.'

'No problem; I'm glad you like it.'

Dennis glanced at his watch. 'Goodness, it's ten to nine. I'd better show my face in the office soon or there'll be hell to pay. How much do I owe you for these by the way?'

'Don't worry about that,' said Winstanley. 'Let's call it recompense for your inconvenience over the door.'

Dennis took the side exit from the shop into the hall and stairway that led up to his first floor flat. A chemical smell from the dry cleaners next door mingled with the aromas of stale cooking and fusty carpet. He turned a Yale key in the door at the top of the stairs and let himself in.

His flat was strikingly bright after the murk of Winstanley's shop. The area that served as his combined sitting room and dining area had a single sash window, providing a view of a Victorian terrace across the road and, beyond it, the Malvern ridge; radiantly green in the morning sunshine, stretching away, in all its undulating glory, towards the south-west. It was a panorama that had provided him with solace and inspiration during some of his lowest periods and he never tired of gazing at it. As he went over to the window to soak it up once again, he tripped over a foot-high stack of books and papers in the middle of the floor. He grabbed the wing of an armchair to steady himself and turned to survey the chaos of his domestic life.

There were similar piles everywhere: some of them

were simply an accumulation of random reading material but others represented specific projects he'd begun at various stages; some of which, to varying degrees, he was still engaged in and others that had fallen by the wayside. He sat down, perching his latest acquisitions on the arm of the chair, and started to examine the heap of documents that had just caused him to lose his footing. He could tell straightaway that this related to the matter he'd just been discussing with Mr Winstanley. The item perched right at the top was a half-folded map of the Malvern area. As he opened it up he recalled that it was the work of an obscure local cartographer called Francis Copley and dated from the early 1850s. It was one of his own discoveries rather than something his landlord had procured: he'd found it a couple of years ago, at the bottom of a box of otherwise unremarkable old maps, in an antique shop in Ledbury. He smiled as he remembered his close friend Margaret's increasingly disgruntled expression that day as he'd dragged her into yet another dismal emporium that stank of the past. It was supposed to have been a pleasant summer Saturday motorcycle tour around the Herefordshire countryside, ending with afternoon tea at the Copper Kettle in Bromyard but somehow, they'd never progressed beyond the junk shops of Ledbury. Afternoon tea had ultimately been a quick stop at a mobile snack bar on the A449 where they'd leaned against the Triumph Tiger, drinking out of cardboard cups. His smile turned to a frown as he concluded that it probably hadn't been his finest hour. He often wondered why Margaret continued to put up with him.

    The map was a smudgy monochrome affair, printed on thick sandy coloured paper that was meant to resemble ancient parchment; presumably to lend it some historical gravitas. This pretension was unnecessary because Copley was, without doubt, one of the most proficient mapmakers Dennis had come across from that period. Despite the crude printing technique, there was a huge amount of detail: the contours of hills and valleys were precisely represented; roads, tracks, railway lines, rivers and streams were easily distinguished, and towns, villages and hamlets were shown as the sums of their parts, comprising clusters and threads of minute, individually plotted buildings. But where Copley particularly excelled himself was in the unusual and, as far as Dennis knew, unique way he portrayed an assortment of "special features." The items he designated in this way, and which he elucidated in an elaborate "Legend" panel at the foot of the map were, to Dennis' mind, not only fascinating but utterly revealing about the cartographer's interests and personality. They made him regard Francis Copley as a kindred spirit.

Copley had designed around fifty symbols to show subtle distinctions – in some cases; very subtle indeed - between the springs and wells to be found on, and around, the Malvern Hills. Some were grouped according to the feature's historical significance, for instance; if it was reputed to have had a ceremonial or ritualistic function at some stage in the past. If this were the case, then the period – Iron Age; Roman; Mediaeval or whatever – would be revealed through each specific symbol's design: "Roman Ceremonial," for example, was represented by a water jar inside an olive wreath, though, because of the poor quality of the printing, a magnifying glass was required to pick out such details. Others were placed in a topographical category and each was differentiated according to criteria such as: whether it had been adopted as a "Civic Amenity," meaning people continued to use it as a free source of Malvern water, or as a "Civic Ornament" where it had taken on a primarily decorative function. More enigmatically, the topographical section included symbols for "Hidden Feature," signified by a skeletal tree superimposed on a human eye and, "Subterranean Feature," where a stylised water droplet was contained within the outline of a hill. If a feature had a joint historical and topographical significance, the two appropriate symbols would be interlocked – in these instances, a magnifying glass was even more necessary.

To Dennis though, the most interesting symbol of all was a depiction of cascading water inside an egg-shaped capsule. It was labelled, "Chamber Spring." Chamber springs, as the name suggested, were springs that burst forth inside underground hollows and then flowed away through a natural drainage system. According to the map, there were five of these; the most famous example having been uncovered during the excavation of the first railway tunnel under the hills in 1852 and subsequently becoming a major source of water for the town, aided by the installation of a steam powered pump. One of the others, however - the one Dennis called the Chamber Spout - was known about, but its precise location had faded into obscurity. Copley's map indicated that it was in the Malvern Wells area, but the symbol was too big, relative to the map's scale, to pinpoint the spring's precise location. There were lots of theories about where it *might* be but, so far, nothing conclusive. Dennis put the map down and then, with a trembling hand, reached for the thin, leather bound volume, "Hidden Realms of Rock and Water," that was balanced on the arm of his chair. Maybe this was the document that would finally reveal the truth. He'd been intending to save reading it until later when he'd have more time but suddenly, despite needing to head off to work, he decided it couldn't wait.

He needn't have been too worried about the delay though because it him took less than five minutes to establish that the thirty-five sparsely printed pages were not going to provide the proof he'd been hoping for. Scanning through them, he could tell they contained nothing but hearsay, half-truths and flimsy speculation, and it was clear that Nathaniel Byng-Hawley had come no closer to pinning down the precise location of the Chamber Spout than he had.

With a resignation learned from countless similar disappointments in the past, he placed the book on top of one of the nearby piles, got out of his chair and headed for the door.

CHAPTER 3
Malvern Gazette

Wednesday 27th March 1957

9.10 a.m.

The Gazette offices were in Langland Parade, just around the corner from Dennis' flat. As he went in through the main entrance at ten past nine he almost collided with Brian "the Whippet" Fairclough, resplendent in dogtooth tweed jacket over a red and yellow Argyle sweater.

'Where's the fire?' said Dennis.

The Whippet had already surged past, but he turned, mid-stride and said, 'It's a big story. The police are crawling all over Symbiosis House, up in Malvern Wells, someone's dug up human remains in the garden there.' His eyes were darting impatiently in all directions; his wiry frame poised to move on.

'I know, my landlord told me half an hour ago. Why aren't you up there then?'

'I just nipped back to brief Jeff and to get that lazy lump of a photographer, Larry Frazer, up there, ASAP.'

'What else do you know?'

'Nothing yet. The police are being tight-lipped as usual, but they probably know bugger all anyway. A lot of people think it's the body of that Kraut psychiatrist who disappeared in the war but, you know me: I don't deal in rumours, I only deal in facts.'

With that, he was gone.

Dennis carried on through the vestibule and into the big, ground-floor room that served as a newsroom for seven reporters. It was a labyrinth of desks, filing cabinets, bookshelves and storage cupboards. The only person there now was Julian Croft, the theatre correspondent. He was hunched over his desk, typing fluently and shrouded in a haze of smoke from one of his pungent French cigarettes. He gave no sign of noticing that anyone else had entered the room; and continued to tap away on his typewriter as Dennis squeezed past. He was humming quietly to himself and seemed totally engrossed in completing a review of whichever show he'd been to see the previous evening. But then, as soon as Dennis had sat down at the desk behind him, he swung round and sang lustily, in a rich baritone,

'"Your eyes beseech me in the moonlight
Reveal the yearning in your heart
Those words unsaid that make me bright
And tell me that we'll never part"'

Not quite knowing how to react to the performance, Dennis shrank back into his chair.

'Sorry,' said Julian, stifling a chuckle. 'I'm obviously embarrassing you.' He inhaled deeply from his cigarette before breathing out a perfect smoke ring. 'I was at the Festival Theatre last night, for the premiere of Princess Apple Blossom, written by my old friend Vernon McPherson. That's one of the songs; it's been going around in my head for hours now, so, once I realised I'd got company, I couldn't resist giving it a quick blast. Sadly though, I can tell my spontaneous rendition has discombobulated you somewhat. I wasn't *really* serenading you; I promise.'

'Don't worry. You just made me jump that's all.'

'I know; I know. I'm afraid my naturally exuberant nature is forever getting me into trouble. Having said that, I'm not going to let old Vernon off the hook so easily; it's his fault for turning out such an insanely catchy tune.'

'Is that his real name, Vernon McPherson?'

Julian launched another smoke ring and watched appreciatively as it floated away towards the window on the other side of the room. 'I'm not sure. It sounds made up doesn't it but then he *does* come from a theatrical family. They probably decided to give him a stage name at birth to save him the bother of adopting one later.'

'It sounds as if you had an enjoyable evening anyway.'

'Not really,' said Julian with a sigh. 'None of the other songs were as good as that I'm afraid. In fact, most of them were downright awful – dirge-like is probably the best way to describe them.'

'Oh dear.'

'*Oh dear* indeed and it's left me with a classic dilemma: do I speak the truth, or do I compromise my journalistic integrity to spare the feelings of a dear old friend?'

He stubbed out his cigarette and then raked both hands through his thick brown hair. It was cut in a style that Dennis always thought of as foppish and which, at a distance, made him look about twenty years younger than the sixty he almost certainly was.

'Is that the review you're working on now?' asked Dennis.

'It's the one I've been working on since seven o'clock this morning, as my wastepaper basket will testify,' said Julian, indicating the overflowing receptacle next to his desk. 'This is version five I'm writing now; versions one to four have been filed in the bin. The long and the short of it is that professionalism is finally winning out over sentimentality which means I'll have to soothe Vernon's damaged ego with numerous G and T's after this has gone to press.'

He lit another cigarette. 'Anyway, changing the subject, did you happen to see the Whippet as you came in? Now there's a man on a mission if ever I saw one.'

I know. He almost knocked me flying. He was rushing

back to Symbiosis House where this body is supposed to have turned up.'

'The body of Mathias Friedman: that's what they're saying isn't it?'

'And do you agree?'

'Not really. What about you?'

'I don't have an opinion either way. In fact, my landlord had to remind me what had happened because I'd forgotten all about it. He was hounded out for being a Nazi sympathiser, wasn't he?'

'That's right, but there was never any suggestion of foul play – well, not at the time anyway.'

'I think my landlord would differ with you about that. He's convinced the body's Friedman's.'

'But would he have thought that, two years ago; before the Gazette decided to whip the story up again?'

'What do you mean?'

'Don't you remember? It all started because of a feud between a couple of local estate agents. We did a big splash on it, two weeks running.'

'Sorry, I've got no recollection of it at all.'

'I'm amazed. Is that because you were off on holiday or something?'

'I doubt it. I was probably just engrossed in other things. Maybe I was busy doing research in the library or down in the archives; that's the most likely explanation.'

'Well it must have been pretty damned absorbing for you to have missed all that, but there we are. Anyway, it all started because that big agents on Bellevue Terrace, Trubshaw and Co., had a millionaire client who was keen to buy up some of the bigger hillside residences and establish a string of prestige hotels. Three of the four properties he'd got his eye on were with Trubshaw and Co. and the deals on those were done quite quickly, but the fourth, Symbiosis House - the one he liked most of all - was with their competitors, Crawford, Davies and Withers. He was a busy man and he didn't have the time to be dealing with two estate agents, so he set Trubshaw and Co. the task of negotiating with Crawford, Davies and Withers, on his behalf, to secure his fourth and final purchase. What he hadn't realised, however, was that, although Symbiosis House was lying vacant, it wasn't officially for sale. Naturally, being immersed in the local property market, Trubshaw and Co. knew this very well but, in their eagerness to pull off four big sales, they'd decided to gloss over the matter with their rich client. Anyway, they were confident that the generous offer they'd be putting on the table would be more than enough to clear any petty obstacles out of the way, but they soon found out how wrong they were. Crawford, Davies and Withers made it crystal clear that they wouldn't be negotiating with them.'

He stubbed his cigarette end in the ashtray, and immediately lit another before continuing.

'The reason they gave – and this is how they were quoted in the Gazette - was that, "due to historical circumstances, current ownership could not be clearly established, so they'd been instructed to keep the property off the market until the situation could be clarified." Are you honestly saying you don't remember any of this?'

'Yes,' replied Dennis. 'So, what happened next?'

'A lot of tongues started wagging, that's what. The events at Symbiosis House were just ancient history for most people in Malvern by then, but there's nothing like a bit of intrigue to revive interest in a subject is there? I remember being in the bar at the Festival Theatre after the article appeared and just about everyone there was busy speculating about Mathias Friedman and what had actually happened to him on that night in 1939.'

'Just because of some ambiguity about who owned Symbiosis House?'

'It doesn't sound much in itself, I know, but what it did was remind people that Friedman's disappearance had never been properly explained. It re-opened an old debate between those that thought he'd made a clean getaway, back to Austria and those who were convinced he'd been bludgeoned to death and buried in the garden. Interestingly, Norman Trubshaw and his wife were also there in the bar, no doubt stoking things up nicely.'

'Why would they have been doing that?'

'Because of the feud between Trubshaw and Co and Crawford, Davies and Withers that I mentioned before. I haven't got a clue how it started but Norman Trubshaw had a longstanding grudge against old Joe Crawford – that's the original Crawford of Crawford, Davies and Withers – despite Joe having died way back in the thirties. After Joe's death, the partnership went to his son James who's still one of the senior partners.'

'James Crawford's my brother-in-law,' said Dennis. 'He's married to my younger sister, Susan.'

'Is he indeed?' said Julian. 'In which case, I'm surprised this has never come up in conversation between you.'

'You wouldn't be if you knew how little I see of them.'

'Something of a strained relationship, is it?'

'Distant more than strained, I'd say. James is quite a stuffy character and he likes to keep himself to himself. Some of that's rubbed off on Susan I'm afraid.'

'Maybe that's why the feud persisted then: like father; like son and all that. Anyway, this complication over the sale of Symbiosis House was hugely inconvenient to Norman Trubshaw so I'm sure he leapt at the chance to get back at his old rival – albeit posthumously - by stirring up trouble for Crawford, Davies and Withers.'

'How exactly?'

'By encouraging people to think that Mathias Friedman was buried at Symbiosis and that Crawford, Davies and Withers were complicit in keeping it a secret.'

'Hence their unwillingness to sell.'

'Yes. Which is why Trubshaw and his wife made a point of being there that evening, at the Festival Theatre.

They were going around, planting the idea in everyone's head.'

'Stoking things up, as you said before.'

'Only to have them stoked up even further by the Gazette, in its next two editions.'

'Was that thanks to you by any chance?'

'*Me?*' exclaimed Julian, looking genuinely offended. 'That's not my style and you know it. How could you suggest such a thing? I was there to write a theatrical review, not a scandal column. No, it was a freelancer, Ted Crabtree, who picked up the story. I noticed him as soon as I arrived: skulking in the bar; listening to the various conversations. His report made the following week's front page and, from then on, tongues were wagging all over town.

'What did he actually say?'

'Effectively, he re-wrote the original story about the millionaire being thwarted in his attempt to buy Symbiosis House but, this time, he put a lot more emphasis on the Mathias Friedman debacle in 1939, and the way some people thought he'd never left the place alive. He didn't directly accuse Crawford, Davies and Withers of covering up the existence of a grave on the site, but it didn't take much to read between the lines. It was very clever actually; a typical Ted Crabtree piece.'

'So, who was responsible for the original report?'

'Bill Fletcher, the chap who used to write the property page. It was just before he retired. Bill's been friendly with Norman Trubshaw for years so that'll explain why he got the tip-off.'

'So how come Ted Crabtree got involved if Bill Fletcher was already working on it?'

'Because Bill's essentially a bricks and mortar man so it wasn't really his sort of thing at all. Once he'd got the ball rolling he must have phoned Ted Crabtree and asked him to come and spice the story up a bit – just the way he knew Norman Trubshaw wanted it.'

'Which is why Ted was lurking in the Festival Theatre bar that night.

'Precisely,' said Julian, lighting yet another of his small, black cigarettes.

'To be honest, I'm surprised Jeff allowed it; he's usually pretty damning about these fly-by-night freelancers, isn't he?'

'Ah, but that's the point: Jeff wasn't here. He'd gone abroad for three weeks and left Don Blackmore in charge. And you know what Don was like: he didn't have an ethical bone in his body, which is probably why he's doing so well on that Fleet Street rag he works for now.'

'That explains why I don't remember anything. If Don Blackmore was in charge, I'll have made myself scarce for the duration.'

'He was hell to deal with, that's for sure. Looking back, I'm amazed I didn't do the same.'

'He and Ted Crabtree obviously pulled it off though if they got everyone talking the way you described. I bet the Gazette's circulation figures went up a fair bit too.'

'They certainly did - for a while anyway.'

'And now, the discovery of this body at Symbiosis House has got everybody talking again.'

'That's right, the Blackmore legacy lives on. I'll be fascinated to see how the Whippet covers it.'

'Presumably he'll be desperate to get some inside information: he just told me he only deals in facts; assumptions are anathema to him apparently.'

'That's rubbish though, isn't it? He's just as happy to feed the rumour mill as Ted Crabtree is, if it suits his purpose. Do you remember that piece he did about…?'

He stopped mid-sentence and switched his attention to a point beyond Dennis' left shoulder; a broad smile appearing on his face. 'Oh, it's you,' he said. 'Welcome to our little hive of industry. To what do we owe this unexpected pleasure?'

Dennis turned around to see Jeff Stephenson looming in the doorway.

'Hive of industry my foot,' said Jeff. 'Gossip shop more like, and it stinks like a Paris bar at closing time. Open a window will you Julian? It feels as if I'm being smoked alive upstairs. And Dennis, come with me; I need a word with you in my office.'

He turned abruptly, and they heard his footsteps receding along the hallway.

'Oh dear,' said Julian, 'he didn't sound very happy, did he? You'd better get a move on and see what he wants. Meanwhile,' he added with a sigh, '*I'd* better get back to this confounded review - Princess Apple Blossom, version six; here we come.'

He started typing again; a thin black cigarette dangling from the corner of his mouth.

***

Jeff was renowned for being a snappy dresser and today was no exception. He was perched casually on the front of his desk; immaculate in a bespoke, double-breasted tweed suit, red and green silk tie and crisp white shirt, with striking red enamel, star-shaped cufflinks. He was rumoured to be in his fifties but, other than a few crow's feet around the eyes and flecks of grey in the dark brown hair at his temples, his matinee idol looks were largely unblemished by the ravages of time. Dennis made a mental comparison with his own sagging, blotchy features and receding hairline, last glimpsed in the bathroom mirror an hour or so before. He realised, with a shudder, that he must be at least fifteen years younger than his editor was reputed to be.

'Thanks for coming up,' said Jeff, indicating the low armchair that faced his desk.

Dennis sank into the yielding upholstery and gazed up at his boss. 'Is there a problem?' he said.

'Why do you say that?'

'You seemed a bit annoyed just now, when you looked in downstairs.'

'I told you, didn't I? Julian's bloody cigarette smoke was getting on my nerves and, when I came down to complain, I found you both nattering rather than working.'

'Sorry.'

'Never mind, I've made my point now so let's just forget it. I've got an assignment that's going to be right up your street and it's all thanks to a letter from one of our readers, a Mr H. Parsons of Hereford. Mr Parsons is a big admirer of your "Wells and Springs of Old Malvern" column and he's very keen to meet you. Here, you can read for yourself.'

Dennis took the letter from him and was immediately struck by the old-fashioned elegance of the copperplate script. He leaned back in his chair to read:

The Editor

Malvern Gazette

Edith Walk

Great Malvern

Worcestershire

25th March 1957

3, Weobley Villas,

Hobart Street

Hereford

Dear Sir,

I have been a dedicated reader of the Gazette for many years now. Although I live in Hereford, some twenty miles distant, I have spent much of my professional life, working in and around Malvern and so I retain a general interest in local news. However, being a hydraulic engineer by profession – a mantle I took on from my late, well-respected father, Matthew Parsons - my primary reason for subscribing to your organ, is the monthly feature. "Wells and Springs of Old Malvern," written, with great dedication, insight and expertise, by Mr Dennis Powell.

Recently, my interest in this column was particularly aroused by the reference to structures the author referred to as "chamber springs;" naturally occurring subterranean springs which it became fashionable, amongst certain wealthy Victorians, to turn into elaborate architectural features, to impress their friends. As the article so eloquently explained, many of these impressive structures fell into disuse during the late nineteenth century. Naturally this has imbued them with an enigmatic allure for aficionados like the estimable Mr Powell and me. It so happens that, during the 1890s, my father had the good fortune to restore one of these "lost treasures" - indeed, I believe it is that which Mr Powell knows as the Chamber Spout; the "holy grail" that has so far eluded him - and consequently I am in possession of his notebooks, containing sketches, plans, descriptive material and other related esoterica that I am sure Mr Powell (and ultimately your readers) would find extremely interesting and informative. With your permission, I would very much like to meet with Mr Powell so that I can hand over the material to which I have referred and provide a brief elucidation that will hopefully enable him to make best use of it. I propose that we rendezvous this Thursday morning, on the eight-thirty train from Hereford to Worcester. If Mr Powell would be good enough to join the train when it reaches Ledbury at one-minute past nine and then alight at Great Malvern, twenty-five minutes later, it should allow sufficient time for all that I need to say.

The reason I have suggested this rather elaborate arrangement, rather than simply coming to your offices or requesting that Mr Powell visit me at home, is that I would like to request a small favour in exchange for the valuable information I am providing. The basis of my request is as follows: -

I travel to Worcester twice a month (i.e. every other Thursday) because, in my capacity as a (now semi-retired) hydraulic engineer, I am advising the Cathedral authorities on the renovation of some ancient stone drainage conduits. Our discussions tend to become rather involved which means that I cannot always accurately predict the time of my return journey, hence my being so specific about the morning train. The train continues to be my favoured mode of transport and, until recently, I always considered the Hereford to Worcester service to be quick, safe and reliable. However, during the last three months, there has been an irritating tendency for the carriage lights to fail as we pass through the long tunnel under the Malvern Hills. This has caused me much inconvenience, not to mention anxiety. Being of a nervous (and increasingly frail) disposition, I cannot abide being plunged into total darkness without any warning. Naturally, I have complained to the train guard on each occasion (I have experienced eighteen such incidences to date and no doubt there have been countless more in my absence), but his response has been consistently unsatisfactory. He always seems surprised that I do not take the stoical attitude of the average British Railways passenger and simply accept that such things are par for the course. Three weeks ago, I wrote a stiff letter to his regional manager, hoping that this might result in the matter being taken more seriously, but I still haven't had a response and consequently my patience has run out. I now conclude that the only option available to me is to circumvent the normal channels of complaint and to draw attention to the issue through the local press - hence the favour I referred to earlier.

If you would be good enough to allow Mr Powell to rendezvous with me, on the Hereford to Worcester train, this coming Thursday morning, I am reasonably confident that he will experience the electrical problem at first hand – the odds are *certainly in favour of it. However, even if the lights continue to shine resolutely (and, I'm inclined to say, perversely!) during our journey through the tunnel, it will still provide me with an opportunity to describe my experience, in all its distressing detail, so that he can accurately report on the matter in the next edition of the Gazette. In exchange for your co-operation, I can promise that he will return with a collection of exclusive documentary material of considerable historical interest.*

Let me assure you that, given the short notice, I do not expect a reply to this letter. Mr Powell's appearance or (and I sincerely hope this is not the case) non-appearance will suffice. Regardless of your decision, I will be travelling on the eight-thirty train as usual this Thursday and, should you agree to Mr Powell gracing me with his presence, he will find me sitting in the first compartment of the first carriage to the rear of the buffet car.

Yours very sincerely,

H. Parsons

'So, what do you make of all that?' said Jeff when Dennis looked up again.

'He's certainly got a way with words, hasn't he?'

'You can say that again. Maybe we should start using "the estimable Mr Powell "as your by-line, what do you think?'

'Complete with a photo of me wearing pince-nez and holding a quill pen no doubt.'

'Now don't start giving me ideas. But seriously, do you think all this information he says he's got could be genuine?'

'Possibly, but I've been let down so many times before, I'm not going to get too excited about it. Apart from which, if he's such a devotee of my column, why has he left it so long to get in touch?'

'I haven't got a clue.'

'It's encouraging that he's a hydraulic engineer though. It makes him sound more plausible than a lot of other people who write in.'

'So, can I take it that, despite your reservations, you're happy to rendezvous with Mr H. Parsons?'

'Of course. If nothing else I might find out what the "H" stands for. I'm guessing it's Horace or maybe Herbert?'

'It's Harry; I looked him up in the Kelly's Directory and there's a tiny entry for, "Harry Parsons, Consulting Hydraulic Engineer." Blink and you'd miss it. Nevertheless, he's there in black and white so he seems legit. His gripe about British Railways has the makings of a nice little campaigning story for us. Add to that a few possible revelations about lost subterranean springs and I reckon it'll prove well worth the cost of a train ticket.'

CHAPTER 4
Blue Bird Tea Rooms

Wednesday 27th March 1957

11.45 a.m.

Julian had disappeared by the time Dennis came back downstairs. It seemed that he'd either finished his difficult review or had decided to abandon it completely. A cloud of pungent smoke lingered in the room as a reminder of his recent presence and the window remained closed, suggesting that Jeff's plea for ventilation had gone unheeded. Dennis went over to lift the sash and poked his head through to take in a few welcome breaths of fresh air. The window faced the back yards of shops that lined Church Street but, looking up, he could see the blotchy, pinkish stone-work of Malvern Priory which towered above all the surrounding buildings and, beyond it, the hump of Worcestershire Beacon, misty in the morning sunshine.

He sat at his desk and was just starting to read Harry Parsons' letter again when the telephone rang. It was his sister-in-law, Judith.

'What are you up to Dennis?' she said.

'Not much.'

'Why don't you join me for lunch in the Blue Bird Tea

Rooms then? We can order before the rush starts.'

He glanced at his watch; it was ten to twelve. 'It's a bit early for lunch, isn't it?'

'We can order coffee first; there are a couple of things I need to talk to you about but only if you've got time.'

'It should be all right.' He flicked through his diary as he was talking. 'I'm due to meet a woman from the WI about their annual baking competition, but that isn't until one-thirty and it's only over at the Baptist church hall on Abbey Road.'

'That sounds perfect then,' said Judith. 'I'll see you in fifteen minutes.'

The Blue Bird Tea Rooms were busy when he got there. Judith was nowhere to be seen but he managed to find a table for two in the corner and told the waitress that he was expecting someone and would order as soon as she arrived. The aromas of coffee and baking reminded him of childhood and of school holidays when he, Nigel and Susan had come here with their mother. He couldn't remember his father ever coming with them and he presumed that was because he'd always been at work. Then, as now, Charles Powell was the warehouse manager at Malvern's oldest wine merchants, Thomas Radford and Co. Dennis remembered his mother explaining to the children that their father had a very important job and that Mr Radford relied on him to maintain the good reputation of the company. Charles always came home at seven o' clock in the evening, his clothes exuding the sweet, spirit smell of the warehouse. He was usually tired and bad tempered but sometimes he'd surprise them by bringing home a big cardboard box or some old wine racks for them to play with. Dennis recalled the spark of affection he'd felt for his father on those occasions; it was like remembering a completely different person; someone who had long since died or who had simply been a figment of his childish imagination.

Roused from his daydream by a sudden flurry of activity by the door, Dennis looked across to see that Judith had just come in and was making her way over to him. She was laden down with shopping and was having difficulty manoeuvring between the tables. Her muttered apologies were received with gracious nods as people drew their chairs in to let her pass. She pushed her bags under the table and leaned over to give him a peck on the cheek. As her long chestnut curls brushed against the side of his face, he found himself imagining, as he'd done countless times before, what it would be like if she were married to him instead of Nigel. Embarrassed, he pushed the thought away.

'Sorry I'm a bit late,' she said, 'I was looking at the sandals in Brays and I lost track of time.' She leaned back and perused the menu, which gave Dennis a chance to surreptitiously admire her features; especially her large brown eyes, which sparkled as ever with a mixture of intelligence and impish humour.

'What are you gawping at?' she said, staring directly at Dennis before he'd had a chance to look away. 'Have I got a smudge on my face or something?'

'No,' said Dennis sheepishly, 'I was just deep in thought. I tend to stare blankly like that when I'm concentrating.'

'You'd better be careful,' she said with a chuckle, 'someone's going to get the wrong idea if you do that too often, they might think you're ogling them.'

'Good grief, I've never ogled anyone in my life.'

'How's Margaret by the way.'

'She's all right.'

'That's an evasive answer if ever I heard one. I'm asking

after your girlfriend, not some old maiden aunt.'

'Calling her my girlfriend makes her sound about sixteen; she turned forty last month.'

'Anyway, how are you two getting on?'

'Well enough I suppose. To be honest, we only manage to see each other a couple of times a week: her job up at the college keeps her busy and you know all about the odd hours I have to work.'

'Don't be so abstruse Dennis. I want to know if you're any closer to getting engaged. How long have you been together for goodness sake? It must be nearly twenty years now.'

'It's seventeen, to be precise.'

'Seventeen, twenty; what difference does it make? The fact is; it's a long time. What does Margaret think about it?'

'She agrees with me that we're perfectly fine as we are so why change anything?'

'I can see I'm on a hiding to nothing here. Anyway, I just wanted you to know that I've arranged a family tea party tomorrow and I'd like you and Margaret to be there, just like a proper couple.'

'A family tea party? I thought we gave up on those years ago.'

'Well I've decided to revive them.'

'That's a terrible idea and you know it. Apart from which, you haven't given me enough notice: I'll check my diary when I'm back at the office but I'm sure I won't be able to make it. I doubt if Margaret will either.'

'Well that's where you're wrong because I've already phoned Margaret and she says she's free and she assures me that you are too.'

'How can she possibly know that?'

'Because she says you'd both already arranged to meet up for a drink at five o'clock tomorrow but she's perfectly happy to come to tea instead.'

'Like a lamb to the slaughter, she hasn't got a clue what she's letting herself in for. I take it you've asked my father as well?'

She answered with a nod.

'Well there you are then; talk about a recipe for disaster.'

'Stop being so negative.'

'I'm not being negative; I'm simply facing facts. You know what he's like on these occasions as well as I do; he just uses them as an excuse to pick an argument with one or other of us and we all end up feeling terrible and wishing we were a thousand miles away.'

'Except, this time, Margaret's going to be there, so I expect he'll be on his best behaviour.'

'And pigs might fly. Margaret's presence won't make the slightest difference. If anything, it'll make him worse. Why do you keep deluding yourself Judith? We're never going to be the big happy family you want us to be, however many cosy gatherings you drag us all along to.'

''I just want us all to get on, there's nothing wrong with that is there? You'll thank me for it one day.'

A waitress appeared, and they ordered coffee. After she'd gone, Dennis said, 'Anyway, is that why you were so keen to meet me here; just so that you could invite me to your wretched tea party?'

'That was one reason yes: I knew you'd take some persuading, so I thought I'd better ask you face to face. But the main reason was because I wanted to tell you about a really odd encounter I had earlier on.'

At that moment, a police car roared past outside with its emergency bell clanging. Dennis stood up to get a better view through the window and was just in time to see it swerve left onto Belle Vue Terrace before accelerating away along Wells Road.

'I expect it's heading for Symbiosis House,' he said, sitting down again. 'I assume you've heard what's happened up there?'

'Yes, Nigel's part of the investigation He was called out just after seven this morning. He didn't even have time to finish his toast.'

'So, do you know any juicy details?'

'I'm not supposed to talk about it.'

'Why not? Everyone else is. I've had at least two other conversations about it already.'

'Even so, I promised Nigel I wouldn't say anything.'

'But a body's definitely been found there?'

'Yes,' she whispered, her eyes darting around to see if anyone was listening.

'And has Nigel got any idea who it might be?'

'No I don't think so. Not yet anyway.'

'Everyone's saying it's Mathias Friedman.'

'The Austrian psychiatrist you mean? I doubt it. Anyway, Nigel wouldn't be swayed by that sort of tittle-tattle I can assure you.'

'So where does that leave your plans for tomorrow? Nigel's bound to be tied up with all this going on, so what's the point of holding a family tea party if your own husband can't be there?'

'Oh, I think it'll all be over by then. Apparently, it's what they call an open and shut case.'

They were interrupted by the waitress, returning with their order.

After she'd gone, Dennis said, 'But they haven't even established whose body it is yet, so how can it be an open and shut case?'

'I don't know, I'm only repeating what Nigel's Superintendent says. It seems that the man who dug the body up is already well-known to the police. He was an odd-job man up there. Apparently, he telephoned the police station to report what he'd found and then fled the scene. The police are searching for him everywhere and Nigel's been told to treat him as the prime suspect.'

'What are they planning to charge him with?'

'I haven't got a clue. I assume they think he was responsible for the body being there in the first place.'

'So, it's murder then?'

'Presumably, but I'm not sure what evidence they've got. Nigel certainly wasn't aware of any.'

'Who is this man anyway?'

'His name's Morrigan.'

'Not Andrew Morrigan?'

'Yes, that's it. Why, do you know him?'

'My dad used to employ him, on a casual basis, to look after the old delivery lorry at the warehouse. He was pretty good at it to start with, but later he developed a bit of a drink problem which made him less reliable.'

'Well he's definitely the one they're after.'

'But it doesn't sound as if Nigel's convinced?'

'Oh, you know Nigel, he's a good detective and he's methodical to the core; he hates being party to a fait accompli, however compelling it might seem.'

'I don't blame him. I wouldn't be too pleased if I was sent out on an assignment, only to come back and find my editor had already written the report.'

'Jumping through hoops Nigel calls it; he has to do a lot of that these days. Superintendent Goodall's a bit of a tyrant. Basically, he's lazy and he's always pushing for a quick result. It drives Nigel mad, but he tries not to let it show. He'd be furious if he knew I'd been talking to you about it.'

'I'd better not press you any further then. What's the other thing you wanted to tell me?'

Judith leaned forward, conspiratorially. 'Guess who I saw as I was coming out of the baker's this morning.'

'I've no idea.'

'Your sister, Susan.'

'Susan?' I haven't seen her for ages.'

'Neither had I. The last time was two years ago at your mother's seventieth birthday party. If you recall, Susan and James dropped in with a present and Susan went around chatting happily to everyone while James stayed in the background, looking completely fed up as usual. After half an hour, he dragged her away because he reckoned they were due somewhere else. I remember feeling really sorry for her and wondering how on earth such an attractive woman could have ended up with a husband as dreary as that.'

'I thought the same,' said Dennis. 'She looked so forlorn as he was bundling her out of the front door, I really wanted to say something but, in the end, I didn't.'

'Well you can't really interfere in those situations, can you? But, getting back to this morning, there I was, coming out of Challengers' Bakery when who should I see on the other side of the road but Susan, walking up Church Street, lugging a heavy suitcase. I waited for a gap in the traffic and, by the time I got to the other side; she'd stopped for a rest further up and was leaning against a pillar box with her suitcase at her feet. She had a headscarf pulled tightly around her chin. Now I come to think of it, I'm surprised I recognised her at all because she was a shadow of how she'd been two years before. In fact, I don't think I've ever seen anyone look as worried and worn out as she did at close quarters; it was as if she had all the cares of the world bearing down on her shoulders.'

She took a sip of coffee before continuing.

'I said hello and asked her if she was all right but all I got in return was a blank stare. She didn't seem to have a clue who I was, so I said, "It's me, Judith." There still wasn't the faintest glimmer of recognition, so I said, "You know, your sister-in-law; Nigel's wife." After a few seconds, her eyes seemed to come back into focus and she said, "Yes, of course. I'm sorry; I must have been daydreaming.' Then she picked up her suitcase again and started to move on.'

'That's strange, isn't it?' said Dennis

'Oh, believe me; it gets a lot stranger than that. She continued up Church Street like a bat out of hell. She's obviously a lot stronger than she looks because her suitcase must have weighed a ton and yet I still had to put on a spurt to catch up with her. It wasn't easy going up that hill I can tell you. When I caught up with her again, I asked if she needed a hand, but she just shook her head and kept walking. I felt a complete idiot trying to keep up with her like that. People probably thought we'd had an argument or something and I was running after her to make amends; I got some very funny looks, that's for sure. By now we were nearly at the top of Church Street and the penny suddenly dropped that she was making for the bus stop outside the post office; I don't know why it hadn't occurred to me before really. I asked her if she was going far and, to my surprise, she stopped in her tracks and looked at me properly for the first time. She said, "No, not far, only to Droitwich; I'm staying with my friend there for a few days." As she spoke, a huge tear rolled down her cheek. As you can imagine, it was quite an awkward situation, made worse by the fact that we were standing in the middle of the pavement with her suitcase between us and lots of people grumbling because they had to keep stepping into the road to get past. In the end, I gave her hand a little squeeze and said maybe we should find somewhere less busy and have a chat.

'We went and sat on one of the benches just below Belle Vue Terrace. It was still noisy there because of all the traffic but it meant we could keep an eye on the bus stop to see when the 144 to Droitwich pulled in. It seemed as if we'd been there for ages before she spoke again. I'd already made up my mind not to say anything before she did. I was amazed she'd come with me at all, so I didn't want to make some silly remark, just for the sake of it, and risk scaring her off.'

Judith stopped to look at her watch. 'It's quarter to one now,' she said. 'Shall we order a sandwich? I'm suddenly feeling ravenous.' She signalled to the waitress and after a quick perusal of the menu, they ordered two ham and tomato sandwiches.

'Go on then,' said Dennis, after the waitress had departed, 'what happened next?'

'Well I was absolutely convinced she'd get up again at any moment and haul her suitcase off without saying a word but to my huge relief, she suddenly turned to me and said, "I'm sorry I was so rude and unfriendly just now. The thing is, I've had rather a nasty shock and I think I was in a daze.

I didn't really know what I was doing." I told her not to worry and that I'd be pleased to help in any way I could but if she preferred to confide in her friend in Droitwich rather than me I'd completely understand. She shook her head and assured me that I was just the person she wanted to talk to. She said her friend was a spinster and, although she was very kind, the fact she'd never been married would make it very difficult, if not impossible, for her to understand the dreadful situation that she, Susan, now found herself in. She said it would actually be embarrassing to try and explain it to someone who'd lived such a sheltered life and that was why, now that she'd had a chance to calm down and collect her thoughts, she felt so pleased she'd bumped into me.'

At that moment lunch arrived and they concentrated hungrily on their sandwiches before Judith took up her story again.

'So,' she said, dabbing her mouth with a serviette, 'from that point onwards, there was no stopping her. First, she told me that James is in the habit of going off late at night and not returning until the early hours of the morning. When she asks him where he's been he just gets angry and refuses to tell her. The more she presses him, the more agitated he gets. I should have let her carry on, but I suddenly felt so indignant on her behalf that I butted in and said if Nigel ever treated me like that; he'd be banished to the spare bed until he mended his ways.'

'How did she respond?'

'Well, for a few seconds, she didn't say anything at all, and I could tell she was weighing up her words carefully. Then she said, "But if you weren't sleeping with him in the first place, banishing him to the spare bed wouldn't be an option, would it?"'

Judith stared directly at Dennis. 'So, what do you make of that?'

'It confirms they're just as incompatible as we'd always

thought they were.'

'But we didn't think they were as incompatible as *that*, did we?'

'I don't know; James is so stiff and starchy; it's hard to imagine him having an intimate relationship with anyone, isn't it? Anyway, how did you react to this revelation?'

'I apologised for my insensitivity and told her my big mouth was always getting me into trouble, but she assured me there was no need to be sorry because she'd learned to cope with the shortcomings of her marriage a long time ago. Even as she was saying it though, tears were pouring down her cheeks again. I squeezed her hand to try and comfort her and then she said, "To be perfectly honest, I'm not coping very well at all. Things have just taken a terrible turn for the worse and I'm not sure I can bear it anymore."'

'I didn't want to put my foot in it again, so I just waited until she was ready to continue. After a couple of minutes, she pulled her hand away and dabbed her face with her hanky. When she started talking again, her voice was monotonous, and she seemed to be gazing into space, almost as if she'd forgotten I was there. She said she knew perfectly well that everyone wondered why she and James were so unsociable. It wasn't her choice because she loved seeing people, but she'd decided long ago that it was easier to go along with his preference for a quiet life rather than try to change him. He was a very orderly man who thrived on routine and organisation and being an estate agent was right up his street because he loved producing inventories for big property auctions and rummaging through catalogues and valuation tables. She said he'd liked the army for the same reason: the structure and the order of it all suited him down to the ground. He served in Burma during the war and he oversaw all the regimental supplies. Apparently, he was in his element doing that as well, but he got seriously ill while he was out there and was eventually shipped back here.'

'And about six months later they got married,' said Dennis.

'I'm surprised you remember that.'

'I do my best to blot out these gruesome family occasions, but I don't always succeed. That wedding is still etched on my memory unfortunately.'

'I know it caused a few ructions, but Nigel was away, serving in France and I was staying with my parents in Cirencester, so I wasn't actually around at the time.'

'You were well out of it. My parents only found out about the wedding by chance. They didn't know Susan was seeing anyone, let alone about to get married and they were almost incandescent when they realised she'd been planning to keep them in the dark about it. After that, they made up for lost time and got involved in every detail. In the event though, the ceremony was a dismal affair. James looked like death, presumably because he still wasn't well and, apart from Susan and James, there were only my parents and me at the register office – oh and the best man; a wiry chap with a limp who was never introduced and hardly exchanged a word with James the whole time.'

'Oh, I know who that was,' said Judith. 'His name's Percy Franklin, I often see him around town. I'm surprised you haven't noticed him as well. He works at James' firm, Crawford Davies and Withers. In fact, we had some dealings with him after we bought our house in Abbey Road.'

'So, he's an estate agent like James?'

'Not exactly, He's a sort of assistant; he goes around houses when they're put up for sale, measuring up and listing all the routine information they put in property details. After we moved in, we couldn't work out where the fuse box and the main stop-cock were. In the end, we phoned Crawford, Davies and Withers and they sent him over to show us. I remember he turned up with another man who looked just like him, a twin brother we guessed. This brother, or whatever he was, seemed to be acting as his chauffeur: he just waited outside in the road, leaning against an odd, American-looking car that was painted in two colours, grey and silver – two-tone they call it, I think.'

'Presumably Percy couldn't drive himself because of the limp.'

'That would explain it I suppose. Apparently, he'd served in Burma with James and got shot in the leg while he was out there.'

'He told you all this, did he?'

'No, he turned out to be a very uncommunicative fellow; definitely not the conversational type. I heard about the Burma business from your mother and I assume she heard it from Susan.'

Dennis glanced at his watch and said. 'Sorry, I took us off at another tangent there. You'd better get on with the story before I have to go.'

'We've got plenty of time yet and I don't suppose your WI lady will mind if you're a bit late, will she? Anyway, Susan said she felt quite content after they were first married but after about three months James started to reveal a disturbing side of his nature that hadn't been apparent before. The first time she noticed it they were out for an afternoon walk on the hills: they'd parked their car at Wynds Point and taken the path up to British Camp. At the top, they stopped to catch their breath and to take in the view of Eastnor Castle and the hills and woods of Herefordshire out to the west. Despite being so high up, there was barely any breeze and she could hear the skylarks twittering overhead. She said it lifted her spirits no end but when she commented on the beauty of their surroundings and how happy they made her feel; James' response was really strange. What do you think he said?'

'I haven't got a clue.'

'Apparently, he stood there, staring into the distance for a few seconds and then he said, "It's all just shadows and gloom to me."'

'What a depressing thing to say.'

'It is, isn't it. Susan said she felt utterly deflated but, when he didn't elaborate, she decided to let the moment pass. Eventually, she managed to push it to the back of her mind. A few months later though, something very similar happened: this time they were walking up through the woods to St Ann's Well on a bright, frosty morning in February. She said the trees were sparkling in the sunshine, everything around her seemed magical, and she felt her spirits lifting again. She started to imagine that even James must be moved by it but then he stopped abruptly in his tracks and announced that they had to go back straightaway. Susan said she was shocked to see how terrified he looked; almost as if he were staring into some dreadful abyss. When she hesitated, he tugged roughly at her sleeve and said, "No I mean now, right now; before darkness falls and swallows us up." This happened on a sunny morning, remember.'

'How odd. It sounds like someone on the edge of a nervous breakdown to me. Not that I'm an expert but I honestly can't think of another explanation.'

'That's what Susan thought, and she was really frightened. As they went back down the path towards the town; she pleaded with him to tell her what was wrong, but he claimed it wasn't anything significant; he'd just remembered how much pressure he was under at work and realised he ought to be at home, attending to a backlog of paperwork rather than walking on the hills.'

'But presumably she didn't believe him?'

'No, and even if she had, she'd have been setting herself up for a rude awakening because it started happening regularly after that: they'd be doing something together and then, out of the blue, he'd utter another ambiguous but equally chilling little phrase with that same expression on his face, signifying abject horror. Each time, she implored him to tell her what was on his mind but he'd either say she'd been imagining things or make out it was just something trivial.'

'And she's been putting up with it ever since?'

'It seems so, yes. She said she quickly realised that she had to choose between seeking divorce or staying with James and trying to help him. She reckons that, once she'd made the decision to stay, she started seeing things much more clearly. It suddenly became obvious to her that the reason James liked order so much was because it provided an antidote to the chaos he felt inside. She thought that if she was patient and helped him to live a quiet and organised life; he might eventually feel able to share his troubles with her. She knew it wasn't a recipe for true happiness but at least she might achieve a kind of contentment. And, apparently, that's how it worked out – until last Saturday night, at least.'

'What happened on Saturday night?'

'They'd gone to bed early and she'd gone straight off to sleep. At eleven-thirty though, she was woken up by a loud cry coming from his room across the landing. She got up and listened outside the door. Apparently, he was calling out the same phrase, repeatedly: "Hold him down; put a bullet in his head; die, die, die". She said it made her go icy cold because it sounded as if he was actually killing someone.'

'He was obviously having a nightmare.'

'Exactly. I thought it must be to do with his time in Burma.'

'Did Susan agree?'

'No, she didn't. She said he'd never seen any action out there because he'd always been in camp, looking after the supplies.'

'But he'd have heard the other soldiers talking, wouldn't he? He'd have known what was going on. It was a brutal business out there by all accounts, so he's bound to have been exposed to it one way or another.'

'You'd think so wouldn't you, but Susan wasn't convinced. Anyway, it happened again the following night: he was shouting out the same phrase, almost word for word, and woke her again. She said, if anything, it was even more upsetting the second time.'

'It must have reminded her of his original outbursts as well.'

'It did but she reckoned these were far worse. "More real" was how she described them: as if they were linked to actual memories rather than being the products of a disturbed imagination. But that wasn't the end of it.'

'Go on.'

'Apparently, James went out at eleven o'clock last night and, as usual, he didn't tell Susan where he was going. She said she waited up for him, just as she always does and, at about two-thirty in the morning, while she was out in the kitchen making a cup of tea, she heard him come in through the front door and go straight into the sitting room. When she went through she found him slumped in a chair with his head in his hands, sobbing convulsively. Between sobs, he was muttering something. She couldn't hear what he was saying at first because he was crying so much. Gradually though she realised he was just repeating the same phrase, "It's time for a reckoning; it's time for a reckoning," on and on and on.'

'What did she make of that?'

'She was completely baffled so, after he'd calmed down, she asked him, point blank, what he'd meant, but he just denied it and told her she was imagining things. That's why she's gone to stay with her friend for a few days. She's finally reached a point where James' coldness and secrecy, his oppressive moods, and the feeling she's treading on eggshells all the time have just got too much for her. She's not sure she can take it anymore.'

'I'm not surprised. Anyone else would have given up on him years ago.'

'Well *I* certainly would. Though having said that, I wouldn't have got myself into the situation in the first place.'

'No, I'm sure you wouldn't. Anyway, how do you think James is coping now she's gone? It sounds as if he needs professional help; perhaps I should put him in touch with my friend Dr Gajak at Powick Hospital.'

'Maybe you should. He'd have to acknowledge he'd got a problem first though, wouldn't he? And I can't honestly imagine James doing that.'

'That's true; it's hard enough discussing the weather with him, let alone the delicate matter of his mental state. So, did Susan say anything else or was that it?'

'No, that was about it really. I asked if she'd have far to walk when she got to Droitwich and she said it was a little way, but she'd be all right because her friend was meeting her off the bus and would be able to help her with her suitcase. I tried to find out her friend's name and address, but she said it was better I didn't know. I suppose she didn't want me to be in an awkward position if James asked. Shortly after that, her bus pulled in outside the post office and she got up. Before she went she leaned over and kissed me on the cheek and the next thing I knew, she was already halfway down the path with her big suitcase.'

They both gazed down at their half-eaten sandwiches and cold cups of coffee as they collected their thoughts. Eventually Dennis glanced at his watch. 'I'd better go,' he said, 'I'm already five minutes late for my meeting.'

'You don't sound very keen.'

'I'm not. I've got so much swirling around inside my head, it's hard to summon up the slightest interest in a WI baking competition - not that I had much in the first place.'

'You mustn't get yourself into trouble with your editor though.'

'Oh, I doubt if he'll be particularly bothered,' he said, signalling to the waitress for the bill. 'All this excitement at Symbiosis House is bound to overshadow anything I come up with.'

CHAPTER 5

An Evening Tour on the Tiger

Wednesday 27 March 1957

3.45 p.m.

After his meeting with the woman from the WI – during which he'd dutifully listed the different classes in the baking competition and noted down the judges' criteria for a perfect Victoria sponge – Dennis walked slowly along Abbey Road, debating how to spend the rest of the afternoon. He knew he should go back to the Gazette and type up his report but the prospect doing of that didn't inspire him at all.

Passing through the Priory Gateway, he went down the steps to the yew shaded churchyard and then followed a diagonal path across to Church Street. A narrow passageway between shops provided a short cut home, past the front of his office. As he came to the other end of the passage, he paused to scan the Gazette's windows and to peer up and down the street. Reasonably satisfied that he wasn't being observed, he crossed over and scurried around the corner to Pierrepoint Terrace. Retrieving his motorbike from the alleyway, he rolled it out onto the road, mounted it and kicked hard on the starter pedal. Miraculously, the engine roared into life straightaway.

He had no particular plan in mind but, after taking a

left turn on Belle Vue Terrace, he realised that latent curiosity was taking him up towards Malvern Wells and Symbiosis House. He continued along Wells Road, past the Tudor Hotel and on towards Lower Wyche. Beyond Lower Wyche, rambling houses, built during the town's Victorian boom years, perched grandly on the wooded foothills above the road. He recalled that Symbiosis House – a typically ostentatious property from the same period - was a mile or so further up, standing on the lower reaches of Pinnacle Hill.

He didn't need to see the house to know that he'd arrived. A crowd of about twenty people had formed on the roadside, next to the gateway. A police car was blocking the entrance and two uniformed police officers were standing on either side of it, hands on hips, braced to deal with anyone attempting to come through. Dennis slowed down and took in the scene as he rode past. Beyond the police car, a drive, bordered by laurel bushes, extended steeply upwards before disappearing around a sharp bend. The dense evergreen foliage obscured most of Symbiosis House from this angle but two turrets with conical roofs, topped by golden weathervanes of a strikingly abstract triangular design, were just visible above the trees. After he'd passed the gateway, he accelerated and continued up the road to where he remembered seeing a stopping area for buses cut into the side of the hill. He brought the motorbike to rest there and switched off the engine. As he gazed at the panoramic view across the Severn Plain to Bredon Hill and to the Cotswolds beyond, he contemplated his next move. It was obvious he wouldn't be allowed anywhere near the house while there was a major police investigation going on and he wasn't supposed to be here anyway; this was Brian Fairclough's territory not his. The Whippet had been nowhere to be seen amongst the crowd gathered at the gateway but then the Gazette's ace reporter would never demean himself by hanging around with the "hoi-polloi." It was far more likely that he'd gained access to the property by means of some obscure back entrance and was probably, at this very moment, gathering all the material he needed for another headline story. Despite himself, Dennis had to respect the man's sheer audacity.

After a few minutes weighing up his options, he decided there were more fruitful things to be done than trying to compete with Brian Fairclough. Once again, the Tiger started on his first kick and he edged out into the road with the intention of carrying on up to Wynds Point. However, just as he was about to ride away, he saw a small red car speeding up the hill towards him, coming from the direction of Great Malvern. On a reflex he withdrew into the shadow of the trees that overhung the pull-in. He'd recognised the car immediately; it was Jeff Stephenson's distinctive crimson Morgan. There wasn't another one like it in Malvern or anywhere else for that matter. He remembered Jeff saying how he'd insisted on this particular colour when he'd ordered it from the factory and how they'd mixed the paint to his specification. The car raced past, scattering grit, twigs and dead leaves in its wake. As the roar of its engine faded into the distance, Dennis stood tensely astride his idling motorbike, convinced that he'd been spotted. Gradually though it dawned on him that he was probably far too deep in shadow to be seen from a passing vehicle; especially one travelling as fast as that. Nevertheless, he decided to let another couple of minutes pass before he left the pull-in and continued up the hill.

Reaching the top of the meandering, tree-lined road and turning into the car park opposite the British Camp Hotel, it occurred to him that this was where Susan and James must have parked before their fateful walk up Herefordshire Beacon. Then, with a jolt, he realised that Jeff could quite easily have been heading here too and might, at this very moment, be waiting to reprimand him for having gone AWOL in the middle of the afternoon. He anxiously surveyed the rows of parked vehicles: there were lots of greys and blacks and dark blues but, to his great relief, no sign of a bright Crimson Morgan lurking amongst them.

At some point, during the ride from town, he'd decided it would be a good opportunity to visit the Collis Spring and take a few photographs to use in a future Wells and Springs of Old Malvern column. The Collis Spring was one of his favourite local water features, mainly because - the Chamber Spout aside - it had been one of the hardest to find. He'd lost count of the number of musty documents he'd scoured - many of them supplied by Mr Winstanley - looking for references to it. Nine times out of ten, there'd be no mention at all and even when there was, it would only amount to a second or third hand acknowledgement of its existence. He'd finally tracked it down seventeen years ago but to this day he remained cagey about its precise location. He didn't mind true aficionados making excursions there, but he didn't want it to become just another magnet for sightseers. Margaret often took him to task about what she called his "small-minded, petty attitude" to such things but, rightly or wrongly, he stuck to his guns.

He opened one of the Tiger's rear panniers and took out his camera, an old Leica in a battered leather case, which he'd once bought for three pounds in an antique shop in Bromyard and which took such clear, sharp pictures that Larry Frazer, the Gazette's chief photographer, was forever trying to persuade him to sell it. His latest offer was twenty-five pounds, but Dennis was still loath to let it go. He struck out up the main path that led to the Beacon, the camera, slung over his shoulder on its long strap, banging against his hip as he walked. It was busy today and twice he had to stand aside to make room for large groups of ramblers, coming back down the hill. It suddenly reminded him of why, seventeen years ago, he'd first abandoned the path for the overgrown and unfrequented woods below; a decision that had led to his discovery of the Collis Spring. He'd come up here for some much-needed peace and quiet but had forgotten how popular the route to Herefordshire Beacon could be. Before long he'd become engulfed by throngs of ebullient hikers whose bulky haversacks had pressed against him and whose constant cries of "Hello" and "Good morning," though well meant, had soon begun to get on his nerves. In frustration, he'd made for the sanctuary of the woods below and as he'd careered down the slope, the brambles savagely tearing at his trousers, he'd felt a surge of relief mixed with exhilaration. Eventually the ground had levelled out and he'd slowed to walking pace. It was then, above the soughing of the breeze in the treetops, he'd first heard the sound of running water.

Later he'd identified a natural signpost; a rotting tree stump colonised by frills of light brown fungus, to show him where to leave the path, but when, a few days after his first impulsive retreat, he'd tried to retrace his steps, it had taken numerous abortive forays into the trees before he'd found the right spot. Drawing level with it now he paused, habitually, to caress the stump's gnarly contours before he stepped over the edge. The brambles tore at his legs as he went but he'd already tucked his trousers into his high motorcycle boots hoping this would ensure he reached the bottom of the slope, relatively unscathed. The camera case swung around wildly as he made his barely controlled descent.

Once he was on level ground, he stopped to catch his breath and to check his bearings. It was quiet with just a gentle rustle of branches overhead. Wending his way through the trees, his destination soon came into sight: a rocky outcrop beyond a screen of silver birch. As he got closer, he could make out the Z-shaped crack that split it down the middle with a tell-tale clump of bright green ferns, about halfway up.

Using a series of convenient hand and foot holes, he climbed the rock face until he reached a ledge that was level with the ferns. He parted the fronds and peered into a small cave beyond. As his eyes became accustomed to the darkness, he was able to make out a steady flow of water emerging from deep in the rock and cascading into a natural bowl where it settled briefly before spilling in a sleek sheen over the rim and then swirling and eddying down the crevice to join a stream far below. This was the Collis Spring. He removed his camera and its flash attachment from the case and took some shots of the spring from various angles. He restricted himself to close ups so as to ensure that he didn't make the spring's location obvious to the casual observer.

As soon as he was satisfied he'd taken enough photographs, he packed everything away and then stood up to look at the view. He was now facing north-east, the opposite direction from the one in which he'd just come. The woods stayed level for a short distance before rising steeply again, towards the main road where he could see the occasional flash of a vehicle moving along the same route he'd followed on his motorbike earlier. Then his attention was caught by sunshine glinting on something amongst the trees, just below road level. He squinted, trying to get a clearer view but it was too far away to make out with the naked eye and his binoculars were back at the car park, in the Tiger's other pannier. On impulse, he decided to go and take a closer look. It wasn't really out of his way because he could follow the road round to where he'd parked instead of retracing his steps back up to the path. He scrambled back down the rocks and on through the woods, trying to keep as straight a course as possible. As soon as he started climbing again, the rumble of traffic grew louder and before long he was almost level with the road. Realising he'd overshot his target; he took a diagonal line to his left, back down the hill. The choice of direction was a gamble but, after only a few yards, it seemed to have paid off. His path intersected with a trail of utter devastation: churned up earth, mangled vegetation and fractured branches, extending from the road to a point, about thirty yards below, where a black car was wrapped around the trunk of a large oak tree.

His heart raced as he clambered down the slope to the car. He fully expected to be confronted with a scene of bloody carnage so, when he peered through the open driver's door, he was relieved to find it empty. Nevertheless, there was a lot of, what looked suspiciously like, dried blood smeared on the steering wheel, dashboard and scattered shards of windscreen glass. It was obvious that the injured occupant, or occupants, had managed to get away but how far away remained to be seen. He went around to the front of the vehicle and rested his hand on the badly crumpled bonnet. It was stone cold. He went around to the back of the car again and checked the number plate: OAB 283. It rang a bell, but he wasn't immediately sure why.

Despite the damage that had been caused on its way down, he doubted if there'd be much sign at road level that a vehicle had gone over the edge and speeding motorists would have little time to spot it anyway. It seemed likely, therefore, that he was first on the scene. His heart sank as he realised he ought to undertake a search and make sure no-one was lying injured or, heaven forbid, dead in the surrounding undergrowth. He knew it was ridiculous to think that he could cover much ground by himself, but he felt duty bound to scour the immediate area at least. Having decided to restrict himself to a radius of about twenty feet from the car, he immediately set off on a complete circuit of the outer limit, planning to work inwards from there.

After fifteen minutes or so, he decided that he'd searched as thoroughly as he could. He stood by the wrecked car and listened hard in order to make certain there were no desperate cries for help coming from anywhere in the vicinity but, apart from the sound of traffic from above, there was nothing. Satisfied there was no more he could do here, he started climbing up towards the road. Then, just a few feet up the slope; he realised, with a jolt, why the number plate had seemed familiar: it was because he'd seen it in town, just a week or so before, outside the offices of Crawford, Davies and Withers Estate Agents. It belonged to his brother-in-law, James Crawford.

He'd been out shopping with Margaret and they'd both noticed the gleaming, black Rover parked at the kerb. Jokingly, Margaret had said, "Now that's the sort of car you need, to replace that horrible old motorbike. Look, it's even got a number plate that rhymes – well, almost anyway, OAB 283." He'd just started to ask why she didn't buy one herself if she was so impressed when James Crawford had come out of Crawford, Davies and Withers, climbed into the Rover and promptly driven away.

Deep in thought, he continued up the slope and emerged at the point where the car had gone over the edge. His prediction there'd be little to see had been right: the undergrowth was relatively sparse at this point and apart from tyre tracks on the verge and a few flattened saplings, it didn't compare to the damage caused lower down, where there'd been far more vegetation to impede the car's progress. The big question was why had it gone over here at all? The angle of the track indicated that it had been travelling uphill, away from Malvern Wells, on a straight section of road. There were no skid marks on the tarmac to indicate sharp braking: the car appeared to have veered off the carriageway for no reason at all – no reason that was obvious anyway.

He knew he should inform the police immediately and the nearest public telephone he could think of was at The British Camp Hotel. However, as he trudged up the road towards Wynds Point, it occurred to him that he didn't have any loose change which meant he'd have to waste time negotiating the use of their private line. He concluded that it would be just as quick if he retrieved his motorbike from the car park and rode to Malvern College where he knew Margaret would be working late in the library. He could phone the police from there.

It was a quarter past six by the time he propped the Tiger up behind the college kitchen and the light was fading quickly. There was a lot of clattering and shouting going on inside and he guessed that high tea, or whatever they called their evening meal in an establishment like this, was currently being prepared. He made for the fire escape at the rear of the library wing. Margaret's office was on the first floor and he knew that whenever she needed a cigarette - which was far too often in Dennis' opinion - she used the little platform, just outside the fire door at the top of the steps, as an unofficial smoking area. She tended to keep the door wedged open while she was at work because the latch mechanism squeaked badly, and she wanted to avoid drawing attention to her regular exits. As he clanked up the metal steps, he smelt the tell-tale cigarette smoke before he saw her.

'Caught you,' he said as he came to the top.

'Dennis,' she exclaimed, spinning round to look at him. 'I wasn't expecting to see you tonight.'

'I had a feeling you might be indulging that nasty little habit of yours.'

She stubbed her cigarette in a saucer on the latticed metal floor before straightening up to peer at him through the gathering darkness. 'I'm only enjoying a quick smoke like thousands of other people do. I hope you aren't going to get all sanctimonious with me Dennis, I'm not in the mood for that.'

'Actually, I'm here on urgent business; I need to use your phone.'

'And there I was thinking you'd come to see me.'

'I *have* come to see you but it's really important I talk to the police first.'

'Why? What's happened?'

'I'll explain after I've made my call.'

'You'd better come in then.'

She turned and led him through the fire door, switching the lights on as soon as they were inside.'

'Goodness,' she said, 'I've only been out there five minutes and it's suddenly gone dark in here. I hope no-one's been trying to read or they'll be suffering from eye strain.'

They both looked around, but the library appeared to be empty.

'Come through to the office.'

She lifted a hinged section of the big counter that formed a semi-circular barrier around her librarian's domain and Dennis followed her through and into a small square room beyond. There was just enough space for a desk, a chair and a bookshelf containing green-bound catalogues, each labelled with Dewey classification codes.

'There you are,' she said, indicating the telephone on her desk. 'Sit down and make your call. I assume you don't mind me listening in.'

'Not at all.'

He watched her as he dialled: she was hovering in the doorway; tugging at the fronds of brown hair that always seemed about to close like curtains and hide her features. The narrow section of her face that remained visible was very pale and the contrast with her black-framed spectacles made it seem paler still.

He knew the police station number by heart because of the countless times Jeff or the Whippet had made him phone Nigel, to extract inside information about some case or other. Not surprisingly, Nigel always refused to give anything away which begged the question why they kept bothering to make him ask.

A gruff voice on the other end said, 'Malvern Police, can I help you?'

'Yes, could you put me through to Detective Chief Inspector Powell please?'

'He's not here, can anyone else help?'

'I'm not sure, I suppose they could yes.'

'What does it concern?'

'I want to report an abandoned car I found earlier. I think it might have been in an accident.'

I'll put you through to Sergeant Collins. He's the one on duty tonight. You can give all the details to him.'

'Fair enough,' said Dennis unenthusiastically. He'd far rather have spoken to Nigel.

There was a series of buzzes and clicks and then another voice came on the line.

'Collins.'

He said it in such a bored tone that Dennis' heart sank, and, for a few seconds, he was unable to summon up a response

'Anyone there?' Boredom had quickly turned to impatience.

'Yes, sorry, I want to report something. I was up near Wynds Point earlier and I....'

'Slow down, I need to take your name and address before

we get into all that.'

'Er, my name's Dennis Powell and I live at Flat 1, 15, Pierrepoint Terrace.'

'Powell eh; are you any relation to…?'

It was the question they always asked him and so, as usual, he answered through gritted teeth, trying to hide his irritation.

'Detective Chief Inspector Powell, yes I'm his brother.'

'So, what was it you wanted to report?

'I was up near Wynds Point earlier and I came across a car; a black Rover, registration number OAB 283. It had come off the road and crashed into the woods.'

'Near Wynds Point. Can you be a bit more precise?

'It was actually about half a mile before Wynds Point, as you're approaching the British Camp Hotel from Malvern Wells; down in the woods on the left-hand side.'

'Were there any casualties?'

'There must have been because there was quite a lot of blood on and around the steering wheel but there was no-one in the car.'

'So, did you check the immediate vicinity?'

'I looked around as best I could, but I didn't find anything.'

He waited for a response but, other than crackling on the line, there was silence.

'The thing is though,' he continued, 'I'm sure the car belongs to my brother-in-law, James Crawford. He's a partner at Crawford, Davies and Withers, the estate agents. I recognised the registration plate.'

He sensed Margaret recoil at the mention of James'

name.

'You did, did you?' said Collins.

'Yes, OAB 283, I'm certain that's his number.'

He looked at Margaret who nodded in agreement.

'My... er... my girlfriend can verify that.' He silently winced at his use of the word "girlfriend;" he blamed Judith for that.

'I see. And this girlfriend of yours; she's there with you now, is she?'

'She is.'

'And what's her name?'

'Margaret Jobson; why do you ask?

'Because I'm trying to build up a full picture,' said Collins. 'Simple as that. Now, let's go back to your discovery of the wrecked vehicle: what time was this exactly?"

'About quarter to five I think.'

'You think?'

'Well I didn't actually look at my watch, but I remember checking the time at half past four and I reckon I got to the car about fifteen minutes later.'

'So, what were you doing there then? It's a bit off the beaten track isn't it?'

'I'm a reporter on the Gazette and I was doing some research for an article I'm writing.'

'In the woods? That's a funny place to be doing research isn't it?'

'Not really; not in my line of work anyway.'

'What sort of reporter goes wandering around in the woods at quarter to five on a Wednesday afternoon?'

'I write a monthly column about wells and springs, so it takes me to all sorts of places.'

'So, it seems. Anyway, you said you found this car at quarter to five but it's twenty past six now, what took you so long to report it?'

'I spent about a quarter of an hour looking around and then I had to walk back up the road to the British Camp Hotel where I'd left my motorbike.'

'But it would only have taken you ten minutes at most to walk up there. What have you been doing in between; having a couple of pints in the bar?'

'Of course I haven't; it's just that when I got there I realised I hadn't got any change for the phone, so I decided to ride down to Malvern College where my girl... where my friend, Miss Jobson works. That's where I'm calling from now.'

'Why didn't you get change from someone at the hotel or ask if you could use the phone on reception there?'

'I don't know,' said Dennis, wiping beads of perspiration from his forehead with the back of his hand. 'Now you come to mention it, I suppose that's what I should have done but, at the time, coming here just seemed easier somehow.'

'I take it you and this brother-in-law of yours aren't particularly close then?'

'What makes you say that?'

'It's obvious, isn't it? If you were really bothered about him you'd have reported the incident as soon as possible; not left it an hour because it happened to be easier for you.'

'Why are you trying to turn all this on me?' said Dennis. Sweat was pouring freely down his face now and dripping onto the blotter on Margaret's desk where it formed an amoeboid rash. He dabbed his brow futilely with his handkerchief.

'I'm not trying to turn anything on you,' retorted Collins, 'I'm simply trying to understand why you didn't take the first opportunity to phone from the hotel like any normal person would have done.'

'I honestly don't know. How many times do I have to say it? I accept I made a bad decision, but I really resent the implication that there's any more to it than that.'

'Well let's just concentrate on practicalities, shall we? if we'd known about all this at five o' clock there'd still have been enough light for us to go out and assess the situation properly, but now it's almost dark so there's nothing much we can do before tomorrow is there?'

'You've got torches, haven't you?' You could at least send a patrol out to see if James is lying there injured somewhere.'

'There's no point, those woods are hard enough to get around in the daytime, let alone at night. The fact remains; if you'd just phoned from the hotel in the first place, it would have saved us all a lot of trouble.'

By now Dennis was too dispirited to even attempt a reply.

'Anyway,' continued Sergeant Collins, 'I've taken down the details such as they are. Is there anything else you want to tell me?

'Not that I can think of no.'

'Well I daresay we'll want to talk to you again once we've had a chance to look into things. Can we telephone you at the address you gave me?'

'No, I haven't got a phone at home, so you'll have to give me a ring at the Malvern Gazette if you need to. I can't imagine why it would be necessary though, there's nothing I can add to what I've told you already.'

'Well we'll just have to see about that won't we,' said

Collins, abruptly cutting the connection and leaving a high-pitched tone reverberating in Dennis' right ear.

'And "goodbye" to you too,' said Dennis as he slammed the receiver down on its cradle.

'Well,' exclaimed Margaret, peering down at him and shaking her head, 'that sounded absolutely dreadful. What a rude man. It's enough to put you off ever bothering to phone them again if they're going to treat you like that.'

Dennis mopped his face again with his, by now, sodden handkerchief. 'I know; it makes me appreciate what Nigel has to put up with if he's forced to work with ignoramuses like that all the time.'

'I don't suppose he's typical though; you were probably just unlucky.'

'I suspect he's more typical than you think: according to Judith, Nigel's superintendent's hell to work with too, but that's another story.'

'Well, it's obvious, just from looking at you, how upsetting it's been. I'll put the kettle on and then you can tell me the full story over a cup of tea.'

CHAPTER 6
Dennis brings Margaret up-to-date

Wednesday 27th March 1957

6.20 p.m.

'You look a bit better now,' said Margaret. She and Dennis were sitting on high stools at the library counter, drinking tea. 'I thought you were about to keel over when you came off the phone. Who were you talking to anyway? It sounded as if he was being really nasty.'

'His name's Sergeant Collins and yes, he was being very nasty indeed.'

'I thought you were pretty restrained considering.'

'Maybe that's because part of me thought he had a point.'

'What about, for goodness sake?'

'I should have phoned straightaway from the British Camp Hotel, then they'd have been able to get out there before it got dark.'

'But it's perfectly understandable why you didn't. He was just looking for a reason to pick on you, that's all; he's obviously a dreadful bully.'

'I'm sure he is but that doesn't stop me feeling bad

about it.'

'Well it's too late to change anything now so stop worrying.' She paused and then she said, 'It was definitely James' car you found, was it?'

'Definitely. You obviously recognised the number as well.'

'Yes, it was the same as we saw in town that time. That's awful, isn't it? Shouldn't you let your sister know...? She gasped. 'Oh dear, you don't think she was in the car as well, do you?'

'No, I don't.'

'How can you be so sure?'

'Because she went to Droitwich to stay with a friend this morning. Judith told me all about it over lunch in the Blue Bird Tea Rooms. She bumped into her in town and they had a long chat before Susan caught her bus.'

'Well you should contact her at her friend's house then.'

'I can't. All I know is she's gone to Droitwich; I haven't got an address or telephone number or anything. I don't even know her friend's name.'

'Why don't you ask Judith?'

'She doesn't know either; Susan wouldn't tell her.'

'Why all the secrecy if she's just gone to visit a friend?'

'Because she doesn't want James following her. Apparently, she's decided she needs to get away from him for a few days.'

'Why, for goodness sake?'

Dennis gave her an abridged version of the story Judith had told him in the Blue Bird Tea Rooms.

'Well,' she said after he'd finished, 'that's incredible. I'm almost lost for words.'

'We always knew things were strained between them though, didn't we?'

'We did, but I never imagined they were as bad as that. Poor Susan.'

'Poor James as well, don't you think?'

'No, I don't. This is all his own doing, surely?'

'What if he's been ill though? Some sort of mental problem. He couldn't be held responsible then, could he? Well, not entirely anyway.'

'What are you saying?'

'I'm no expert but the way he's been behaving suggests to me that he's been traumatised at some stage – probably during the war. He served in Burma, which was a notorious hell hole, so he could have been experiencing flashbacks from his time out there.'

'But I thought James was an administrative officer or something. He wouldn't have seen much violence doing that surely?'

'That's what Susan thought apparently, but, as I said to Judith, even if he wasn't directly involved, I'll bet he heard some pretty horrific reports from the other men. Those could easily have tipped him over the edge, couldn't they?'

'It's possible I suppose.'

'And it might explain why the army invalided him back home in the middle of a major campaign.'

'But he contracted malaria, didn't he? That's what I heard.'

'They'd have treated him in a field hospital in Burma

for that, they wouldn't have gone to the trouble of sending him all the way back to England.'

'You don't know that for certain though, do you?'

'No but I bet It's true all the same. I think the real reason he was sent back was because he had a mental breakdown, but he preferred people to think it was because of the malaria.'

'Because the stigma of a breakdown would have been too embarrassing for him?'

'Precisely. I can't imagine James being prepared to admit he'd ever suffered from anything like that: he's the type who'd consider it a terrible sign of weakness. I think he'll have tried to carry on as normal, pretending nothing was wrong but, periodically, it all became too much for him, and he'd have one of his outbursts.'

'But now it's happened once too often, and Susan's run away.'

'Leaving James to face his demons all on his own. Maybe that explains why he decided to crash his car into a tree.'

'You think he might have been trying to commit suicide?'

'It certainly crossed my mind but, thankfully, he doesn't seem to have succeeded, does he?'

'He could still be lying injured somewhere though.'

'Yes, but as you said yourself, there's nothing we can do about it now. I've reported it to the police and hopefully they'll start searching at first light. Injured or not, he obviously got a fair distance away from the car because I went over the immediate area with a fine toothcomb, and I didn't see him anywhere.'

'What were you doing up in those woods anyway? I couldn't help noticing how cagey you were with Sergeant Collins when he pressed you on the subject.'

'I was taking some photos of the Collis Spring.'

'Oh, of course, you'd never reveal the location of your precious Collis Spring would you, even if your life depended on it?'

'I just don't want it to turn into another tourist trap, that's all. There are more than enough of those around here as it is.'

'Don't be silly, it's virtually impossible to get up there, unless you're a rock climber or a mountain goat.'

'The council could easily build steps up to the ledge and signpost a way through the woods though, couldn't they. Before you knew it, you'd have trippers everywhere.'

'But why shouldn't people be able to go and see it if they're interested?'

'Because, chances are, they'd vandalise it or leave litter lying around. Sadly, most people – especially people like Sergeant Collins - don't have any respect for our local water heritage at all.'

'Oh Dennis, that's a sweeping generalisation and you know it. You really are a snob sometimes.'

He shrugged but said nothing.

'Anyway,' said Margaret, 'changing the subject: how was your meeting with Dr Gajak this morning?'

'Interesting actually,' said Denis, perking up again. 'We spent most of the time discussing my father and, in particular, what might account for his obnoxious ways.'

'Sounds a bit psychoanalytical to me. I thought that sort of thing was supposed to be out-of-bounds – from Dr

Gajak's point of view at least.'

'It is usually but he decided to make an exception this time.'

"I assume this is all to do with how your father reacted when you asked him about the St Werstan Spa Hotel.'

'That's right. Dr Gajak was intrigued when I told him about it, so I went on to regale him with one or two other examples of the old man's unpleasantness over the years.'

'That must have taken a while then.'

'It would have done, if I'd given him the whole sorry saga, but I restricted myself to a few selected highlights instead.'

'Did you tell him about those family tea parties during the war when your dad used to make you read out Nigel's letters?'

'I did actually. Whatever made you think of that?'

'Because you told me the very same story soon after we met, and you said what a big effect it had had on you.'

'That's true. Even now, just thinking about those dreadful family tea parties brings me out in a cold sweat... Which reminds me,' he added more sternly.

'What?'

'When I saw Judith at lunch time she let it slip that the two of you had come to a little arrangement behind my back.'

'Oh, you mean the invitation to tea,' said Margaret, blushing. 'I'm sorry about that. I knew you wouldn't be very happy about it, but she caught me off guard and somehow, I ended up agreeing we'd go. You know how persuasive she can be.'

'I do, but I still wish you'd tried harder to resist. I don't think you realise quite how gruelling it's going to be.'

'Sorry.'

'Well we'll just have to grit our teeth and get through it I suppose. I doubt if Nigel will make it though, I expect he'll still be tied up with this Symbiosis House business.'

'Yes, Judith told me he'd been called away on a big case but that was all she said about it. I only found out the details later. Hearing it was Symbiosis House made me feel quite strange actually.'

'Why was that?'

'It stirred up old memories: my father was a member of a club that used to meet there in the early twenties.'

'What sort of club?'

'Astronomy club. They called it the Black Moon Society. It was started by the owner, Mathias Friedman. That's all I know really. It's just that when I heard about Symbiosis House, it suddenly made me think of my father.'

'I hope it didn't upset you too much.'

'It always upsets me to be reminded of him.'

'You were seven when he died, weren't you?'

'I was, but only just. I remember my birthday cards were still on the mantelpiece when the police came with the news he'd been knocked over and killed. I've hated receiving birthday cards ever since.'

'I made the mistake of sending you one, not long after we first met, didn't I.'

'Yes, I still feel awful about that. You don't expect someone to burst into floods of tears when they're given a card do you?'

'Not really.'

'It's what they call the power of association. I suppose I should have got over it by now but obviously, I haven't.'

'What if they'd found the person responsible? Do you think that would have made any difference?'

'A bit perhaps but it isn't going to happen now, is it? We're talking about something that happened in 1923; that's thirty-four years ago.'

'There was a witness though wasn't there?'

'Yes, but he was much too far away to see anything useful. He was walking his dog further down College Road when he heard a screech of tyres. He turned around in time to see a car mount the pavement and hit a pedestrian, after which it spun round and sped off in the direction it had come from. He rushed up to see if there was anything he could do, and he found my poor father lying there. He used a telephone in one of the houses to call an ambulance, but I think he already knew it was too late.'

'I'm amazed you can talk about it so calmly.'

'That's the odd thing: I can relate the facts without getting upset at all; it's the unexpected reminders that get me going.'

'And yet now you're working here, in the same college he taught at: surely that's a constant reminder of him?'

'It is but it's a comforting reminder, which is why I was so keen to come and work here. You see they were so nice after he died; they set up that special science library here and named it the Greville Jobson Science Wing in his memory. I showed you around once, didn't I?'

'You did. It's very impressive.'

'They built a special extension and everything, so it must have cost a fortune. They got some money from a charity called the Mitarbeit Trust, to help them fund it.'

'And you went to the opening with your mother.'

'Yes, they held a little ceremony on the first anniversary of his death and there were quite a few important people there who'd known him; people from the college obviously, like the headmaster, but others as well. Anyway, it was a lovely occasion and I remember thinking it was the first time

I'd felt happy since my father died. That's when I decided I was going to come back and work here one day.'

'And then, five years ago, you did.'

'That's right. It took a long time, but I managed it in the end.'

She rose abruptly and started gathering the tea things.

'I've just thought of something,' said Dennis.

She shook her head. 'Actually, I'd prefer to drop the subject if you don't mind.'

'This isn't to do with your father; it's to do with the wrecked car in the woods.'

'What about it?' said Margaret, sitting down again.

'What if I'm wrong and it wasn't James' at all?'

'Don't be silly, you recognised the registration number, didn't you?'

'I might have misread it though.'

'OAB 283; the rhyming number plate. There couldn't be any confusion about that surely?'

'But OAB's just a Worcestershire code; lots of cars have the same and I could easily have mistaken a six or a nought for an eight, it would still have rhymed.'

'For goodness sake Dennis, stop worrying. We've already agreed there's nothing more we can do about it tonight.'

'Except if we can confirm it isn't James' car after all, it'll give me one less thing to worry about, won't it?'

'So, what are you suggesting?'

'We simply phone James at home and if he's there we've got our answer. It's so blindingly obvious I can't imagine why I didn't think of it before. Even if it turns out it *was* his car, at least we'll know he managed to stumble home safely.'

'Do you know his telephone number?'

'Not off hand but I can look it up in the directory.'

'There's one on the shelf above the phone.'

He was already on his feet and making for her little office. He sat down at the desk and reached for the directory. Leafing through the pages, he soon located the entry for "Crawford J., Hibiscus Lodge, Foley Terrace, Great Malvern" and dialled the number. He let it ring and ring for over a minute, but no-one picked up. He sighed and placed the receiver back on its cradle.'

'Why don't you call his office?' said Margaret.

'It's seven in the evening; no-one's going to be there now, are they?'

'They might be working late for some reason, you never know.'

'It's worth a try I suppose.

He dialled the number for Crawford, Davies and Withers but, once again, there was no answer.

'Oh well,' said Margaret as he put down the receiver, 'at least you tried. You'll have to phone them in the morning as soon as they open. You've exhausted all your options for now so maybe you should start to relax.'

'You must be joking; I'll never relax with all this on my mind.'

'Think about something else then.'

'I know, why don't we adjourn to the Foley Arms for a drink, that'll do the trick?'

'I've got a better idea,' she said, jingling a bunch of keys. 'I've got a new bottle of Johnnie Walker in my bottom drawer. If you move out of the way a second, I'll get it out.'

He backed his chair against the wall so that she could squeeze in next to the desk.

'Are you sure we should be drinking on college premises?' he said as she stood up again, brandishing a bottle and two whisky tumblers.

'Everyone will be scoffing away in the refectory by now, so I doubt if we'll be interrupted. We might be a bit exposed here though. It's all right for drinking tea but whisky calls for somewhere slightly more secluded.'

She led the way through the library. At the end of a section of shelves labelled, "100: Philosophy and Psychology," they came to an anonymous blue door. She turned and handed him the bottle and glasses.'

'You'd better hold these while I let us in.'

She pulled out her keys again and unlocked the door.

They went through into a windowless storeroom lined, from floor to ceiling, with metal shelves. These were stacked densely, but haphazardly with an assortment of cardboard boxes. The air was thick with the mildly fetid aroma of musty paper. Two canvass chairs and a battered school desk stood in the centre of the floor.

'What do you keep in here?' asked Dennis as he placed the whisky and tumblers on the desk.

'Things we can't find a home for but can't bear to throw out; not just library material, there's stuff here from all over the college. I call it the Random Repository. Most of it's just rubbish, but occasionally you'll come across some interesting documents from when the Telecommunications Research Establishment were based here.'

'Of course, the TRE requisitioned the College during the war, didn't they?'

'Yes, they moved up from Dorset in '42 and stayed until '46 when they moved to where they are now. When it's quiet I like to come in here and look at some of the old papers. I just lift down any old box and rummage through the contents for ten minutes or so before I go back to work. Usually, they'll just be boring old college ledgers but sometimes a batch of TRE papers will turn up and they can be fascinating.'

'What sort of papers?'

'The sort that make you wonder if you should really be reading them,' she said, pouring a generous measure of whisky into each of the glasses.

'What makes you say that?'

'Because a lot of them are marked "Top Secret" for a start.'

'How on earth did they end up here then?'

'I don't know. Apparently, the move to their permanent premises was quite fraught and sometimes there were crossed wires between the college and the TRE about what was supposed to be happening. Maybe a few boxes went astray in the confusion.'

'Shouldn't you report what you've found?'

'I will when I'm ready. No-one's missed them for eleven years, so I doubt if hanging onto them a bit longer is going to make any difference.'

'They're to do with radar presumably?'

'As far as I can tell, yes. And it all seems to be the work of someone called Laurent Morel.'

'A Frenchman by the sound of it.'

'Yes, it seems there were quite a few émigré French scientists working for the TRE in those days.'

'All making their contribution to the Allied war effort.'

'Something like that, except, between you and me, I don't think all of Laurent Morel's efforts were entirely official.'

'Really? What makes you say that?'

'It looks as if he was working on two things at once: the project he'd been tasked with and something else he turned his mind to when he got bored or when nobody was looking. It reminds me of pupils we get in the library who pretend to be studying but, all the time, they've got a comic hidden inside their book.'

'So, you reckon Laurent Morel was working on a secret within a secret?'

'That's what it looks like to me. His papers are organised in a series of cardboard files. Inside each file, there's all the official stuff, neatly arranged in numbered page order but, in quite a few of them, there'll be some additional pages, folded in half, tucked in at the back.'

'Perhaps they're just rough jottings; his workings out and that sort of thing?'

'No, they're definitely part of a separate project.'

'How can you be so sure?'

'Because each set of folded pages has the same heading: "Astrred," spelt, A-S-T-R-R-E-D.'

'A secret research project, how fascinating. Is this to do with radar as well?'

'It's connected I think but I get the impression it's a lot bolder than the official work he was doing - futuristic you might even say.'

'Good grief, what do you mean?'

'Don't laugh but it looks as if it's to do with sending wireless signals up into space.'

'As in *outer* space you mean?'

'Yes, I know it sounds far-fetched but that's exactly what it looks like to me.'

'It's not far-fetched at all. I've been reading about that sort of thing for years.'

'Only in those silly Dan Dare comics of yours though.'

'They're not silly, they're intelligent predictions of the future based on proper science.'

'The fact remains, they're still just comic strips written for children.'

'Well I'm not going to argue with you about it now, I'm more interested in what Laurent Morel was working on. Are you sure it was to do with space?'

'That's certainly what it looked like to me, especially going by the drawings and diagrams in there.'

'Can you show me?'

'Not yet. I want to go through the rest of the boxes first and see what else there is.'

'Why don't we both go through them? Two heads are better than one after all.'

'No Dennis, this is my discovery and I'm going to keep it like that for the time-being. I shouldn't have mentioned it at all really, I knew you'd want to go wading straightaway.'

'Well just make sure you tell me as soon as you've finished. This could be the scoop I've been waiting for all these years. I can see the headline already: "Project ASTRRED - Top secret papers the TRE forgot."'

'You can put that idea out of your head right now.'

'Don't worry,' he said, downing his whisky in one gulp. 'I've got quite enough on my plate to be going on with. Jeff's actually given me something interesting to work on for a change.'

He told her about Harry Parsons' letter and about his planned rendezvous with the retired hydraulic engineer the following morning.

'That's exciting, isn't it?' she said when he'd finished

'Possibly, but I'd rather see what he's actually got for me before I get too carried away.'

Margaret drained the rest of her whisky. She put her empty glass on the desk and yawned loudly.

'It sounds as if you're ready for bed,' said Dennis.

'I am, and so should you be if you're getting up early to catch a train. Give me a lift home and then you can stay the night. One condition though: just make sure your wretched motorbike doesn't wake me up at the crack of dawn. I've got the morning off tomorrow and I'm planning to have a nice long lie-in.'

CHAPTER 7
A Return Journey on the Train

Thursday 28th March 1957

8.10 a.m.

Mindful of Margaret's instructions the night before, Dennis pushed the Tiger along St James' Road to the junction with Albert Road before finally starting it up. It was only a ten-minute ride to Great Malvern Station and so by twenty past he'd parked next to the metal railings that separated the car park from the west-bound platform and was ready to go. Then, with a jolt, he realised that he'd left his notebook behind, so he had to rummage around in the motorbike's rear panniers, trying to find something to write on. Having located a few scraps of paper and the stub of a pencil, he stuffed them into his jacket pocket, went through the little gate to join a straggle of people waiting for the eight forty-five to Hereford.

The London express was just leaving from the other side as he took up position next to one of the colourfully painted wrought-iron pillars on platform two. Billows of industrial smelling steam filled the air as the first thrusts of the pistons strained to build momentum. The carriages creaked as they lurched forward and then, with a brief toot from the whistle, the train gathered speed, and, within seconds, it had gone, leaving a heavy silence in its wake.

A murmur of conversation, interspersed with birdsong, gradually began to fill the void left by the train's departure. Beyond the Victorian station buildings on the opposite platform, the hills rose precipitously to meet a pale blue sky.

As he gazed at the view, Dennis reflected on his relationship with Margaret and specifically on what Judith had asked him in the Blue Bird Tearooms, yesterday. *"I want to know if you're any closer to getting engaged. How long have you been together for goodness sake? It must be nearly twenty years now...."* He'd said that they were all right as they were, but he was starting to wonder if Margaret, left to her own devices, would have given the same answer. Was she waiting for him to propose to her? He didn't think so but the more he thought about it, the more he realised he wasn't sure.

He'd first met Margaret in May nineteen forty-four. His old editor, Jack Ferguson, had sent him to Malvern Public Library to write a piece about some diaries they'd recently acquired. They were a Victorian gentleman's graphic account of a series of hydropathic therapies he'd undergone at the Crown Hotel during the early eighteen forties. His descriptions of being "packed" in layers of wet sheets and eiderdowns at six o'clock in the morning and subsequently being subjected to descending and ascending "douches" of freezing cold Malvern water were gruesomely fascinating. Dennis' resulting article proved such a success with readers that Jack asked him to write further reports on the subject over the following weeks. Ultimately these metamorphosed into his monthly feature, The Wells and Springs of Old Malvern.

In those days, Margaret had worked at the public library and one of her duties was to oversee local history acquisitions. On that May morning, fourteen years ago, she'd greeted him shyly at the main desk and led him to a little storeroom at the rear of the building – not unlike the Random Repository at the college – where she'd shown him the rather battered, leather-bound diaries and read him a selection of extracts she'd bookmarked with old library tickets. Dennis had been entranced: partly by the descriptions of arcane hydropathic procedures but mainly by her mellifluous reading voice and her pale face, half obscured behind dark curtains of hair.

After she'd finished reading, he'd asked some questions and noted down a few notable quotes for inclusion in his article. Normally, after that, he would have declared himself satisfied with the information he'd gleaned and, after saying thank you and politely shaking hands, have simply gone on his way. This time though he'd been surprised to find that wanted to prolong the meeting and, more to the point, he was keen to move on from the subject of hydropathic diaries and ask her about herself. It wasn't something that came naturally to him but something about her gave him the confidence to press on.

After an initially awkward and stilted exchange, they'd started to relax, and he'd found himself telling her about his family and all the tensions caused by his father's cantankerous personality. In turn she'd admitted to difficulties of her own. She explained that her own father had been knocked down and killed by a car in 1923, when she was just seven. From then on, her mother had spent most of her days staring blankly out of the window thus forcing Margaret to assume all practical responsibility for their daily lives. This had left her with little time to attend to her own emotions, so it wasn't until her mother's death, just a year before; that the latent trauma of losing her father had hit her and, after plummeting into deep depression, she'd started seeing a psychiatrist at Powick Hospital.

They'd become so engrossed in each other's stories that the knock on the storeroom door, and the message that

Margaret was required on the front desk had come as a complete surprise. Before parting though, they'd arranged to meet for lunch at the Blue Bird Tearooms the following day.

They met regularly after that and one afternoon she invited him back to the house in St James' Road that she'd inherited from her parents. After she'd shown him around they stood together by the mantelpiece while she put names to faces along the row of family photos. Recounting the memories made her tearful so he put his arms around her, and they kissed for the first time.

A few weeks later, they agreed to call in at the Green Man after work. He had a pint and a half of cider and she had two glasses of medium sherry. After an hour in the pub they walked to Pierrepoint Terrace and clambered up the stairs to his flat. Giggling, Margaret reclined on the settee and declared that she wasn't in a fit state to walk home. Without further preamble, they made love, clumsily but enthusiastically, after which Dennis pulled an old blanket over them and they lay in silence for nearly an hour. He remembered his arm turning numb beneath her but not minding at all.

This state of semi-detached companionship interspersed with occasional intimacy was enough for them both - at least that was how Dennis had interpreted it until yesterday when Judith's forthright questions in the Blue Bird Tearooms had stirred doubts he was now finding hard to ignore.

The screech of a whistle, coming from along the line from Malvern Link, interrupted his daydream. Everyone had turned to look expectantly down the track and within seconds the air was filled with smoke and steam. The gentle babble of conversations going on around him was suddenly drowned beneath a cacophonous hissing and rumbling as the train surged into the station, followed by a long squeal of brakes as it came to a halt. He walked up the platform and stepped into a carriage at the front of the train, directly behind the engine. He found an empty compartment, bathed in early morning sunshine, and settled down for the journey to Ledbury.

The train pulled out on time and soon they were rattling along with a view of the Malverns on one side and the backs of houses on the other. Behind the houses he could see a huge dish-shaped object tilted towards the sky and further on, across an expanse of grass, the cluster of buildings that housed the Radar Research Establishment, previously known as the TRE. As they continued beneath the shadow of the hills beyond Malvern Wells Station he noticed that the carriage lights had come on. Then, within seconds, everything outside went black and a deafening roar filled the carriage as they plunged into the tunnel. The clammy air was infused with a chemical stench of steam and burning coal and he found he was holding his breath, fully expecting the lamps in his compartment to go out at any moment. Reading Harry Parsons' letter in the comfort of Jeff's office he'd found it hard to appreciate why anyone should make such a song and dance about the lights failing on a train but now, in this noisy, fume-filled and generally claustrophobic situation, he could tell how unsettling it might be. Nevertheless, the lights held out this time and after a minute or so they emerged from the tunnel and the train braked sharply as they approached Colwall.

As the train rested in the deserted station he reached out to pick up a Daily Express that someone had left on the seat opposite. It was open at an inside page bearing the prominent headline, *"Red Peril! Are the Soviets preparing to launch their first satellite into space?"* He started to read the article but stopped after the first paragraph as it occurred to him that it might be a better use of his time if he started thinking about his impending encounter with Harry Parsons. It was obvious, just from the way the old man wrote, that he was a stickler for high standards in all walks of life, so he wasn't likely to be impressed by a reporter - especially one who wore his trousers tucked into motorcycle boots - who hadn't prepared a few pertinent questions. He folded the newspaper in half to use as a makeshift desk and searched his jacket pockets for the stationery items he'd salvaged earlier.

Doors slammed, the guard blew his whistle and the carriage creaked as the train began to inch its way forward. Dennis leaned back in his seat with his pencil poised over a blank sheet of paper. He decided he had two objectives: first, he wanted to gauge Harry's credibility and establish the provenance of the material he'd promised to hand over. Bitter experience had taught him that there were quite a few fakes in circulation. Old Winstanley traded in historic documents all the time and even he had to admit that he'd been caught out - at considerable cost to his bank balance - on a few occasions. In the right circles, such material could command very high prices, so it wasn't surprising that skilled forgers had homed in on the market with the intention of making a killing. By quizzing Harry about his past and about the way in which the documents had come into his possession, Dennis hoped to avoid wasting his time ploughing through a batch of completely useless information later. He jotted down the points he intended to cover. He soon ran out of space on his scraps of paper, so he started writing in the margins of the newspaper as well.

His second – and, from his point of view, less important - objective was to listen to Harry's gripes about electrical failures on British Railways trains and possibly even share the experience of being plunged into darkness halfway through the tunnel so that he could write about it later in the Gazette. He didn't bother writing down any questions this time, partly because he didn't think Harry would require much prompting on the subject and partly because he didn't want it to dominate the limited time available.

He looked up from his notes and gazed out of the window at the wooded Herefordshire countryside, tinged with spring green. But moments later the vista was blotted out as the train entered Ledbury Tunnel and he knew he was now less than a mile from his destination. He stuffed his notes and the newspaper into his jacket pocket and went out into the corridor.

After alighting, he climbed the footbridge to the opposite platform. He paused halfway across and leaned on the parapet to watch as the train moved off towards Hereford. It soon went out of sight around a bend in the track, but he continued watching as the white plume it had left in its wake rose higher and higher into the air, slowly thinning out before disappearing completely. Then the other track began to vibrate, and he lowered his gaze to see the Worcester train rounding the bend. Within seconds it had squealed to a halt beneath the bridge, enveloping him in billows of smoke and steam. He clattered down the steps to join it, coughing as he went to clear the acrid taste from the back of his throat.

Harry's letter had instructed him to head for the first compartment of the first carriage to the rear of the buffet car. He clambered into the first carriage he came to, slammed the door closed behind him and worked his way along the corridor, guided by the enticing aromas of coffee and warm pastry. After negotiating the connecting doors through to the next carriage he stopped to peer into the first compartment. Its only occupant was a corpulent old man in a stained pin-striped suit. His mouth was wide open as if he was snoring and his bald head was tilted at an awkward angle. There was a tartan shopping bag on the seat beside him and a newspaper lay open on his lap.

Dennis tapped gently on the glass and slid the door open. The old man gave a start and gazed up at him, his eyes hazy with confusion. He glanced out of the window and then back again. 'Goodness me, have we reached Ledbury already? I must have dozed off.' Then he blinked and said. 'Of course, you must be Mr Powell, the reporter.'

'Yes, I'm Dennis Powell from the Malvern Gazette. I assume you're Mr Parsons?'

'Indeed I am and please call me Harry.' As he stood up to shake hands, the newspaper slipped off his lap and fanned out across the floor of the compartment. Dennis quickly bent down, gathered the pages together and handed it to him. 'Very kind of you.' said Harry. 'I'm a little out of sorts this morning. I made the mistake of mixing the grape with the grain last night. I really ought to know better at my age.' He reached inside his jacket and pulled out a hipflask. 'However, I always find the hair of the dog an excellent restorative.' He unscrewed the cap and took a long gulp before returning the flask to his inside pocket.

The whistle gave a double blast and there was a judder and a thrust of pistons as the train started to move forward. Harry fell back into his seat and Dennis took the one opposite.

As soon as they plunged into Ledbury Tunnel, Harry pulled out a handkerchief to mop his brow.

'Sorry,' he said, using his other hand to loosen his already disarranged collar. 'I always find tunnels dreadfully claustrophobic. And engine drivers and firemen particularly dislike this one because the atmosphere's terrible, due to the exceptionally narrow bore. For me though, it's nothing like as bad as the Colwall Tunnel which runs under the main ridge of the hills. Going through there I'm conscious of over a thousand feet of rock bearing down on us, whereas here it's a couple of hundred at most. Also, I've never known the lights fail in this section, though there's a first time for everything I suppose. But enough of that; I'm sure the important matters we have to discuss will be a helpful distraction from such distressing thoughts. Which reminds me, I need to give you this.'

He handed over the tartan shopping bag.

'Thank you,' said Dennis. 'I presume this is the information you referred to in your letter?'

'It is indeed.'

'There seems to be a lot of it.'

'They're my father's notebooks from the 1890s: there are eight in total. He recorded other projects in them of course so they don't pertain to the Chamber Spout exclusively. In fact, at least half of them, the earliest ones, won't make any reference to it at all. I've simply provided you with them for the sake of completeness. Hopefully, they'll give you a feel for the full scope of his work and provide you with some insights into his professional methodology. They're not labelled so you'll have to use your own initiative to navigate your way around them I'm afraid. However, I think you'll quickly see that there's a broadly consistent structure to the way they're set out, so it shouldn't prove too onerous, and I promise you the rewards will more than justify the effort.'

'I'm sure they will and obviously, I can't wait to get started...' He paused and then added, 'in the meantime though I wonder if you could just...?'

'Stop beating about the bush and tell you where the blessed Chamber Spout is,' Harry, interjected. 'That's what you're thinking isn't it?'

'I was going to put it a bit more diplomatically than that, but yes, I suppose it is.'

'It's located at, or should I say *beneath*, a place called Symbiosis House; one of those rambling, Victorian edifices you'll no doubt have observed, perched on the side of the hills above Malvern Wells.'

Dennis frowned, wondering if he'd heard correctly. 'Symbiosis House? Are you sure about that?'

'Of course I'm sure. I might be old, but I can assure you I'm not gaga; not yet anyway.'

'Sorry, I didn't mean it to sound as if I doubted you. It's just a rather odd coincidence that's all.'

'A coincidence? In what way?'

'You obviously haven't heard; somebody found a body there yesterday.'

'A body?'

'Yes. Some people reckon it could be Mathias Friedman, the chap who used to own the place.'

'I see.'

'Did you ever come across him when you were working in the area?'

Harry nodded.

'I did; he was a fascinating and charismatic man. In fact there was a period, during the early twenties, when our paths crossed quite frequently. I met his associate; business partner or whatever, Emery Harcourt, as well. Unlike Friedman though, he was rather a cold fish; no charm at all.'

'So presumably you know what happened to Friedman at the beginning of the war?'

'I know there was a vendetta against him because of his nationality and that he and Harcourt subsequently disappeared. I find it hard to believe that these are his remains though. I didn't know Friedman well, but I think he would have been more than a match for a gang of xenophobic vigilantes.'

'Well it's only a rumour.'

'One of many from that troubled period I imagine.'

'I'm sure you're right.'

Harry was distracted by the return of daylight outside the window. They'd left the tunnel now and were travelling through a deep cutting.

When he turned back he said, '

'Incidentally, there's another notebook I probably should have given you. It's one of my own actually, rather than my father's, but it contains some musings which might also be of interest to you. It didn't seem relevant before, but on reflection I rather wish I'd included it.'

'Is it to do with the Chamber Spout?'

'Not directly, but I'd like you to see it all the same: I think it would help to complete the picture. Unfortunately, it's going to be at least a fortnight until I do this journey again, otherwise I'd have suggested another rendezvous on the train, and I could have given it to you then.'

'What if I came over to Hereford to collect it?'

'Really? Would you?'

Suddenly, Dennis wished he hadn't been quite so impulsive: It was doubtful that Jeff would agree to fund a second rail trip in the same week, especially one without an obvious story attached to it.

'I'd have to get Jeff, my editor, to agree but hopefully that won't be a problem.'

'You wouldn't find it too much of an imposition?

'No, I'm happy to come over if you think it's worth my while.'

'Except now I'm starting to worry that, when you actually see it, you'll think I was wasting your time.'

'I'm sure I won't.'

'But, if it doesn't amount to anything, it will have been a terrible waste of your time, won't it?"

The more Harry back-tracked, the more intrigued Dennis became.

'No,' he said, 'I've made up my mind. I won't worry about clearing it with Jeff; I can easily fit it in around the rest of my work.'

'Well, just so long as you're sure. I'd hate you to fall out with your editor on my account.'

The train pulled into Colwall, but no-one left or got on. Apart from a distant hiss from the resting locomotive, everything was quiet.

'I could come over tomorrow evening if you like,' said Dennis. 'I know your address from the letter you sent to the Gazette. How about six o'clock?'

'I live alone,' said Harry, 'so I can accommodate whatever suits you.'

'Six should be all right. It's usually quiet at the Gazette on a Friday afternoon so I could probably get away earlier if I wanted to. Still, I'd better play it safe just in case my editor lumbers me with something at the last minute.'

He glanced out of the window and noticed that the guard had got off the train to talk to the station master. They were both gesturing up the track in the direction of the tunnel entrance. Looking back at Harry he said, 'it looks as if we've been delayed.'

'That's typical on this route I'm afraid. There are hold ups all the time.'

'What's going on do you think?'

'Oh, it could be anything, not that we'll ever be told. I've known the train sit here for fifteen or twenty minutes before now and no-one's had the courtesy to come and say what's going on.'

'Going by your letter, it sounds as if you think standards have slipped badly in recent times.'

'They certainly have I've been a regular passenger on this line for over fifty years now but for the last ten I've seen all the things that once made rail travel a pleasure systematically destroyed by the incompetent idiots who've taken it over. Once upon a time the staff had immaculate uniforms, the carriages were pristine, and the locomotives were gleaming. But have you seen the engine that's pulling us along today? It's caked with soot and grime. I doubt if anyone's even thought of cleaning it since nineteen forty-seven.'

'And you said you had a particular concern about the carriage lighting.'

'Yes, it fails with alarming frequency. The worst incident was just a week ago. I'd been to the lavatory at the other end of this carriage and, on my way back, the train was suddenly plunged into total darkness. It unsettled me a great deal because I've always had a fear of the dark and my phobia has become worse as I've got older. So much so that it sometimes gives me dreadful palpitations. I must have panicked because I walked straight into one of the connecting doors and banged my head quite badly. The experience has taught me never to go wandering off along the corridor just before we pass under the hills. As you can imagine, I wrote an extremely stiff letter of complaint to British Railways. '

'But there's been no reply?'

'Nothing at all; they couldn't care less. That's why I resorted to contacting the Gazette.'

'You said in your letter that you still use the train for

work reasons.'

'Yes, I'm currently advising the authorities at Worcester Cathedral on how to best deal with their troublesome medieval drainage system. As I'm sure I mentioned; I've dedicated the whole of my professional life to the management of water: that element upon which we all depend but which continually resists our efforts to contain and control it.'

'That's a good description; I'm going to write that down.'

'You'll see testimony to my struggle throughout this area. Most of the evidence is hidden away of course: pumps; conduits; pipes; sumps; filters beds, valves; stop-cocks; chambers. Malvern's water heritage has provided me with a particularly interesting variety of challenges over the years but of course I'm preaching to the converted: you know all about that because of your own interest in the subject, don't you?'

'I know some of it but it's just the tip of the iceberg really. I'm finding out new information all the time but each time I learn something, it seems to open countless other avenues to explore. I'm certain that will be the case when I read all this.' He patted the tartan shopping bag on the seat beside him.

Looking up again, he was alarmed to see that the old man had suddenly gone very pale and perspiration was streaming down his face.

'Are you feeling bad again?' he asked.

Harry drank from his hipflask before replying. His hand was shaking badly and most of the liquor seemed to be running down his chin.

'I'm afraid I am,' he said, wiping his face with a pin-striped sleeve. 'I think the delay has brought on one of my turns. I'm usually fine if it's just a quick stop because I don't have time to dwell on the prospect of entering the tunnel. Whenever we're held up like this though it prolongs the period of anxiety. Sometimes I cope perfectly well but today it seems to be affecting me quite badly.'

'Is there anything I can do? Do you want me to call for help?'

'There's no need for that. Just ask me a few more questions to take my mind off things. Nothing else about the train business though; I'd prefer not to dwell on that particular subject now and I don't suppose it was ever your primary interest anyway.'

'A bit more background on your father's notebooks would be helpful if you don't mind.'

'Fire away.'

'You said they're a record of his work during the 1890s: in which year did he come across the Chamber Spout.'

'1896,' said Harry, taking another gulp from his hip-flask. 'Apparently he received an unsolicited letter from the owner of Symbiosis House, a lawyer called Maurice Forbes, asking him if he'd be available to advise on the renovation of a neglected water feature he'd discovered beneath his house in Malvern Wells.'

'Is this what your father told you, or did you get it from his notes?'

'He told me. It wasn't long before he died actually, in 1935. That's when he showed me the notebooks for the first time. I don't know why he'd never mentioned them before, but there it is.'

'So this Maurice Forbes wrote to him out of the blue. How would he have tracked him down?'

'I'm not sure. I daresay he consulted Kelly's Directory

and saw his entry there. That's the most likely way.'

'And presumably your father was happy to oblige.'

'Extremely happy. He'd heard all the rumours about the Chamber Spout, so he was probably just as keen to see it in the flesh as you are. He described how Forbes met him at Symbiosis House at the appointed hour and led him across the grand entrance hall to a wooden trap door, set into the stone floor. It was through this that they descended, via a spiral staircase, into the chamber.'

'And that's when he saw the spout?'

'Heard it rather than saw it at that point I understand. Apparently, they were standing on a wooden platform – the correct term is mezzanine – at the foot of the ladder which gave a view down into the lower part of the chamber. An oil lamp, carried by Forbes, provided the only illumination and all my father could really see below was a rough floor strewn with fallen rocks and general detritus. Forbes said that, because of the chamber's present unstable condition, it was perilous to go down any further. The spout itself was hidden somewhere behind all the debris but it obviously made its presence felt because my father said the sound of water gushing out of it was so deafening that Forbes had to shout directly into his ear whenever he wanted to say anything.'

'It must have been disappointing for him to be held back like that.'

'Not really. He knew he'd be returning soon to begin the renovation and that, as soon as he'd taken steps to stabilise the site and bring more lamps down there, he'd be able to look around to his heart's content.'

'And what did he say about what he saw after he did?'

Harry wiped his perspiring face with the back of his sleeve.

'Sorry Dennis, I'm afraid I'm not up to saying any more. Look at my notes and drawings: they'll tell you everything you need to know.'

'It doesn't sound as if my questions have been much help after all.'

'Oh they've helped a little, but not quite enough I'm afraid. I'm going to get off now and wait for the next return train to Hereford. I'll telephone the people I was seeing in Worcester and rearrange my appointment for another day. I'm far too weak to face the tunnel this morning.'

Without another word, he rose slowly to his feet and slid back the compartment door. Leaving it open behind him, he shuffled off down the corridor.

'I'll see you tomorrow at six then, shall I?' Dennis called after him.

There was no reply. A few seconds later, Dennis heard the carriage door clunk shut and he watched as Harry Parsons made his unsteady way along the platform towards the footbridge.

CHAPTER 8
A Chance Meeting with Nigel

Thursday 28th March 1957

9.40 a.m.

The train finally left Colwall five minutes after Harry Parsons had got off. Dennis peered across at the other platform as they pulled out. He was expecting to catch a glimpse of the old man waiting for his return train but there was no sign of him at all. Within less than a minute they'd entered the tunnel and Dennis stared anxiously at the lamp on the opposite wall, convinced it was going to go out at any moment. Harry's nervousness was contagious but – on this occasion at least – it proved unwarranted. The story about unreliable electrics would have to wait for another day but there were plenty of other things to think about in the meantime.

Back at Great Malvern he stowed the tartan shopping bag in the Tiger's empty pannier. The other held his precious Leica and he looked now to make sure it hadn't been stolen. Margaret kept telling him to fit padlocks to the panniers, but he'd never got around to it. Despite the Whippet's regular tales of petty crime in the town, he chose to think of Malvern as a generally honest, law-abiding place and so he was glad, on finding the camera present and correct, to have his faith vindicated yet again.

As he rode along Imperial Road he debated what to do next. He supposed he should report back to Jeff and explain why his investment in a return ticket hadn't quite resulted in the campaigning story he'd been hoping for. He also supposed he should check if there were any messages from the police, now that they'd had a chance to visit the crashed car in daylight. Neither prospect was remotely appealing.

He swung left onto Church Street but instead of taking a right turn into Graham Road, which would have taken him round to Langland Parade and the Gazette office, he put his foot down and continued straight up the hill to Belle View Terrace. Soon he was heading south along Wells Road, retracing his route of the afternoon before. Although he didn't relish any further discussions with the police about it, he was curious to see if they'd acted on his information. As it turned out, he only had to travel a few hundred yards before he got his answer. A lorry rumbled past him, going in the opposite direction and sitting on the back was the black Rover. It had been secured using thick ropes and its badly crumpled front section was hidden by a tarpaulin. Strands of vegetation were still attached to it at various points and they trailed in the breeze like ragged garlands on a carnival float as the lorry trundled on towards Great Malvern.

As he approached the entrance to Symbiosis House he slowed down to see what was happening. There was still a police car parked in the gateway with a couple of bored looking constables standing next to it. There were only three other bystanders this morning, so it was apparent that the initial flurry of interest had died down and probably wouldn't flare up again until another rumour started circulating or new information appeared in the paper. He wondered how the Whippet was doing with his big story and if he'd been able to coax anyone into divulging inside information.

He put his foot down again and rode on towards Wynds Point. The point where the Rover had left the road was impossible to miss today. The heavy wheels of the lorry had churned the verge into deep ruts and the devastation caused by the salvage process itself looked like the aftermath of a cyclone that had torn everything up in its narrow path. He sat astride his motorbike with the engine still running and peered down the corridor of mangled undergrowth, muddy tyre tracks and scarred trees. At the bottom, he could see the oak tree that had stopped the progress of the rolling car but which, apart from some scuffing on its lower trunk, appeared remarkably unblemished. There was a halo of broken glass around its base that resembled the shattered surface of a frozen pond.

Then he saw something moving through the gloom, just beyond the oak tree and a man stepped out into full view and turned to look at him. He was tall, grey bearded and wearing a long overcoat and countryman's tweed cap. It was Andrew Morrigan. He'd aged a lot since Dennis had last seen him in his father's loading yard at Thomas Radford and Son, but he was instantly recognisable all the same.

After a few seconds Morrigan turned away and, without any apparent urgency, strolled off into the trees Dennis considered scrambling down the slope and following him but dismissed the idea almost immediately. Other than having heard second-hand, via Judith, that Morrigan was wanted by the police; he had no reason to think the man was doing anything other than taking an innocent walk through the woods.

The road was quiet on the way back to town, allowing him to enjoy a burst of speed. The Tiger was remarkably nippy when it wanted to be. He'd decided to put in a brief appearance at the office, check to see if there were any urgent messages and then nip out for an early lunch. With a bit of luck Jeff would be too wrapped up in other, more important, business to be interested in the outcome of his train expedition. He planned to hide in the Gazette's little basement library for the rest of the afternoon and start looking through the material Harry Parsons had given him.

Seeing a car coming out of a gateway, thirty yards or so ahead, he started to slow down. As he got closer, he realised it was the entrance to Symbiosis House. By now the car had come to a halt a little further down the road. The driver had got out and was now walking back up towards him. It was his brother, Nigel.

'I thought it was you,' said Nigel as Dennis drew level with him. 'I'd know that decrepit Triumph anywhere. You were going a bit fast for this road, weren't you?'

'And *you* drove straight out into the road without looking.'

'That's because I'm busy and I had a lot on my mind. What's your excuse?'

'I'm busy too. I'm late getting back to the office, that's why I was getting a bit of a spurt on.'

'Goodness knows how on that heap of junk.'

'That old motorbike has served me well.'

'I'm sure it has. Maybe I'd be nicer about it if I hadn't had such a hard morning.'

'Slow progress is it?'

'You could say that.'

'But at least you know who you're after.'

'How do you work that out?' said Nigel, eyeing him suspiciously.

Dennis realised he was in danger of incriminating Judith if he wasn't careful. 'The Whippet told me. He reckons Dad's old mechanic, Andrew Morrigan, dug the body up early yesterday morning and then ran away.'

'The Whippet, I might have known; that man's a bloody liability. We caught him trying to get onto the property yesterday; he thought he was being clever, creeping round through the woods and coming in the back way, but we soon put a stop to that.'

'How far did he get?'

'Far enough to make me to strengthen the watch around the boundaries. What else did he say?'

'Not a lot but you know what he's like: always making out he's in the thick of things.'

'Well you can take it from me, he doesn't know anything.'

'I also heard it's Mathias Friedman's body that's been dug up.'

'The Whippet told you that too, did he?'

'No, it's just another of the rumours doing the rounds.'

'I don't listen to rumours.'

'Funnily enough, that's what the Whippet said when I asked him the same question.'

'Ah, except the difference is, he's lying and I'm not.'

'But he was right about Morrigan being the man you're after?'

Nigel frowned but didn't answer straightaway.

'So,' Dennis persisted, 'was he?'

After taking a deep breath, Nigel said, 'It's true I need to talk to him but I'm not *after* him; not in the sense that you and the Whippet mean it anyway.'

'You don't necessarily think he's guilty then?'

'Guilty of what precisely?'

'Murder I assume – that and concealment of a body.'

'You're jumping to some hefty conclusions there, aren't you?'

I'm only going by what I've heard.'

'And so, based on a lot of idle gossip, you've decided Andrew Morrigan must be a murderer.'

'I haven't *decided* anything, but he didn't help matters by running off, did he? Having said that, the fact he phoned the police first might count in his favour I suppose.'

The words had barely left his mouth before he realised his mistake.

'How do you know he telephoned the police?' said Nigel, fixing him with a penetrating stare.

'The Whippet told me,' said Dennis, frantically hoping the lie would work a second time.

'That's very strange because, apart from me, only two people know about that phone call and I'm certain neither of them would have told the Whippet about it.'

'He must have just put two and two together then.'

'I suppose he must.' said Nigel, holding Dennis' uneasy gaze. 'It's the only possible explanation, isn't it?'

Dennis nodded. He was desperate to change the conversation, but he wasn't sure how to do it.

'To be honest,' continued Nigel, 'the last thing I need is yet another person telling me what the outcome is before I've had a chance to gather all the evidence.'

'Who else is then?'

'My boss, Superintendent "Bad'n" Goodall.'

'Oh him, I'd heard he could be difficult.'

'*Difficult?*' exclaimed Nigel. 'That's an understatement if ever I heard one.'

He looked up the road towards the gateway where two PCs were chatting animatedly to each other as they stood guard. He watched them carefully for a few seconds before returning his attention to Dennis, 'Listen,' he said, lowering his voice, 'you mustn't repeat what I'm about to say to anyone – anyone at all. Is that clear?'

'Yes.'

'I mean it: you've got to keep all this to yourself or there'll be hell to pay. Are you sure you understand?'

'Of course.'

'All right, the first thing you need to know is that Superintendent Goodall is a lazy bastard who thinks framing someone for a crime is a perfectly reasonable thing to do.'

'But that's blatant victimisation. Why would he resort to that?'

'Lots of reasons: it makes his detection rates look good; it saves him a lot of time and energy, but most of all it means he can put people like Morrigan away where he thinks they belong.'

'People like Morrigan? What do you mean?'

'It's obvious isn't it; people who don't fit in; people who make Malvern untidier than it should be? And for him Andrew Morrigan's a classic case: no fixed abode; doesn't have a steady job; drinks too much; gets into fights; the list goes on and on.'

'If he's such a classic case, why hasn't he been arrested for something already?'

'Oh, he has, lots of times, but only for minor things and that's what drives Goodall mad. For years now, he's been champing at the bit to pin something more serious on him, but he's never managed to make anything stick. But now he's been handed an opportunity on a plate: Morrigan kills a man in a drunken brawl and buries him at Symbiosis House. To all intents and purposes, he's got away with it, but his guilty conscience keeps gnawing away at him until eventually, unable to bear it any longer, he digs the body up again, thereby confessing to his original crime.'

'But you think that's just supposition?'

'I do, because as things stand, there isn't a shred of evidence to support it. But Goodall's not bothered about evidence; he's only interested in how easily circumstances can be swayed to suit his purpose.'

'That's terrible.'

'You say that now, but it isn't what you were suggesting a minute ago, is it?'

'What do you mean?'

'You had Morrigan down for murder and concealment of a body, as I recall.'

'I was only saying what it looked like; I didn't say he was automatically guilty, did I?'

'Not in so many words but you were getting pretty close. It just goes to prove how dangerous rumours can be in this sort of situation. They play straight into the hands of people like Goodall who just want to short-circuit the law and get a quick result.'

'But how does he get away with it? You'd think someone more senior would have got wind of what he's doing by now, wouldn't you?'

'My guess is he's got such a tight grip on things; they

don't realise what's happening.'

'But now you've got a perfect reason to go over his head and tell them, haven't you?'

'In theory yes, but the truth is, I'm worried about what might happen as a result.'

'Because Goodall could make life difficult for you if he found out you'd gone against him.'

'Exactly.'

'But once you'd informed the top brass, he wouldn't be able to do anything about it, would he?'

'But what if they were complicit in it?'

'Do you think that's likely?'

'Who knows? It's certainly possible. I'm not suggesting they're actively involved or anything; more that they just prefer to turn a blind eye. They might be prepared to let him get on with massaging the crime figures because, in the end, it makes them look good too.'

'So, who does Goodall actually report to?'

'The Chief Constable and his deputy.'

'And he's got a second in command presumably?'

'He should have a chief inspector, but currently there's no-one in post; in fact, there hasn't been for six months now, ever since Arthur Jenkins retired.'

'So where did Arthur Jenkins stand on all this?'

'It's hard to tell. He was useless to be honest; he gave up the ghost years ago, and frankly, no-one's really noticed he's gone. My guess is, he didn't know anything about it and even if he had, he wouldn't have let it bother him. Anything for a quiet life with old Arthur.'

'That would have suited Goodall down to the ground

then.'

'It certainly did; you can see why he hasn't been in any hurry to find a replacement can't you.'

'Chief Inspector's the next step up the ladder for you, isn't it'?

'You're right, but I won't get a sniff of it while Goodall's there because there's another man in the running, Inspector Leonard Bates. Him and his sidekick, Sergeant Collins, think the sun shines out of Goodall's arse. Naturally, Goodall loves that, so you can see who he's likely to favour in the superintendent stakes can't you?'

Dennis nodded. 'I've never come across Inspector Bates, but I *have* made Sergeant Collins' acquaintance. It was just last night. I phoned the police station, trying to get hold of you, but they passed me onto him instead.'

'I heard about that. He didn't warm to you at all apparently, but I don't suppose that comes as any surprise.'

'Not in the least. All I was trying to do was report a wrecked car I'd found in the woods. The way he reacted you'd have thought I was guilty of armed robbery or something.'

'That's Collins all over I'm afraid. He said you thought the car belonged to James Crawford.'

'I'm sure it does. It's a black Rover; registration number OAB 283. The letters rhyme with the numbers see; that's why I remember it.'

'I'll take your word for it.'

'You've heard about the latest trouble with Susan, have you?'

'I certainly have. Judith was telling me about it in bed, at one o'clock this morning; it's the only time we get to talk these days so no wonder I'm so tired all the time.'

'What do you make of it then?'

'I don't make *anything* of it. Given the pressure I've been under since this Symbiosis House business blew up, Susan and James' marital problems are well down my list of concerns.'

'Doesn't it worry you that James might have tried killing himself by driving off the road into the woods?'

'Obviously, it worries me but, as things stand, there's nothing I can do.'

'Meaning that whatever happens next is down to Sergeant Collins?'

'Him and Inspector Bates yes.'

'But can they be trusted to do it properly?'

'Hard to say. It depends on how straightforward it is. The less trouble it causes them, the less they'll be inclined to cut corners.'

'Well they've had the car taken away so that's a start I suppose.'

'How do you know that?'

'I've just been up to Wynds Point; that's why I was coming back past here. I saw the car being towed down to town as I was going up the hill.'

'There you are then; hopefully once they've confirmed it *is* James' car, they'll make a reasonable effort to find him. Chances are, he staggered home after the accident and he'll be there now, drowning his sorrows and feeling like a complete fool.'

'Well he wasn't there last night because I phoned and there wasn't an answer. It was the same at his office.'

'He was probably too embarrassed to pick it up. I

should try him again when you get back to work. Just make sure you let Sergeant Collins know if you track him down. I don't want him ranting to me about how my brother's been wasting his valuable time.'

'And if I don't get him at home, I'll try his office again. Even if he isn't there, I can talk to his secretary and see if she knows anything.'

'Good idea,' said Nigel, taking another glance at the gateway before checking his watch. 'Anyway,' he continued, 'I'd better be going before those PCs report me to old Bad'n for loitering on the job.'

'Do you really think they'd do that?'

'Probably not, but you can't be too careful round here. I'm never quite sure how far Goodall's tentacles reach.'

'I don't know how you put up with it.'

'We all have our crosses to bear,' said Nigel with a shrug. 'I don't suppose working at the Gazette is perfect all the time either.'

'No, it isn't, but I don't have to look over my shoulder all the time, wondering who I can trust.'

'Well you should count yourself lucky,' said Nigel, glancing at his watch again. 'Is there anything else you want to get off your chest before we go our separate ways?'

Dennis wondered if he ought to mention his earlier sighting of Andrew Morrigan, but something made him hold back. 'Like what?' he said noncommittally.

'Nothing really, I was just wondering how things are between you and Dad these days.'

'As fraught as ever, how about you?'

'Much the same but I hear he was particularly bad yesterday. Mum phoned Judith during the afternoon to tell her all about it.'

'What set him off this time?'

'I don't know. Judith reckons Mum was a bit confused.'

'That doesn't sound like Mum; she's usually pretty insightful about his mood changes. What did she actually say?'

'At first, she reckoned he was still angry because you'd been pestering for information about that hotel our grandfather used to own, but then she decided it was to do with what's happened up here.'

'Why would that upset him so much?'

'Goodness knows.'

'So, he's likely to be like a bear with a sore head when we all meet up later for this tea party'

'What tea party?'

'The one Judith's arranged; don't tell me you'd forgotten.'

'Completely, but it hardly matters because I couldn't have made it anyway. Never mind, I'll be there with you in spirit.'

He got back into his car and closed the door behind him. He wound the window down before starting the engine.

'Just as a matter of interest,' said Dennis, peering in at him, 'do you have a sergeant, someone like Collins, who works for you?

Yes, his name's Clarke, Sergeant Ronnie Clarke but, unlike Collins, he's as straight as a die. I don't work that closely with him though – or with anyone else for that matter. I'm a bit of a lone wolf at work to be honest.' He suddenly revved the engine and, without a further word, drove off at speed, waving at Dennis through the open window.

As Dennis watched the car disappear around a bend, it occurred to him that he should have asked Nigel when he'd be able to get inside Symbiosis House to look at the Chamber Spout. He knew why he hadn't though: Nigel was obviously far too busy for such trivial matters. He got back on the Tiger and kicked down hard on the starter pedal. It obligingly fired up straightaway, so he cranked the throttle up to maximum to make sure it didn't change its mind.

Back at the Gazette Julian Croft appeared to be the only person around. The reporters' office was gloomy after the bright spring sunshine outside and made even more so by the fog of cigarette smoke that hung in the air. The scene matched his current state of mind perfectly. His mood lifted slightly however when he reached his desk and saw that it was just as he'd left it the day before. There were no new messages.

'Has anyone been trying to get hold of me?' He called across to Julian who was hunched over his typewriter as usual.

The clatter of typing stopped, and Julian turned around to look at him in the languid way that always made it seem as if he was operating in slow motion.

'Not that I'm aware of. The phone's been blessedly quiet all morning. Who were you expecting to hear from?'

'I thought the police might be after me.'

'Really?' said Julian eagerly, 'tell me more.'

'It depends if Jeff's about. I don't want another telling off like the one we had yesterday.'

'Don't worry; he's been out since first thing. He was here when I arrived at eight but, ten minutes later, he raced off in that little red devil of his. He didn't say where he was going but he certainly had the look of a man on a mission.

Anyway, it's quite safe to talk so come on; why are the cops after you?'

Dennis told him about his discovery of the wrecked car and the difficult conversation he'd had with Sergeant Collins when he reported it.

'That's quite a tale,' said Julian after he'd finished, 'but I wouldn't take it personally if I were you; the police can be pretty uncooperative round here from what I've heard.'

'What have you heard exactly?' asked Dennis, wondering if he was going to get a repeat of what Nigel had just told him.

'Oh, nothing really. It's just an impression I get, that's all.'

'So, has anything happened while I've been away?'

'No, it's been as quiet as the grave. I managed to finish my review in the nick of time and ever since then I've either been twiddling my thumbs or smoking like a proverbial chimney. Meanwhile, you've had an exciting rendezvous on a train I hear.'

'Jeff told you I presume?'

'Yes, and he seemed pretty confident it had the makings of a good story.'

'Well, if he's hoping for a campaigning piece about the faulty lights in British Railways carriages, he's going to be disappointed because they worked perfectly in both directions.'

'Actually, I think he was more excited about these documents the old man had promised to give you. They were supposed to reveal the location of your lost underground spring, weren't they?'

'You're seriously telling me Jeff was excited about

that?'

'He certainly seemed to be yes. I know you're always saying he's got no time for your Wells and Springs column, but I think, secretly, he's quite a fan.'

'You could have fooled me.'

'Jeff's a man of many parts: on one level he's the ruthless businessman, dedicated to driving up the readership figures and increasing advertising but, on another, he's interested in people; their heritage and the unique stories they've got to tell. That's why he's such a good editor of a local paper I suppose.'

'I agree he's a good editor; I just wish he'd show me more of his people side and a bit less of the ruthless businessman.'

'I know what you mean but I'm sure he's got a soft spot for your column all the same. Anyway, did the old man on the train come up with the goods or not? Jeff reckoned he was promising to reveal the location of your precious underground spring.'

'That's right, the Chamber Spout, and yes he did. Remarkably, it's supposed to be at Symbiosis House. Can you believe it?'

'Well it's strange that it should come to light at the same time as the other business up there, but these coincidences happen I suppose. What's this chap's name by the way and what's his connection with the place?'

'His name's Harry Parsons and he's a hydraulic engineer by profession. He must be in his seventies now and he claims to be semi-retired. Apparently, his father was a hydraulic engineer before him, and he was taken on by the house's owner in the mid-1890s because the chamber and the spout itself were in a bad state and desperately in need of renovation. Harry's given me a bag full of the old notebooks his father kept when he was working on the renovation project. I haven't had a chance to look through them yet, but I gather they contain all his drawings, measurements and calculations.'

'So, do you think he's reliable?'

'I must admit, I didn't think so at first: he's a scruffy old devil and, going by the way he was gulping down whisky from his hip flask, I suspect he's pretty sozzled most of the time. But the more I talked to him, the more plausible his story seemed to be.'

'Well I doubt if he'd have given you all those notebooks if he was just making the whole thing up.'

'I agree. I just need to find time to look at them properly now and confirm that they're as authentic as he's making out.'

'What did he make of the news about the body up there?'

'He didn't know anything about it until I told him.'

'And how did he react when he found out?'

'On the face of it he seemed to take in his stride,' said Dennis, rubbing his chin reflectively, 'but now you come to ask, I'm not so sure.'

'Why not?'

'Because his mind seemed to drift elsewhere for a few moments and then he told me about another notebook he'd left at home and how he regretted not bringing it along with all the others. He said it was one he'd kept himself, not one of his father's, and that it contained some musings – that was his exact word – which might help to complete the picture.'

'And you think it might have a bearing on current

events?'

'I'm beginning to, yes. I didn't have time to press him much further because he suddenly left the train when we were held up at Colwall. He'd got himself into a panic because he's frightened of the lights going out halfway through the tunnel. Fortunately, I'd already agreed to go over to his house in Hereford tomorrow evening to pick it up.'

'That's good. I'll be fascinated to hear what happens. Don't forget to let me know, will you?'

'No, of course not. I'd be grateful if you could keep it under your hat for now though. It might come to nothing, so I don't want to raise any expectations, especially Jeff's, until I'm sure of what I'm dealing with.'

'Don't worry, mum's the word. So presumably that was all you were able to get out of him before he made his abrupt exit, stage left.'

'There was one other thing actually: I asked him if he knew Mathias Friedman.'

'Really? What did he say?'

'That he did and that their paths had crossed quite frequently for a time during the early twenties.'

'Interesting.'

Julian lit another of his little black cigarettes.

'That's about the time the Black Moon Society started,' he said, releasing a perfect smoke ring into the air.

'The Black Moon Society?' echoed Dennis. 'Funnily enough, Margaret mentioned the same thing last night. Apparently, her late father was a member. What do *you* know about it?'

'Quite a lot as it happens.'

He abruptly got to his feet.

'But before we get onto all that, can I suggest we adjourn to the Lamb and Flag. I'm suddenly in need of refreshment.'

CHAPTER 9
Black Moon Society

Thursday 28th March 1957

1.00 p.m.

They sat down at a small table in the lounge of the Lamb and Flag. 'Cheers,' said Julian, taking a sip of his gin and tonic. 'How's your beer?'

Dennis had ordered a pint of bitter. He gulped down the first half inch which was more head than beer. 'Not bad,' he said, wiping the foam from around his mouth with the back of his hand.

'Actually, I've just remembered something,' said Julian, 'before we get onto the Black Moon Society, I need to tell you about my encounter with the Whippet, earlier on.'

'Let me guess, he's single-handedly solved the Symbiosis House case and will be revealing all in tomorrow's Gazette.'

'Not quite but he does claim to have made a significant breakthrough. He reckons he managed to creep right up to the house and look in through one of the windows. By a huge stroke of luck, it turned out to be the room the police are using as their operations centre and where, at that very moment, your brother was updating his minions on how the investigation was progressing. The window was shut tight so he couldn't hear actually anything but, helpfully, a blackboard and easel had been set up against the facing wall, on which DCI Powell had chalked up the salient points for all to see.'

Julian paused to take another sip of his drink.'

'So, come on then, what were they?' asked Dennis, impatiently.

'He wouldn't say. He told me I'd have to wait until tomorrow for all the details, just like everyone else.'

'Typical Whippet. He's utterly infuriating, isn't he?'

'That's one way of putting it. Slimy, manipulative little bugger are the words I'd use to describe him.' He downed the rest of his gin and tonic. 'But that's beside the point now because, after he'd disappeared, I had a brilliant idea.'

He seized his empty glass and got to his feet.

'Where are you going?' said Dennis.

'Sorry to leave you on tenterhooks but that went down so well I need another one. How about you?'

'Just a half this time, please. This is heavier on the stomach than the stuff you're drinking.'

He watched Julian thread his way between the tables towards the bar and then he turned to look out of the window. Although the glass was frosted to make it harder to see in from the street, limited visibility was possible through a row of three-inch high letters, proclaiming, "Wines, Spirits and Fine Ales." These were transparent in contrast with the otherwise opaque surface of the pane. Through a mirror image of the letter "S" he could see a man leaning against the wall of the Gazette office, across the road. He was small with sharp features and wearing a medium length overcoat and a check cap. To Dennis he looked like an aging jockey. He kept looking up and down the street as if expecting someone to appear at any moment. This continued for about a minute then he glanced at his watch and seemingly deciding he'd waited long enough, set off along Langland Parade before turning right into the alleyway that led directly to Church Street. He moved quickly despite having a pronounced limp.

After a few seconds the penny dropped: it was the mystery best man Dennis had last seen well over a decade before at Susan and James' wedding; the one who, according to Judith, worked with James at Crawford, Davies and Withers.

'Do you know a man called Percy Franklin?' he asked when Julian came back with their drinks and two packets of Smith's crisps.

'I know *of* him,' said Julian as he opened one of the packets and sprinkled salt on the contents from the little blue bag inside. 'Why do you ask?'

'He was hanging around outside the office just then. He looked as if he was waiting for someone.'

'Oh, he'll have been waiting for Jeff.'

'Waiting for Jeff? Why?'

'He's Jeff's personal bookie or, to be more accurate, he acts as Jeff's intermediary with the betting shop down the road.'

'Are you telling me Jeff bets on the horses?'

'Oh, Jeff will bet on anything, but it's mainly horses I think yes.'

'I'm amazed. It seems completely out of character. I'd got him down as an opera buff or something cultural like that.'

'He could be one of those as well for all I know but he's definitely a man who likes a flutter and Percy Franklin's the man who goes and does the business for him.'

'Why can't he go to the betting shop himself?'

'I'm sure he does sometimes but I think there's more to his arrangement with Percy than just getting him to go and place a particular bet; Old Percy's a seasoned gambler in his own right. From what I understand, they've been discussing odds and working out systems together for donkey's years now.'

'He looks as if he might have been a jockey once; you know the small, wiry type.'

'Percy? No, I don't think so. His dad, Alfie Franklin, was quite a well-known character round here in the twenties and thirties. Actually, by well-known I mean notorious. He was a sort of traveling antiques dealer and he used to set up his stall at agricultural shows and race meetings – anywhere there'd be a big crowd of people. Preferably people from elsewhere with lots of money.'

'Why notorious?'

'Because no-one – no-one locally anyway - believed his wares were entirely above board. I don't think he was ever actually done for anything, but he was always seen as someone who sailed a bit close to the wind.'

'You mean he dealt in fakes?'

'That was the general view: fakes and knock-off to put it crudely or items of doubtful provenance if you want to be more polite about it.'

'And Percy was part of this set up?'

'Yes, him and his twin brother Clarry. Clarry's more brawn than brains I think, so he concentrated on fetching and carrying while Percy acted as his dad's understudy. They used to travel around from event to event and eventually Percy's and Jeff's paths crossed, at Worcester Racecourse.'

'When would this have been?'

'The early twenties I think.'

'So, Jeff was quite young.'

'In his teens I'd guess.'

'He's not from round here though, is he? Wasn't he brought up in Norfolk?'

'He was, but he went to school at Malvern College.'

'How would a schoolboy get away with sneaking off to race meetings in Worcester?'

'Who knows? But anyway, that's how Jeff and Percy first got to know each other and, from what I gather, that's when they started working on their little gambling system.'

'Is the twin brother part of it as well?'

'Clarry? No, I shouldn't think so. As I said, he's the brawn and Percy's the brains. These days, Clarry makes himself useful as Percy's personal driver: he's probably parked at the end of the street, waiting, as we speak. He drives a flashy-looking Standard Vanguard, in two-tone silver and grey – you can't miss it.'

'I still find it hard to believe that Jeff's a gambler.'

'He's a man of many parts, that's for sure. For example, not many people are aware that he was posted to Malvern, during the war, to run a specialist military training centre. Where do you think it was based?'

'Symbiosis House?'

'Oh, so you know about that do you?' said Jeff, looking disappointed.

'I know about the training centre because my landlord mentioned it yesterday. I didn't realise Jeff had had anything to do with it though. It's a far cry from editing a local newspaper isn't it?'

'True but Jeff only got into newspapers later: his original field was Physics: that's what he studied when he went up to Cambridge. Have you seen all those scientific tomes on his bookshelf?'

Dennis nodded as he topped up his pint glass with the half that Julian had brought him. 'Yes, I have but I thought they were just a fixture, I didn't know they belonged to Jeff.'

'Oh, they're his all right but I doubt if he looks at them much these days. I expect he's put that phase of his life well behind him now.'

'I've never heard him mention any of this so how come you know all about it?'

'I doubt if he'd have told me either if I hadn't asked him directly. I'd picked up a few snippets of information on my travels, so I simply asked him if there was any truth in them.'

'And he didn't mind?'

'Not at all.'

'So, you're on pretty friendly terms, are you?'

'I wouldn't go that far: we have a chat from time to time if he's passing through the office and I'm here on my own, but no more than that. I've never done this with him for instance. Jeff's not really the pub type.'

'Just the betting shop type.'

'Exactly,' said Jeff with a chuckle.

'Anyway,' said Dennis. 'what was this brilliant idea you were going to tell me about, before you dashed off to the bar?"

'Oh yes, we were talking about the Whippet, weren't we? Well, twenty minutes before he came crowing to me about his big discovery, I'd seen him creeping down to the library in the basement. Now I don't think I've ever seen the Whippet use the library in all the time he's been here so, after he'd gone out, I went downstairs to see if I could find out what he'd been looking at. It wasn't hard because, despite all that swagger, he's actually a bit dim. He'd left a volume of Encyclopaedia Britannica on the desk, open at the page he'd been reading. Of course, I couldn't tell which entry he'd actually been reading but I guessed that, if I looked in the wastepaper basket under the desk, I'd find a clue to help me narrow things down. Sure enough, there was a crumpled-up sheet in there, presumably from his notebook. I smoothed it out and there, before my very eyes, was a rough sketch of what he must have seen on the blackboard at Symbiosis House.'

'Just a sketch; no writing?'

'That's right, he must have held on to his written notes for when he typed up his report. For a moment I thought the sketch was going to be useless without some sort of explanation: he's no artist I can tell you and at first glance it just looked like a vaguely cross-shaped pattern of lines and circles but then I looked back at the open page of the encyclopaedia and suddenly all was revealed. Crude though it might have been, I could see straightway that his sketch matched a photograph on the page that was open: it was an Occitan cross. Does that mean anything to you?'

'Nothing at all.'

'It didn't to me either; not until I'd read the Britannica article. It turns out it's also known as the cross of Toulouse and it's associated with the Languedoc region of France. Basically, it's a stylised cross with three small disks – I think they're supposed to be golden spheres – at each point. The photograph in the encyclopaedia was only in black and white but, according to the description, it appears in heraldry as yellow on a red background. Quite often the background takes the form of a shield. I suppose I could have brought the Whippet's drawing over to show you but it's worse than useless really. You'd be better off looking in the encyclopaedia for yourself.'

'So, what do you make of it?'

'I reckon the police found one of these Occitan crosses on or near the body.'

'A medallion or something like that?'

'A medallion or a ring – something durable that would still be recognisable after being buried for years.'

'That makes sense.'

'It's also the sort of thing that might have a name or a message engraved on it.'

'Which could reveal the body's identity. No wonder the Whippet was so excited.'

'The trouble is, without seeing his notes, there's not a lot more we can find out is there?'

'We've got some useful clues though,' said Dennis. 'We ought to be able to deduce something from them.'

'I'm not so sure but I admire your optimism so let's give it a try. The clues so far are that the body of a French person – we don't know if they're male or female - possibly from the Languedoc region, was, at some point, buried in a garden in Malvern Wells. So, what do you deduce from that, Sherlock?'

'Firstly, that if the victim really was French, it knocks the rumour about Mathias Friedman on the head because Friedman was Austrian not French.'

'Good point. What else?'

'It suppose it begs the question why a French person might have come to Malvern in the first place.'

'Go on.'

Dennis peered at him doubtfully. 'Actually, this is all starting to seem a bit pointless now I come to think about it.'

'No, keep going. Just say the first thing that comes to mind?'

'A holiday? They came to here to walk and look at the scenery? Maybe they came to take the waters. It could be the body of a Victorian water cure patent for all we know.'

'What else?'

'It could be anything – maybe they came here for a job.'

'What sort of job?'

'A chef at one of the hotels or restaurants perhaps, or a teacher at the College or one of the prep schools, or...'

'Go on,' said Julian, leaning forward and staring at him intently. 'something's just clicked, hasn't it?'

'Possibly, I'm not sure. The thing is, last night, Margaret told me about some papers she'd found in a storeroom that dated from the war years, when the TRE was based at the College. They were research notes that one of the scientists had left behind and funnily enough *he* was French.'

'I see,' said Julian. He nodded slowly as if something was clicking into place for him too. 'What was this scientist's name? Do you remember?'

'It was Morel – Laurent Morel.'

'And you're saying that name doesn't ring any bells for you?'

'None at all.'

'You surprise me, but maybe it'll all start coming back to you after I've explained.' He lit a cigarette and inhaled deeply before continuing. 'It's generally known that when the TRE commandeered the College in 1942, Malvern suddenly found itself in the forefront of radar development. Less well-known is the fact that, amongst the whizzes carrying out this pioneering work, was a contingent of émigré scientists. Mainly, they were people who'd become stranded over here after the outbreak of hostilities, and one of them was a Frenchman called Laurent Morel.'

'I already know all this.'

'I realise that but there's something in particular about Laurent Morel you don't appear to know, or at least, you seem to have forgotten. One day, in the Autumn of 1948, he disappeared into thin air. One minute he was there and the next, he was gone. Of course, as he was a TRE scientist, presumably working on new-fangled radar systems, and a foreigner to boot, most people assumed he'd run off with top secret information.'

'Good grief, how on earth could I have missed that?'

'I expect you were so obsessed with tracking down some obscure spring or other at the time, you didn't notice. And, to be fair, the Gazette's reporting on it was low-key to put it mildly. Normally, that sort of thing would be an absolute gift to a small-town rag like ours, wouldn't it? Foreign boffin goes missing with a bag full of secret dossiers, etcetera, etcetera. But, for some unfathomable reason, the Gazette decided to play it down. The week of his disappearance, it just about got onto the bottom of the front page but, incredibly, it didn't make the headline. None of the Worcester or Hereford papers picked up on it, nor did any of the nationals. Then, a week later, we printed a brief paragraph on page two, effectively saying, "panic over", the police now thought Laurent Morel had just been homesick and had chosen to return to France - and specifically, now I come to think of it, to his home town of Toulouse.'

'It almost sounds as if it was being hushed up for some

reason.'

'That's what most of us thought – those of us who were paying attention, that is. But, as you might recall, the Gazette's editorial policy wasn't exactly open to question in those days. Not that it is now really, but at least Jeff's prepared to listen first, and *then* ignore you.'

'Of course, this must have happened while the rebarbative Don Blackmore was in charge. No wonder I made myself scarce. Arthur Cavendish had retired suddenly in the September, and then Blackmore stood in for three months until Jeff arrived. So, do you think the police leaned on him to close the story down?'

Julian shrugged. 'It's possible I suppose. Don always knew which side his bread was buttered on so he could easily have agreed to back off if they made it worth his while somehow. I'm still not sure why they'd have been so bothered about it though.'

'Just as a matter of interest, was Superintendent Goodall around then?'

'Yes, he was. Why do you ask?'

'Because I hear he's got a reputation for bending the rules. "Bad'n" Goodall, that's what my brother Nigel calls him.'

'Goodall, of course. He and Don Blackmore were like peas in a pod so they could easily have come to an agreement of some sort.'

'But why?'

'From what I hear, Goodall likes an easy life, with everything kept neatly sewn up and under his control. Maybe he was worried that, because of the national security implications, the Laurent Morel business was about to take on a life of its own. Special Branch, or whatever, would have to be called in and he'd end up playing second fiddle to them.'

'But I don't understand why they didn't take over anyway. I can see how he might have persuaded Don Blackmore, but he wouldn't have had any influence over Special Branch would he?'

'I shouldn't think so but, in any case, as far as I know, they never got involved and, within a couple of weeks, most people had forgotten about Laurent Morel completely.'

'Do you think there's any chance Blackmore and Goodall knew that Morel was buried at Symbiosis House?'

'It's an interesting idea,' said Julian, exhaling another of his immaculate smoke rings, 'but maybe we shouldn't let our imaginations run away with us at this stage. Let's confirm it really *is* Morel who's buried there before we start speculating any further.'

He stubbed out his cigarette and then leaned forward, conspiratorially. 'Actually,' he said, 'there's another dimension to this you probably need to be aware of.'

'Yes?'

'It was generally understood that Laurent Morel was a homosexual.'

'Oh, I see.'

'And you can imagine how Don Blackmore might make use of that sort of information, can't you? Especially if his friend, Superintendent Goodall, had asked him to distract people's attention from a potentially troublesome story.'

'He'd probably use it to play on people's basest prejudices and try to make them think Morel wasn't really worth bothering about.'

'Exactly.'

'Don was good at writing that sort of stuff, wasn't he?

A few carefully chosen phrases to make people read between the lines. He used to do it all the time. You'd have called it clever if it hadn't been so twisted.'

'And in this particular instance he excelled himself: The final paragraph was loaded with enough innuendo to sink a battleship. It was plainly meant to make everyone think, good riddance to the perverted bastard; we don't want any more of his type round here.'

'Not the paper's finest hour by the sound of it.'

'Far from it and say what you like about Jeff Stephenson, no reporter would ever get away with that sort of scurrilous reporting under his regime and the same was true of Arthur Cavendish before him.'

'But you never confronted Blackmore about it?'

'No, I'm ashamed to say, I didn't.'

'You shouldn't feel bad about it though. I doubt if anyone else would have had the guts to challenge him – *I* certainly wouldn't.'

'Maybe so, but, for me, it was particularly shameful because, although I didn't know Morel, I felt as if I was letting him down.'

'I don't understand.'

'Let's just say I felt a particular bond with him and the reason I didn't press the matter with Blackmore was because I was frightened he'd guess why and use it to destroy me. Now do you see?'

'Yes,' said Dennis, suddenly feeling uncomfortable, 'I think I do.'

'Anyway, enough of all that,' said Julian. He stubbed out his cigarette and downed the rest of his gin and tonic. 'After you've got me another drink, we'll get onto what we came here for.'

Five minutes later Dennis was back with another gin and tonic for Julian, another half of bitter for himself and two packets of crisps.

'Right,' said Julian, 'Mathias Friedman's legendary Black Moon Society: did you say it was Margaret who mentioned it to you?'

'Yes, she told me her father was a member in the early twenties.'

'And that's about the same time your man on the train, Harry Parsons, did some work up there?'

Dennis nodded.

'Harry's a chap in his seventies, is that right?'

'I should think so, yes.'

'In which case he's a prime candidate to have been a member of that particular group. Any man from round here of that age and from a broadly professional background would be the same. Not that they'd ever tell you though. How old's your father for example?'

'He's sixty-seven but he's a lot sprightlier than Harry Parsons. He still works full-time, managing the warehouse at Thomas Radford and Son. He served in the First World War and he's proud of it as he never tires of telling everyone. Are you saying he could have been a member of the Black Moon Society as well?'

'Oh, I'd bet good money on it but, as I say, he'd never let on.'

'Well he's pretty cagey about his past anyway, with the notable exception of his war service of course, but you're making it sound as if members were sworn to secrecy; a bit like the Freemasons.'

'I don't know if they were sworn to secrecy, all I *do* know is that you'd be hard pressed to get anyone who'd been involved to open up about it.'

'Maybe that's because they don't want to be associated with Mathias Friedman: he's been pretty much persona non grata round here since 1939, hasn't he?'

'True but, even when Friedman was at the height of his popularity, I doubt if you'd have got anyone to say anything.'

'So, if they're all so reticent, how come *you* know so much about it?'

'Because I keep my ear to the ground Dennis, that's why. I'm fifty-six now which means I was too young to serve in the First World War but old enough to have been a raw theatre correspondent in the early nineteen-twenties, mingling with the interval crowds in the Festival Theatre bar, listening in to all the local gossip. I found I could merge into the background quite easily and you'd be amazed at the things people will say in your presence when they've stopped noticing you're there.'

'Almost as if you were invisible.'

'Precisely and it's usually down to pure snobbery. Once they've concluded you're outside their social circle you effectively cease to exist. You know as well as I do that there's a certain section of the population that thinks it's a cut above the likes of you and me and they're not afraid to let you know it. In fact, it's become such a habit for them, they don't even realise they're doing it. I daresay you get the same thing everywhere, but I have to say, Malvern seems particularly prone to it. I've learned to take it with a pinch of salt but, between you and me, it's one thing about working round here that really drives Jeff Stephenson mad.'

'But Jeff went to public school for goodness sake. You'd think that made him one of them, wouldn't you?'

'It probably does but he wouldn't admit it. I don't know if I've ever mentioned this before, but our Jeff was a bit of a political firebrand when he was at Cambridge: he had a particular penchant for the philosophy of Karl Marx.'

'He was a communist?'

'A passionate one by all accounts. I believe he visited the Soviet Union a few times while he was at university.'

'Is he still as passionate about it?'

'I doubt it. I'm sure he left all that youthful fervour behind a long time ago.'

'Going back to the Black Moon Society then, what exactly did you learn while you were listening in to all those interval conversations in the Festival Theatre bar?'

'Mainly that, rather than just being an astronomical society, as the name would suggest, it involved strange ceremonies during which copious amounts of alcohol were consumed. Even more interestingly, some people reckoned drugs were taken as well.'

'Good grief,' exclaimed Dennis, 'what sort of drugs?'

'Apparently Friedman had access to all sorts because of his work Powick Mental Asylum.'

'I didn't know Friedman was at Powick.'

'Didn't you? He worked there as a psychiatrist in the early twenties but of course he's much better known for his charity work, the swanky dinners he used to host and the way his photograph was in the papers all the time, along with his associate, Emery Harcourt.'

'Emery Harcourt,' said Dennis, 'that name rings a bell. Harry Parsons mentioned him; he reckoned he was a bit of a cold fish.'

'Yes, Harcourt lived at Symbiosis House with Friedman. He'd been a pharmacist at Powick and that's how they got to know each other. Harcourt was brilliant by all accounts but Harry's right, he seems to have been rather a detached and charmless character.'

'So, while Friedman was running the Black Moon Society, was he still working at Powick?'

'No, he'd left Powick by the time he started the Black Moon Society and there were rumours he left under a bit of a cloud. It doesn't seem to have done him any harm though because, as you know, all through the twenties and thirties he was the talk of the town.'

'How did he make his living then, after he left Powick?'

'I don't think Friedman *needed* to make a living, not in the conventional sense anyway. He just seems to have been one of those fortunate people for whom money never seems to be an issue.'

'So, apart from consuming drink and drugs, what else happened at these ceremonies?'

'Mass hypnotism, ceremonial chanting and that sort of thing apparently.'

'Why though? What was it all supposed to be about?'

'People seemed to think it was all just a bit of a game: Friedman's way of helping a few ex-soldiers forget their troubles and let off steam. Apparently, he'd been working with shell-shock victims at Powick, so I suppose it followed on from that. They didn't approve of it exactly, but they understood why it might play a useful part in certain men's lives; those who'd suffered so much, serving their country. They were inclined to turn a blind eye, but that didn't stop them being intrigued by it.'

'And why the name? Why the Black Moon Society?'

'I haven't got a clue. Sorry, I'm not quite the fount of

all knowledge you were expecting, am I? I can tell you what a black moon *is* though: assuming you don't know already, of course.'

'Is it like a blue moon in some way?'

'Yes. As you know, a blue moon refers to the second occurrence of a full moon in the same month. For that to happen, the first full moon has to appear right at the beginning of the month allowing enough time for the second one, the blue moon, to appear before the end. They're not as rare as people think, they crop up every eighteen months or so, sometimes less than that. A black moon is the same principle applied to a new moon rather than a full moon.'

'Fascinating Is there anything else you can tell me?'

'I'm afraid not. Nothing that springs to mind anyway. Perhaps this Harry Parsons fellow will be able to reveal more when you see him again tomorrow.'

He finished his gin and tonic and glanced at his watch. 'I'd better be getting back. I still need to put the finishing touches to my Princess Apple Blossom review before the editor's deadline.'

'I should go as well,' said Dennis. He gulped down the rest of his beer in one go and got up.

'Funnily enough,' said Julian as they stepped out into the street, it's just occurred to me that there's going to be a black moon this Sunday, the thirtieth of March. We can take a look at the calendar when we get back to the office if you like.'

CHAPTER 10

Tea Party

Thursday 28th March

5.30 p.m.

'What's the matter with you?' said Margaret.

She was waiting for him outside the Gazette office, after work. They were meant to be going to the Foley Arms for a fortifying drink before Judith's tea party but something about the look on her face told Dennis the plan might be about to change.

'Nothing's the matter,'

'Yes it is, you're tipsy. I thought you were as soon as I saw you and now I've smelt your breath, it's obvious I was right. What have you been up to?'

'Julian and I went over to the Lamb and Flag at lunchtime. There were a few things we needed to discuss.'

'It's not like you to drink in the middle of the day,' she said as they strolled round to the rear of the building to retrieve his motorbike.

'I know but, under the circumstances, I thought I'd make an exception.'

'What circumstances?'

'Just that we were having an interesting conversation in the office and Julian suggested we continue it over at the pub.'

'I bet he did.'

'He started knocking back G and T's, so I decided to have a pint of bitter.'

'You didn't have to keep pace with him though did you?'

'I wasn't really thinking about it. Anyway, I stuck to halves after the first one.'

'I don't think you ought to drink anymore now though?'

'But you need one don't you? You can't be expected to endure this ghastly tea party without a stiff whisky inside you.'

'I'll manage. It's no good relying on alcohol to get you through these things is it?'

'I'm not so sure about that.'

They'd reached the Gazette's small parking area by now. It had been empty before lunch when Dennis arrived back but now the Tiger was sandwiched between Jeff's bright red Morgan and Brian Fairclough's mud-streaked Ford Anglia. The Whippet had been ensconced in the editor's office since four o'clock and it was generally assumed by the rest of the staff that intense discussion was underway about the final version of tomorrow's big front-page story.

'I'll tell you what,' said Dennis as he seized the handlebars, kicked back the prop stand and carefully pushed the motorcycle out of the narrow space, 'I've got two bottles of Mackeson back at my flat. Rather than going to the Foley Arms, we could have a drink there and then walk round to Judith and Nigel's, just in time for tea.'

'I don't like Mackeson.'

'I think I've got some lemonade as well. I can make you a shandy. That would be all right wouldn't it?'

'I suppose it'll have to be. Just be careful you don't get drunk Dennis. It's one thing to take the edge off your nerves but I don't want you getting into a state where you might say something you regret.'

'Don't worry; I've got a much stronger constitution than you think. Anyway, the lunchtime beer will have gone through me by now.'

'If you say so.'

Dennis patted the pillion seat of the Tiger and said, 'So, are you getting on, or what?'

'It's hardly worth starting her up now is it? Your place is only just around the corner. Let's walk.'

When they got to Pierrepoint Terrace, Dennis parked his motorbike in the alleyway and let them in through the side entrance to his flat.

'It's about time your landlord got that fixed,' said Margaret after he'd finally dislodged the door with his shoulder.

'I know but I'm worried that the stream of interesting documents will dry up if I pester him too much about it.'

'A pile of musty old books isn't going to be much use if you do yourself a nasty injury is it?'

'Maybe not,' said Dennis, straining as he forced the door closed behind them, 'but I don't want to look a gift horse in the mouth. Winstanley might be a lazy toad when it comes to basic maintenance but there aren't many landlords who provide their tenants with a ready supply of local history material are there?'

'That's because most people prefer their landlords to behave like landlords rather than purveyors of antiquarian texts,' said Margaret as she followed him up the stairs. 'Just don't expect me to come round and type up all your reports after you've broken your shoulder.'

Inside the flat, Dennis went straight through to his little kitchen and took down two bottles of Mackeson from the shelf above the sink. They clinked together loudly as he put them down on the table

'I think I'd prefer a cup of tea actually.' Margaret called through from the other room.

'No this will definitely be better for us. It says on the label it contains "energising carbohydrates of the highest purity."'

'If you believe that you'll believe anything.'

'So do you really want tea?' he said as he levered off the caps.

'It's a bit late now. I'm certainly not letting you drink two bottles on your own.'

'Do you want a drop of lemonade in it?'

'No, I'll drink it straight thanks. In for a penny, in for a pound.'

'So what time did Judith say we had to be round there?' he said as he brought the drinks through.

'Six-thirty,' Margaret replied. She was sitting at his rickety dining table, absent-mindedly leafing through one of the dusty tomes Mr Winstanley had given him.

'It's a bit late for tea isn't it?' said Dennis, sitting down in the chair opposite.

'Oh that's because of Penny and Carol. Apparently Judith and Nigel make it a rule that both girls have to get their homework done before the family sit down to eat in the evening.' She took a sip of Mackeson and nodded approvingly. 'Actually this is better than I remember.'

'Well make the most of it, I doubt if there'll be any alcohol round at Judith and Nigel's if it's a homework night.'

'Don't be so cynical Dennis. Judith's not like that at all. She always seems refreshingly easy-going to me.'

'Judith might be, but Nigel's quite the opposite: he's a stickler for doing the right thing. He and Judith are like chalk and cheese when you think about it.'

'Opposites attract: that's what they say, don't they?'

'It doesn't apply to us though.'

'Of course it does.'

'No it doesn't, the reason we get on is because we're both so alike.'

'We're nothing of the sort. The business with your front door is a case in point: if I lived here I'd have insisted he fixed it months ago, but you just put up with it. That's how different we are.'

'It doesn't mean we're different, it just means we've got slightly different priorities.'

'No, it proves I live in the here and now, where practicalities matter, whereas you tend to live in a… well, in a different place.'

'You mean, in the past?'

'I think so, yes. You've only got to look at the teetering piles of books and maps in here to know that.'

'But you're the same aren't you? Only last night you were telling me how much you liked rummaging through those old files in that Random Repository of yours.'

'It's true, but the main reason I started looking through all that stuff was simply because it was getting in my way. I decided there were much better uses for a room like that than storing rubbish from all over the college. I went in there one day with the intention of sorting it out, and a few of the files captured my interest. I admit I've been distracted from the practical task I'd set myself but it's only temporary.'

'Maybe it is but I bet those files will interest you even more after you've heard my latest news.'

'Go on,' she said, peering at him over the rim of her glass.

He reprised his conversation with Julian about the sketch of the Occitan cross and how it had led them to suspect that it was Laurent Morel who had been buried at Symbiosis House.

'Interesting,' said Margaret when he'd finished. 'So, do you think his death might have had anything to do with this secret project he was working on?'

'I don't know but it's an angle worth exploring, isn't it?'

'Definitely. I'll see if I can find any clues when I go back to his papers.'

'So, when will you be able to do that?'

'Tomorrow maybe, if isn't too busy in the library. Failing that, I can always go in on Saturday.'

Dennis nodded approvingly as he took a sip of his beer.

'Of course,' said Margaret, 'if it really is Laurent Morel who's buried there, it might put an end to all the Mathias Friedman rumours.'

'I'm not so sure. I reckon that, until we discover what actually happened to Friedman, those rumours will carry on regardless. That's just human nature for you, I'm afraid.'

'I suppose you're right. So, how do you think Nigel's feeling about the case at the moment?'

'Going by his mood, when I saw him earlier, I'd guess he's still got a lot more questions than answers.'

'Oh, you've seen him have you?'

'Yes, he pulled straight out in front of me as I was coming past Symbiosis House, so we stopped to have a chat.'

'What were you doing up there?'

'I went to Wynds Point to check if anything had been done about James' car. I saw Nigel on the way back.'

'Did you tell him about the Whippet?'

'We discussed the fact that he'd trespassed on the crime scene, but I didn't let on about what he found out. Nigel still thinks he was stopped before he got anywhere near the house.'

'He's going to be furious when he sees the paper tomorrow morning then isn't he.'

'That's true but, hopefully, all his fury will be directed at the Whippet. There's no reason for him to think I knew anything about it.'

'So you didn't mention the files in the Random Repository?'

'Of course not. It would really have given the game away if I'd have done that.'

'But you'll have to tell him at some stage.'

'Of course, but we'll need to do a bit more digging around before we start sharing anything.'

'I don't know Dennis. All this skulduggery feels wrong to me.'

'It's not skulduggery. We're following up a theory that's all. As soon as we come up with something solid, I promise I'll pass it straight on to Nigel. If I tried telling him about it now, he'd just say I was wasting his time.'

'I still don't like it.'

'Don't get involved then. I'm perfectly happy to look through Laurent Morel's papers on my own if it bothers you so much.'

'Hang on,' said Margaret, wagging her finger at him. 'You can't fool me that easily. I'm the one who's going to be looking through the papers, and that's how it's going to stay.'

'Fair enough, but you can't have it both ways.'

'Maybe not but I'm telling you now, if I find out anything significant, I'll be passing it onto Nigel whether you like it or not. She took a sip of her Mackeson and frowned. 'Actually, I've changed my mind, I'm not enjoying this drink at all.'

'Do you want some lemonade, or shall I make you a cup of tea?'

'She checked her watch. 'There isn't time. It's coming up to a quarter-past six and we're due at Judith's by six-thirty. It'll take us at least fifteen minutes to walk round to Manor Road.'

As she turned away, Dennis took the opportunity to drain both glasses.

'I saw that,' she said.

'Saw what, have you got eyes in the back of your head or

something?'

'Now that would be telling,' she said with a chuckle as she pulled on her coat.

The streetlamps were just coming on as they stepped outside. They set off along Pierrepoint Terrace and then turned right into Priory Road. To the west, the dark mass of the hills rose above the town to meet a pink-tinged sky. Lights from the windows of elevated houses formed a sparkling tiara along the lower slopes.

As they crossed Church Street into Victoria Road Dennis said, 'I haven't told you about my meeting with Harry Parsons yet have I?'

'The man on the train? No you haven't, how did it go?'

'It was interesting.'

'He wasn't a time-waster then?'

'Not as far as I could tell.'

'Does that mean you're a bit closer to discovering where the Chamber Spout is?'

'Actually, assuming Harry's telling the truth, I think I know exactly where it is.'

She stopped in her tracks and stared at him incredulously. 'And there was I thinking you'd been let down again and didn't want to talk about it. So why aren't you jumping up and down with excitement. More to the point, why wasn't it the first thing you told me?'

'Because you didn't ask me and because we'd already started talking about something else. If I remember rightly, you accused me of being drunk.'

'Tipsy's what I said, not drunk. Anyway, stop prevaricating and spill the beans will you?'

'All right, but you'd better brace yourself for a big surprise, he reckons it's at Symbiosis House.'

'No that can't be right. It's far too much of a coincidence

surely?'

'Coincidence or not, that's what he said. It all sounded pretty plausible actually.'

As they walked on he told her the rest of the story.

'What is it about that place?' said Margaret, after he'd finished. 'Nobody's given it a second thought for years, then suddenly it's cropping up all the time.'

'You're right, it's strange.'

'Did he know about the body?'

'No, he seemed genuinely surprised when I told him.'

'But the news must be everywhere by now.'

'I think he's a bit of a recluse. He lives alone in Hereford and, even when he's out and about, he's probably too sozzled to notice very much.'

'Did he have any theories about who it was?'

No, only about who it wasn't.'

'That it wasn't Mathias Friedman you mean?'

'Exactly. He reckoned Friedman was far too wily to be picked off by a mob of ignorant vigilantes.'

'But he might know more about who it really is than he's saying.'

'I agree, especially given that, within seconds of the subject coming up, he suddenly remembered another notebook – his own this time, rather than one of his father's - he thought I ought to see. He said he hadn't considered it relevant before which was why he'd left at home in Hereford. He described it as his musings, so I'd guess it's some sort of diary or journal.'

'And you think this journal might provide a clue as to the identity of the body?'

'I do, which is why I agreed to go to Hereford to collect it. Of course it's possible I've got the wrong end of the stick; in which case it'll be a wasted journey. Almost as soon as he mentioned it, he started backtracking, saying he was worried he might be dragging me over there on false pretences.'

'But you're still going?'

'Yes, I'll be heading over there straight after work tomorrow.'

'Is this one of the things you and Julian were discussing in the pub?'

'One of them, yes, but the main reason we went there was to talk about the Black Moon Society. I happened to mention that your father had been a member and Julian reckoned Harry Parsons might have been one too. He said he was the right age, had the right sort of background and, of course, he already knew Friedman because of the work he'd been doing for him at Symbiosis House.'

'What did he mean by the right sort of background?'

'Broadly professional – that was the phrase he used – the sort of man who had a certain standing in the community. That and the fact that he needed to be young enough to have served in the Great War. On that basis, it seems highly likely that my dad was a member as well.'

'Why should that have anything to do with joining an astronomy club?'

'Well, that's the thing: according to Julian, astronomy wasn't as central to the club's activities as you'd think.'

He explained about the drug and alcohol-fuelled ceremonies that were rumoured to have taken place and how these were viewed as Friedman's way of helping the men get over their war memories.

'I can't imagine my father getting involved in that sort of thing.'

'What if he was going through a bad period though? Lots of men found it hard to settle after they came home and maybe having access to an escape valve like that was helpful to him. After all, you were only a child at the time, weren't you? You wouldn't necessarily have known how he was.'

'I know my own father though,' said Margaret, wiping away a tear, 'and I'm certain he'd never have participated in anything like that.'

'No, you're probably right,' said Dennis, realising it was time to drop the subject. Anyway, we're only going by a lot of gossip Julian overheard in the theatre bar. I doubt if it amounts to much really.'

'Maybe this mysterious journal you're collecting tomorrow will shed some light on the issue.'

'It's possible I suppose, In the meantime, I could always pick my dad's brains about it while we're having tea.'

'You won't do that will you?' said Margaret, anxiously.

'Of course not. Surviving this ordeal is going to be hard enough as it is, without adding even more stress to the situation.' He tugged at her hand. 'Come on, we'd better get there before they polish off all the sandwiches.'

***

The first thing that struck Dennis, as soon as Judith had ushered them in and sat them down, was how ill his father looked. Charles Powell had taken his customary place of honour at the head of the table but, his face was drawn, and he seemed a pale shadow of his usual belligerent self.

Dennis and Margaret were sitting on the side of the table to Charles' right. Penny and Carol, still wearing their navy-blue grammar school uniforms, sat opposite, with their grandmother, Rosemary, positioned between them. Judith had the chair at the other end of the table – there was no sign of Nigel.

'I was just explaining to Charles and Rosemary,' said Judith, 'it looks as if Nigel's going to have to work late tonight after all.'

'The case is turning out to be a bit more complicated than he thought then?' said Dennis.

She flashed him a warning glance. 'His superintendent's called a meeting to review the situation that's all. I expect they're working on a press announcement or something like that.'

'Nigel's their top man, he's bound to have things well in hand.' growled Charles.

Rosemary turned to look at Penny and then Carol. She said, 'I expect you're a bit disappointed your daddy can't be with us though aren't you?'

'It *is* a shame he's not here,' said Penny, 'but he often gets called away at short notice. We're used to it by now.'

'Irregular hours are a policeman's lot I'm afraid,' said Judith. 'Anyway, help yourselves to sandwiches and I'll go and make a fresh pot of tea.'

'Sorry we're a bit late,' said Margaret, after Judith had disappeared into the kitchen. 'We decided to leave Dennis's bike in Pierrepoint Terrace and walk over here. It took us a little longer than we expected.'

'Very wise too,' said Rosemary. 'I'm sure walking is a lot better than perching on the back of that horrible old motorcycle. I really think it's about time you got yourself a proper car Dennis. I always notice all the second-hand models Anderson's Garage has for sale whenever I see their advert in the Gazette. One of those little Fords or Austins would suit you nicely and I'm sure Margaret would appreciate it wouldn't you dear?'

'Oh we never go very far afield so it probably isn't worth the expense.'

'He hasn't got a car licence anyway,' said Charles. 'Probably couldn't be bothered to make the effort.'

Dennis was about to say that he'd actually had a licence for years, but Rosemary chipped in first.

'That's enough Charles. We agreed there'd be no unpleasantness this evening didn't we?'

He frowned and reached for a sandwich.

'I hear you work at Malvern College,' said Rosemary, as she turned to face Margaret across the table.

'Yes, I'm the librarian there. I've been at the College five years now. It can be quite hectic but generally I enjoy it a great deal.'

'Are the boys well behaved?'

'Usually they are but I suppose boys wouldn't be boys if they weren't a bit boisterous sometimes.'

'I'm sure girls can be exactly the same,' said Rosemary, glancing playfully at Penny and Carol but getting no response. She returned her attention to Margaret. 'So have you always worked there?'

'No, before that I was at the public library in town. I mainly worked in the reference section. I also had responsibility for organising and displaying special collections.'

'That's how you and Dennis met isn't it?' said Judith as she came back into the room carrying a steaming teapot.

Margaret blushed. 'Fancy your knowing that. Yes, I suppose it is. I'd arranged a small exhibition and Dennis came to interview me about it for the Gazette.'

'And the rest is history,' said Judith. Noticing Dennis' strained expression, she added, 'sorry, I'm being embarrassing. How do you take your tea Margaret, milk and sugar?'

'Just milk please.'

While Judith was pouring, Rosemary said, 'So what made you decide to move to the college?'

'There were quite a few reasons really. One of them was that my father used to work there so I was very familiar with it.'

'Was your father a librarian as well?'

'No he was a science master there during the twenties. He taught physics and some chemistry as well. He used to take me up there sometimes when I was a child, especially during the holidays when it was quiet. I had the run of the place and got to know it like the back of my hand so, for a while, it felt like a home from home.'

'And did your father move on to teach somewhere else later?'

'No, sadly he was killed in a road accident when I was seven.'

It was Rosemary's turn to blush. 'Oh I'm so sorry my dear, I didn't realise.'

'There's no reason why you should and, anyway, it happened a long time ago.'

'No but it was insensitive of me. The trouble is Margaret, Dennis is so secretive I know almost nothing about what goes on in his life. He'll think I'm getting at him now, but I don't mean it like that; I just wish we'd had a chance to meet before. After all, I understand you've been friends for quite a while.'

'Well at least you're meeting now,' said Judith diplomatically as she came around behind Dennis and Margaret and passed them their tea.

'Yes,' said Rosemary gazing up at her, 'This tea party was a wonderful idea of yours. It's so important for families to get together from time to time. It's just a shame that Nigel wasn't able to be here… and poor Susan of course.'

'Are Auntie Susan and Uncle James going to get divorced?' asked Carol abruptly, the gleam in her eyes indicating she thought the conversation had just taken a more interesting turn.

Judith looked daggers at her. 'That's not the sort of question you ask young lady.'

'Why not,' said Penny, exchanging a conspiratorial glance with her younger sister, 'everyone knows that Auntie Susan's run off to Droitwich to get away from Uncle James so why shouldn't we talk about it?'

'Because we don't know anything of the sort, that's why,' said Judith, 'And even if we did, it would be wrong to gossip about it around the tea table.'

'But you were discussing it with Grandma earlier,' said Carol, 'We both heard you.'

'That's because we're grown-ups,' said Judith, moving back to her seat at the end of the table. 'And we're allowed to discuss whatever we like. I'm ashamed of you both for listening to a private conversation, I thought you knew better than to do that.'

Both girls bowed their heads sulkily and returned to eating their sandwiches.

'What was your father's name?' barked Charles, seemingly oblivious to the intervening conversation.

Realising that the question was directed at her, Margaret turned to reply. 'Jobson,' she said, 'Greville Jobson.'

Dennis caught his father's reaction: an agonised seizure of the facial muscles that came and went in a flash.

'Why do you ask dear,' said Rosemary, 'do you think you knew him?'

Charles placed both of his hands on the table and slowly pushed himself up into a standing position. 'Excuse me,' he said, 'but I need a bit of fresh air. I'm going to step out into the back garden for a few minutes.'

Rosemary stood up and went around to seize his arm. 'Whatever's the matter with you Charles? Have you got a pain or something? Is it your chest?'

'Stop fussing,' he said irritably as he moved towards the door with Rosemary still clinging to his arm. 'I told you, I just need some fresh air for a moment.'

'Well I'm coming with you.' Rosemary looked back at Judith from the doorway and said, 'Sorry about this.'

'Don't worry,' said Judith. 'It's probably a good idea to let the sandwiches settle before we have our cake.' She turned to her daughters. 'Why don't you two go and play in your room for a while? I'll call you down again when Grandma and Grandpa are ready.'

Penny and Carol got up and silently left the room.

'Poor Rosemary,' said Judith, shaking her head sadly, once

she'd heard the girls' bedroom door close and could be certain that she, Dennis and Margaret were on their own. 'She's having a dreadful time at the moment. Apparently Charles has been more cantankerous than ever recently, and she's been at her wit's end wondering what to do about it. Ironically though, he's hardly said a word since he got up this morning. The ranting and raving's bad enough but this brooding silence is *really* unsettling her.'

'He looks different as well doesn't he?' said Dennis. 'It struck me as soon as we arrived.'

'Yes, I was horrified when he walked in this evening. It was as if he'd aged ten years since I last saw him.'

'And, even when he made that jibe about my lack of a driving licence, his heart didn't really seem to be in it.'

'You're right,' said Judith. 'It was as if he was just going through the motions.'

'And why did he suddenly ask what my father's name was?' said Margaret. 'It came completely out of the blue and, when I told him, he had a really odd look on his face. It's hard to describe but I didn't like it at all.'

'It was fear,' said Dennis. 'I recognised it straightaway. For some reason, when you told him your father's name was Greville Jobson, it shook him to the core.'

CHAPTER 11

No Hiding Place in the Basement

Friday 29th March 1957

6.10 a.m.

Dennis woke up before dawn and lay in bed, staring at the ceiling. He was keen to go out and buy a copy of the Gazette so that he could read the Whippet's report, but he was afraid to move in case he disturbed Margaret. She was sleeping fitfully, and he knew how annoyed she'd be if he woke her. It was only after she turned over and started to snore, that he decided it was finally safe to get up.

The luminous hands of his alarm clock told him it was ten past six. He took his clothes through to the next room, got dressed in the dark and then crept down the stairs. The front door was as stubborn as ever and it took three arm-wrenching heaves to get it open. He left it ajar to avoid having similar trouble on the way back.

At the corner shop, he joined a short queue of early starters who'd called in to buy newspapers and stock up with cigarettes for the day ahead. There was a pile of Gazettes on the counter, so he could see the headline, *"Malvern Wells body – latest news"* even before he got his hands on a copy. As soon as he'd paid, he went outside and stood under the nearest lamppost to read the whole story.

"Police seek local man after gruesome discovery of shallow grave in garden – exclusive report by Brian Fairclough, Gazette Crime Correspondent

Police were called to Symbiosis House, Malvern Wells at seven o'clock on Thursday morning, after the discovery of a shallow grave containing human remains in the garden there. The remains were uncovered by itinerant labourer, Andrew Morrigan. Morrigan subsequently fled the scene and Malvern Police are urgently trying to establish his whereabouts in order that he may assist with their enquiries.

It is understood that Morrigan was employed, on a casual basis, as a gardener and odd-job man at the vacant property and was in the habit of arriving for work soon after first light. A witness reports that, at around ten to seven on Thursday morning, Morrigan had gone off to dig over a patch of ground in a remote part of the garden but reappeared five minutes later, in a visibly distressed state, and announced that he had found a body. He then ran away and has not been seen since.

Morrigan, 63, is approximately six foot two inches tall, of muscular build with an unkempt beard and greying hair. He is thought to be wearing a dark tweed overcoat and matching cap. He is of no fixed abode but drives an olive-green Land Rover, registration number 726 PUY.

A police spokesman said that Andrew Morrigan has previously been arrested several times for committing violent acts whilst intoxicated. He also has a history of mental problems and should not be approached under any circumstances. There is no information so far concerning the possible identity of the body or the length of time it had been buried there.

The public are asked to report any sightings of the missing man to the detective in charge of the investigation, Detective Inspector Nigel Powell, at Great Malvern Police Station, telephone number, Malvern 216."

Dennis mulled over what he'd just read, all the way back to Pierrepoint Terrace. As soon as he stepped inside the hallway, he saw that Margaret was peering down at him from the top of the stairs. The light was on in the flat behind her and he could see she was wearing one of his jackets as a dressing gown.

'Where have you been,' she asked.

'I just slipped out to the newsagents,' he said, waving his copy of the Gazette. 'I couldn't sleep thinking about the Whippet's story, so I decided to get a copy straightaway rather than waiting until I got into the office. I tried not to wake you.'

'It doesn't take much to wake me, you ought to know that by now, especially when I'm squashed up in that tiny bed of yours.'

He kicked the door shut behind him and rushed upstairs to join her.

'Shall I make some tea?' she asked as he followed her into the flat.

'Not yet, I need you to read this front page first and tell me what you think.'

He handed her the paper and she sat down at the table to read.

After a while she turned to look at him. 'It's a bit bland, isn't it?' she said. 'Or have I missed something… is there more inside?'

'No, that's it.'

'But what about all those juicy clues he left behind that you and Julian pieced together yesterday?'

'I don't know. Maybe they weren't really clues at all. Maybe we just got carried away and jumped to the wrong conclusions."

'Or maybe he misled you on purpose: planted a false trail to make you think he knew more than he actually did?'

'No,' said Dennis, shaking his head emphatically. 'That doesn't sound like the Whippet at all.'

'So, does this sound like him then?' said Margaret jabbing the front page of the Gazette.

'What?'

'This report: is it the sort of thing he normally turns out?'

'No, it isn't. Despite his many faults, he's got a brilliant way with words but there's no evidence of that here.'

'It's almost as if he's just paraphrased a police statement.'

'Exactly.'

'So, what's going on do you reckon?'

'I think someone wants this business tied up as quickly as possible and he's determined not to let anything get in his way.'

'Who's that?'

'Nigel's boss, Superintendent "Bad'n" Goodall. Apparently, he's been giving Nigel a hell of a time over it. He's convinced Morrigan's guilty and he wants him arrested and charged as quickly as possible.'

'But Nigel doesn't agree?'

'No, he reckons Goodall's cutting corners, partly to make his clear-up rates look good, and partly because he hates vagrants like Morrigan. Nigel's the first to accept that Morrigan didn't do himself any favours by running away but he certainly doesn't think it proves he's a killer.'

'So, do you think Goodall put pressure on the Whippet to tone his story down?'

'He might have, but that means he'd have to have put pressure on Jeff Stephenson as well and I find it hard to imagine Jeff backing down without a fight.'

'But, in the end, Goodall's the law, isn't he? Even the editor of the Gazette would be hard pressed to take a stand against that.'

'I suppose you're right. He certainly seems capable of putting the fear of God into everyone else. Nigel was looking over his shoulder all the time yesterday, while we were talking: he suspects Goodall's got a cohort of people, including police officers, who report back if they see or hear anything suspicious'

'The name Andrew Morrigan rings a bell with me for some reason,' said Margaret. 'I've got a feeling you've mentioned him before.'

'I'm sure I have. He used to do odd jobs for my dad, when I was a kid. Handy Andy we used to call him. One of them was repairing the old Dennis delivery lorry at Thomas Radford and Son whenever it broke down, which was quite often, as I recall. It had a big Dennis badge on the bonnet, and I used to think I was named after it. Whenever I visited the yard with my mother and Andy was there, he'd let me sit in the cab while he worked on the engine.'

'He sounds nice. A lot different from how he sounds in the paper.'

'Oh, he was nice enough, but I never wanted to get too near him because his clothes were filthy, and he looked as if he hadn't had a wash for months. And he did like a drink, in fact that's why my father got rid of him in the end, because he'd turned up under the influence once too often. I never got the impression he was violent though and children are pretty sensitive to that sort of thing, aren't they? If anything, he seemed a bit lost and helpless.'

'The perfect scapegoat, in other words.'

'For anyone unscrupulous enough to exploit it, certainly. That's why, in my opinion, the longer he stays at large the better, and I'm sure that's what Nigel thinks too. Interestingly though, I happened to see him only yesterday. For the first time in years.'

'Really?' said Margaret staring at him. 'Where was that?'

'Up at Wynds Point. I'd gone there to take another look at the spot where the car left the road. I was looking down into the woods and I saw him wandering through the trees.'

'Have you told Nigel?'

'No.'

'You're going to get yourself into serious trouble if you're not careful Dennis. Just because Morrigan's someone you want to protect, doesn't give you the right to withhold important information about him. The fact remains he went on the run, so it's perfectly understandable that the police want to talk to him.'

'I suppose so, but the way he looked at me made me feel as if there was some sort of pact between us. I know it sounds ridiculous but that's just how it felt.'

'He saw you as well?'

'Yes, he looked up the slope and our eyes met for a couple of seconds. Then he just moved off into the woods as if he didn't have a care in the world.'

'*How* did he look at you exactly?'

'As if he knew I wasn't going to follow him.'

'Or send the police after him.'

'That as well I suppose.'

'I think he was just taking you for a mug. He obviously recognised you and played on the fact that you'd remember him kindly from when you were a little boy. Meanwhile, you're left at risk of being arrested for obstructing a police investigation.'

'So, what do you suggest I do?'

'You need to tell Nigel about it as soon as possible and say it slipped your mind.'

'He's hardly going to believe that, is he?'

'It doesn't matter if he does or not, it's just a way of saving your bacon. Maybe Nigel's superintendent is putting pressure on him, but you can't use that as an excuse for keeping important information to yourself. Make sure you phone him as soon as you get back to the office.'

'And what if he's not there and I have to talk to the rebarbative Sergeant Collins?'

'Leave a message, and say you need to speak to him urgently. At least then you'll have the excuse that you tried to tell him.'

'I've been a bit stupid, haven't I?'

'Not stupid exactly, just hasty. I know this sounds a bit holier than thou but, in my experience, it's never a good idea to rush to conclusions without making sure you've checked your facts first.'

Dennis sighed. 'I'm sure you're right. I'll try and do a bit more digging around. Before that though, I need to find why the explosive story the Whippet was promising us turned out to be such a damp squib.

He glanced at his watch. 'It's coming up to seven. Hopefully Julian will be in the office by now, *he'll* know what's going on.'

'And don't forget to phone Nigel,' shouted Margaret, as he bounded down the stairs.

***

Outside, in the alleyway, Dennis retrieved the tartan shopping bag from the Tiger's pannier before setting off for the office. He intended to spend a good part of the morning, reading through the notebooks to satisfy himself that they were as authentic as Harry Parsons had claimed.

In Langland Place, Jeff's red Morgan was parked outside the Gazette offices and, as Dennis entered the vestibule, he could hear the editor's muffled, but plainly agitated, voice coming from upstairs. Intermittent silences suggested that he was having a phone conversation. Dennis was tempted to creep up and listen to what he was saying from outside the door, but he feared that the notoriously creaky stairs would give him away.

Apart from Jeff, no-one else seemed to have arrived yet. He went over to Julian's desk and wrote a message on the back of an old envelope,

"I'm downstairs in the crypt. Please come and see me as soon as you arrive. Thanks, DP."

He propped the note up against Julian's telephone and then he made for the door at the side of the reporters' room that opened onto the steep wooden staircase leading down to the archive library.

It was always pleasantly cool in the basement because an elaborate ventilation system had been installed years ago, along with thick insulation to keep any subterranean damp at bay. The Gazette offices weren't particularly extensive, so all available space had to be utilised. No-one wanted to work in a windowless cellar, so it had long been designated as a combined reference library and storage room for back numbers. It was a rectangular, stone floored room, equivalent in area to the entire ground floor above but without any dividing walls. Two rows of six pillars that held up the low ceiling gave it the crypt-like appearance that Dennis had alluded to in his note to Julian. Wooden boxes, specially designed to protect the old newspapers from the effects of air and moisture, were stacked on shelves that took up three of the four walls. The fourth wall, at the end of the room, furthest from the staircase, was entirely taken up with an ancient bookcase whose shelves groaned under the weight of encyclopaedias, atlases, dictionaries, thesauruses and other bulky tomes. Adjacent to the bookcase was a desk that, despite its current shabby state, would have been extremely imposing in its day. Dennis always thought it looked as if it belonged in a bank manager's office: a huge expanse of mahogany with deep drawers and brass fixtures and fittings. It was twinned with an equally grand leather-upholstered chair.

On top of the cup-ringed and cigarette-burnt surface of the desk were a telephone, a reading lamp and a volume of Encyclopaedia Britannica, still open at the page labelled "OCC" – OCC for Occitan Cross. Right in the centre of the page was the black and white photograph Julian had told him about. It looked like a flower with four short, arrow-shaped petals, each of which was adorned by three little disks – what Julian had described as golden spheres – arranged in a triangle at its point.

He pushed the book to one side, switched on the reading lamp and, with a deep sigh of resignation, reached for the telephone receiver. He was about to dial Nigel's number when he heard footsteps clattering down the staircase. He placed the receiver back in its cradle and looked up with a smile, expecting to see Julian coming through the door. But it wasn't Julian, it was Jeff, and he wasn't looking happy. He strode over to the desk, his shoes clicking urgently on the stone floor.

'What are you doing down here?' he barked, looming over the desk and making Dennis feel even more dwarfed than usual by the vast leather chair.

'I was about to make a phone call,' said Dennis, realising, as soon as the words left his mouth, that he'd used the wrong excuse.

'Why not use the phone on your own desk? There's no-one else around now. And what's so secret that you need to hide away in the basement anyway?'

'Nothing really,' said Dennis feebly.

'As soon as I saw you coming in through the front door, I could tell you'd be heading down here. You had a distinctively furtive look about you. What's going on?'

Dennis shifted awkwardly in his seat; it hadn't occurred to him that Jeff might have been watching from his office window.

'Nothing's going on. I was planning to check something in the archives when I'd finished my call, so I was just killing two birds with one stone.'

'I don't want you adopting this room as your unofficial office Dennis. I know you like it down here, but you've got a perfectly good desk and telephone upstairs. I don't expect to have to waste time searching for you high and low, especially when there's something important I need to talk to you about.'

'Is it to do with the electrical problems on the train? I'm sorry I didn't get much out of Harry Parsons about it yesterday but...'

'It's nothing to do with that,' said Jeff, interrupting him. 'That story's a dead duck now, as far as I'm concerned. No, this is to do with the business at Symbiosis House. You're the one who's going to be covering it from now on.'

Dennis stared at him aghast. 'Is this some kind of joke?'

'Do I look as if I'm joking? No, I'm deadly serious. I want you to start working on it now, ready for our next edition.'

'But that's the Whippet's assignment, everyone knows that.'

'Brian's gone; he won't be doing any more assignments for the Malvern Gazette.'

'Gone where?'

'Fleet Street. He's been offered a plum job with one of the nationals.'

'And he's left just like that? Isn't he supposed to serve a notice period or something?'

'Strictly speaking, yes, but the horse has already bolted so there's nothing I can do about it now.'

'But that must mean he's broken his contract? Doesn't the Gazette have lawyers who can challenge that sort of thing?'

'These big papers have got lawyers too remember and their pockets are much deeper than ours. Take it from me, there's no point even thinking about it. The Whippet's well and truly gone and so, as from today, you've got the Symbiosis House assignment.'

'But why me? You'd never let me anywhere near a story like this, normally. Surely it would be better if someone else took it on?'

'No, I've made my decision. In fact, I've already arranged your first interview with Superintendent Goodall, at eight-thirty this morning. He's agreed to brief you on current developments so that you can get off to a flying start with your report.'

'What report?' protested Dennis. 'Going by this morning's front page, it looks as if the whole thing's sewn up already. Once Andrew Morrigan's in custody, the case will be closed, meaning that, by this time next week, it'll be ancient history.'

'We'll still have to set out the facts and put the record straight.'

'In other words, you're expecting me to act as a mouthpiece for Malvern Constabulary, and deny that there's any substance to what the Whippet claimed to have found out?'

'Be careful,' said Jeff, staring at him menacingly, 'you'll get yourself into deep water if you carry on talking like that. The Gazette isn't going to be anybody's mouthpiece while I'm editor. Do I make myself clear?'

'Sorry, I shouldn't have said that. It's come as a bit of a shock that's all.'

'I'm sure it has, but that doesn't give you the right to start casting aspersions about the way the way I run this paper. So, did the Whippet say what he was planning to write?'

'No, he just said he was planning a big revelation in today's edition. Then, when I saw the front page this morning, I realised that either he'd been bluffing, or you'd made him tone down the report for some reason.'

'You thought the police had got wind of what we were going to print and forced me to change it?'

'Either that, or you'd decided not to run with it for legal reasons.'

'But you chose to conclude that I crumbled under pressure?'

'I suppose I did. Sorry.'

'I'm disappointed Dennis, but never mind. As it happens, your second assumption would have been the correct one. The Whippet had come up with a complete work of fiction. The police would have had a field day in court if we'd printed any of that.'

'So, what was he saying?'

'It was such complete nonsense it doesn't bear repeating.'

'And is that why he decided to leave, because you wouldn't print his story?'

Jeff shook his head. 'No, I'm sure he'd decided to leave long before that. The story was probably just a parting shot to embarrass me.'

'Nasty.'

'Yes, but entirely predictable I'm afraid. I won't deny I had respect for him, he was one of the most tenacious reporters I've ever known, but people like Brian are a double-edged sword and, sooner or later, they turn against you. He always thought he was destined for greater things and I suppose he got it into his head that I was holding him back.'

'But how can you be so sure he was making the story up?'

'Let's just call it an editor's instinct. Don't get me wrong, I'm prepared to back the wildest sounding reports provided they've got an essential whiff of authenticity, and what we end up printing stays within the law. It's those sorts of stories that sell newspapers after all and, to be fair to the Whippet, he's brought me quite a few in his time. This one didn't pass the test though, it started ringing alarm bells, so I phoned Superintendent Goodall, just to check it against his side of the story.'

'Did you tell him what the Whippet had come up with?'

'No, of course not. I simply asked how the investigation was going and if he was prepared to give me a statement for our next edition, which it turned out he was.'

'And *his* statement passed the test, did it? The same one the Whippet's had failed?'

Jeff glared at him. 'What exactly are you implying?'

'I'm not implying anything; I'm just trying to understand how you judge what's plausible and what isn't. I need to be clear about that if I'm going to take this story on.'

'There's no *if* about it Dennis. You're taking it on, and that's that.'

'But what about all my other work.'

'What other work? You've got nothing earth-shattering on that I'm aware of.'

'But I'm supposed to be seeing Harry Parsons again later, to follow up what we discussed on the train yesterday.'

'But we're dropping the faulty electrics story. I've already told you that.'

'I know but this is something different: he's got another notebook he wants to give me.'

'Another one? Why wasn't it with the others he brought for you?'

'This one's different apparently. He only remembered it after I told him about the business at Symbiosis House which made me think it might shed some light on things.'

'You seriously think that, do you?'

'Why not? He obviously saw a connection between current events and whatever he'd recorded in this old journal. It might provide an interesting angle for our story, especially as I'm the one who now appears to be covering it.'

'But don't you see what's going on here Dennis?'

'I haven't got a clue what you're talking about.'

'Haven't you, really? In which case, you're a lot more gullible than I thought you.'

'You'd better tell me what I'm missing then,' said Dennis tetchily.

'This Harry Parsons is a compulsive attention-seeker. He's plainly a lonely old man whose heyday, if he ever had one, is long behind him. First, he uses your obsession with the Chamber Spout to draw you in and then he hints at being able to provide some insights into the Symbiosis House situation to get you even more interested. He's wasting your time just to make himself feel important.'

'That isn't what you were saying a couple of days ago, after you received his letter. You were all for me going to see him then, weren't you?'

'I was, but at that stage he just seemed to be a harmless old man with an interesting story to tell.'

'Maybe he still is, but you're more jaundiced now because the Whippet's gone off and left you in the lurch.'

'Give me some credit, will you? I'm quite capable of separating my feelings about the Whippet from all this. There's no two ways about it I'm afraid, Harry Parsons is taking you for a ride.'

'So, are you telling me I can't go and see him?'

'Not at all. You can do what you like in your own time, provided you don't let it affect your job.'

'Meaning that, even if there does turn out to be something interesting in this journal of his, I won't be allowed to use it in my Symbiosis House report?'

Jeff shrugged. 'As I said, Harry Parsons is just leading you up the garden path, so I can guarantee the issue will never arise.'

He glanced at his watch. 'I make it seven thirty-five now, which means you've got less than hour before your meeting with Superintendent Goodall. I suggest you go back to your desk and start focusing on the matter in hand.'

With that, he turned on his heels and headed for the stairs.

CHAPTER 12
One Bad Apple
Friday 29th March 1957
7.40 a.m.

After Jeff had gone, Dennis sat at the big desk, chin in hands, mulling over the situation he found himself in. He'd been handed an assignment he didn't want, and which he feared would end badly. Somehow, he had to maintain his own, unofficial, lines of enquiry whilst appearing to do Jeff's – and presumably, Superintendent Goodall's - bidding. It was going to be a hard balance to strike without getting himself into deep water. After a few minutes' fruitless consideration, he decided it was time to do something more productive. He reached for the phone, mindful that Jeff's interruption had stopped him from letting Nigel know about his sighting of Andrew Morrigan. However, just as he was about to dial the police station number, it occurred to him that there was a good chance he'd bump into his brother when he went to see Superintendent Goodall, and that way he'd be able to tell him face to face. He opened the telephone directory and looked up the number for James Crawford's office instead. It was only twenty to eight, but he knew that auctioneers and estate agents often started early if they were preparing to attend a market or a big sale somewhere. Sure enough, the phone was answered on the third ring.

'Crawford, Davies and Withers,' said a woman at the other end

'Hello, I'd like to speak to Mr. Crawford if possible.'

'Hold on please and I'll put you through to his secretary, Miss Collingford.'

There was a click and a buzz and then another female voice came on the line. 'Hello, may I help you?'

'I hope so. I'm Dennis Powell, James' - Mr Crawford's - brother-in-law. Sorry to call so early but I was hoping to have a quick word with him if he's available.'

'Oh Mr. Powell, is it really you? I'm so glad you phoned.'

'It sounds as if were you expecting me.'

'Well, to be perfectly honest, it was your brother the Inspector I was waiting to hear from, but I'm just as pleased to hear from you. I assume he's told you what I phoned about?'

'No, he hasn't told me anything. The reason I'm phoning has nothing to do with my brother. I wanted to speak to Mr. Crawford about something that's all.'

'But that's exactly why I tried to contact Inspector Powell - about Mr. Crawford I mean. The fact is I'm terribly worried about him. He hasn't been into the office for three days now. I've tried to reach him several times at home by telephone but there's never an answer.'

'Has Mr. Crawford ever been out of contact like this before?'

'A few times yes. In fact, I probably wouldn't have thought anything of it if it wasn't for the fact that he didn't come in to wind up his clock yesterday.'

'His clock?'

'Mr. Crawford has an antique grandfather clock in his office.' She laughed. 'Oh dear, he'd be dreadfully annoyed if he heard me calling it that; I should have said long case clock, that's the correct term apparently. Anyway, he owns this valuable long case clock that I believe is about two hundred years old. It stands in the corner of his office and it chimes every quarter of an hour, you can hear it throughout the building. It isn't annoying though, it's rather homely and reassuring. And it doesn't just tell the time; it's one of those clocks that show the phases of the moon as well. It's a beautiful piece of craftsmanship and Mr. Crawford's very proud of it indeed. So much so that he never lets anyone go anywhere near it and of course that means the only person who can wind it up is Mr. Crawford himself. He does it every Thursday, by noon at the latest. He says that antique clocks are very delicate objects and adhering to a strict winding routine is essential to ensure their long-term well-being.'

'I can just imagine James saying that.'

'Yes, he's pernickety to say the least, but I find it rather an endearing quality.'

'So, when James didn't come and wind up his clock, you started to think something must be wrong?'

'Yes, and after mulling it over for a while, I decided to telephone your brother at Malvern Police Station. I didn't want to make a big fuss in case it was nothing at all, but I knew that Mr. Crawford's brother-in-law was a detective inspector, so I thought a quiet word with him about it was probably the best thing to do under the circumstances.'

'So, did you speak to him?'

'No, I was put through to the sergeant on duty and he told me that Inspector Powell was out, so he'd have to take a message and pass it on.'

'Do you remember this sergeant's name by any

chance?'

'Colley, something like that… Sorry, I'm not sure.'

'Sergeant Collins?'

'Yes, that's it, Sergeant Collins.'

'And, apart from taking a message for my brother, did Sergeant Collins ask you anything else about it?'

'What do you mean?'

'Did he take down any other details so that they could start a search for Mr. Crawford?'

'Oh no, nothing like that. Sergeant Collins said it was far too soon for a missing person enquiry, but he did assure me that he'd draw the matter to Inspector Powell's attention as soon as he saw him.'

'What time was this?'

'About two o'clock. I'd been on tenterhooks ever since midday, but I didn't like to trouble your brother too soon in case he thought I was being silly.'

'And you haven't heard anything back since you left the message?'

'No, that's why I was so pleased when you called. I thought perhaps your brother had asked you to phone me instead. After I telephoned the police station yesterday, the penny dropped that he must be involved in that big police investigation in Malvern Wells and that he was probably far too busy to deal with my trivial concerns.'

'As I said before, Nigel hasn't mentioned any of this to me at all. I only phoned James because I haven't heard from him for a while either and I wanted to make sure he was all right.'

'So, *you're* worried about him as well, are you? You

don't think I'm being hysterical?'

'No, and I'm sure Nigel won't either. James is a creature of habit, so I can understand why you'd be worried about him not coming back to wind up his clock.' He paused, and then he said, 'Just as a matter of interest Miss Collingford, have you any idea what sort of car he drives?

It was a long shot, but he wanted to be sure that James hadn't changed to a new model since he and Margaret had last seen him getting into the Rover, outside Crawford, Davies and Withers.

'Why do you want to know that?'

He wondered whether to come clean about the wrecked car in the woods but decided against it. There seemed little point in adding to her anxieties at this stage.

'Just in case I see it while I'm travelling around.'

'Of course, how silly of me. Yes, it's a Rover 90. Mr. Crawford's forever singing its praises: I think it means almost as much to him as his long case clock. He says it's got a ninety horse-power engine and can do ninety miles per hour.'

'What colour is it?'

'It's black – *classic* black he likes to call it - and so highly polished you could almost use it as a mirror.'

'And do you remember the registration number?'

'Yes, it's OAB 283.'

'Thank you, that's very helpful,' said Dennis, trying to keep his voice neutral.

'When he didn't come in to wind up his clock, one of the first things I did was check if his car was in its private parking space outside,' said Miss Collingford, 'Obviously, it wasn't, otherwise I would have mentioned it. It isn't in his garage at home either – or, at least, it wasn't when I checked.'

'You've been to his house? When was this?'

'Yesterday evening, after I finished work. I suddenly realised how foolish I'd look, having raised the alarm with the police, only for it to turn out he'd been safely at home all the time. It was getting towards dusk by the time I got there and there were no lights on, even though most of the neighbouring houses were well lit up by then. I stood outside the gate for about twenty minutes, waiting to see if anything happened. Even if Mr Crawford was prepared to sit in darkness, I couldn't imagine his wife putting up with it for very long. A few people came past while I was waiting, and they all looked at me strangely as if they were wondering why a middle-aged woman was lurking there like that. In the end, I plucked up the courage to go and knock on the front door. The thing that had been holding me back all that time was that Mr Crawford hates anyone making a fuss and I knew he'd be angry if he thought I was checking up on him. By that point though I'd passed caring what he might think because I was so worried. I knocked for ages but there was no answer. I could tell there was no-one there because the noise just echoed around and around inside the house. In desperation, I went and peered through the window at the side of his garage to see if the Rover was there. Luckily there's a streetlamp just by the front gate so there was plenty of light to see inside but the garage was empty. I hardly slept at all last night, worrying about what might have happened to him. Actually, we should be concerned about his wife as well shouldn't we because there doesn't seem to be any sign of her either?'

'Don't worry. I understand she's gone away to see a friend for a few days. It probably isn't worth troubling her with any of this just yet. Not until we're sure what's happened.'

'No, I'm sure you're right.' She gave a sniff and then

went silent. Dennis waited patiently, assuming she was fighting back tears. After a few seconds she said, 'You will try to find him won't you Mr Powell? The longer this goes on, the more I think something really bad must have happened to him.'

'I'll do my best, but I'm sure he'll turn up, sooner or later, anyway. Going by what you said earlier, it's not the first time he's gone off the radar.'

'But it's the fact he didn't come back and wind up his clock that bothers me. Well, that and ...'

The line fell silent.

'Yes?' prompted Dennis.

'Oh, I suppose I might as well tell you: he's been acting very strangely for the last two weeks so I was already concerned about him, even before he disappeared.'

'Acting strangely? How?'

'Locking himself in his office, for one thing.'

'That's unusual, is it?'

"It's certainly never happened in the twelve years I've worked for him. Even when he's engrossed in something complicated – a big auction inventory for example – he never locks his office door. As senior secretary, I've got keys to lock and unlock the building, but only the three partners have keys to their own offices. They work with important documents every day of the week so it's important that they take personal responsibility for keeping them secure. Despite that, I can't recall a single occasion when any of them - Mr Davies, Mr Withers or Mr Crawford - has locked himself inside his room while he's been at work. I don't think this has anything to do with work though.'

'What makes you say that?"

'Because he's been crying.'

'While he's locked away in his room you mean?'

'That's right. Several times now, I've heard him sobbing in there.'

'And you're sure it was him.'

'I am now but, at first I wondered if he was listening to something on the wireless. I knew there was no-one else in there with him, so it was the only other explanation I could come up with. But then I realised that I'd never seen a wireless in Mr Crawford's office and even if he had kept one in there I could never imagine him listening to it in the middle of the day – he'd think he was setting a terrible example to all the staff. Anyway, the longer I stood there, the more ridiculous the idea seemed: you might get a bit of crying in one of those plays they broadcast on the Home Service, but it wouldn't just go on and on like this did.'

'Have you got any idea what might have set him off?'

'I've been racking my brains, and the only thing I can think of is the argument he had with Mr Franklin.'

'Is that *Percy* Franklin?'

'Yes, Mr Crawford's assistant. Do you know him?'

'We've never met, but my sister-in-law mentioned him yesterday, and then, by coincidence, I saw him in town. He's got a bad limp, hasn't he?'

'Yes, I understand he took a bullet in his knee when he was serving in Burma, so it's a miracle he can walk at all. He and Mr Crawford were invalided home from there at the same time. As I'm sure you know, Mr Crawford contracted a serious bout of malaria that nearly killed him. When he took over the partnership from his father, he offered Mr Franklin the job as his assistant. I think Mr Franklin was finding it hard to secure a job anywhere else, because of his leg problems, so Mr Crawford helped him out. It was kind of him really because I don't think they were particularly friendly or anything.'

'So, could you tell what this argument was about?'

'No, I was down in the typists' room, at the time and all we could hear was raised voices up in Mr Crawford's office. The girls wanted me to go and check what was going on, but when I went out into the hallway, Mr Franklin was already coming downstairs with a face like thunder. He brushed past me without saying a word, and went out into the street, slamming the front door behind him.'

'So, when was this?'

'About a fortnight ago.'

'Had you ever heard them argue before?'

'No, they're often a bit terse with each other, but no worse than that.'

'And soon after this argument, James started shutting himself away in his office?'

'Yes. It might just be a coincidence of course, but that's what happened? As I said, they're not friends, just colleagues. And seeing them together, you'd never think Mr Crawford was Percy's boss, you'd think it was the other way around: almost as if Percy had some sort of hold over him.'

After bringing the telephone call to a close, Dennis wandered around the basement room, trying to assimilate what he'd learned. He wove his way between one row of pillars and back between the other. After his second circuit, he looked at his watch and, seeing that it was now five past eight, decided he might as well bite the bullet and make his way to the police station for his appointment with Superintendent Goodall. He retrieved Harry Parsons' tartan shopping bag from under the desk and made his way back upstairs.

The reporters' office was still deserted. He picked up the note he'd left on Julian's desk earlier and dropped it in the bin. As he went out into the hallway, he could hear Jeff talking on the phone upstairs, but as before, it was impossible to hear what he was saying.

Outside, on Langland Parade, he turned into the alleyway he'd seen Percy Franklin take the previous day. Turning left at the end, onto Church Street, he slowed down. He was going to be early, and the prospect of sitting like a lemon, outside Superintendent Goodall's office didn't appeal to him at all. He paused at a bakery window, feigning interest in the bread and cakes on display. He repeated the charade at a flower shop a little further on before consulting his watch again and deciding the time had finally come to keep his appointment.

The police station was a square, relatively modern building by Malvern standards, with a Union Flag flapping from a pole on the roof. Inside it smelt of pine disinfectant, fried food, and perspiration. He walked across the echoing entrance hall to a hatch with a sliding glass window, and a sign above that read, "Enquiries." There was no-one there but a push-button bell, mounted on the wall next to the window was labelled, "Ring for attention." He gave the bell a quick blast and waited. He'd feared having a face-to-face encounter with the brusque Sergeant Collins but, to his relief, the policeman, who emerged from a rear office, showed no sign of recognition when he announced his name. He was signed in and then a PC was tasked with taking him up to the first floor.

He was told to wait outside a door bearing the name "Superintendent R.P. Goodall" in one-inch high, gold letters, and on the other side of which, a muffled but plainly agitated conversation was taking place. Suddenly it flew open and Nigel came out looking angrier than Dennis had ever seen him. Their eyes met briefly then Nigel strode away, kicking open the swing doors at the end of the corridor, and clattering off down the stairs.

A voice boomed out, "Are you coming in or not? I haven't got all day you know.' Dennis turned to see a red-faced man standing over him. He was wearing police uniform trimmed with such an elaborate array of silver insignia that no-one could possibly have doubted his importance. His tightly curled, steel grey hair looked like chainmail, adding to the general aura of ruthlessness and impregnability.

He ushered Dennis into a thickly carpeted office with a view of the main road. The room was almost as big as the one Dennis shared with five other reporters and was dominated by a desk, equally as grand as the one in the crypt, but much better cared for. On the wall, behind the desk, was a large, elaborately framed portrait of the Queen in full coronation regalia. Goodall went and sat behind his desk and motioned Dennis to sit down opposite.

'I take it your editor has briefed you on the situation we find ourselves in,' he boomed.

'He just said I had to take over the Symbiosis House story because the reporter who was covering it previously has left for another job. That's all I know.'

'I see,' said Goodall, looking pointedly at his wristwatch. 'I suppose I'd better put you in the picture then. You're a reporter so no doubt you're used to grasping the gist of things quickly. If you listen hard and don't ask any inane questions, I'm sure we can get this all tied up within the next five minutes.'

Dennis felt duty bound to protest at this point, but the Superintendent was already ploughing on

'The first thing to say is that, just before your predecessor jumped ship, he'd started peddling a cock and bull story about the body that's turned up at Symbiosis House. Laughably implausible as it was, if it had made it into print it would have seriously undermined our police investigation, not to mention the reputation of your newspaper. Fortunately though your editor is a shrewd man and as soon as this work of fiction came to his attention, he spiked it – that's what you say in newspaper circles isn't it?'

Dennis managed a perfunctory nod as Goodall continued.

'But there's no point dwelling on the past. It's time to start with a clean sheet, which is why I agreed to meet with you this morning. The long and the short of it is, there's absolutely no mystery about this case: no conspiracy; no intrigue; no murky history. Our one and only suspect is a man called Andrew Morrigan, a local itinerant, well-known for bouts of drunken violence. He also has a serious mental disorder which exacerbates his aggressive tendencies. We believe he killed someone during a drunken altercation and then buried them at Symbiosis House because he knew it to be a remote and unfrequented spot. Three days ago, however, he was overcome with remorse, and dug the body up again, which, in our view, is tantamount to a confession to his original crime.'

He stopped and fixed Dennis with a gimlet stare. 'Why aren't you writing anything down? You haven't even got your notebook and pencil out yet.'

'But this is just background, isn't it? Most of it's been in the paper already.'

'That's not the point, I need to be sure you know what your boundaries are, and that you're not suffering under the delusion that you can just go away and write what you damned well like. Am I making myself clear?'

'Perfectly.'

'Good, because if I ever get the impression that you're heading down the same duplicitous road as your predecessor you'll wish you'd never been born. Do you understand?'

'Yes,' said Dennis weakly

'In which case, I just need to outline how I see matters proceeding henceforth. Obviously, our priority – or should I say, your brother's priority - is to arrest Andrew Morrigan. As I said to him before you arrived, there's no excuse for allowing a man like that to evade capture in a small town like ours. By the time your next edition comes out, I expect Morrigan to have been charged with murder, and to be languishing behind bars, awaiting trial. At that point, your job will be to report the facts in a supportive way and to dampen down any unhelpful speculation that the public might choose to indulge in.'

He pressed a button on his desk causing an electric bell to ring somewhere in the distance.

'Right,' said Goodall standing up and walking over to the door.' Time for you to be on your way.'

He pulled the door open and ushered Dennis into the corridor where the PC who'd shown him up earlier was already waiting, presumably summoned by the bell. Within two minutes Dennis was out on the street again, weighing up where he might go to gather his chaotic thoughts.

Then he felt a tap on his shoulder and turned to see his brother standing there.

'Come with me,' said Nigel. 'We need to talk.'

CHAPTER 13

A Meeting of Minds

Friday 29th March 1957

9.15 a.m.

Nigel strode off with Dennis in his wake. Crossing Church Street, he led the way into the Priory churchyard and flopped onto a bench under the canopy of an ancient cedar tree.

'Any more of that and he'll be getting my letter of resignation,' he exclaimed, as Dennis sat down beside him.'

'Goodall, you mean?'

'Of course. Who else?'

'He was charm itself when I saw him.'

'Really?'

'No, he was utterly obnoxious.'

Nigel scowled at him. 'Don't do that to me Dennis, I'm not in the mood. Why were you there anyway?'

'Jeff Stephenson sent me. It turns out the Whippet's gone off to join a national paper and left him in the lurch. I'm supposed to pick up the Symbiosis House story where he left off – except it isn't really where he left off because the last thing I heard; he was planning to write a completely different story from the one in this morning's Gazette.'

'It sounds as if Goodall's got to Jeff as well.'

'That's what I thought but he wasn't very pleased when I suggested it.'

'I bet he wasn't. What did he say?'

'How dare I question his editorial integrity, that sort of thing. He reckoned he'd dropped the story because he thought the Whippet had written a fake story just to embarrass him.'

'Why would the Whippet do that?'

'He's got it into his head that Jeff's been holding his career back and stopped him from rising to the dizzy heights he thinks he deserves, so it was an act of revenge before he headed off for pastures new.'

'So, has he *really* got a job on a national paper, do you think?'

Dennis shrugged. 'I assume so, why do you ask?'

'It seems a bit of a coincidence, that's all.'

'I don't know. The Whippet's always looked after number one so if he was offered a plum job on a plate, he'd take it. He wouldn't think twice about leaving Jeff in the lurch.'

'Except I'm pretty sure the story he'd written wasn't a fake at all. More like the best scoop the Gazette's had in years.'

'What makes you think that?'

'You remember me telling you how we caught him trespassing the other day?'

'Yes, you said you'd had him ejected and then you strengthened the guard around the boundaries.'

'That's right, but that was only after we'd caught him looking in through the window while I was briefing everyone about how the investigation was going.'

It suddenly occurred to Dennis that he'd better be careful how he responded because he wasn't supposed to know any of this. He said, 'But he couldn't have heard what you were saying from outside could he?'

'No, but stupidly I'd set up a blackboard and easel with all my points chalked up on it, in full view of the window.'

'I see.'

'It wouldn't have been hard for him to piece together what we'd discovered from all that so, by the time we kicked him out, he wasn't bothered anymore because he'd got everything he'd come for.'

'And more, by the sound of it.'

'A lot more,' said Nigel. Then, peering at him quizzically, he added, 'You don't seem all that surprised.'

Dennis blinked. 'What do you mean? Of course, I am.'

'Don't lie to me Dennis, you're dealing with a detective here remember. Reading people's expressions is second nature to me and yours tells me you've heard most of this already. Did the Whippet tell you what he saw?'

'No, he didn't. He was boasting about uncovering a big story, but he didn't let on about any of the details. He said we'd have to read it in today's Gazette, just like everyone else. That's why I was so disappointed when I saw what had been printed.'

'How did you find out then?'

'I didn't find out, I…'

Conscious of Nigel's unrelenting gaze, he realised that further evasion was pointless. 'All right,' he sighed, 'You've rumbled me. I think I know what the Whippet found out but it's only because he left a couple of clues behind and Julian and I managed to build up a bit of a picture from them.'

'Who's Julian?'

'Julian Croft, the Gazette's theatre correspondent.'

'What's a theatre correspondent got to do with any of this?'

'Nothing really. He's just got an enquiring mind, so I suppose he thought it was an interesting puzzle to solve.'

'He obviously hasn't got enough to keep him busy, either that or he's missed his vocation. What did you and this enquiring theatre correspondent come up with then?'

'Well, for a start, we deduced that you'd found an interesting object in the grave.'

'I assume you mean the Occitan cross, otherwise known as the cross of Toulouse. I didn't recognise it but one of my men is fanatical about heraldry and he knew what it was straightaway. How did you work that out then?'

'The Whippet had made a rough sketch of it which we found screwed up in the wastepaper basket. It didn't mean anything to us on its own, but he'd helpfully left an encyclopaedia open on the desk, with a photograph of the same cross slap bang in the middle of the page. We couldn't see its significance straightaway, but we worked on the assumption that it was probably a ring, or a medallion, or something like that. Then, by a process of elimination, we decided it could have belonged to Laurent Morel, the French TRE scientist, who disappeared in 1948.'

'Interesting.'

'Really? I thought you'd say it was a ridiculous idea.'

'Not at all, I reckon you're spot on, I just wish you'd come clean in the first place. What were you planning to do? Carry out your own private investigation?'

'I don't know. Possibly I suppose.'

'You need to be straight with me Dennis. I realise Dad's done his best over the years to stir up trouble between us but that's just the mischief making of a discontented old man. If you just stopped and thought about it for a moment, it might dawn on you that we're both on the same side.'

'You're right, I'm sorry.'

'Well just remember it in future, will you? That's all I ask.'

Dennis gave a sheepish nod.

'Anyway,' Nigel continued, 'the long and the short of it is that you and this theatre correspondent of yours are thinking along the same lines as me but, nobody else, especially Superintendent Goodall, seems ready to do the same. I'm guessing he gave you the party line when you saw him just now; something along the lines of unknown man gets killed during a drunken confrontation with Andrew Morrigan; Morrigan buries the victim at Symbiosis House but later, out of remorse, decides to dig the remains up again. Am I close?'

'You are. He made it sound like a classic, low-life brawl, where one of the parties ended up getting killed. Unfortunate perhaps, but no particular mystery attached to it.'

'Which might be a reasonable theory if the victim had been stabbed or bludgeoned, but, in my experience, being shot in the side of the head at point blank range isn't the usual outcome of a brawl, especially the crude, knockabout type that Goodall's describing.'

'You're saying he was shot?' exclaimed Dennis, staring at him in astonishment.

'That's surprised you hasn't it,' said Nigel. 'I'm glad there's still *something* about this case you don't know.'

'We only had that sketch of the cross to work with really, so he must have held onto any other notes he made.

That's assuming he knew about the shooting of course.'

'Oh, he knew about it all right because I'd obligingly written it all up on the blackboard, in full view of the window. I even wrote what type of revolver was used. It was quite an unusual one actually, I've never come across it before.'

'What was it?'

'It won't mean anything to you, but it was a Nagant M1895. It's a Russian revolver, first used by the Imperial Russian Army, and then adopted by the Red Army after the Revolution. One particularly interesting fact about it is that, unlike most other revolvers of that period, it could be fitted with a silencer.'

'Is that significant do you think?'

'Maybe, maybe not. The thing is though, shooting someone in the temple, at point-blank range, suggests a premeditated, assassination-style killing to me, and the use of a silencer would certainly be consistent with that sort of M.O.'

'I see what you mean now about Goodall's version, it doesn't add up at all when you look at the facts does it?'

'Not really.'

'But how do you know all this? Did you find the revolver in the grave with him?'

'No, just the bullet. I'm basing it on the analysis I got back from our ballistics experts in Birmingham. They can glean a remarkable amount of information from the marks made during firing. I don't think they've come across many M1895s, so they were quite excited about it, hence all the extra historical blurb they gave me.'

'They can't tell you how a revolver was actually used though, can they?'

'*They* can't but a halfway competent pathologist can. Dr Reeves could see straightaway that it was a point-blank wound to the side of the head. I'd already worked that out for myself before he arrived, but, obviously, his professional knowledge carries a lot more weight than mine where that sort of thing's concerned.'

'What about the pre-meditated nature of it?'

'I admit that's down to me, and the experience I've had of other, similar, situations. I think the victim was taken there and executed and that the whole thing had been planned well in advance, even to the extent of digging a grave in readiness for what was going to happen.'

'But Superintendent Goodall doesn't agree.'

'No, he's worried that if he gave credence to that sort of theory, it would open a huge can of worms that he wouldn't be able to control, and that's something he could never allow to happen.'

'So, he's using Andrew Morrigan as a scapegoat to make life easier for him?'

'That's how it looks to me. Morrigan might have been part of it in some way but never in a million years would he have been capable of carrying it out on his own.'

'And what about the likelihood that Laurent Morel was the victim? How does Goodall react to that?'

'By completely ignoring it, that's how. He's the one who brushed the Morel story under the carpet in the first place, so he's hardly likely to let it come to light again now.'

After a moment's pause, he said, 'I can't believe I'm having this conversation with you, especially when it's so obvious you were holding back on me before.'

'So why are you then?'

'Because it's been preying on my mind, but there hasn't been anyone else I could talk to about it.'

'What about the people working on the investigation with you; your sergeant and all the others? They were there when you were explaining it all on the blackboard yesterday they must know about it anyway.'

'Except, since then, Goodall's given them the same bilge he gave you. He's told them that, whatever they've heard to the contrary, there's no mystery about what happened; Morrigan's the culprit and once he's been apprehended, the case will be well and truly closed.'

'Even though you've already told them you think it's a lot more complicated than that?'

'It doesn't matter what I think because Goodall's far more powerful and intimidating than I'll ever be so what he says is what people believe – or pretend they do anyway.'

'What about the revolver though? You said yourself it makes the drunken brawl theory look pretty thin: how does he explain that away?'

'He just says Morrigan must have got hold of it by chance: won it in an illicit poker game or something like that.'

'And then used it to shoot someone at point-blank range?'

'Again, he makes out it was a chance occurrence. The gun went off, mid-tussle, and happened to be up against the victim's head at the time.'

'Won't your pathologist have something to say about that?'

'I doubt it. Dr Reeves is a good pathologist but he's not going to go out on a limb if it means falling out with Goodall. Anyway, all he's said is that the barrel of the revolver was in contact with the skull at the time of firing. He makes it clear that working out the rest – the how and why business – is entirely down to us.'

'What about the forensics people in Birmingham?'

'They're the same. They've carried out an analysis of the material they've been sent, but they won't get involved in the case beyond that.'

'And you're sure there's no-one more senior you could appeal to?'

'No-one at all. As I told you yesterday, Goodall's got the whole place sewn up.'

'Have you talked to your sergeant about it?"

'No, I haven't.'

'Is that because you don't trust *him* either?'

'Oh, I think Ronnie's trustworthy enough, it's just that I'm not entirely sure how well he'd bear up under questioning.'

'If Goodall nobbled him you mean?'

'Goodall or one of his cronies, yes.'

'So, you've got no-one else to turn to.'

'Apart from you it seems.'

'What about Judith or Dad?'

'Nigel stared at him aghast. 'You must be joking. I'd never burden either of them with something like this.'

'Why not?'

'Because Dad doesn't need any more worries in his life than he's already got and, as far as Judith's concerned, I prefer to keep my home life and my work life separate.'

'Does that mean you don't tell Judith when your job's

getting you down?'

'Sometimes I'll have a moan about Goodall's bad moods or my sergeant being a lazy toad but no more than that.'

'But she's tough, isn't she? She's bright as well. I'd have thought she was the perfect person to confide in about something like this.'

'Hang on a second Dennis,' said Nigel, wagging his finger at him. 'I'm prepared to discuss the case with you but I'm not about to let a confirmed bachelor advise me on what I should and shouldn't share with my own wife.'

Dennis nodded. 'Fair enough, let's stick to the case then. You said you thought it looked like an execution and that you'd come across similar situations before. Where on earth was that then? Not in Malvern surely?'

'It was while I was serving in France towards the end of the war. I came across a couple of people who'd been killed in the same way.'

'Who were they?'

'French citizens who'd been collaborating with the Germans. One was a man and one was a woman. As we advanced, and the Germans retreated, their neighbours decided to take revenge. They both got bullets in the head at point-blank range but, unlike our current victim, were left unburied as a warning to other informants about what might happen to them.'

'But in every other respect, they were like the body at Symbiosis House?'

'Yes, a bullet in the side of the head; a neat entry wound and a much messier exit hole on the other side. I'm guessing they were chased or dragged to the spot by their killers, and then forced to kneel down and take their punishment.'

'Do you think the Symbiosis House victim would have

been forced to kneel down like that as well?'

'Yes because, when we sifted through the soil at the bottom of the grave, we found the bullet. What that indicates is that the victim must have been made to kneel at the side of a pit that had already been dug. The killer would then have been firing downwards into the head and, on exit; the bullet would have continued that trajectory and embedded itself in the freshly excavated earth below.'

They sat in silence for a few seconds and then Dennis said, 'actually, I've got another confession to make.'

'Another one,' said Nigel, with a chuckle. 'You're turning out to be an even darker horse than I thought. Come on then, what is it?'

'I saw Andrew Morrigan, up in the woods near Wynds Point.'

'When was this?'

'Yesterday morning, just before I bumped into you outside Symbiosis House.'

'I knew it,' said Nigel, shaking his head in exasperation. 'I could tell you were holding back on something at the time. Why on earth didn't you say.'

'You weren't in the best of moods, so I wasn't sure how you'd take it.'

'Rubbish, you thought you'd got a lucky break and you were planning to use it to your advantage. Come on, be honest.'

Dennis sighed. 'You're probably right. Sorry'

'So you should be. Did you see where he went?'

'No, I just got a glimpse of him and then he disappeared into the trees again. I didn't call out or try to follow him.'

I'm assuming you didn't tell the charming Sergeant Collins about this.'

Dennis shook his head

'That was probably wise under the circumstances,' said Nigel more thoughtfully. 'But it's no excuse for keeping it from me.'

'I know, I'm sorry.'

'As it happens, something else has come up about James since you mentioned finding his car. I asked Sergeant Clarke to get me some background information on the current ownership status of Symbiosis House, and it seems that James' firm acts as agents for the property. It means they've got access to all the legal paperwork.'

'And did your sergeant try getting hold of him?'

'Yes but, unsurprisingly, he wasn't available, so he ended up speaking to a man called Percy Franklin instead.'

'That's James' assistant.'

'So I understand, but according to Ronnie Clarke, he wasn't helpful at all.'

'What about Miss Collingford, James' secretary? Have you or Sergeant Clarke tried talking to her?'

'*I* haven't but it's possible Ronnie has. I'll check when I next speak to him.'

'It's just that I was in contact with her earlier about James and she mentioned she'd been trying to contact you. She left a message at the police station and they promised to pass it on.'

'Who did she leave it with…? No, let me guess, this is Sergeant Collins again, isn't it?'

'I'm afraid so.'

'He probably dropped the message straight in the bin. That's assuming he wrote it down at all. What was she so keen to speak to me about?'

'Her concerns about James. I phoned first thing this morning because this car business was preying on my mind and it turned out that she's been at her wit's end since yesterday lunch time because he didn't come in to wind up his precious long case clock. Apparently, he does it every Thursday, before noon, without fail. He won't let anyone else near the thing because it's so old and valuable. She reckons he's been acting strangely for a couple of weeks now so the fact that he didn't appear yesterday finally brought matters to a head for her.'

'Acting strangely? How?'

'Locking himself away in his office which is something he's never done before. She thinks she's heard him crying in there too.'

'Now that *is* strange. Especially when you consider it's James we're talking about here. He's not exactly known for wearing his heart on his sleeve, is he?'

'You can say that again. I asked her if she knew what might have set him off and the only thing she could think of was that she'd overheard him having an argument with Percy Franklin, around the time it all started. She didn't catch any of what they were saying but it was definitely an angry exchange.'

'It sounds as if old James has been having more than his fair share of troubles recently.'

'And it looks as if they might have finally come to a head which makes it all the more important to track him down before he does anything drastic again.'

'I'll try and find out what's happening when I go back

to the station,' said Nigel. 'In the meantime, we'd better decide how we're going to play this Symbiosis House business?'

'I don't know, you're the one in charge of the investigation. I'm just a humble reporter.'

'*In charge*? That's a joke. The only one in charge is Superintendent Goodall and if he thinks, for one moment, I've disobeyed his instructions, he'll have me out of the force so fast, my feet won't touch the floor.'

'There's your answer then: you just have to make him think you're doing as you're told. Meanwhile, I could carry on digging around on your behalf and report back anything I find.'

'That's reasonable I suppose, provided you *do* report back, and promise to tell me everything, not just the edited highlights.'

'Why wouldn't I?'

'Because you've kept information back from me at least twice now so, naturally, I'm wondering just how trustworthy you are.'

'In which case, all I can do is give you my word as your brother, that it won't happen again. We're both on the same side, I see that now.'

'I hope so Dennis because this isn't a game anymore. This is deadly serious, and I need to be certain I can rely on you. Do you understand?'

'Completely. From now on, as soon as I discover anything, you'll be the first to know.'

As they stood up to go, Nigel grabbed Dennis by the elbow and whispered urgently in his ear.

'Did you see that?'

'No, what?'

'A man just ducked out from behind that tree over there. Look, there he is, heading for the steps up towards Belle Vue Terrace.'

Dennis peered in the direction his brother was pointing and saw a limping figure starting to negotiate the steps, just beyond the Priory entrance.

'That's Percy Franklin, James' assistant. Do you think he was watching us?'

'I'm certain he was. 'What's he up to, do you think?'

'I don't know. That's the second time I've seen him in two days. He was hanging around outside the office yesterday. Julian reckoned he was waiting for Jeff.'

'Why would he have been waiting for Jeff?'

'He places bets for him apparently. According to Julian, they share an interest in horse racing that goes back years.'

'That's an odd association, isn't it?'

'Very odd indeed. I still find it hard to believe, but Julian swears it's the case. Seeing him here again now though makes me wonder if it was me he was interested in, rather than Jeff.'

'What would his interest in you be?'

'Again, I don't know. I'm probably just being paranoid.'

'He was definitely watching us though. Fortunately, he wouldn't have been able to hear anything from that far away.'

'You don't think he's one of Goodall's spies, do you?'

'I hardly think so. What possible connection could they have?'

'We were just saying the same about him and Jeff though, weren't we? And you did say you were worried about how far-reaching Goodall's tentacles might be.'

'You're right, I did. It seems as if we're both going to need eyes in the backs of our heads from now on, doesn't it?

CHAPTER 14
Back to an earlier time

Friday 29th March 1957

9.45 a.m.

After parting from Nigel at the gateway to the Priory churchyard, Dennis crossed over Church Street and then turned into Graham Road, heading for the public library. It was still only quarter to ten and he was relishing the prospect of a working day with nothing urgent to do. Although Jeff had ordered him to concentrate on the Symbiosis House report, the deadline was still nearly a week away and the story was a fait accompli anyway. The only pressing thing was to make sure he caught a late afternoon train that would get him to Hereford in time for his six o'clock meeting with Harry Parsons.

  A free day like the one stretching ahead of him now provided an ideal opportunity to scour the local newspaper archives at the public library. He wanted to see if he could find out any more about Laurent Morel and the half-hearted police enquiry into his disappearance in 1948. He was also keen to pursue the separate matter of his grandfather's involvement in the St Werstan Spa Hotel and discover why the mention of it had upset his father so much. Before he did any of that though, he intended to look through the notebooks that Harry Parsons had given him on the train. He was still clutching the tartan shopping bag they'd come in and, although he was fascinated to see what its contents might reveal, he was getting a bit sick of lugging it around.

There were two good reasons for choosing the public reference library over the Gazette's crypt: firstly, it had a far wider range of publications on offer, including back numbers of Berrow's Worcester Journal and the Worcestershire Chronicle if he needed them; secondly, Jeff Stephenson was far less likely to come looking for him there.

He established himself in one of the reading booths furthest away from where most of the library's users tended to cluster and spread the notebooks out on the desk in front of him.

There were eight of them in total; all about three quarters of an inch thick, and all bound in black leather; dog-eared through age and heavy use. They weren't labelled so it was impossible to tell, at a glance, which years they related to. Opening one of them, however – the most dog-eared of all and therefore, he thought, likely to be the oldest – he saw that Harry's father, Matthew, had dated each of his projects and provided location details and names of the clients who'd engaged him in an immaculate copperplate script. This notebook had been started in October 1890 and ran through to May 1891. To introduce each new project there was an overall sketch of the site in question, cross-referenced with more detailed illustrations of features that required special attention. Dennis was impressed: they were beautifully executed: each of them, a little work of art. All the drawings were meticulously annotated with dimensions and headings. Next came a summary of the commission, including objectives and estimated timescales. Finally, there was a three-column table, listing: materials required; likely supplier, estimated cost.

Interspersing each of these introductory descriptions,

were review notes on projects already underway. These followed a similar pattern, with drawings to show any modifications to the original plan, followed by revised objectives and an adjusted resource table to reflect the changes deemed necessary.

As he worked his way through the notebooks, it became clear to Dennis that Matthew Parsons had been a very busy man indeed. He'd often been managing three complex projects at the same time and had plainly been versatile because his work ranged from the installation of huge agricultural drainage systems, through the construction of interconnected lake features on country estates, to the renovation of leaky plumbing systems in ancient Herefordshire manor houses.

Having got a feel for the way in which the records were organised, Dennis skimmed through the other notebooks until he came to Matthew Parsons' first mention of Symbiosis House in April 1896. Turning the page he saw a beautiful, ink-drawn diagram of the chamber that made him catch his breath. He'd seen various other depictions before – the one in "Hidden Realms of Rock and Water", for example; the slim volume his landlord had given him two days ago – but they'd never been as clear and meticulously detailed as this one was.

It stretched across two adjoining pages and showed a space like the inside of a slightly flattened egg, served by a network of drainage channels, valves and tanks. Paler lines and shading around it showed how it sat in relation to the layout of the house above.

As with the other project notes Dennis had seen, this general representation of the site was supported by a series of drawings that showed specific features in more detail. The one that fascinated Dennis the most was of the spout itself: a swan's neck and head, intricately cut from stone; water gushing from its beak, into a rough-hewn trough, below. Many accounts referred to the possible existence of this swan's neck feature, but this was the first time he'd seen an actual depiction of it.

He turned back to the main drawing again and re-read the heading above it.

21st April 1896
Proposed refashioning of subterranean water feature
Symbiosis House, Malvern Wells, Worcestershire

'Refashioning,' thought Dennis. 'What a quaint word to use.'

As he flicked through the rest of the pages a small black and white photograph fell out onto the desk.

Picking it up, he saw that it was a shot of the spout and trough taken from above. He'd noticed on the plan that there was a mezzanine platform half-way up the chamber, and he presumed that this was where the photographer had stood. On the opposite side of the chamber from the trough was a ladder that appeared to be fixed to the wall. There had been no such ladder on the plan and Dennis assumed it must have been a temporary fixture for construction purposes. It also struck him that in the drawing the trough was shown as being to the right of the mezzanine, looking down, but here it was to the left. He pondered on it for a few seconds before concluding that, as sometimes happened during the development process, the photograph had been printed the wrong way around. He slid it back between the pages, making a mental note to look at it again later.

What he most wanted to do now was go to Symbiosis House and see the Chamber Spout for himself, but he knew that was out of the question while a police investigation was going on. He gathered up the notebooks, returned them to the tartan shopping bag and placed it on the floor, next to his chair. He decided that the next task was to search out information that might shed some more light on the disappearance of Laurent Morel.

Over the years, the public reference library had become a home from home to him and he knew it inside out. Within five minutes he'd located the first batch of newspapers he planned to search through. He'd focused on editions of the Malvern Gazette for October and November 1948. The first was dated Friday 1st October. He flicked through the pages twice, but he couldn't find any references to a missing TRE scientist. He turned his attentions to the Friday 8th October edition that had been published a week later. He read from the front page to the back but still there was nothing.

He combed all the newspapers for October but without success. He started on the next month's editions but wasn't until he reached the one for Friday 26th November that he found what he'd been looking for. Julian had been right: although the report had made the front page, the headline feature concerned a legacy, bequeathed by a wealthy local resident, ensuring, "Great Malvern's display of Christmas lights will shine more brightly than ever this year."

The Laurent Morel story appeared towards the foot of the page.

Police baffled by disappearance of French scientist
Possible risk to national security?
Malvern police have so far failed in their attempts to locate TRE scientist Laurent Morel (31) who was reported missing three days ago. Morel, originally from Toulouse, was a French émigré who had been working in this country since 1939. Said to be a brilliant physicist he was formerly based at Worth Matravers, Dorset until the TRE moved to Malvern College in August 1942. Morel was one of several émigré scientists who were stranded in England during the early days of the last war. However, police are at pains to reassure the public that, despite Morel's proximity to

sensitive research work, he no longer had any involvement in projects that could have a bearing on national security.

No-one from the top-secret research establishment was available to speak to the Gazette before we went to press, but we have learned from colleagues of the missing man that he was last seen at around 10.30 pm on Tuesday 23rd November. They say he rode a bicycle to and from his flat in Malvern link where he lived alone. Staff say they were worried when he failed to appear the following morning because he had never been known to miss a day's work. The police were notified of his disappearance after a colleague went around to his flat and found no-one there. Speaking to the Gazette, Superintendent Albert Goodall, of Malvern Police, admitted that they had yet to establish what had happened to Morel and that they were attempting to locate his relatives in Toulouse. Superintendent Goodall went on to say,

"We are keen to hear from anyone who thinks they might have seen Morel after 10.30 last Tuesday night. If you have any information that might help you should call in at your local police station or telephone Great Malvern 216."

Dennis put the paper to one side and opened the next one: it was the edition for Friday 3rd December 1948. Julian was right again: the follow-up was just a short piece on page two.

Police wind down search for missing scientist

Local police announced today that they are discontinuing their search for missing TRE scientist Laurent Morel. He is believed to have returned home to France and it has been confirmed that his disappearance does not pose any threat to national security. It appears that Morel's access to top-secret information had been restricted for some time and that this could have been in response to rumours about some of his personal associations.

Superintendent Albert Goodall confirmed that although Morel was undoubtedly a brilliant scientist and had worked on advanced technical projects in his early days at the TRE, the Frenchman had been confined to non-sensitive, low level duties at the top-secret government establishment for the last five years. Superintendent Goodall expressed regret that, currently, he was not at liberty to disclose the reasons behind this decision. However, one of Morel's former colleagues, who wished to remain anonymous, has since informed the Gazette of longstanding concerns about aspects of Morel's social life, particularly the types of exclusively male clubs he was known to frequent, which could have compromised his position, if his access to sensitive information had been allowed to continue.

Recently, Morel had been working as a librarian in the Greville Jobson Science Wing at Malvern College. The special wing, funded through the Mitarbeit Trust and which was established after the untimely death of science teacher, Dr Greville Jobson in 1923, is still used as a reference library by those scientists who continue to be based at the College during the TRE's transfer to new premises.

A spokesman for the TRE said that it was now presumed that M. Morel had had personal reasons for leaving the area and it was very likely that he had returned to France.

Dennis recalled the phrase Julian had used in the pub the previous day, "good riddance to the perverted bastard; we don't want any more of his type round here." Now he'd read it for himself he could see what Julian meant; it was just the sort of bigoted reaction the report was intended to provoke.

He leafed through the rest of the newspaper, half-heartedly looking for any other references to the Morel disappearance but, as expected, there was nothing at all. He decided to give up on missing scientists for the time-being and try another angle. Given that Margaret had spoken about it only a couple of days before, the report's reference to the Greville Jobson Science Wing had leapt out of the page at him. He remembered she'd mentioned attending the opening ceremony with her mother in March nineteen twenty-four, one year after her father's death so he decided to look out copies of the Gazettes from around that time and see how the event had been reported.

The library had a similar arrangement for storing back numbers to that at the Gazette: flat boxes, each capable of holding a dozen newspapers flat and unfolded were stacked on narrowly spaced shelves in five vast metal cabinets, no doubt specially designed for the purpose. He recalled Margaret telling him that the reference library in Birmingham had long ago transferred its entire newspaper archive to microfilm that could be read through a special reader and that Worcester Reference Library was now going through the same process. He guessed it wouldn't be long until Malvern adopted the system as well and it made him wonder how they'd use all the space they'd gain after the massive cupboards had been moved out. He carefully returned the newspapers he'd been reading to their boxes and slid them back onto the appropriate shelf. Then he turned his attention to the cabinet holding local newspapers from the turn of the century, through to the early thirties. A single box contained editions of the Malvern Gazette published during January, February and March 1924. He pulled it out, placed it on the table in front of the cabinets and removed the lid. Each newspaper was encased in its own paper sleeve with a cellophane window to reveal the front page He extracted the four copies for March 1924 and took them back to his reading booth. He found the report he'd been hoping to see in the one dated Friday 14th March. It appeared halfway down the third page.

New Science Wing at College Named in Honour of Late Teacher

A special ceremony took place at Malvern College on Tuesday evening at which the new science wing of the library was officially opened and named in honour of the late Dr Greville Jobson. Dr Jobson taught Physics and Chemistry at the college until his sudden death in March 1923 when he was run over by a passing car whilst walking home. The driver of the vehicle that killed him has never been found. During his career, Dr Jobson amassed an extensive personal library, comprising works of an advanced scientific nature and this collection has been bequeathed in its entirety to Malvern College under the terms of Dr Jobson's will.

Host of the ceremony, Headmaster of Malvern College, Dr Nicholas Montague, told the Gazette, "Throughout an eminent career; one that was so tragically curtailed a year ago whilst he was still in his prime, Dr Jobson made an invaluable contribution to Malvern College which will never be forgotten by all those who were privileged to know him and to be taught by him. We are the very grateful beneficiaries of a large collection of scientific texts that would be the envy of any school in the Kingdom. After first hearing of the bequest, we all agreed that the least we could do under such circumstances was to provide Dr Jobson's library with a permanent home and, in so doing, that we should achieve two essential goals: firstly, that it should be worthy of the collection's immense academic worth and secondly, and of far greater import, that it should do justice to Dr Jobson's illustrious memory. Today I believe I can say with confidence that this magnificent, newly constructed, extension to the college library has more than achieved both objectives and we are therefore proud to name it the Greville Jobson Wing. I would like to add that we are very grateful to the Mitarbeit Trust for providing much needed funds and thus ensuring that this project came to fruition. As some of your readers may already know, the Mitarbeit Trust is a charity dedicated to the furtherance of international understanding through science."

Mrs Edna Jobson, Dr Jobson's widow, and their only daughter, Margaret (8) were special guests at the opening ceremony. In addition to the Headmaster, the following representatives of the College were present: Major J. Townsend, Chairman of the Board of Governors; Mr M. Crosby-Nash, Assistant

Headmaster; Dr L. Phillips, Head of Physics; Mr F. Edwards, College Librarian. Others present included: Councillor C. Bennett-Jones, Mayor of Malvern; Mrs V. Bennett-Jones, Lady Mayoress; Professor P. Caruthers, Cambridge University; Mr B. Summers, Architect; Mrs A. Delaney, Malvern Library; Dr M. Friedman, Mitarbeit Trust.

'Now that's interesting,' said Dennis under his breath. 'Mathias Friedman and the Mitarbeit Trust seem to be one and the same thing.'

Something made him glance round and he saw that one of the librarians was standing there peering at him. She'd been transferring a load of books from a trolley onto the shelves across from his booth and plainly thought he was one of those eccentric library users who disturb everyone else by having conversations with himself.

'Sorry,' he mouthed silently.

He emphasised the apology with, what he hoped was, a reassuring smile. It seemed to work because she responded with a vague, though possibly reproving, nod before continuing with her work.

He left the newspaper open on the desk while he went over to the shelf containing foreign language reference books and located a thick German dictionary. He took it back to his booth and flicked through the German-English pages until he came to the M section. Turning the flimsy pages over more carefully as he narrowed his search, he soon found the entry he was looking for,

mitarbeit *f. - cooperation; collaboration*

He jotted it down in his notebook and then went and exchanged the German dictionary for a copy of the Oxford Concise English Dictionary from the shelf above it. Back at his desk, he looked up the word "symbiosis,"

symbiosis n. Association of two different organisms living attached to each other or one within the other to their mutual advantage

He copied the definition down and sat staring at everything he'd written for a minute or so. It was clear that Friedman had had a bee in his bonnet about co-operation, collaboration and mutual support but what it signified he couldn't think. What struck him as interesting though was the way that the Mitarbeit Trust had been mentioned in two separate reports, nearly twenty-five years apart. The earlier reference was more explicable because it was obvious that, without the support of Friedman's charity, the Greville Jobson Science Wing could never have been built. The mention in the second Laurent Morel report, however, seemed oddly out of context; an unnecessary piece of information that added nothing to the main thrust of what was being said. It began to bother him so much that he went back and fetched the 3rd December 1948 paper so that he could take another look.

Recently, Morel had been working as a librarian in the Greville Jobson Science Wing at Malvern College. The special wing, funded through the Mitarbeit Trust and which was established after the untimely death of science teacher, Dr Greville Jobson in 1923, is still used as a reference library by those scientists who continue to be based at the College during the TRE's transfer to new premises.

There was no doubt about it; this penultimate paragraph changed the flow of the whole report, very nearly neutralising all the poison that had been laid in the words that preceded it. It left the reader with an almost benign image of the quiet librarian supporting his colleagues in the pursuit of scientific knowledge rather than that of the deviant foreigner everyone was glad to see the back of that the article had set out to create. And then the report ended with a remarkably limp sentence that seemed to have been inserted almost as an afterthought,

A spokesman for the TRE said that it was now presumed that M. Morel had had personal reasons for leaving the area

and it was very likely that he had returned to France.

Dennis frowned as he tried to think his way into the mind of the person who had written it. There was no name attached to the article and the same applied to the one that had appeared the week before. He guessed that Don Blackmore, in his capacity as acting editor, had tasked some hapless reporter to turn out a piece that met his muck-raking specifications and then, for some reason – possibly at the last minute –insisted that a paragraph about the science library be added.

He closed his eyes and leaned forward, cupping his head in his hands. It still failed to make any sense: if Don Blackmore had wanted to convey a negative picture of Laurent Morel as the first section of the report plainly showed he had, why would he then dilute the message by telling the reporter to insert a completely unnecessary paragraph? Of course, there was always the possibility that the reporter had added it on his own initiative as a way of stamping his identity on a mindless piece of production-line journalism. He smiled as he recalled the times Jeff had taken *him* to task for adding personal flourishes to an otherwise bland report. But it still didn't make proper sense because a blatant addition would stick out like a sore thumb and would never get past the editor unless the editor wanted it there. Which took him back to his original theory: Don must have wanted the paragraph included and might even have written it himself, just before the paper went to press. In fact, the more Dennis thought about it, that was what had struck him about the report in the first place; it read like a piece that had been written by two different people.

He sat up straight again and stretched his arms as he tried to clear his head. Experience told him that when thoughts became blurred, as they were now, it was best to turn to something else and let the sub-conscious get on with its work in the background.

He carefully returned all the back numbers to their respective homes and then selected the storage box for January, February and March 1923. He was looking for a report on the hit and run incident in which Margaret's father had been killed. As he pulled out one of the folders, something interesting caught his eye through the wrinkled, yellowing cellophane: a photograph of the St Werstan Spa Hotel, right in the centre of the front page of the Friday 2nd February edition. It appeared below a banner headline that read,

Spa Hotel with a dark history to be sold again

He pulled the newspaper from its wrapping and began to read.

A notable Malvern landmark, with a morbid tale to tell, has come onto the market for the third time in ten years. The St Werstan Spa Hotel in St Ann's Road has just been placed on the books of Crawford, Davies and Withers a mere eighteen months since it was last sold. Once again there has been a great deal of local speculation as to whether the frequent changes of ownership have anything to do with the St Werstan Spa's association with the unfortunate demise of Oktav Baader in the autumn of 1889. At that time, The St Werstan Spa was owned by a prominent Malvern entrepreneur, Henry Powell. He had established a successful business offering hydropathic cures for a variety of ailments, like those pioneered by Doctors Wilson and Gully in the middle of the last century. The hotel's prosperity grew as Powell actively promoted his therapies throughout Great Britain and the continent. It was as the result of a visit Henry Powell made to Gräfenberg, Austria earlier in 1889 that Oktav Baader decided to come and stay at the hotel. Herr Baader suffered from a respiratory illness and was persuaded by Powell that the special treatments provided at the St Werstan Spa would help to relieve some of the debilitating symptoms of his condition. He subsequently travelled to Malvern and began an intensive programme of hydropathic therapy. Unfortunately, his constitution proved to be much weaker than either he or his host had anticipated and during one of the procedures he suffered a heart attack and died. Although Henry Powell was exonerated by the Coroner at the subsequent inquest, his reputation was seriously damaged by the episode and shortly afterwards he decided to sell the hotel. Since then, because of its imposing position on the side of the hills, the St Werstan Spa has continued to serve as a popular base for visitors to the area. However, it has never offered any hydropathic remedies since that fateful day in 1889 when Oktav Baader met his untimely end, and it has changed ownership more often than any other hotel in the town.

Henry Powell himself died on 30th October 1921, while taking an evening walk on the hills, as was his habit. He is thought to have strayed from the path above Gullet Quarry and fallen into the lake below where his body was found by a fisherman, the following morning. Despite the Coroner's verdict of accidental death, questions have persisted to this day as to how a man, so familiar with the hills and who had taken that route so many times before – both during the day and at night - could have made such a fatal mistake. The incident only served to reinforce local superstition that something of Herr Baader's misfortune rubs off on those who become too closely associated with the location of his tragic and untimely demise.

Property details are available by request from Crawford, Davies and Withers Estate Agents and Auctioneers, Belle Vue Terrace, Great Malvern.

As he finished reading, he realised that he'd been gripping the edge of the table so tightly that his hands and wrists were aching. He gave them a shake to relieve the tension and then he took the newspaper back to his reading booth, along with the four editions for March. He sat down and read through the report twice more. Was this why his father had been so unwilling to talk about the family connection with the St Werstan Spa Hotel? Was he worried that the reputational damage Henry had suffered might transfer to him if the subject ever came up again? And might it explain why he'd been so desperate to leave the area after Henry died? Had he been afraid that public interest in the inquest would bring the Oktav Baader scandal to the surface again and endanger his own jealously guarded reputation?

He decided that, before he did anything else, he should dig out the original reports from 1889 when Oktav Baader had had a fatal encounter with hydropathy at the St Werstan Spa Hotel. That would mean looking through copies of a much earlier newspaper - the Worcestershire Chronicle.

Just as he was getting to his feet, he heard a familiar voice coming from the desk at the entrance to the reference section. It was Jeff Stephenson and he was talking, in hushed tones, to one of the librarians. As Dennis peered warily over the top of the partition, the librarian selected a book from the shelf behind her and passed it over the counter. Jeff nodded his thanks and withdrew to the reading booth nearest the exit. The last thing Dennis wanted was to have to explain what he was doing here but how could he escape without being observed? Possibly Jeff would be so absorbed in whatever he was reading that he wouldn't look up, but it seemed too big a risk to take. Then he remembered that if he turned right out of his booth instead of left, he could go out via the staff cloakrooms into the back yard. That was the way Margaret had crept out for a cigarette when she'd worked here.

He stood up cautiously and stuffed his notebook and pencil into his jacket pocket. He'd have to abandon the papers he'd been reading without returning to them to their cabinets. To do that was against library rules but he could always phone them later to apologise. Keeping his head low, he crept out of the booth and made his way towards an unmarked door at the end of the narrow walkway, desperately hoping that it wouldn't be locked. To his relief, the door opened without even a squeak and within seconds he was out in the back yard and walking quickly towards the lane that led back round to Graham Road and freedom.

By the time he reached the junction with Church Street, he'd already formulated a new plan of action. He cut back through the alley way that led to the Gazette, then turned right along Langland Parade and into Pierrepoint Terrace. He wheeled his motorbike out from the passageway between Relics of Sabrina and the dry cleaners and kicked down hard on the starter pedal. The engine roared into life straightaway inspiring him to give the Tiger's petrol tank a gentle pat to show his gratitude. He'd just started accelerating along Albert Road, taking advantage of an unusual absence of traffic, when an awkward thought came into his mind, causing him to ease off the throttle again. He'd been intending to call on his mother at home; confident that, between the hours of eight a.m. and six p.m. on a working Friday, Charles wouldn't be around. It had seemed safe to assume that he'd be supervising the loading of the old Dennis lorry in preparation for Thomas Radford and Son's afternoon delivery run, just as he'd done every weekday for the last forty years or so. But it suddenly occurred to him that, because of his strange turn the evening before, there was a slight chance Charles might not have been well enough to go into work today. It was only a slim chance because it was hard to imagine his father ever missing a day at the warehouse, but it was still one he didn't want to take. He turned right at the cricket ground and then turned immediately right again, into Priory Road, heading back towards the town centre.

Thomas Radford and Son's wine and spirits shop was halfway up Church Street. The warehouse round the back was reached via Langland Parade and then by taking a left turn, just after the Gazette Office, into Wilson's Entry, a narrow thoroughfare hemmed in by parallel stone walls. Occasional gateways provided access to the yards of businesses to the rear of Church Street on one side and Langland Parade on the other. Dennis nosed the Tiger slowly along the road until he reached the entrance to Thomas Radford and Son. He propped the bike on its stand but left the engine idling while he tentatively poked his head around the gatepost to see into the yard. The Dennis delivery lorry, complete with canvass canopy sheltering its cargo platform, had been reversed up close to the building. The warehouse's big wooden doors had been opened flat against the wall on each side of the entrance and standing nearby was the hunched figure of his father, clipboard in hand, overseeing two men as they loaded cases of wine into the lorry.

Returning to his motorbike, Dennis manoeuvred the machine so that it was facing back in the direction he'd come from. Not for the first time, he wondered how the old delivery lorry managed to pass to and fro along the narrow lane without constantly scraping against the walls on either side. He couldn't recall ever seeing a single blemish on its gleaming paintwork. He turned into Langland Parade and along to Albert Road where, once again, he could pick up speed before turning left at Woodshears Road and finally into Court Road where his parents lived.

He rang the bell and was surprised to see Judith appear at the door rather than his mother. She looked tired and anxious.

'I'm certainly glad to see you,' she said as she ushered him in. 'Your mother's in a right old state and I don't think I'm being any help at all.'

'Is this about Dad again?'

'It is actually but there's no point in me trying to explain. Come on through and she can tell you herself.'

He followed her into the dining room where his

mother was sitting, facing the door, with her spectacles perched on top of her head. She was dabbing her eyes with a lace hanky. There was a metal box on the table in front of her. The hinged lid hung open and was badly buckled, as if it had been forced. A large screwdriver – presumably the means of entry – lay alongside.

'Hello Dennis,' she said, blinking away more tears as she looked up at him.'

Kissing her on the cheek he said, 'Judith tells me you're a bit upset. What's been going on?'

'It's your father,' she sniffed. 'We had a terrible row this morning, the worst one ever, and we've had some real humdingers in our time I can tell you.'

Dennis sat down beside her while Judith took a chair opposite.

'Is this to do with last night, when he had that funny turn and you went out into the garden with him?'

'That's what set it off yes, but he's been in a state for a couple of days now. Ever since he heard about that wretched body at Symbiosis House.'

'Why would that upset him so much? Did he explain?'

'Of course not, he never does. That's why we argued, because I told him how sick I was of his secretiveness, not to mention all the bad moods and nasty remarks. It didn't get me anywhere though: he just stomped out, with a face like thunder, slamming the door behind him. That's when I decided enough is enough.'

'Is that what this is about?' said Dennis, indicating the screwdriver and the broken box.

She nodded and started mopping away tears again.

Dennis gave her free hand a sympathetic squeeze but, as he did so, a terrible thought came to him, unconnected with his mother's woes. In his desperation to avoid an encounter with Jeff, he'd forgotten to pick up the tartan bag containing Harry's notebooks. It must still be where he'd left it: on the floor, next to his chair, in the reference library reading booth.

CHAPTER 15

A box of secrets

Friday 29th March 1957

11.10 a.m.

'Sorry,' said Dennis, getting up, 'I've got to make a quick phone call.'

'What, now?' protested Judith. 'Can't it wait?'

'No, it's important. I've left something at the library, and I want to make sure they put it in a safe place for me.'

'That's all right dear,' said Rosemary. 'Just go and make your call. I'll explain everything when you get back.'

Dennis went out into the hall and dialled the number for the public library. It was etched on his memory from when Margaret had worked there.

'Hello,' said a woman on the other end, after three rings. 'Great Malvern Public Library, can I help you?'

'It's Dennis Powell here, from the Malvern Gazette, I wondered...'

'Dennis Powell?' she exclaimed, before he could continue. 'This is Jane - Jane Cooper. Margaret and I used to work together in the reference section, do you remember?'

'*Jane*, of course, how are you?'

'Very well thanks. How's Margaret getting on? Are you two engaged yet, by the way?'

'Oh no, nothing like that,' he said with a nervous laugh. 'She's fine thanks, working at the College seems to suit her very well. Listen Jane,' he continued without a breath, keen to pre-empt any further chit-chat, 'I need your help if that's all right?'

'Of course, is this to do with something you're working on? Do you want me to look out some information for you?'

'No, nothing like that. It's just that I was in the reference section earlier and I left something behind. I wondered if you could check if it's still there.'

'No problem at all. I don't work in the reference section anymore, that must be why I didn't see you, but I can easily pop in and see. Do you want to hang on a minute, or should I phone you back?'

'I'll hang on thanks if you don't mind looking now. I was in one of the reading booths – either the third or fourth one along from the exit, sorry I can't remember which exactly - I left a tartan shopping bag on the floor, next to the chair. It's got some notebooks in it that I'm very keen to get back as quickly as possible.'

'On my way, back in a tick.'

There was a clatter on the end as she placed the receiver on the desk. Dennis could feel his heart pounding in his chest, but he couldn't think why he was so worried: it was still probably where he'd left it: the reference library was never that busy after all. Even if it wasn't, surely someone would have handed it in or the reference librarian would have seen it herself and put it in safekeeping.

After what felt like an eternity but was probably no

more than a couple of minutes, Jane picked up the receiver again. 'Sorry about the delay,' she said, but Sally, the reference librarian, is in a meeting with someone upstairs and can't be disturbed. She didn't mention anything to Felicity - that's the girl standing in for her - about your bag but we both think she'll have locked it away somewhere secure. She shouldn't be long. We'll ask her as soon she comes back down and one of us will give you a ring.'

'You're positive it isn't still in the reading booth where I left it?' said Dennis, trying to suppress his impatience.

'No, it definitely isn't there. I checked all the booths, just to be on the safe side, and there was no sign of a tartan shopping bag. Sally's very diligent about dealing with lost property though. She wouldn't leave something like that lying around, she'd put it away safely in one of her cupboards. The trouble is, we won't know which one until she comes back from her meeting. Please don't worry, I'm sure it'll turn up all right.'

Dennis wasn't convinced about that, but he thanked Jane anyway, gave her Judith's telephone number, and said goodbye.

Judith and his mother looked enquiringly at him as he came back into the dining room.

'Is everything all right dear?' asked Rosemary. 'Did you manage to track down whatever you were looking for?'

'I'm not sure. The person I needed to speak to is in a meeting and they're going to ring me when she gets back. Are you ready to tell me about this?' he said, pointing at the mutilated metal box on the table.

Rosemary nodded. 'We found it inside a drawer in Charles' desk that he always keeps locked. It drives me mad that he won't tell me what he's got hidden in there and, whenever I try to raise the subject with him he just flies into one of his dreadful rages which makes matters even worse. Anyway, after he stormed off this morning, I decided that was the last straw and that I wasn't going to put up with his secretiveness a moment longer. I phoned Judith and asked her if she'd mind coming round. I didn't tell her what I was planning to do, I just said that Charles and I had had another argument and that I'd appreciate a bit of moral support. After she arrived, and I'd got everything off my chest, I told her I was going to break into his desk drawer. I explained that Charles had the only key so there was no point in searching for a spare.'

'That's when I suggested going out into the garage to find a suitable implement,' said Judith. 'We saw this big screwdriver straightaway and it proved to be perfect for the job: it splintered the wood quite badly, but we had the drawer open in seconds.

'It was his father's desk,' said Rosemary, 'so he's going to be furious about the damage we've done to it but I'm past caring now.'

'And presumably this metal box was inside,' said Dennis

'Yes,' said Judith, 'and, as you can see, we had to use the screwdriver to force that as well. It was a lot more resistant than the desk but eventually it buckled and gave way. We'd just managed to open it when we heard you ringing the doorbell.'

'Have you checked what's in it yet?'.

'No,' said Rosemary, 'that's what we were about to do.'

She picked up the box and peered inside before removing three items: a photograph, a handwritten sheet of paper, and, what appeared to be, a scrap of screwed-up tinfoil.

'Is that it?' said Judith. 'Are you sure there's nothing

else in there?'

'Not that I can see but my eyesight isn't what it was so maybe you'd better look for yourself.' She pushed the box across the table.

Judith tilted it towards the window so that she could see inside more clearly. 'Nothing,' she confirmed, shaking her head. 'It seems like slim pickings after all that effort, don't you think?'

'Maybe' said Dennis, 'but they must have been important to him if he felt it necessary to lock them away like that.'

He picked up the photograph and studied it carefully. Then he got up and took it over to the window, his heart beating faster now because he recognised the two subjects. One was a studious-looking, bespectacled man in his early forties. The other was of a similar age but with a fleshier, more lived-in, face. They appeared to be posing in a garden with an elevated view across open country.

'I know these people,' he said. 'I met one of them yesterday. His name's Harry Parsons. He's changed a bit over the years but I'm sure it's him. The other man is Margaret's father, Greville Jobson. I recognise him from other photos I've seen.'

'What's your connection with Harry Parsons?' asked Judith.

'He's an engineer; a hydraulic engineer to be precise. He specialises in building and renovating drainage systems and water courses. I met up with him on the train yesterday because he's got a gripe against British Railways and he wants the Gazette to do a piece on it. He promised to bring along some interesting documents to make it worth my while.'

'What sort of documents?'

'They're to do with the Chamber Spout I've been looking for. It turns out it's at Symbiosis House. Harry Parsons' father did some work on it in the 1890s and one of the notebooks contains a record of what he did.'

'Interesting,' said Judith. 'Let's see what the note says, shall we? I take it this *is* Charles' handwriting?' she added, turning the sheet of paper for her mother-in-law to see.

'Definitely,' said Rosemary.

'There's no heading or salutation,' said Judith, 'it just launches straight into the business in hand.'

She began to read.

'"*After giving the matter much thought, I feel I must do everything I can to dissuade you from taking, what I fear could be, a highly dangerous course of action. I know you sincerely believe you witnessed the incident you described to me, but I beg to suggest that you were mistaken. After all, the eye can easily be deceived, especially when singular circumstances, such as those we have both experienced, contrive to distort perception.*

You will remember that when we first joined this group, we had to swear that we would accept whatever occurred thereafter, without comment or complaint. We were assured that the rewards would far outweigh any discomfort we might suffer on the way but were told that, if we ever spoke to anyone outside about our experiences, we would pay a high price which would be extracted without mercy. It was a harsh condition certainly, but I remain convinced that, in making it, "our host" had only our best interests at heart.

And so, I beg you, please give up this notion of speaking out. Otherwise, I fear that there will be dire consequences, not just for you but for the rest of us as well."'

'What on earth does it all mean?' exclaimed Judith, looking up again.

'It's to do with that wretched club,' sighed Rosemary.

'The Black Moon Society.'

Dennis stared at her.

'So, it's true that Dad was a member, then?' he said.

'Yes, but I'm surprised to hear *you* know anything about it. He's never mentioned it to a soul, as far as I'm aware.'

'It was just an educated guess. Margaret told me about her father being involved and then I got talking to Julian, a colleague of mine, about it and he thought there was every chance Dad would have been part of it as well.'

'Why?'

'He reckoned Mathias Friedman set up the Black Moon Society to help local ex-servicemen deal with their bad memories of the trenches and given his age and war experience Dad would have been a prime candidate.'

'Did he say anything else?'

'Only that, going by the rumours, the Black Moon Society wasn't quite what it seemed. Apparently, people talked about all sorts of strange things going on there, including the use of drugs.'

'That wouldn't surprise me in the least.'

'Really? Why do you say that?'

'Because you only had to see how Charles was when he came back to know that something very peculiar had happened to him.'

'How was he then?'

'Either in ridiculously high spirits, verging on the manic, or in a terrible depression where I wouldn't get a single word out of him for twenty-four hours. But it was the high spirits that disturbed me most, because it was so out of character. He was like a man possessed: energised but strangely absent at the same time. I thought it must be the drink at first - he certainly reeked enough of it - but as time went on, I realised alcohol wouldn't have had that effect at all.'

'You thought it was down to some sort of drug?' said Judith.

'Not exactly, because I had no idea about such things in those days. Possession was the only way I could explain it. I think I'd seen a newsreel at the cinema about some African tribes' people being possessed by a spirit and it reminded me of that. It was only later that I started to wonder if it had been to do with something he'd taken.'

'It certainly bears out the rumours about the Black Moon Society not being what it seemed. And now this body has turned up at Symbiosis House and plunged him into a dreadful state again. Maybe he thinks it's the person he wrote the note to: a fellow member who died because he ignored his warning.'

Dennis shook his head.

'It doesn't fit with the facts unfortunately.'

'What facts? You haven't been taken in by that cock and bull story Superintendent Goodall's putting about I hope.'

'No, this is to do with what Nigel told me.'

'When did you see Nigel?'

'Earlier, at the Police Station.'

'And what did he say?'

'He reckoned the body was buried there in the late 1940s. There's evidence to suggest that the victim was a French scientist called Laurent Morel who went missing in

1948.'

'He hasn't mentioned any of this to me.'

'I just happened to catch him at a weak moment. He'd just had another set to with Superintendent Goodall and I think he needed to get things off his chest.'

'It isn't connected with the Black Moon Society at all then?'

'It doesn't look like it.'

'So, why has it upset Charles so much?'

'Maybe it was news he'd been expecting, so he leapt to a logical, but erroneous, conclusion.'

'You think he'd been *expecting* a body to turn up?'

Dennis shrugged. 'Possibly. What did his note say again…?' He picked up the handwritten sheet of paper and scanned it until he found the sentence he was looking for. 'Here we are, "…if we ever spoke to anyone outside about our experiences, we would pay a high price which would be extracted without mercy." He was plainly fearing the worst when he wrote that, wasn't he?'

'But, to fear that someone was going to die, that's a bit extreme, isn't it?'

'Not if you knew it was one of the risks you signed up to when you joined the Society.'

'Who was the note meant for, do you think?'

'Maybe one of the men in the photograph: Greville Jobson or Harry Parsons. We know that Greville was a member of the Black Moon Society because Margaret said so. I'm not certain about Harry yet but I'd be very surprised if he didn't turn out to have been one too.' He turned to his mother. 'I don't suppose Dad ever mentioned either of them, did he?'

'Never,' she replied. 'He barely talked about the people he worked with let alone the ones he mixed with up there.'

'I'd put my money on it being Greville,' said Dennis. 'If only because of Dad's shocked reaction when his name came up last night.'

'What are we to make of this then?' said Judith, picking up the third item from the box: the piece of screwed-up tinfoil.

She carefully pulled it apart to reveal a small, grey lozenge-shaped object. She passed it to Dennis.

'It looks like a rather grubby sugar lump,' said Rosemary, leaning over to look. 'But why would he lock away something like that?'

'Perhaps he was keeping it as evidence,' said Dennis.

'Evidence of what?'

'Of what went on at the meetings.'

'You think it's to do with the drugs, don't you?' said Judith. 'You think this sugar lump, or whatever it is, was impregnated with something.'

Dennis nodded.

'Sugar lumps impregnated with drugs?' exclaimed Rosemary. 'How ever do you know about these things dear?'

'Because of other drug cases Nigel's told me about. Being married to a detective inspector can be quite instructive you know.'

'Have you any idea what sort of drug it was?' said Rosemary

'No, according to Julian, this colleague of mine, Friedman had access to all sorts because he'd worked at Powick with a man called Emery Harcourt who was the pharmacist there.'

'So was this Emery Harcourt part of the Society as well,' asked Judith.

'I think so, yes. It seems that Friedman and Harcourt lived at Symbiosis House together, so they were obviously close personally as well as professionally.'

This must be terribly unsettling for you dear,' said Judith, turning to her mother-in-law.

Rosemary sighed. 'Not really. In a funny sort of way, it's a relief because it confirms everything that, deep down, I think I've always known. Believe it or not, back in the 1920s, Charles and I sometimes went to the theatre and, while we were having a drink before the show or during the interval, I'd overhear the same sort of gossip Dennis' colleague did. Naturally Charles would hurry me along to my seat if he thought I might be listening in to something I shouldn't. I should have confronted him about it really, but I never did. I took the easy option and pushed it to the back of my mind. It's all coming back to me now though. He was always moody and absent-minded, but he got far worse after he started going to the Black Moon Society. I'm not talking about how he was when he got back from the meetings, that usually passed within a day, I'm talking about his general state of mind. The first meeting was in March 1921. From then on, I had to put up with more and more of those vicious little outbursts that have become so typical of him. I remember him having a particularly bad one on the fourteenth of September, our wedding anniversary, and it upset me terribly. Then, at the end of October, his father suddenly died and, after that he was angrier than ever, as you know.'

He nodded as he recalled how he'd borne the brunt of that fury because his illness had prevented them from making a new start in a new town as his father had wanted,

'I've had a thought,' said Judith, interrupting his reverie. 'Maybe Nigel could send this sugar lump off to his forensics people in Birmingham and get it analysed.'

'Good idea,' said Dennis. 'Provided Superintendent Goodall doesn't get wind of it.'

'Why should he?'

'According to Nigel, he's got eyes and ears everywhere. I don't suppose he'd take too kindly to police resources being used for something unconnected to a current investigation.'

'Let Nigel worry about that. Goodall's his problem, not yours.'

'That's not strictly true now, actually.'

'What do you mean?'

'I've been told to liaise with him about the big investigation. That's why I was at the Police Station earlier. Jeff Stephenson's handed the Symbiosis House story over to me.'

'But that's good, isn't it?' said Rosemary. 'For your career anyway.'

'It would be. except my instructions are to produce a report that supports Superintendent Goodall's version of events, and which can only be signed off with his approval.'

'It sounds just like the same position Nigel's in,' said Judith. 'But Jeff's a newspaper editor, he isn't accountable to Goodall. Why's he playing along like that?'

'Search me, I can't understand it either.'

'What's happened to your ace crime reporter then?' asked Judith. 'The Whippet or whatever his name is?' I thought *he* was covering the story.'

'It seems he's jumped ship and run off to join one of the big nationals.'

'Presumably because he objected to being told what to write?'

'I assumed so, but Jeff denies it. He says the Whippet had been planning to go for ages.'

'And Jeff thinks you'll be so flattered he's asked you to take over from him that you'll write whatever you're told?'

'Probably.'

'And is he right?'

'Of course not. At least, not if I can help it. There's still a week to go until the deadline so hopefully there'll be plenty of room for manoeuvre in the meantime.'

'How did you leave it with Nigel when you saw him earlier?'

'I agreed to make a few enquiries behind the scenes; look through newspaper archives and that sort of thing.'

The telephone started ringing and Rosemary sat up with a jolt. Dennis wondered if she'd been dozing while he and Judith had been talking, or just deep in thought.

'I'll go,' he said, 'I expect it's the library phoning back about my lost property.'

As he went out to the hall, he realised that he was still clutching the sugar lump. He pushed it into his jacket pocket for safe keeping.'

'Dennis Powell,' he announced into the receiver.

'My name's Sally Jenkins,' said the woman at the other end. 'I work in the reference section of the public library. I understand you phoned earlier about a missing bag.'

'That's right,' said Dennis, his heart starting to race. 'It's a tartan shopping bag, containing a set of notebooks. Have you found it?'

'I'm afraid not,' the woman replied. 'We've just done another thorough search but nothing of that description has turned up anywhere.'

CHAPTER 16

Historical analysis

Friday 29th March 1957

11.40 a.m.

After several forceful, but unsuccessful, attempts to kick-start the Tiger, Dennis decided to give it a rest for a few seconds. Taking his frustration out on the hapless machine wasn't going to bring the notebooks back. He hadn't bothered explaining to Judith and his mother what had happened, he'd just poked his head around the door and announced he had to go. They'd looked surprised but were already well into a new conversation, so they didn't offer any resistance.

He took a few deep breaths before pushing down on the starter pedal again, this time with a more controlled movement. The Tiger immediately spluttered to life and, despite his troubles, he gave its petrol tank an appreciative pat.

His first thought was that he should go straight back to the library and undertake a search of his own, but he quickly saw that, not only was this likely to be a waste of time, it was likely to irritate the staff there who had already done everything they could. It crossed his mind that perhaps Jeff had spotted him after all and had gone into his booth, after he'd gone, and retrieved the tartan bag. It seemed highly unlikely though because he was sure Jeff had been far too absorbed by whatever he'd been reading to notice anything else and it was hard to think why he'd go and look in another booth without good reason. It was much more likely that someone else had used the booth later; discovered the bag and decided to keep it for themselves. He imagined they'd be disappointed when they saw the contents though: a collection of old notebooks, full of strange diagrams, tables and meaningless figures. They'd probably just throw them away.

Instead of going into town, he headed along Court Road, towards Malvern Link. Soon he was passing the Morgan works on Pickersleigh Road and preparing to take a right turn at the junction before continuing towards Powick Mental Hospital.

He wasn't due there again until the following week, but he knew that Dr Gajak was in the habit of taking an early lunch, so he hoped he'd be able to waylay him en-route to the staff refectory. After leaving the Tiger in the parking area, he thought about how he was going to persuade Stanley, the gatekeeper, to let him through without an appointment. As it turned out though, it was Stanley's day off and the stand-in attendant barely gave him a glance.

'So much for a tight ship,' Dennis whispered to himself as the metal trellis slid shut behind him and he set off across the courtyard.

The tower clock started striking twelve as he arrived outside Dr Gajak's annexe and just as it rang out its final chime, the old psychiatrist came out of the door. He paused on the step for a moment, peering at his watch with a faint smile of satisfaction on his face.

He slipped the watch into his waistcoat pocket and then waved at Dennis, as if seeing him there was no surprise at all.

'Still six minutes slow,' he said. 'I've told them it needs adjusting but by the time they get around to doing anything it will probably have put itself right again. 'Anyway, to what do I owe this unexpected pleasure?'

'I was wondering if you'd mind me picking your brains about a few things. Only if you've got time of course. I'd be more than happy to buy lunch in return.'

Gajak waved the offer away. 'Not at all Dennis, lunch is on me. One of the perks of working in this fine institution is that meals are generously subsidised and surprisingly good as well. Being Friday, there will certainly be fish and chips on the menu. If we hurry, we'll probably be at the front of the queue.'

They were soon sitting facing each other in a corner of the echoing refectory, surveying their plates of cod, chips and peas.

'Big portions as well,' said Gajak. 'I doubt if either of us will need to eat again today after this. Let's tuck in, shall we? I'm afraid I only have about half an hour until my next appointment, so we'll have to talk while we eat and hope that we both don't end up with indigestion. How can I help?'

He wondered if he should admit that, after losing the notebooks, he'd needed a distraction and coming here was the first idea he'd come up with. He decided against it though, partly because it would have sounded rude and partly because, now he was here, he had some questions that he hoped Dr Gajak would be able to answer.

'After our chat, the other day, I did some more research and a few things came up I'd like to ask you about.'

Gajak waggled his fork in the air encouragingly as he started to eat.

'I keep coming across the name, Mathias Friedman and I wondered if you knew him. I understand he was a psychiatrist who worked here in the nineteen twenties.'

'Yes,' Gajak replied, after a slight pause. 'He left a few months before I arrived, so I didn't know him personally, but, as you'll know, he had quite a reputation, so I certainly knew *of* him.'

'Someone told me he left under a bit of a cloud: do you know anything about that?'

'Nothing at all. As far as I'm aware, everyone was extremely sorry to see him go.'

'Do you know anything about the club he set up after he left: The Black Moon Society.

Gajak drank some water before answering.

'A little, why do you ask?'

'Because I think my father might have been a member.'

'And you think this could have a bearing on what we were discussing last time?'

'Possibly, yes.'

Gajak stopped eating and nodded slowly as if turning the idea over in his mind.

'Are you sure you don't mind discussing this?' said Dennis.

'Of course not, why do you ask?'

'I'm not sure. You seem a bit hesitant, that's all. It makes me wonder if you find it a sensitive subject for some reason.'

'I suspect, in truth, we're both feeling a little sensitive,' said Gajak, smiling suddenly, and picking up his knife and fork again.

'I don't understand,' said Dennis, suddenly feeling uncomfortable.

'Oh, I think you do. When you arrived, you weren't entirely sure why you'd come here were you?'

'What makes you think that?'

'Because it was written all over your face and, as you must know by now, I'm adept at reading such things.'

Dennis sighed. 'It's true: when I set off earlier, I wasn't planning to visit you at all. It's almost as if I came here on automatic pilot.'

'Lured by a siren voice, promising answers.'

'Something like that I suppose. I felt at a bit of a loose end, so I just headed for the first place that came into my head. Sorry, you'll think I'm wasting your time even more now, won't you?'

'Not at all. *I'm* the one who should be apologising really, for making you feel uncomfortable. My only excuse is that your line of questioning has rather taken me by surprise. Glancing at Dennis' plate he added, 'please don't let your food get cold, it really is just as delicious as I promised.'

Dennis took his first mouthful and nodded approvingly as Gajak continued.

'The hesitation you observed stems from a habitual reluctance to discuss the reputation of a professional colleague, albeit one with whom I never worked. We medical men tend to close ranks when we think one of our number is being scrutinised from outside. But of course, we're talking about things that happened decades ago and Friedman's long gone now so there's no earthly reason why I shouldn't tell you what I know about him. I should warn you though, it probably won't amount to much more than you know already.

'As I said, Friedman left here a couple of months before I arrived, but my colleagues still talked about him a lot because he'd plainly made quite an impression on them. It seems they were intrigued from the start because they couldn't understand why someone with a reputation like his should choose to come and work in a provincial English mental institution like Powick. It was well known that he'd been a star medical student at the University of Vienna and the medical journals were full of praise for the neurological research that - like Freud, his venerable predecessor - he'd undertaken at Vienna General Hospital. With credentials like those, he could have worked anywhere he wanted: somewhere like Burghölzli maybe, where Jung worked in the early 1900s.'

He paused to eat some more of his meal and washed the food down with a sip of water before continuing.

'The truth is, I think everyone felt a little intimidated by his reputation but, when he arrived, he turned out to be extremely personable and they took to him straightaway.

'The only slight issue of concern, as I recall, was his relationship with one of the pharmacists; a man called Emery Harcourt. It seems they'd struck up a friendship straightaway which surprised everyone because, in contrast to Friedman's sunny disposition, Harcourt came over as something of a cold fish; someone who generally kept himself to himself. As I say, it wasn't something people were overly concerned about, just an incongruity they'd refer back to from time to time.'

'And, from what I hear, Harcourt left his job at the same time and went to live with Friedman at Symbiosis House.'

'My, my, you are well informed.'

'Was that when they started the Black Moon Society?'

'I believe it was, yes.'

He paused before adding, 'You said you thought your father was a member: can I ask why?'

'A colleague of mine, Julian Croft, said that Friedman selected local men from professional backgrounds who'd recently served in the trenches. Apparently, he thought they'd benefit from the opportunity to let their hair down a bit and escape from their wartime memories. He reckoned Friedman's interest in that sort of thing stemmed from his work with shell-shock victims at Powick.'

'I suppose that's possible. Powick certainly had more than its fair share of those poor devils: I dealt with a lot of them myself.'

'But you don't know for sure?'

'As I said before, I've learned a little about the Black Moon Society over the years, but, until now, I've honestly never heard anyone make that connection.'

'What have you heard then?'

'Just the standard gossip really: that, as part of his contribution to local life, Friedman started an astronomical society for the sorts of men who might have an interest in that sort of thing - meaning those who were relatively intelligent and well-to-do, I assume. The general understanding seems to be that, after a while, the astronomy gave way to more frivolous activities in which the consumption of alcohol played a not inconsiderable part. Harmless enough I suppose and, supposing what you said before is true, possibly even therapeutic to some extent.'

'Have you heard anything about drugs being part of what went on?'

'Drugs?' exclaimed Gajak, putting down his knife and fork and staring at him wide-eyed. 'Where did you get that idea from?'

'From Julian. It's just another of the snippets of information he picked up in the Festival Theatre bar, back in the early 1920s. People reckoned Friedman still had access to them; presumably through Emery Harcourt, the pharmacist.'

Gajak shook his head as he started eating again. 'I think that's highly unlikely. As far as I'm aware, Harcourt was no longer a practising pharmacist after he left Powick, meaning that he'd have no more access to drugs of the type I think you're referring to, than any other member of the public.'

'He'd have known people though, wouldn't he? Other pharmacists I mean. He might have been able to get hold of supplies through them.'

'No, as I told you, Harcourt was a cold fish, he didn't associate with anyone – apart from Friedman, of course. Anyway, no pharmacist, worth his salt, would ever pass on drugs informally like that.'

'How would you explain it then? According to Julian, the rumours were pretty consistent and now my mother tells me she remembers hearing them as well.'

'You've spoken to your mother about this?'

'Yes, just before I came here. I wasn't planning to because I thought it would upset her too much, but she'd obviously been thinking about it anyway.'

'Why?'

'Because my father's been worse than ever over the last two days and they'd just had a huge row. After he stormed out, she phoned Judith and asked her to come over. She'd decided to take action, but she needed some moral support before she went through with it.'

'What sort of action.'

'It's been irritating her for years that my father keeps one of his desk drawers locked: it's made her feel as if he's been keeping secrets from her. Anyway, this morning she and Judith broke into it and found three items that seem to relate to his Black Moon Society days. I arrived just as they'd turned them out onto the dining room table.'

'How fascinating. Can you tell me what they were?'

'Of course. There was an old photograph, featuring Greville Jobson, Margaret's late father, and Harry Parsons, a semi-retired hydraulic engineer, I met on the train yesterday. Apparently, Harry's father was in the same business and was commissioned to renovate the Chamber Spout, back in the 1890s.'

'So this Harry Parsons must know where it's located then?'

'Yes, believe it or not, he reckons it's at Symbiosis House.'

Gajak put down his knife and fork.

'Remarkable,' he said, staring at him intently. 'And do you think it's true?'

'I do actually. He gave me his father's work notebooks from the time and all the specifications, sketches and technical diagrams he produced, bear out his story completely. He says he's got another notebook for me as well – one of his own – which he thinks might shed even more light on the situation. I'm not sure what's in it exactly, but it sounds intriguing, so I'm heading off to his house in Hereford later, to pick it up.'

'Well this is truly marvellous news Dennis, I'm very pleased for you.'

Gajak dabbed his mouth with a serviette. His plate was

now completely empty.

'But going back to this locked drawer of your father's: tell me about the other two items he'd hidden in there?'

'One was a short note, in my father's handwriting, to an unnamed individual, warning him not to speak out about an incident he thought he'd witnessed. It included a reminder that they'd sworn an oath of silence to someone referred to as "our host', in the full knowledge that anyone who broke it would pay a very high price indeed.'

'And you think this was to do with something that happened at the Black Moon Society?'

'Yes, I do. Although it doesn't look as if the note was ever sent, I think the intended recipient was Greville Jobson and I'm more or less certain now that he and my father were both members.'

'In which case, "our host" would be Mathias Friedman?'

'Exactly and it sounds as if he was extremely sensitive about anyone outside the group finding out about what they got up to.'

'The alleged use of drugs you mean?'

'Possibly, but I've got a feeling it was more than that.'

'What then?'

'I don't know yet. Maybe Harry's journal will shed some light on the matter.'

'Maybe it will,' said Gajak, distractedly.

Then he said, 'So, what about the third item?

'It's a sugar cube wrapped in tinfoil. I thought it might contain traces of whatever substance it was they were supposed to be taking.'

'Did you bring it with you?'

'Yes, I've got it here.'

He reached into his jacket pocket, pulled out the discoloured object and passed it across the table.

'Would you like me to get this analysed in our laboratory?' asked Gajak, peering at it intently from behind his tiny, gold-framed spectacles.

'That would be marvellous.' said Dennis. 'I was going to ask my brother to send it up to the police forensics people in Birmingham, but it would be much better if you could do it here.'

'Of course, there's no guarantee we'll be able to detect anything. It's probably badly degraded by now, but we can certainly try.'

He pulled out a pristine white handkerchief and wrapped the sugar lump in it, before placing it in his own jacket pocket. At that moment, the tower clock struck the half hour.

'Sorry,' he said, 'My time's up I'm afraid. I really must be going.'

He looked at Dennis' uneaten food and added, 'But there's no reason why you shouldn't stay on and finish your lunch. It would be a pity to waste it.'

'That's all right. It was delicious, but my appetite isn't as big as it used to be. Anyway, it's time I was off too.'

They both got up from the table and walked back through the refectory to the exit.

'Thank you for a most thought-provoking conversation,' said Gajak, when they were out in the courtyard. 'I'm so glad you came.'

They shook hands.

As Dennis watched the old psychiatrist shuffle off towards his consulting room, it struck him how uncharacteristically formal their leave-taking had just been. Almost as if they'd been doing it for the last time.

CHAPTER 17

Out on a limb

Friday 29th March 1957

2.00 p.m.

Heading back to Malvern Dennis spotted a roadside telephone kiosk and, on impulse, decided to give Julian Croft a call.

Julian answered on the second ring. 'Malvern Gazette, Croft here,' he said in a strange, mid-Atlantic drawl that was only ever noticeable on the telephone. Dennis could imagine him blowing one of his nifty Gauloise smoke rings as he spoke.

'Hello Julian, its Dennis. Are you free to talk?'

'Good grief Dennis, where are you? Jeff's been looking for you all morning. I think you'd better come in before he finally blows a gasket.'

Dennis felt a knot in his stomach. 'Is he there with you now?'

'No, he's rushed off somewhere in his little red devil, but he could be back at any moment. He's been darting in and out all morning with a face like thunder and every time he appears he demands to know if anyone's set eyes on you or if you've been in touch.'

'I can't come back now, I've got to catch a train over to Hereford to see Harry Parsons, the old man I was telling you about yesterday. The thing is Julian, when I was in the library earlier, I stupidly left the bag of notebooks he gave me, in one of the reading booths. I phoned to check if anyone had found them, but they seem to have completely disappeared. I was hoping you'd listen out for my phone on the off-chance they get in touch to say they've turned up after all.'

'Is this a tartan shopping bag you're talking about?'

'Yes, why, how do you know?'

'Because it's right here in front of me, sitting on top of your desk.'

Dennis felt beads of perspiration starting to form on his forehead. 'Are you sure?'

'Of course, I'm sure. You can hardly miss it, can you? It's a riot of red, yellow, blue, white and green: The Royal Stewart if I'm not mistaken.'

'How did it get there, do you know? Did Jeff bring it in?'

'No, he was asking about it too. He was complaining about how untidy the desks are in here. Then he asked what the bag was doing there and made a sarcastic comment about the office becoming a repository for your groceries.'

'So, you didn't see anyone else leave it there?'

'No, I've been in and out myself all morning. Unfortunately, the times I've been in have coincided with Jeff screeching up outside in his Morgan, and then stomping around the place like a bear with an extremely sore head.'

'Perhaps they *did* find it at the library, and someone brought it round.'

'That's the most likely explanation, isn't it?'

Dennis' anxiety began to melt away. 'I expect one of the library staff put it in a safe place without telling the others and it only came to light after I phoned. Is there a note with it by any chance?'

'Hang on a sec, I'll have a look.'

There was a rustling at the other end as Julian got up to investigate. Seconds later, he picked up the receiver again and said, 'no, I'm afraid not, just a bag of old notebooks.'

'I don't suppose you could bring them to me, could you?'

'Bring them where?'

'I was thinking of the Abbey Gatehouse, in about fifteen minutes.'

'Why can't you come here to get them?'

'Because I don't want to run into Jeff, that's why. I'm due over in Hereford in a couple of hours and if he gets the faintest whiff of what I'm up to, he's bound to stop me going.'

'I'm not sure this is a good idea Dennis. Jeff will have your guts for garters if he finds out you're working on something behind his back.'

'What's the matter? I thought you liked a bit of intrigue.'

'I do normally, but this is an exception.'

'You were happy enough adjourning to the pub for a gossip yesterday: what's changed?'

'If you'd seen how Jeff was earlier, you wouldn't need to ask.'

'But Jeff's often like that, isn't he: storming into the office in a bad mood and telling everyone off. It always blows over after a couple of hours.'

'Not this time. Thanks to the Whippet's sudden departure and the continuing Symbiosis House saga, he's jumpier than I've ever seen him.'

'I expect you've heard about me taking over the Symbiosis House story, haven't you?'

'Of course, it was the first thing he told me when he came in. That's why he's so keen to track you down: he wants to make sure you're sticking to the task in hand rather than chasing after stories that don't concern you.'

'And now you're relaying the message to me, as instructed?'

The pause that followed told him he'd hit the nail on the head.

'That's right isn't it?'

'Yes,' said Julian, sheepishly. 'I wasn't going to, but now you've told me what you're up to, it feels as if it's for your own good.'

'So, does that mean you won't bring the notebooks?'

'No,' he sighed, 'It doesn't mean that. I'll be there in fifteen minutes as requested, but heaven help us if Jeff finds out.'

Dennis rode up Worcester Road with the open space of Link Common to his left and the dark bulge of North Hill straight ahead. When he reached Belle View Terrace, he turned down Church Street, and then right into Grange Road. He parked the Tiger next to the kerb, crossed over and passed through a gap in the wall into the Priory Churchyard. He followed a winding, yew shaded path over to the western side and then climbed the steps up to the medieval gatehouse, once the entrance to the original Benedictine priory.

Julian was waiting inside the archway, shooting nervous glances left and right. When he saw Dennis approaching he raised his hand and then backed away into the shadows.

'I hope you know what you're doing,' he said, as Dennis joined him, 'because I'm damned if I do.'

He produced the tartan bag from under his coat and handed it over.

'What's got into you?' said Dennis 'You were jittery enough on the phone, but now you seem even worse.'

'I don't know. Maybe it's because I haven't been getting enough sleep. It can have that effect on you, can't it? I was reviewing a play in Birmingham last night and the night before that I was at another one in Cheltenham. It's obviously starting to take its toll.'

'Are you sure that's all it is? I get the impression you're not telling me something. What else has Jeff been saying?'

'Nothing much. He was just complaining about the trouble the Whippet had caused him with that story about the body at Symbiosis House.'

'The story he's just spiked, you mean?'

'Yes, and with good reason by the sound of it.'

'But I thought you agreed with me that the Whippet was on to something. That's why we spent so long in the pub yesterday, piecing all the clues together that he'd left behind.'

'But what if planting those clues was just a practical joke? He must have known we'd go down to the basement to check what he'd been doing, so maybe he left the scrap of paper and the open encyclopaedia there to send us off on a wild goose chase.'

'No, you know as well as I do, that the Whippet isn't the type to indulge in practical jokes. He's far too serious and single-minded for that sort of thing. Anyway, it turns out that everything we deduced from the clues he left there was spot on.'

'How do you know?'

'Because I've spoken to my brother and he's confirmed it.'

'I thought your brother never talked about his cases.'

'He doesn't usually, but he's getting a lot of pressure from above over this one, so that's made him unusually willing to open up.'

'Pressure from Superintendent Goodall you mean?'

'That's right, the man whose influence seems to know no bounds. He's got to Nigel, he's got to Jeff and, through them, it seems as if he's getting to you and me as well.'

Julian shook his head. 'Nobody's got to me I can assure you.'

'Why are you so frightened of being seen here with me now then? Why were you imploring me to play ball with Jeff and abandon my trip to see Harry Parsons?'

'I'm not frightened, and I wasn't imploring you to do anything. I was simply offering you some friendly advice.'

'If you say so.'

'The thing is, bitter experience has taught me when it's better to back off and take the path of least resistance. Being resolute is an admirable trait, but it can be a very dangerous one as well.'

He suddenly reached out and squeezed Dennis' shoulder. 'Take good care of yourself,' he said, gazing earnestly into his eyes.'

Then he turned on his heels and scurried away.

***

It was just after half past five when Dennis alighted at Hereford Station. He passed through the ticket office and out onto the station concourse where luggage was being loaded into cars, buses and taxis. Doors were slammed, and engines roared into life as arriving passengers rushed off on the next stages of their journeys. He stood to one side of the main entrance, watching the flurry of activity until, after a few minutes, everything calmed down again, and a relative silence descended on the scene.

He followed the pavement that ran alongside the station approach, down a slight incline, towards the main road. From studying the Hereford street map earlier, he knew that, after turning right out of the station exit, Harry Parsons' road was the third one along, on the left. Sure enough, after about a hundred yards, he saw the sign for Hobart Street and found himself in a quiet suburban thoroughfare with dark-bricked Edwardian houses on either side. A row of pollarded lime trees bordered each pavement, resembling two opposing ranks of badly wounded but still upstanding soldiers, lined up in the afternoon sunshine. The houses were grouped in terraces, each comprising five individual dwellings, and each bearing the name of a Herefordshire village. After passing Almeley Villas, Madley Villas, Broxwood Villas and Vowchurch Villas, he finally came to Weobley Villas on his right. Harry's was the last house along, number 5. Its square of weed-ridden front garden was split in half by a short path, leading to the front door.

He banged the knocker three times and waited. Nothing happened. He could hear a dog barking, children shouting to each other as they played further up the street, and a rumble of traffic from the main road. It all reinforced his impression that the house was cocooned in a silent world of its own. It was ten to six by his watch, so he was a little early. Perhaps Harry was out and wouldn't be back until six on the dot. He knocked again, more loudly this time, but there was still no response. He stepped sideways and tried to see through the front bay window. Grey net curtains obscured his view, but he could make out the diffused glow of what appeared to be a two-bar electric fire. He moved further round and managed to find a sliver of a gap where two sections of net weren't quite pulled together. He put one eye against the glass and peered into the room. At first his vision was dominated by the orange light from the fire and it was difficult to make out much else but gradually, as his eye adjusted, he could see the black rectangle of an open grate behind and framing it, a tiled mantelpiece with two picture frames and a big old-fashioned clock on top. Turning slightly, he saw that there was an armchair to the right of the fireplace and slumped in it, with his head lolling forwards, the large and instantly recognisable shape of Harry Parsons. The glow from the fire was reflected in something metallic lying on the floor next to one of his splayed-out feet. As he strained to focus, Dennis realised it was the hip flask he'd seen the old man tippling from on the train the day before.

'He's drunk himself into a stupor,' he thought. 'I've made all this effort to get here and I'll be lucky to get anything out of him at all now.'

He rapped hard on the windowpane, but Harry still didn't respond. He went back to the front door and shunted it with his shoulder, wincing as he did so because of bruising caused by the stubborn door at Pierrepoint Terrace. It was as solid as a rock.

Then he remembered that each of the terraces he'd passed had had an alleyway at each end that provided access to the houses' backyards. He retraced his steps along the pavement and through the alley leading to the rear of Weobley Terrace. Some of the backyards were protected by six-foot-high wooden fences but most, including Harry's, had nothing more than a low brick wall that did little more than mark out the boundary. He stepped over and ducked under a low-slung washing line to reach the back door of number five. It was built into a rickety wood and glass porch which must have been added to the house at some stage to act as a makeshift extension to the kitchen.

He gave a cursory knock before trying the door handle. To his surprise the door swung back on its hinges and banged against the inner wall, causing the window to vibrate alarmingly in its frame. He stepped into a vestibule thick with cobwebs and smelling of damp soil. Last season's tomato plants; yellowed and wilting in their ceramic pots, lined each wall. Passing through the kitchen he held his breath to avoid the rank aroma emanating from unwashed plates and cooking utensils that filled every surface. He closed the door behind him and made his way along a dark hallway to the front room.

A wall of heat met him as he opened the door; a dry, electric heat, infused with burnt dust. He made straight for the armchair in which Harry lay sprawled like a grounded whale and shook the old man gently by the shoulder.

'Mr Parsons, Harry, its Dennis Powell. You invited me to come over to see you this evening do you remember? You didn't answer when I knocked on the front door, so I came around the back. I hope you don't mind.'

He shook harder, but Harry still showed no sign of stirring. Looking round he noticed that, apart from the discarded hip flask on the floor, there was an open bottle of Johnny Walker perched on the tiled fender, next to the electric fire and a whisky tumbler lying on its side on the floor nearby.

'I reckon you've had even more than I thought,' he muttered to himself.

He was about to give Harry's shoulder another shake

when an alarming thought came to him: what if he wasn't in a drunken stupor, what if...? He rested his hand on the old man's chest but there was no rise and fall; no sign of breathing. Next, he lifted his limp right arm and tried to find a pulse but, once again, there was nothing. Then, it struck him how cold the skin felt, and he knew, without doubt, that Harry Parsons was dead.

He backed away and looked out into the hallway, hoping, ridiculously, that someone else might have come in who could tell him what to do next. It was the first dead body he'd ever encountered, and he didn't have the faintest idea how he was meant to respond. It crossed his mind that maybe he should try giving Harry mouth to mouth resuscitation or try to massage his heart back to life but, apart from not having a clue how to do either of those things, he knew that he'd be wasting his time.

As he took in the rest of his surroundings, he started to notice something about them that hadn't registered before. They were untidy certainly, just as the kitchen and no doubt the rest of the house was, but this was more than just neglect. The contents of the bookcases, that filled the wall opposite the fireplace, seemed to have been swept onto the floor, leaving just a few volumes standing there like the last stumps in an otherwise toothless mouth. Likewise, a bureau to the left of the fireplace, over towards the bay window, had been disembowelled and sheaves of bills, receipts and invoices lay fanned out across the carpet around it. His field of vision had been so limited through the crack between the net curtains that only the tableau of Harry, the armchair and the fireplace had been perceptible. However, it was now apparent that at some point – before, during or straight after Harry's death – this room, and probably all the other rooms in the house, had been ransacked. But why? Could they possibly have been seeking the same thing he'd come here for, Harry's notebook?

His first inclination was to dismiss the idea out of hand: It seemed highly unlikely that anyone else would know about, let alone have the slightest interest in, the musings of a retired hydraulic engineer. But then he remembered how, immediately after mentioning it, Harry had tried to backtrack on its significance, and had claimed to be concerned that he might be dragging Dennis over to Hereford under false pretences. Even at the time, those protestations hadn't rung true; in fact, he recalled that they'd seemed so disingenuous that they'd whetted his appetite even more. And now, standing in this plundered room, in the presence of Harry Parson's body, he was starting to think that his musings might be very significant indeed; possibly significant enough to cause, or at least contribute to, their owner's death. It could well be that the shock of being interrogated about its whereabouts had caused the old man's seriously ailing body to finally give up altogether. But had the search proved successful? On balance, Dennis thought not. Its frenzied nature suggested that that Harry had died before the intruder had been able to extract from him where the notebook was hidden.

Then, it struck him that there was something telling about the way the body' was positioned, but what exactly? He considered the splayed feet; the lolling head; the right hand resting on the arm of the chair – just as it had been before he'd tried to find a pulse – and the left hand, hidden down the side of the chair... as if it had been thrust in there on purpose. Dennis knelt and tentatively pushed his own hand into the tight space. He was fighting back nausea now because, having finally assimilated the fact that Harry was dead, it felt like an intrusion; an assault on the old man's dignity. It was only his growing certainty that he was on to something that made him continue.

The hand was further down than he'd expected, deep in the crevice between the inner arm of the chair and the cushion. Dennis shuddered as he felt the end of Harry's cold fingers. They seemed to be pressed against something flat and hard. He carefully pulled the object out and examined it in the orange glow from the electric fire. It was a small blue, hardback notebook with a handwritten title on the front cover, "Journal, 1921."

CHAPTER 18

Appearances and disappearances

Friday 29th March 1957

6.10 p.m.

He stuffed the journal into the tartan bag with the other notebooks and tried to focus on what to do next. The obvious priority was to report what had happened to the police, but he suspected he'd have to go out and find a telephone kiosk to do that because he hadn't seen a phone in the hall, and he doubted if Harry would have bothered installing one anyway. He was about to go exploring, just to make sure, when he heard a loud battering on the front door that made him jump out of his skin.

Someone called through the letter box, 'Police, open up please.'

While he was fumbling with the latch he heard a scrape of boots on the tiled floor behind him. He swung around to see a man with a thick black moustache peering at him through the murk. He was a good three inches taller than Dennis and the way he filled the hallway suggested he was probably a good bit wider too.'

'Who are you?' asked Dennis, tremulously.

'Tell me who you are first,' the man retorted. 'You're

not Mr Parsons, that's for sure. Not going by the description I've been given, anyway.'

'I'm Dennis Powell, an acquaintance of Mr Parsons. I've just come over from Malvern to visit him.'

'Well. I'm Detective Sergeant Bowen and the one shaking the door on its hinges is Detective Inspector Gwilliam. I think you'd better let him in before he breaks it down, don't you?'

As soon as Dennis turned the latch, the door was thrust open from the other side and he was forced to step back. Another man stood there, silhouetted against the fading, early evening sunlight.

'Who have we got here then?' he said, addressing the sergeant over Dennis' shoulder.

'This is Mr Powell. He says he's come over from Malvern to visit Mr Parsons.'

'So, where's Mr Parsons?' said Gwilliam, stepping inside.

'He's in there,' said Dennis, gesturing towards the front room. 'I think he's dead… actually, I'm sure he is.'

'You'd better show us.'

The two policemen followed him in. The ruddiness of the setting sun through the net curtains and the matching radiance from the electric fire lent a cosiness to the scene that belied the presence of death. Gwilliam knelt next to Harry and felt for a pulse. He tried the right arm first and then he pressed his thumb against the old man's flabby neck. He looked up at them and shook his head. 'Nothing there,' he said. 'But he's not quite cold yet so it hasn't been long.'

He stood up again and said to the Sergeant. 'Put the light on will you, so we can see what's been going on in here.'

Bowen flicked the switch.

'Not that it makes a lot of difference,' observed Gwilliam, glancing up at the dim, yellow bulb.'

'But enough to see the place has been well and truly turned over,' said Bowen.

'Either that or Mr Parsons' housekeeping skills left a bit to be desired,' said Gwilliam. 'Is this how it was when you arrived?' he added, turning to Dennis.

'Yes, of course. I'm certainly not responsible for the mess, if that's what you're getting at.'

'Just checking,' said Gwilliam. 'What time did you get here?'

"About ten to six. My train got to Hereford just after five-thirty, but it was a quicker walk from the station than I expected. I'd arranged to meet Mr Parsons here at six o'clock so, when he didn't answer, I guessed he must have gone out somewhere and that he'd be back shortly. Then I looked through a crack in the lace curtains and saw him slumped here. I assumed he was asleep, so I knocked again but I couldn't rouse him. The front door was shut tight so that's when I thought I'd see if there was a back-way in.'

'Like I just did,' interjected Sergeant Bowen.

'I suppose so, yes.'

'And the back door was unlocked?' said Gwilliam.

'Yes.'

'You didn't have to force it?'

'No, I just told you, it was unlocked.'

'You'd better go and check for damage,' said Gwilliam to his sergeant.

Bowen nodded and left the room.

'Why's he checking?' Dennis protested. 'Don't you believe me?'

'It's got nothing to do with that, we just need to know if someone else forced the door, before you arrived.'

Bowen reappeared. 'No damage as far as I can see,' he said.

'Thanks,' said Gwilliam. Then he added, 'Mr Powell's worried we think he's a potential housebreaker.'

Bowen looked Dennis up and down. 'No,' he said, shaking his head. 'He's not the type.'

'But even if he was, there'd be mitigating circumstances in this instance, wouldn't there?'

'Concern for the old man's wellbeing you mean?'

'Exactly.'

'But I *wasn't* concerned about him at that point,' interrupted Dennis. 'I thought he'd been drinking and was having a doze to sleep it off. If the back door hadn't been open, I'd just have kept knocking until he woke up again.'

'You'd have been knocking for a hell of a long time then, wouldn't you?' said Bowen, looking down at Harry's body again.

Dennis and Gwilliam followed his gaze.

'How well did you know him then? asked the Inspector.

'Hardly at all,' said Dennis. 'We met for the first time yesterday.'

'But you knew he liked a drink.'

'Well you can see that from the hip flask on the floor here, can't you? He was quaffing from the same one all the time I was with him.'

'So why *were* you with him?'

'I'm a reporter on the Malvern Gazette and he'd written in complaining about the poor quality of service on the train journey from Hereford to Worcester. I was assigned to meet him, en-route, to experience the problems at first hand. In the event, the story didn't really add up to anything, so we started talking about other things. He reads the Gazette, so he was familiar with a monthly column I write: The Wells and Springs of Old Malvern. He said he had some information at home I might find useful. It sounded quite interesting, so I arranged to come over today and pick it up.'

'What sort of information?'

'Some notes connected with a historic water feature I'm interested in.'

'Fair enough,' said Gwilliam. 'So, you came over from Malvern, expecting to pick up this information, only to find Harry Parsons, conked out, in his armchair.'

'That's right. As I said, I thought he must have had a few too many and dozed off in front of the fire but, when he wouldn't wake up, I realised it was more serious than that.'

'About as serious as it gets,' interjected Bowen.

'I tried taking his pulse, but I couldn't feel anything. I was shocked obviously and for a few seconds I wasn't quite sure what to make of it all. I knew he wasn't well because he had a funny turn while we were on the train yesterday. He told me he was prone to palpitations which made me think he'd probably got a weak heart.'

'Was there any sign of the information he'd promised you?'

'No.'

'That must have been disappointing.'

'Not particularly. At that point, I was more concerned about finding a telephone and calling the police.'

'I'm sure you were but I'd be very surprised if part of you wasn't still itching to get your hands on those notes of his.'

'What are you getting at?'

'Just that no-one would blame you if you'd had a bit of a dig around to find what you'd come here for.'

'So you still think I'm responsible for all this mess?' said Dennis, indignantly.

'I'm not sure what to think just yet, I'm just considering all the possibilities.'

'Are you seriously suggesting I'd search through a dead man's personal belongings? What sort of person do you think I am?'

'A perfectly normal person. You've already told us you didn't really know this man so there's no reason why you should have been particularly upset by his death - apart from the natural shock of finding a body, obviously. But after you'd got over that, why not have a quick rummage to make your journey worthwhile?'

'Well that might be normal behaviour in your world, but it certainly isn't in mine.'

'So, you still say the state of this place is nothing to do with you?'

'That's precisely what I'm saying. Someone else must have been here before me.'

'Someone who shares your interest in obscure historic water features.' said Gwilliam. 'That's quite a coincidence, isn't it?'

He wondered if now was the time to come clean about finding the journal down the side of Harry's chair but immediately decided against it. There were certain things he just wasn't ready to share.

'Perhaps they were looking for something else,' he said.

'Perhaps they were,' said Gwilliam sounding far from convinced. 'But let me make one thing clear Mr Powell, if I later discover that you haven't been completely honest with us, I'm going to be very annoyed. Do you understand?'

'I understand,' said Dennis morosely.

'We'd better establish a time and cause of death, hadn't we?' said Bowen, gesturing towards the body.

Gwilliam nodded. 'Yes, you'd better get on the radio and ask them to send Dr Evans up here along with a forensics team. We'll also need as many PCs as they can spare to secure the premises and conduct door to door enquiries. In the meantime, I'll stay take a good look around while you drive Mr Powell back to HQ and take his statement. You can come back and join me here later.'

'Right you are,' said Bowen. He motioned for Dennis to go ahead of him.

'Don't forget, we'll need his fingerprints too,' Gwilliam called after them.

'Why do you need my fingerprints?' asked Dennis as they walked down the front path to the black Wolseley parked at the kerb. It was dark now and the streetlamps had come on along Hobart Road.

'For elimination purposes,' said Bowen from behind him. 'If someone really *did* go through the old man's things before you arrived on the scene, we'll need to distinguish their prints from yours.'

They got into the car and Bowen switched on the internal light before pulling a radio microphone out of a cubby hole in the dashboard. He pressed a button and said, 'Three-seven-nine here, are you receiving, over?'

There was a burst of static from a hidden loudspeaker and then a female voice came back tinnily over the airwaves, 'Central control here, receiving you three-seven-nine, over.'

'Deceased adult male at five Weobley Villas, Hobart Street. Possible suspicious circumstances. Request urgent attendance of Dr Evans at the scene, over'

'Message received and understood three seven nine. Will notify Dr Evans immediately, over.'

'Inspector Gwilliam has also requested the forensics team attend and at least five PCs for support, over.'

'All requests noted. Will pass on straightaway, over.'

'Yes, just one more thing Irene,' said Bowen, suddenly abandoning his stilted radio manner. 'It looks as if I'm going to be late home tonight, over.'

'Well there's a surprise. Try not to make too much noise when you come in then, over and out'

'The wife,' explained Bowen, grinning at Dennis as he returned the microphone to its cubby hole. 'Otherwise known as Central Control.' He switched off the light, started the engine and then they drove off down Hobart Street, towards the junction with the main road.

'So how come you and Inspector Gwilliam turned up there anyway?' said Dennis after a while.

'You were spotted by an observant neighbour who thought you were behaving suspiciously so he phoned the police station. Inspector Gwilliam and I happened to be in the area, so we decided to come and take a look.'

'So, am I still under suspicion?'

'It remains to be seen. We'll take your statement, consider it in the light of all the other evidence and see what we think after that.'

'It's a bit much having all those questions fired at me by Inspector Gwilliam and then being carted off to the police station just because I happened to be in the wrong place at the wrong time.'

'That's the way it goes sometimes I'm afraid,' said Bowen, glancing in his mirror as he prepared to turn right.

'Your big mistake was going into the house. You need to try and see it from our point of view: we find an unidentified male preparing to make his exit from a scene where there's a dead body in an armchair and signs of a possible burglary. It doesn't look very good, does it?'

'I suppose it doesn't when you put it like that,' said Dennis gloomily.

'Anyway,' said Bowen, 'just to change the subject for a minute, I want to ask you something that's preying on my mind ever since you told us your name and said where you came from. Are you related to Inspector Nigel Powell of the Malvern Constabulary by any chance?'

Dennis turned to look at him in surprise. 'Yes, he's my brother, how did you guess?'

'I heard he had a brother who worked for a local paper, so I just put two and two together.'

'Presumably you know him through the job. I expect the Hereford and Malvern forces work quite closely together, don't they?'

'Not as much as you'd imagine but, in any case, my knowing your brother hasn't got anything to do with the police, it's because I served in his platoon in France during the war, along with Inspector Gwilliam.'

'And you've kept in touch ever since?'

Bowen laughed. 'Let's put it this way: *we've* tried to keep in touch, but your brother doesn't seem quite so keen. In fact, he's totally ignored all the letters we've sent him and telephone messages we've left. We always make a point of reminding him about the regimental reunion that happens every year and saying how much everyone would like to see him again, but he never turns up.'

'Why do you think that is?'

'You'd need to ask him that.'

'But you must have an idea.'

'Possibly but he's the only one who could say for certain, so it would be wrong to speculate.'

'He's always been proud of what he did in the war, so it seems a bit odd that he doesn't leap at the chance to reminisce about it with all his old comrades.'

'Less of the *old* please,' said Bowen. 'I've only just turned forty so I'm a bit sensitive about that sort of talk these days.'

He turned a sharp left into a police station compound that was bathed in the glow from overhead arc lights and came to a halt between two identical black Wolseleys.

'Here we are,' said Bowen. 'We'll just get you processed and then, provided you behave yourself, I might be prepared to chauffeur you back to the railway station.'

Dennis followed him into an echoing foyer that was like the one at Malvern Police Station, but bigger. Bowen nodded to the desk sergeant who waved them through into a dimly lit corridor lined with numbered doors. They exited into a brighter, but entirely windowless waiting area with four rows of bare wooden chairs facing a plaque of the royal coat of arms mounted on the wall.

'Take a seat,' said Bowen. 'I just need to sort out a couple of things and then I'll be with you.'

There were twenty chairs in total, five to a row, and Dennis sat down in one at the back so that he could survey his fellow occupants. Two men were sitting at opposite ends of the front row and, just in front of him; an elderly couple were engaged in an urgent, whispered conversation about a troublesome neighbour who'd been lighting bonfires too close to their garden fence. He assumed they were here to make a formal complaint.

As his interest in the couple's litany of ruined washing and charred fence posts began to wane, Dennis' attention was drawn to the man at the left-hand end of the front row who seemed to be just as worked up about something but was plainly talking to himself. The man on the other end had obviously just noticed it too because, with a disdainful sideways glance, he stood up and left the room. Thirty seconds later, the elderly couple did the same.

Dennis was transfixed as the agitated man continued to conduct a mumbled debate with himself.

'Incredible isn't it. We get all sorts in here.'

He looked up to see Bowen standing there. It was clear that he'd been taking in the strange performance as well.

'What's the matter with him do you think?' said Dennis.

'I haven't got a clue. They've called the doctor in to find out.'

'Has he said why he's here?'

'You must be joking. All he does is talk to himself. It obviously makes sense to him but no-one else has the foggiest idea what he's on about.'

'He just walked in, did he?'

'No, someone dropped him off – literally, in fact. The desk sergeant says he was bundled out of a Land Rover, just outside the main entrance, twenty minutes ago. Apparently, it screeched to a halt, the passenger door flew open, and our friend here tumbled out before the vehicle roared off again at top speed. A couple of PCs helped him to his feet and brought him in. It seems that he was rambling on just the way he is now, making no sense at all so in the end the decision was made to bring him in here out of the way until medical help arrived. He's obviously bonkers but he seems harmless enough.'

Suddenly there was a bustle behind them and they both turned around to see two police constables enter the waiting area followed by a stout, balding man in a brown tweed suit.

'And here comes the doc, right on cue,' said Bowen.

The trio made straight for the front row and the two policemen stood on either side of the agitated man while the doctor bent down and started talking to him in a quiet, solicitous tone. This continued for a minute or two but then, plainly deciding he wasn't getting anywhere, the doctor raised himself to full height again. As he did so he nodded to the two PCs who each took hold of an arm and gently but firmly lifted the man to his feet. They manoeuvred him slowly across the front of the room with the doctor leading the way this time.

'They're taking him to the medical room,' Bowen whispered. 'Given the state he's in, that's probably where they should have taken him in the first place.'

As the little group turned to walk down the side of the room towards the exit, Dennis saw the man properly for the first time. His clothes and hair were dishevelled, and his eyes were glazed but, despite all that, he was instantly, and shockingly, recognisable. The procession passed by and, within seconds, had disappeared through the swing doors at the back of the room.

'Are you all right?' said Bowen. 'You look as if you've just seen a ghost.'

'It certainly feels like it,' said Dennis hoarsely.

'I assume that means you recognise him?'

'Yes, his name's James Crawford. He's married to my

sister, Susan.'

'Blimey, that *will* have been a shock for you then. Is he from Malvern as well?'

'Yes, he went missing a couple of days ago after crashing his car into a tree.'

'That would explain the odd behaviour then. He's probably suffering from concussion.'

'I think he's been having a few personal problems recently as well. Susan's been really worried about him.'

'We'll need to let her know where he is then and put her mind at rest. Who's the police officer dealing with it at Malvern, do you know?'

'I spoke to a Sergeant Collins. I think there's an Inspector Bates involved as well. Apparently, they work together.'

Bowen smiled. 'Bates and Collins eh? Well I wish you luck with that pair.'

'Funnily enough, Nigel said much the same when I mentioned them to him. It sounds as if they've got a bit of a reputation.'

'You could say that but, if they're the ones involved, they're the ones we'll have to deal with.'

'Actually,' said Dennis cautiously. 'I'm not entirely sure my sister knows anything about James' disappearance yet.'

'But I thought you said she'd been really worried?'

'That was *before* he disappeared. The thing is, she's gone away for a few days and we haven't got an address for her.'

'This is starting to sound complicated.'

'It's very complicated.'

'I'll tell you what,' said Bowen. 'Let's find somewhere we can talk properly. I'll get us a cup of tea as well.'

'Thanks, but I'd prefer to go and see James if you don't mind. I might be able to help.'

'You'd be wasting your time. You saw the state he was in, didn't you?'

'I know, but if I could just speak to him quietly it might bring him round.'

'I think it would be better if we left all that to the doctor, don't you?'

'But I expect he's just an ordinary doctor isn't he, not a psychiatrist or anything, so all he'll do is give him a sedative and make him even more dazed and confused.'

'And you think you could do better?'

'No, of course not but I *am* a relative of sorts; someone he actually knows.'

'He didn't appear to know you very well just then, did he?'

'That's because he's shocked and concussed but I'm sure he'll start to focus better when he hears a friendly voice.'

'All right, I'll let you see him on one condition.'

'What's that?'

'From now on, whenever one of us asks you a question, do you think you could be a bit more forthcoming?'

'I don't understand.'

'Yes, you do, you're a master of evasion and you know it. I could tell as soon as you opened your mouth, so could Inspector Gwilliam; that's why he gave you such a hard time.'

'I thought it was because that neighbour told him I'd been acting suspiciously?'

'No, you were in the clear by then because, afterwards, another neighbour got in touch to say they'd seen someone enter the house twenty minutes before you even arrived.'

'So why didn't he mention it?' said Dennis angrily.

'I expect he thought if you could be sparing with the facts, so could he.'

'That's not a very professional, is it?'

Bowen shrugged. 'It depends on your point of view. Personally, I think it was perfectly justified under the circumstances.'

'Give me one example of where I've been evasive then,' said Dennis, not really wanting an answer but feeling it incumbent upon him to ask.

'It's not about specific examples, it's just your general attitude: your slightly prickly manner; the way you don't always make eye-contact when you reply. A variety of things really.'

'I don't suppose I'm any different from anyone else being interrogated by the police. Most people are a bit edgy in that situation, aren't they?'

'It's more than that with you though. I get the feeling you're on some sort of mission but you're not quite sure where it's taking you, and that's what's making you cagey. Am I right?'

'There could be some truth in that I suppose.'

'Good,' said Bowen, giving him a broad smile. 'I think we're starting to make progress.'

'So, someone else was seen entering Harry's house,' said Dennis, keen to change the subject.

'Yes, one of the neighbours was hanging up curtains in her bedroom and happened to see a short, skinny man, limping up the alleyway and then enter the house via the back door.'

'He was limping you say?'

'That's right. Why, does it remind you of someone?'

'I'm not sure.'

Bowen cocked an eye at him. 'It does though, doesn't it? Come on, you might as well admit it, your face has given the game away already?'

'It sounds a bit like someone I saw in Malvern recently; a man called Percy Franklin.'

'How do you know him? What does he do?'

'He works for an estate agent in Great Malvern, Crawford, Davies and Withers, the one where James is a partner.'

'That's interesting. Do you know anything that might connect him with Harry Parsons as well?'

'Nothing at all. It probably isn't the same man anyway. He won't be the only man in Malvern with a bad leg, will he?'

'True,' said Bowen, 'it's probably nothing. Then again, in our game, you'd be surprised how many of these little coincidences turn out not to have been coincidences at all.'

Suddenly the swing doors behind them burst open and they both swung round to see a police constable standing there. He was one of the men who had escorted James and the doctor out of the room a few minutes before.

'What is it Fraser?' said Bowen.

'Sorry to interrupt Sarge, but we were wondering if you'd mind having a word with this chap who's come in. We've all tried, but we can't get a squeak out of him. It's like talking to a brick wall.'

CHAPTER 19

Connecting some dots

Friday 29th March 1957

7.30 p.m.

Dennis followed Sergeant Bowen and PC Fraser along the corridor that led away from the waiting area and back towards the main entrance hall. Bowen knocked on a door, halfway along and he, Dennis and the constable went straight in.

The medical room was brightly lit with a heavy aroma of disinfectant in the air. Yellow blinds were pulled down over the windows to the left. To the right, an examination bed, covered with a single white sheet, was just visible through a gap in the curtains that surrounded it. There were two chairs against the far wall, one empty and the other occupied by the second PC who'd accompanied James earlier.

Bowen nodded to him. 'Evening Bentley,' he said.

'Evening Sarge,' replied Bentley. 'This is Dr Crowther.'

He indicated the bald-headed man they'd seen before who was now sitting at a table in the middle of the room. Opposite the doctor sat James; bolt upright in his chair and gazing fixedly into space.

Crowther stood up to shake Bowen's hand.

'Good evening Sergeant,' he said. 'I'm most grateful to you for sparing the time to join us. 'I'm afraid I'm having considerable difficulty communicating with this gentleman, so any assistance you're able to provide would be much appreciated.'

'This is Mr Powell,' said Bowen, nodding in Dennis' direction. 'He was here to see me about something else, but he happened to see your patient here and identified him as his brother-in-law, James Crawford.'

He crouched down next to James and spoke directly into his right ear. 'Mr Crawford, James - do you mind if I call you James? - How are you feeling?'

James continued to stare directly straight ahead.

Bowen tried again. 'James, Dennis is here with me; Dennis your brother-in-law. He'd like to talk to you, is that all right?'

Still James didn't answer.

'We think you've had a shock,' Bowen persisted. And it's obviously shaken you badly. Dennis would like to help you sort things out, in fact, we'd all like to help if we can. Is there anything you'd like to get off your chest?'

Yet again, there was no reaction.

Bowen got up and turned to Dennis. 'You'd better see if you can get through to him.'

Dennis came forward and crouched next to James just as Bowen had done. 'Hello James,' he said, 'I just wanted you to know that Susan's very worried about you. She'd like you to come home so that you can both sort things out.'

He felt bad making false promises on behalf of someone he hadn't spoken to in ages but concluded that it hardly mattered because James wasn't hearing him anyway. He could have recited a series of nursery rhymes into his brother-in-law's ear for all the difference it was likely to make.

'This is a waste of time,' he said, standing up and looking at Bowen. 'I think he needs to see someone who knows how to deal with this sort of thing.'

'What do you think Doctor?' said Bowen.

'I tend to agree,' said Crowther. 'I'm a general practitioner, so this isn't really my domain. All I can do is offer a sedative to settle him down.'

'He seems to have calmed down a bit since we brought him in here, so perhaps we should leave the sedative for now. I'm all for calling a specialist in though. Who would you recommend?'

'I'm not sure. I'd need to make a few enquiries.'

'Do you know Dr Gajak at Powick Mental Hospital?' said Dennis.

'Not personally, but I know he's got an excellent reputation and he'd fit the bill perfectly if he's available. May I ask how you know him?'

'He's a friend. We share an interest in local history. I can give you his direct telephone number if you like. I'm sure he won't mind, and it'll be a lot quicker than going through the hospital switchboard.'

He wrote Gajak's number down on a scrap of paper and handed it over.

'Thank you,' said Crowther. 'I'll call him straightaway and see if he's willing to assist.'

He turned to Bowen. 'What are you proposing to do with Mr Crawford in the meantime?'

'I'd be grateful if you could stay with him until the psychiatrist arrives. I'll leave PC Bentley and PC Frazer in here with you though, just in case he needs restraining or anything.

'What if the psychiatrist says he's got to be taken to the hospital?' said Bentley.'

'That's fine. In fact it would probably be the best thing all round. Just make sure you get all the relevant forms signed when you hand him over. Understood?'

There were nods all around.

'Good. In that case Mr Powell and I have got some other business to finish off in the interview room next door. After that, I'll be re-joining Detective Inspector Gwilliam at the scene of an incident we were called out to earlier. You can try and contact me there on the car radio if you need to, but I'll be calling in from time to time anyway, just to see how you're getting on.'

The interview room next door was a smaller but equally brightly lit version of the one they'd just left, containing a desk, positioned side-on to the window, with a single chair on either side.

'He's in a right old state, isn't he?' said Bowen as they sat down facing each other.

'He is,' said Dennis. 'It's a shock seeing him like that, it really is.'

'So, what's set him off do you think? You mentioned personal problems earlier.'

'It's to do with his marriage I'm afraid. He's a gloomy sort of chap, so I don't think Susan, my sister, has ever found him easy to live with. But she's stoical to the core and somehow, for the last thirteen years or so, she's managed to put up with it. He's got a lot worse lately though and, by all accounts, she's reached the end of her tether and gone off to stay with a friend.'

'She hasn't left him permanently then?'

'Not as far as I know, but if you knew Susan you'd understand what a big step it was for her to finally walk out like that, even just for a few days.'

'Has he been violent with her do you think?'

'No, I'm pretty sure it's his state of mind that's driven her away rather than anything physical. He was always prone to black moods, but it seems that recently he's been having terrible nightmares and screaming out things like "die, die, die," in his sleep as if he was in the middle of killing someone.'

'Good grief. What's all that about, do you think?'

'Flashbacks to the war probably. He served in Burma and it got pretty nasty out there from what I understand.'

'Does he strike you as the suicidal type?'

Dennis thought for a moment, then he said, 'I didn't think so before but, after I found his crashed car the other day, it occurred to me he might be, yes.'

'That's why I asked. You said those two reprobates Bates and Collins were dealing with that didn't you?'

'Yes, not that they seemed particularly bothered. At least Sergeant Collins didn't; I can't speak for Inspector Bates because I've never met him.'

'Oh, you can take it from me, Bates will be the same. And they'll both be even worse now because they'll be able to claim that the big case is taking up all their time.'

'Which big case?'

'You know which one I mean: the body in a shallow grave at that big house in Malvern Wells.'

'Oh, you've heard about that, have you?'

'Of course, I have. What do you take me for? Nigel's heading up the investigation, isn't he? What's *he* told you about it?'

'I'm not sure I should say, it's supposed to be confidential.'

'I think you've forgotten who you're talking to here. I'm a police officer: nothing's confidential where I'm concerned. So come on, what have you heard?'

'Not a lot because, understandably, Nigel's pretty cagey about it as well. All I know is that one of the gardeners dug up a body, early on Wednesday morning and the police are sifting through clues to try and find out whose remains they are and how they got there.'

'You'll have to do better than that. What else has he told you?'

'Well, this isn't anything Nigel told me but, given what we've just been discussing, I suppose it's an interesting coincidence that the agents for Symbiosis House, the place where the body was found, are none other than James's firm, Crawford, Davies and Withers.'

'That *is* interesting. Anything else?'

'Nothing much.'

Bowen peered at him across the desk. 'In other words, quite a lot. Come on Dennis, spill the beans.'

'But Nigel will go mad if he finds out I've been blabbing about his case.'

'No he won't. He might be a bit of a lone wolf, but he'd be the first one to tell you that the key to a successful investigation is sharing information with colleagues.'

'Maybe he would but…' Dennis' voice tailed off.

'But *what*?'

'He's finding things a bit awkward at the moment. He's not sure who he can trust.'

'Is this to do with that charming boss of his by any chance? Superintendent "Bad'n" Goodall

'You know him?'

'Not personally, but I've heard a lot about him; none of it complimentary. So you're saying he's giving Nigel a hard time.'

'I think he's *always* given Nigel a hard time but now it's worse than ever.'

'Why?'

Because of this Symbiosis House business. Goodall's decided that Andrew Morrigan, the man who found the body, is bang to rights and refuses to accept anything to the contrary.'

'But this Morrigan's gone missing, hasn't he? That's what I read in the paper.'

'But that doesn't automatically make him guilty, does it?'

'No, but it doesn't do him any favours either, especially as he appears to have been in trouble before.'

'Only for being drunk and disorderly, nothing more serious than that. Lots of people in Malvern know Andrew Morrigan lives rough and likes a drink, so he's an easy target. But we're talking about a shooting here, not drunken fisticuffs'

'What if Morrigan whipped out a revolver in the heat of the moment?'

'It doesn't sound as if there was anything heated about this killing. Nigel's pretty sure the victim was shot through the head in cold blood because it reminded him of revenge killings he came across in France at the end of the war.'

'Does he indeed?'

'You said you served in his platoon, didn't you? Do you

know the sort of thing he means?'

'Oh, I know the sort of thing he means all right. What did he say about it?'

'He said the victim would have been made to kneel by his own grave and take his punishment; a bullet in the side of the head. He said it was always obvious because of where the bullet ended up.'

'Embedded in the earth at the bottom of the grave, having been fired downwards from a standing position.'

'That's it exactly.'

'Yes, we saw quite a few of those in France. They always seemed to follow the same pattern. That's the psychology of revenge I suppose: the perpetrators adopt a well-tried ritual to guarantee maximum satisfaction.'

'Chilling.'

'It is but we saw far worse things than that over there, I can assure you.'

'Like what?'

'Better you don't know. I still get nightmares about it all even now. You won't meet a soldier who doesn't.'

'Even Nigel?'

'*Especially* Nigel.'

'You wouldn't know it to hear him talk, especially when he's talking to my father about it. His stories sound as if they're straight out of Boy's Own.'

'I can just imagine.'

'Why do you say that?'

Bowen shrugged. 'Because I served with him, I know what he's like.'

After a pause he said, 'I'm guessing you never served.'

'No I didn't. How can you tell?'

'I just can. What was it, health problems?'

'A chronic respiratory condition.'

'It must have been hard hearing Nigel talk like that then?'

'It was but I didn't really blame him. It was more to do

with my father egging him on.'

'I doubt he needed much encouragement.'

'I get the impression you don't like Nigel very much.'

'I wouldn't say that. There's a bit of unfinished business between us, that's all.'

'From your time in France?'

'That's right, from our time in France.'

'And it's still an issue, twelve years on?'

'Not an issue as such, more of an irritation: an itch that just won't go away.'

'And does this involve Inspector Gwilliam as well?'

'Of course. We were both there; we both remember what happened.'

'So what *did* happen exactly.'

Bowen shook his head. 'This might sound like tit for tat, but I don't think it would be appropriate to say. It would be better if you asked Nigel.'

'Tell him you let it slip that he'd done something to irritate you during the war but wouldn't tell me what it was, so could he explain please? That wouldn't go down too well, would it?'

'No,' said Bowen, smiling, 'I suppose not.'

'So, now you've let the cat out of the bag, perhaps it would be simpler if you just told me yourself.'

'Perhaps it would.

He closed his eyes, as if collecting his thoughts, before continuing.

'It was June 1944; we were advancing across northern France and Nigel was commanding our platoon. We saw some horrific things as we went along I can tell you, but we had a job to do so we did our best to push it all to the back of our minds and concentrate on surviving. Although the Germans were in retreat it was still extremely dangerous, and we were regularly getting involved in skirmishes where close comrades got killed. It was ugly and utterly terrifying, but we just had to grit our teeth and carry on.

'One morning, around ten o'clock, we started to advance on yet another village. We were ultra-cautious as usual, just in case the enemy had taken up a defensive position there and tried to pick us off as we approached. The closer we got though, the more we became convinced that the village had been abandoned: there was total silence and absolutely no sign of life. I sometimes think I had a premonition of what lay ahead but that's probably just the benefit of hindsight. Anyway, premonition or not, nothing could have prepared me for the shock of what we found. I'll spare you the grisly details but, suffice to say, we were confronted by a bloodbath: the aftermath of a massacre of men, women and children that was more gruesome than anything you could possibly imagine. I'm sure I'm not exaggerating when I say that every soldier in the platoon immediately bent over and threw up the at the sight of it.

'Even so, this was war and we knew we needed to pull ourselves together and properly appraise the situation before moving on. That was when we realised that our platoon commander, Second Lieutenant Nigel Powell, was nowhere to be seen. Gwilliam and I started looking around, thinking that he might have wandered off a bit further so that he could do a bit of a recce of the countryside beyond to assess how safe it was to proceed. We checked a few outbuildings on the edge of the village because we knew they were places he'd probably choose as observation posts. They were mainly old stone barns with little slit windows; ideal for peering through with your binoculars without making yourself a sitting duck for any enemy snipers. We'd looked in about five before we found him. The one he'd chosen had four pigs penned up inside, snuffling and snorting away. They were desperately hungry, poor buggers, and Nigel was sitting on the floor amongst them, covered in straw and muck; holding his head in his hands and crying like a baby.'

'He sounds traumatised,' said Dennis, aghast at this image of his normally steadfast brother.

'Traumatised and sitting in pig shit: incapable of saying or doing anything, least of all leading a platoon.'

'How did you feel?'

'Shaken obviously – angry as well if I'm honest - but mainly sorry for him. No-one can predict how they're going to stand up to the horrors of war and we knew that it could just as easily have been one of us sitting there. Our main concern was getting him back to some semblance of normality before the other men saw him.'

'So, what did you do?'

'First we hauled him up like a sack of potatoes and literally dragged him round and round that stinking barn until his feet started working for themselves and he was less of a dead weight. It was knackering I can tell you. Even when he started walking again, it was hard to get any proper sense out of him. He just kept going on and on about how nightmarish everything was. Eventually though, he relaxed a bit and started apologising for letting us down and saying how he'd never be able to thank us enough for the comradely way we'd supported him in his hour of need. We were quite buoyed up by that and we felt even better after he'd gathered the men together again and given them a bit of a pep talk. It was as if nothing had ever happened. We were pleased because we knew we'd done a good job and seen off a potentially sticky situation.

'But then, a couple of days later, he took us to one side and asked us to promise we'd never utter a word to anyone about what had happened. We'd assumed that was taken as read so we were surprised he felt the need to ask. Even so, we obligingly gave him the promise he wanted and went back to our duties. We thought we'd finally drawn a line under the matter, which was right in a way but not quite in the way we'd imagined. The thing is that, from then on, he started giving Gwilliam and me the cold shoulder. We understood why of course, we were an embarrassment to him. We'd seen him at his most vulnerable so the less he had to do with us, the less he'd be reminded of his weakness. It was hurtful though and it made our, already difficult, jobs even harder because he'd never talk to us. And that's how it was for the remainder of the time we served under him.'

'How long was that?'

'Not long as it turned out, just a month or so. Once things had calmed down a bit over there, he got a promotion and we never saw him again.'

'So that's what you meant by unfinished business?'

'Yes. It might sound petty, but it still rankles to this day that he reacted like that. All Gwilliam and I want is an opportunity to sit down with him and talk about it. We're not looking for thanks or a grovelling apology; we'd just like him to acknowledge what happened and then we can all go away again and get on with our lives.'

'Incredible,' said Dennis. 'I'm not sure what to say.'

'I'm not surprised. I daresay you see your brother in a completely different light now. It's not exactly Boy's Own material, is it?'

'No, but I suppose I'm a bit torn really: on one hand, it makes him seem a lot more human. All that heroic talk never seemed real to me to me anyway, I suspect it was just for the benefit of my father – actually, I'm sure it was. But, on the other hand, it sounds as if he treated you and Inspector Gwilliam appallingly, after the decent way you treated him.'

'So, hopefully you now see what I meant about the itch that won't go away.'

'I do, I'm just not sure how I can help, that's all. Nigel would be furious if he thought I knew something about him like that. He'd probably give me the cold shoulder, the same way he's done with you.'

'I wasn't expecting you to help anyway. The only reason I told you about it was because you pressed me.'

'That's not entirely true though, is it? You were the one who mentioned unfinished business, you must have known I'd take the bait.'

'Yes,' said Bowen, nodding, 'I'm sure I did. I was just giving that itch another scratch: I can't help myself sometimes, I'm afraid.'

'I'm glad you did tell me though. It's the sort of information that's unsettling but helpful at the same time. I just need a bit of time to think about it, that's all.'

'In which case, why don't we change the subject? I need to take a statement from you but, before that, perhaps you'd like to tell me a bit more about what's been going on at Symbiosis House?'

CHAPTER 20

... And some more

Friday 29th March 1957

8.15 p.m.

Dennis spent the next few minutes bringing Bowen up-to-date about developments at Symbiosis House. He recapped on how the bullet had been found lodged in the bottom of the grave, described the discovery of the Occitan cross, and reiterated Nigel and Superintendent Goodall's difference of opinion about the direction the investigation should take. Finally, he explained how he'd been put in charge of the story after the Whippet's sudden departure and the pressure he was now under to accept Goodall's version of events.

'Nigel's not the only one feeling the Superintendent's heavy hand on his shoulder then,' said Bowen when he'd finished.

'No, I get the impression his influence reaches everywhere: even Jeff Stephenson, my editor seems to have been persuaded by him.'

'And you're convinced Nigel's on the right track?'

'Pretty much so, yes.'

'I certainly prefer his theory to Goodall's, at least there's some evidence to back it up whereas Goodall's just building a case on assumptions and prejudice. But why would he do that when it's so obvious the facts point in a different direction? What's he got to gain?'

'I don't know yet, but I'm determined to find out.'

Bowen peered at him. 'And are you sure you've told me everything now?'

'Of course,' said Dennis, holding his gaze as steadily as he could. 'I know I was a bit economical with the truth earlier but now I've seen the error of my ways.'

'I wish I could believe that, but I still think you're a slippery customer.'

Dennis felt a prickle of perspiration break out on his forehead. 'What do you think I'm not telling you?'

'I just find it odd that, so far, you haven't expressed an opinion about the identity of the body.'

'Most people think it's Mathias Friedman, don't they?'

'That's what I've heard but what do you think?'

'It's possible I suppose. After all, he never turned up again, did he?'

'What about this cross they found in the grave? An Occitan cross, that's what you said, wasn't it? What do you make of that?'

'I'm not sure.'

'Sorry I don't believe you.'

'Why not?'

'Because I reckon you think it's Laurent Morel, the missing TRE scientist.'

Dennis stared back at him in amazement.

Bowen grinned back at him. 'I'm right aren't I?'

'Yes,' said Dennis. But how on earth did you know?'

'It's all down to a man called Dan Yeats, Sergeant Dan Yeats. He transferred over to us from Malvern not long after Morel went missing. He hated Goodall's guts, and by all accounts, the feeling was entirely mutual.'

'There seem to be quite a few like that.'

'But, unlike Dan Yeats, most of them can't escape his clutches.'

'Why not?'

'Because Goodall's capable of making your life very difficult indeed if he thinks you're working against him. That'll be the predicament Nigel's in now, I'm sure.'

'How did Yeats get away then?'

'I don't know. Maybe he was more determined than most... or more reckless.'

'So, he transferred because he didn't like the way Goodall handled the Morel enquiry?'

'I don't think he liked the way Goodall handled *anything*, but the Morel enquiry's certainly what swung it for him. He couldn't understand why the search for Morel had been so lacklustre. Given that a top scientist had gone AWOL, possibly taking top secret information with him, he imagined the police would pull out all the stops to get to the bottom of it but the instruction coming down from the top was to simply go through the motions and then wind it down as quickly as possible. Unofficially, it was put about that Morel was just a French pansy and therefore a waste of valuable police resources. Apparently, Morel was known to have a penchant for wearing jewellery which made him a complete degenerate as far as Goodall was concerned. Colleagues at the TRE kept referring to a medallion he was particularly attached to, an Occitan cross, otherwise known as a Cross of

Toulouse. When you mentioned that one had been found in the grave, I knew you must have made the same connection.'

Dennis shook his head. 'I didn't actually. I couldn't find anything in any of the newspaper reports that referred to an Occitan cross. I only worked it out because I looked it up in the encyclopaedia and made the Toulouse connection.'

'And you've confirmed all this with Nigel, have you?'

'I have now, yes.'

'Anyway, in the end Goodall decided Morel must have been homesick and run off back to Toulouse - case closed.'

'I keep wondering how he gets away with it. After all, he's only a superintendent, isn't he? There's at least another four ranks above that.'

'Dan Yeats wondered the same thing.'

'What was his explanation?'

'He never came up with one. All he knew was that Goodall reigned supreme. Even the top brass over here were wary of him.'

'How do you know that?'

'Because of how they treated Yeats after he arrived. It was made crystal clear to him that his transfer was conditional upon his keeping schtum about his time at Malvern, especially his fall-outs with Superintendent Goodall.'

'You mean they gagged him?'

'They tried to yes, but Dan Yeats wasn't having any of it. He was forever shouting his mouth off about the corrupt way Goodall operated: how he always closed things down whenever they started to get complicated. He reckoned it was all part of some big conspiracy.'

'What sort of conspiracy?'

'He never made that clear. Anyway, most people stopped listening to him whenever he got onto that subject; me included.'

'Why?'

'Because we thought he was being obsessive about it, as if he'd got a persecution complex. It was obvious to all of us that Goodall was a complete bastard, but he was miles away, working in another force so why should we worry about him? Whenever Dan started one of his rants we'd either switch off or tell him to pack it in and think about something else.'

'Is he still around?'

'No, he's dead poor devil. He'd only been here a month before a car ran him over while he was out on point duty him and killed him outright. It was a hit and run so no-one was ever arrested for it.'

'Were there any witnesses?'

'A few, but all they could remember was a black car with dirty number plates knocking the policeman over and then racing away at speed.'

'And the car was never found?'

'Not as far as I know. Are you all right, you've gone as white as a sheet?'

'It's just that it rings a bell. A friend of mine, Margaret Jobson, told me very a similar story, a couple of days ago. That's how her father died in 1923.'

'Hit and runs aren't common fortunately but, when they happen, they always leave a nasty taste in the mouth.'

'Could Dan Yeats have been targeted, do you think?'

'Run over on purpose, you mean? Why, is that what happened in the case of your friend's father?'

'I don't know.'

'But you must have your suspicions, otherwise you wouldn't have asked.'

'Possibly, but that doesn't mean I've got any evidence to base them on.'

'I must admit, I did wonder about Dan myself, at the time.'

'Because of Goodall, you mean?'

'I suppose so. It certainly crossed my mind that Dan's death was pretty convenient for him under the circumstances.'

'In that it put an end to all the bad-mouthing?'

Exactly. However dismissive everyone was about Dan; it must have annoyed Goodall to know that his name was being taken in vain all the time.'

'So, what did you do?'

'Nothing?'

'Why not?'

'Because I decided I was getting carried away.'

'Do you still feel the same?'

'I did until we started having this conversation, but now I'm starting to think I should have listened to Dan a bit harder. No-one else can explain why Goodall wields all this power, so maybe he *was* on to something.'

'On to what though? Can you remember anything of what he said?'

'Not really, just that he thought Goodall had got friends in high places: people who were prepared to pull strings for him behind the scenes because he was useful to them where he was.'

'You scratch my back and I'll scratch yours.'

'That sort of thing, yes.'

'But he didn't mention any names?'

'Other than Goodall, no.'

'You said earlier that Goodall's capable of making people's lives very difficult if he thinks they're working against him: do you think that extends to having them killed?'

'I've only met him once, so it's hard to say. I found him pretty intimidating though, so it certainly wouldn't surprise me.'

'What about this other hit and run then? Tell me about that.'

'Greville Jobson, that's Margaret's father, was a teacher at Malvern College. He was walking home one afternoon in 1923 when a speeding car mounted the pavement, knocked him over and killed him. Apparently, it then did a quick turn in the road and raced away in the direction it had come. There was one witness, a man walking his dog, who described what happened, but he was too far away to get a registration number or identify the driver. Needless to say, neither car nor driver were ever seen again.'

'It's a lot like the Dan Yeats incident I agree, but, to be honest, so are most hit and runs. Why do you think this was different?'

'Greville Jobson was a member of a group called the Black Moon Society that met at Symbiosis House during the early 1920s. It turns out my father was a member too, and I'll explain why that's relevant in a minute. The Black Moon Society was established by Mathias Friedman, the psychiatrist who owned Symbiosis House. It was ostensibly a group that provided ex-soldiers with support in coming to terms with their experiences in the trenches but there seems to have been quite a lot of alcohol consumed there as well, not to mention drugs.'

'How do you know all this?'

'I've heard bits and pieces about it from various people but the most striking piece of evidence I've come across is a note, written by my father to a fellow member – I'm pretty sure it was Greville Jobson - urging him not to tell anyone about something that occurred at one of the Society's meetings.'

'What was that?'

'I don't know but it must have been serious if Greville was planning to tell people outside the group about it. Especially as, in his note, my father reminds him of a warning, presumably issued by Friedman, that anyone breaking their oath risked paying a high price that would be extracted without mercy.'

'And the price Greville paid was being run over and killed on his way back from work?'

'That's what it looks like to me. I'm guessing Friedman got wind of what he was planning to do and had him silenced before any damage could be done.'

'It's quite a theory.'

'I know, but the more I think about it, the more plausible it seems.'

'Have you talked to your father about this? Assuming he's still alive, of course.'

'Oh, he's very much alive, I can assure you. The trouble is, he's the last person I'd broach the subject with. You could ask anyone in my family, and they'd say the same.'

'He's touchy about it, is he?'

'He's touchy about everything but especially his past. Even my mother can't get any information out of him, that's why she broke into his desk.'

'Your mother broke into your father's desk?' exclaimed Bowen. 'What on earth made her do that?'

'It's a long story but, suffice to say, ever since the body turned up at Symbiosis House, he's been like a bear with a sore head. He's been driving my mother up the wall and this morning, after they'd had another big argument, she decided enough was enough and that she was going to break into the desk drawer he always kept locked. There was a secure box in there which she broke into as well. Inside that was the note I mentioned, along with a photograph of two men, one of whom was Greville Jobson.'

'Who was the other?'

'Harry Parsons. I think he belonged to the Black Moon Society too but, as I said, I'm almost certain Greville's the one the note was intended for.'

'What makes you so sure?'

'It's complicated but essentially it's because of the way my father reacted when his name came up in conversation yesterday. I've never seen him look so shaken. It was obvious it had struck a very raw nerve indeed.'

'As did this body turning up by the sound of it. Do you think he knows something about that as well?'

'I doubt it. Not if the body's Laurent Morel's, as we assume. I just think the Symbiosis House connection has stirred old memories, that's all.'

'Do you know if Greville Jobson ever talked about what was going on?'

'Not that Margaret remembers, but then she was only seven when he died so she might not have known about it even if he did.'

'Intriguing,' said Bowen. 'It makes you wonder if Harry Parson's death ties in with any of this, doesn't it?'

'Because he was a member of The Black Moon Society you mean?'

'Exactly.'

'I bet you'd have said I was getting carried away if I'd suggested that.'

'Maybe I would, but it might have got me thinking all the same. Anyway, thanks for being so candid, it's certainly an improvement on how you were earlier.'

'That's all right. It's been good to have a chance to get it off my chest actually.'

'And I'm sure there'll be more to get off your chest in the not too distant future, won't there?'

'Why do you say that?'

Because you're like a dog with a bone and you're just going to keep gnawing away at it. I'm right aren't I?'

'Probably.'

'Meanwhile, I'll have a chat with Inspector Gwilliam and see what he thinks about it all.'

'Not a lot probably.'

'We don't know that yet though, do we?' said Bowen. 'He's actually a lot more open to this sort of thing than you might think. Having said that though, he wouldn't be too impressed if he found out I'd been talking to you all this time without taking your statement.'

'Fair enough,' said Dennis. 'We'd better get down to it then. After that, perhaps you'd be good enough to drop me off at the railway station.

***

Leaping out of the police car on the station concourse, Dennis saw that the 8.15 to Great Malvern was already in. After pushing his way through a crowd of new arrivals, he raced along the platform and wrenched open one of the carriage doors just as the train was pulling away. Breathless from exertion, he sought out an empty compartment and slumped down in a forward-facing seat.

He sat still for a while and watched the lights of Hereford drift past his window. As they reached the edge of the city, the lights thinned out and the train began to gather speed. He sat listening to the hypnotic click of the rails for a minute or two and then he reached into the tartan bag he'd been carrying everywhere since Julian had returned it to him and pulled out Harry Parsons' journal for 1921.

Opening it at the first page, he was surprised to find that, rather than 1st January, the opening entry was dated Wednesday 9th March. He shifted slightly in his seat to maximise the meagre glow from the lamp mounted on the wall behind him and began to read:

"This evening I had the honour of being present at a gathering of local gentlemen at a prestigious residence in Malvern. The residence of which I speak nestles in the bosom of the hills and enjoys glorious, panoramic views across the Worcestershire countryside. I will not commit its name to paper because our esteemed host wishes us to exercise discretion both regarding the location of our meetings and the identities of those present. I am happy to respect his wish. Indeed, I embrace the clandestine nature of our affiliation with a lusty enthusiasm. I cannot deny that the idea of belonging to a secret society fills me with a boyish thrill. I am sure many people would find it risible that a thirty-nine-year-old bachelor should be so excited by such a thing and would no doubt dismiss it as a silly, childish game, but the fact

remains, that's exactly how I feel. I'm so excited, in fact, that I'm itching to relate every extraordinary detail to someone. However, because I have sworn (on my life no less) to maintain total secrecy about what occurred, confiding in this journal will have to suffice.

Once we were all gathered, our host made formal introductions while EH, his close friend and professional associate served glasses of the same fine Champagne with which we had been welcomed when we first arrived. There were eight guests including myself: AF, a dealer in antiques; AG and NC, two police officers; GJ, a schoolmaster; JM who runs a fleet of lorries and charabancs; HF, his business partner and CP who is in the wine and spirits trade.

On seeing the clear reference to his father, Dennis felt his heart begin to pound. He took a few deep breaths before reading on.

On the face of it we seem to have little in common other than that we are all male and of a similar age. In fact, without wishing to sound snobbish, there are many in our company who are far from top notch, either intellectually or socially. To be truthful though, I doubt if any of us could rival the palpable intellect of our host or even that of EH, his trusted friend and associate – yes, that includes me (and I rate myself as being well above average intelligence) and GJ, who has already impressed me as someone in possession of a first-class brain.

I don't know how anyone else was approached but my presence here is the consequence of an earlier encounter I had with our host, over a professional matter. He had engaged me, in a professional capacity, to remedy a drainage issue on his land. I willingly undertook the project and I am delighted to report that he was highly satisfied with the results. After the business was concluded, he asked me if I had an interest in astronomy. I replied that I certainly had an interest, but that I could not claim to have any significant knowledge of the subject. He then informed me that he had a rather fine telescope and that I would be very welcome to join his little astronomy group. I can only guess that the other members were enlisted in a similar way: perhaps each of them undertook a task for him that met with his satisfaction and, like me, was subsequently invited to join his group. However, I'm still left with the question, why us? To be completely frank, we just don't seem 'his type' or, dare I say, his equal.

Nevertheless, we all find ourselves members of this select astronomy group. I call it an astronomy group because that is how it was initially described to me, just as I assume it was to all the others. However, we have quickly discovered that there is far more to this affiliation than looking through a telescope and learning about the universe. The long and the short of it is – and I know it sounds queer for a practical, matter of fact person, like myself (a hydraulic engineer for goodness sake!), to be talking like this - but I believe our host is offering us a path towards true enlightenment. This evening, at our inaugural meeting, he spoke persuasively of how a study of the cosmos might be analogous with an exploration of the darkest reaches of the mind. He developed his theme in such an articulate and moving way that I'm sure we were all deeply affected by him – but more of that later.

He is indeed the proud owner of a large and extremely powerful telescope which he keeps in one of the turret rooms. It was to this room that we were first led this evening and our host informed us that it would be the gathering place for all future meetings.

To backtrack for a moment, I must record that each of us arrived separately at around nine o' clock this evening. After EH had served us the first of many glasses of our host's fine Champagne, we stood and chatted about inconsequential matters for perhaps fifteen minutes while the group assembled. I should make it clear that it was only after we were all present and correct that our host made his grand entrance and said a few words of welcome. His aura was palpable, and it was imme-

diately apparent that he is a man who lends gravitas to even the simplest action or utterance.

He called for attention and told us a little about what we could expect to see in the heavens this evening. Interestingly however, although it was a clear, moonless night and therefore perfect for stargazing, most preferred to carry on drinking, smoking and socialising, myself included I'm slightly ashamed to say. Once the remaining twilight had faded I think one or two members of the group might have taken it in turns to look through the telescope and, at one point, our host remarked on some prominent constellations that could be seen and mentioned the new, and presently invisible, moon. He announced that he would use the occurrence of a new moon to determine the dates of all our future meetings.

I note that I have referred to our consumption of alcohol several times so far and I am conscious that I might be at risk of portraying this gathering as being little more than an exclusive drinking club. However, as I have already intimated, and as I will go on to explain at greater length, this would be doing it a great injustice. Nevertheless, it cannot be denied that our host was remarkably generous with his excellent Champagne and by ten o' clock we were all quite inebriated. Even now, three hours later, as I write this, I am still feeling a little fuzzy-headed. Thinking about it though, this is probably attributable to something else that I will return to shortly.

So, let me describe what happened during the remainder of this extraordinary evening. At the stroke of ten, our host called for our attention once more and we all sat down on chairs that had been placed around the perimeter of the turret room while he took centre stage, next to his gleaming brass telescope. He then addressed us in a most unusual and poetic manner. I swear I have never heard anyone speak like that before and his words had a strangely hypnotic effect on the whole group. I wish I could quote everything he has said to us but I'm afraid a lot of it has faded away into the ether. Having said that, there is one section I can remember almost exactly. It was part of a long discourse about the moon and it went as follows:

"...things are different with Luna: every month she is darkened and extinguished; she cannot hide this from anybody, not even from herself. She knows that this same Luna is now bright and now dark - but who has ever heard of a dark sun?"

I believe he was quoting the noted psychoanalyst Carl G Jung, for whom he seems to have a very high regard. Then he went on to say – speaking in his own words now – that he believed this strange, dark state of the moon achieved its fullest potency on the rare occasions it manifested itself for a second time in a single lunar month. He called these occurrences Black Moons and he proposed that we cease using the rather prosaic term Astronomy Group to describe our association and henceforth call ourselves The Black Moon Society.

I wish I could remember more, but it is astonishing that I am able to recall even this much when I think about what happened next.

While our host was expounding on the mysterious qualities of the moon, EH came around with a tray on which were eight fresh glasses of Champagne. As each of us took a glass from the tray he also - rather incongruously I thought – handed over a sugar cube. He gave a slight inclination of his head, making it clear that he wished us to swallow it straightaway. Without further question, that is what we did – I remember it had a dry, bitter taste which, though not completely rebarbative, wasn't something one would choose to consume again in a hurry! We were then urged to swill it down with the Champagne which, of course, was considerably more palatable.

The subsequent period is something of a blur. Except, on reflection, 'blur' is not quite the right description because, although I couldn't comprehend what I was seeing I can clearly recall some quite astonishing images (I would almost call them *visions) of objects and events that felt more real than anything I had ever seen before and yet seemed to be projected from somewhere I couldn't reach. In one way, they felt part of me and yet, in another they felt alien as if I'd been temporarily given someone else's thoughts and memories. Am I sounding confused? I expect, when I read this back, I will think I lapsed into madness for a while. There are three particular images that have stayed with me: firstly, a torrent of running water that seemed to fill my head with a strange amalgam of sound and vision which was unlike any representation of water I have ever known before ; secondly, a huddle of dark figures, each of which seemed to be formed out of the shadowed portion of a crescent moon; thirdly, the neck and head of a swan that sometimes became part of the running water and had a disturbing aura that was simultaneously ominous and benign. This image preoccupies me more than any other because I'm convinced it has a precise significance for me but, try as I might, I cannot think what it is.*

So, I must accept that is all the sense I am going to be able to make of it for now, even though I have the uncomfortable feeling that something that would bind it all together and give it solidity is lying just below the surface of my thoughts. It reminds me of Malvern stone which is so irregular after it has been blasted that the only way to build a straight wall with it is to apply copious amounts of mortar. My recollections are like those misshapen blocks but, presently, I'm lacking the mortar with which I might join them up.

At least I can remember how the meeting ended, albeit in the same hazy way as one remembers a dream after suddenly waking up. I recall that, around midnight, EH poured us a generous measure of Scotch and within half an hour we'd all gone our separate ways. Of course, none of us was in a fit state to drive a car, let alone navigate along dark country lanes or through town but, nevertheless, I am now safely within my own abode; apparently unscathed and feeling... Feeling what exactly? Excited I think. In fact, euphoric might be a more accurate description.

But, in my experience, euphoria can be a troublesome emotion; something of a double-edged sword. I keep thinking of that swan's neck: both ominous and benign. What can it all mean?

The train slowed, and Dennis peered out of the window to see scattered points of light from houses on the outskirts of Ledbury. He suddenly had the odd feeling that he too was emerging from a dream but, if so, it was only a fleeting wakefulness because, by the time the train squeaked to a halt in the deserted station, he'd turned the page and was already immersed in the next section of Harry Parson's extraordinary journal.

CHAPTER 21

The Strange Journal of Harry Parsons

Friday 29th March 1957

8.45 p.m.

Saturday 12th March 1921

At noon today, quite by chance, I bumped into a fellow Black Moon Society member, GJ. I was in Great Malvern around lunch time when I saw him walking towards me along Belle Vue Terrace. I remembered from the brief conversation we'd had at our inaugural meeting, that he was a local schoolmaster – a teacher of science to be precise. I'd found him extremely intelligent and personable and had taken to him immediately. After exchanging pleasantries, I suggested we adjourn to the lounge of The Abbey Hotel for some liquid refreshment. He readily agreed, and we continued our conversation there with a couple of stiff whiskies to hand.

After talking for a while about the ups and downs of our respective professions, we moved on to the subject of the previous meeting. It soon became clear that he shared my confusion about some of what had occurred but that his perspective on it differed significantly from my own as I will now explain.

I described the disturbing visions I'd had after swallowing the mysterious sugar cube and asked him if he'd been affected in the same way. He shook his head and explained that he had left the room soon after swallowing it because it had immediately made him feel unwell. He'd gone out into the garden for some fresh air and immediately vomited into the rhododendron bushes. He said he'd felt much better after that and so he'd returned to the meeting. Having ejected whatever substance it was from his body; he was now in the unique position of being able to observe what happened next with a completely clear head.

He said that the members of our group (including myself of course) slowly fell silent. Our eyes stared straight ahead, and faces became expressionless as if we were slipping into a trance. Observing this state of affairs, he quickly decided to feign the same behaviour in order to blend in. As our host continued his impassioned discourse, we rose from our seats and followed him like sleepwalkers, down the winding staircase from the turret room. We descended the main staircase, along a passageway and then down another, even narrower spiral staircase, accessed via a trap-door. The stairs led down to an egg-shaped chamber where our host and his assistant, EH, were waiting for us. They were standing, side by side in front of a stone trough into which water flowed from a spout shaped like the head and neck of a swan.

GJ went on to recall how, once we were all assembled in front of the water spout, our host had begun to wax lyrical about something he described as the black moon's masked radiance. He said that, by learning to see beyond its dark shroud, we might achieve enlightenment and he likened this quest to the way that alchemists had worked to turn base metals into gold. I noticed a pained expression on my friend's face at this point and so I asked him what was wrong. He said he was always irritated by this sort of whimsical mythologizing, especially coming from the mouth of such an obviously intelligent man.

He then described the singular ritual that followed. Our host instructed the group to help him to hold EH's head under the water in the trough. Apparently, we all responded without hesitation. However, GJ said he could tell, from observing our glazed expressions, that we had little or no awareness of what we were doing. The "victim" appeared completely relaxed throughout the process, despite his head being submerged for a distressingly long time. During the immersion, our host continued his spurious pontificating (my friend's phrase, not mine) until, upon a signal, the man was released, and he stood up, bedraggled, but seemingly none the worse for his experience. After that, the company returned to the turret room and were gradually brought back to their senses with liberal measures of fine Scotch whisky.

As soon as he'd finished, I asked why he'd decided to act out this elaborate charade rather than admitting he'd had an adverse reaction to the "sugar lump." He looked a bit taken aback and then he replied, rather lamely, that he enjoyed amateur dramatics and that he'd seen it as an unexpected opportunity to test out his acting skills. It struck me that, despite his previous candour, something had suddenly caused him to have cold feet.

I tried bombarding him with all the other questions that had been bubbling up in my mind. What did he think it all meant? What did he think we'd been dosed with? What was the immersion business all about? How had we been chosen to take part? How had he first been approached?

Again, all his answers were frustratingly vague and non-committal, and he started glancing hither and thither as if afraid that someone might be watching us. Then he abruptly gulped down the rest of his Scotch, glanced pointedly at his watch and announced that he needed to be on his way.

Finding myself unexpectedly alone, I decided to order another whisky to keep me company while I pondered what I'd just learned.

Friday 8th April 1921

I have spent the past month in turmoil of indecision about whether to continue or end my association with the Black Moon Society. The morning after my conversation with GJ in the lounge of the Abbey Hotel I woke from fitful sleep, intent on writing to our host to say that, on reflection, I didn't think the group was for me after all and that I wished to withdraw with immediate effect.

During breakfast, however, I began to wonder why I'd been so ready to accept the testament of a man I hardly knew and who had proved to be so reticent when I'd pressed him for further information. It also occurred to me that, if I pulled out of the Black Moon Society now, I would forever be haunted by questions about the this mysterious, and therefore utterly beguiling, enterprise.

And so, over the last four weeks, my attitude towards our host and the Black Moon Society has swung wildly between these two extremes. One moment – especially in the early hours of the morning after another restless night's sleep – I have been ready to put pen to paper and end my association once and for all but, shortly afterwards, I've found myself eagerly looking forward to the next meeting and speculating about ways in which I might contrive to assume the unadulterated observer role that GJ inadvertently took on last time. It has also crossed my mind several times that I should attempt to arrange another rendezvous with GJ, to share my dilemma with him and to try once again tease out some of the thoughts he'd suddenly become so reluctant to express towards the end of our previous encounter. Once or twice I've even reached the point of picking up the telephone receiver with the intention of calling him at Malvern College where he works but, almost immediately, I've put it down again – I'm not precisely sure why –and resolved to let circumstances take their natural course.

It so happens that this evening I had sunk back into my most negative frame of mind about the whole venture, so it was with a heavy heart that I set off for the second gathering of the Black Moon Society.

Of course, my mood lifted as soon as I had a drink in my hand. This time the atmosphere was akin to any standard drinks party as opposed to the rather stilted ambience of our inaugural gathering. It was notable however that, despite ostensibly being as affable as before, GJ seemed at pains to ensure that we only conversed as part of a wider group. He wasn't avoiding me exactly, but it was clear that something between us had changed.

When the time came for our host to call us together, I expected him to give us a further lecture on lunar matters but, to my astonishment, I was proved completely wrong. Instead he began to talk about the horrors of the 1914-18 war, acknowledging that many of us were survivors of that conflict and probably still bore the scars: if not physically then certainly psychologically. He was greeted with affirming nods from all present (including me) when he reached this point. It hadn't really occurred to me before that most men of my generation are condemned to live with nightmarish memories of the war and yet it's a subject we rarely discuss. It seems to have become something of a taboo; as if it were a sign of weakness to talk about the past rather than simply gritting one's teeth and moving on. Our host was giving voice to the silent preoccupation of every man in the room and the collective appreciation of this was palpable. He told us that his specialism was treating damaged minds and that, with the help of EH, his trusted assistant, he had developed some pioneering methods that were proving extremely effective in this field. He said he hoped that we would forgive the deception but, during the previous meeting, he had employed one of these methods without our knowledge. He believed he could justify this because, if forewarned, our natural scepticism might have made us less receptive to the technique's full effect. He explained that he was offering his skills to help each of us find peace and enlightenment but if anyone had been offended by his duplicity or simply did not wish to proceed they should say so now and take their leave, *assured of his best wishes.*

A dramatic silence hung in the air and I am sure that each of us was waiting with bated breath to see if anyone would speak or make a move towards the door. Then, after what seemed an age, our host raised his hands as if blessing us for our tacit (and unanimous) acceptance of his offer. It also seemed to be a signal to EH to bring round the champagne and soon a buzz of animated conversation filled the room.

Since it appears to be at odds with my earlier antipathy, perhaps I should explain why I complied so readily with the prevailing mood. The explanation is simple: I was genuinely touched by what he said. I was, perhaps, the least receptive man in the room and yet I found it impossible to doubt the sincerity of his words. Indeed, they were so moving that some of my fellow members (GJ included) had tears in their eyes. Nevertheless, despite my more positive frame of mind, I'd hatched a plan that I fully intended to carry out.

After the address, our host and EH dissolved into the background and we were left to chat informally for about an hour. There was excitement in the air and the noise level in that little turret room became quite deafening. Then, as the clock struck nine, there was a sudden lull and EH reappeared with his drinks tray. I noticed that, amidst the glasses, there was a small wooden box which reminded me that we had reached a critical point in the proceedings, He gave each man a glass of champagne followed by a sugar cube (I'm not sure what else to call it). Each time he watched for a moment, like a nurse ensuring the patient has taken his medicine, before moving on. It was interesting to note that, this time, GJ appeared to swallow without hesitation and showed no immediate signs of excusing himself from the room. I, on the other hand, was ready to take the role of abstainer in his place. When my turn finally came, I placed the sugar cube in my mouth but manipulated it with my tongue so that it rested in the space between my lower teeth and the inside of my cheek. I meant to keep it securely contained there until EH had moved on and I could discreetly transfer it into my handkerchief. At least that was my intention until I met his eyes which were pale blue – cornflower blue I think you would call it – and very piercing. Ridiculous as it might sound, I was suddenly convinced that he could read my mind, and, without further hesitation, I released the cube and meekly washed it down with a gulp of champagne. I must say I felt rather humiliated by the situation, but there was nothing I could do now except give way to the inevitable.

The experience was subtly different this time. Many of the weird images were the same but the colours were less vibrant and infused with melancholy. To use a musical analogy; it was as if a tune had switched from a major to a minor key. Also, I was more conscious of external events than before because I could hear a droning voice in the background and I distinctly remember holding someone under water (disturbingly, I'm fairly sure it was GJ this time) and being conscious of desperate fear and resistance.

Once again, I've arrived home with little recollection of driving here and, once more, I'm in a troubled frame of mind. In part this is because I'm angry with myself for allowing my resolve to be broken so easily but mainly it is because of concern for my friend. Was he really struggling? Was he frightened? If so, was I to blame? I simply don't know; I'm not even certain that it was him at all. Despite the lateness of the hour, I have a strong urge to contact him, but it is impossible because I have neither his home address nor his home telephone number.

Saturday 7*th* May 1921

Re-reading my last entry I feel rather ashamed. Despite having expressed such anxiety about the wellbeing of my friend, I subsequently made no attempt to contact him; either the next day or at any time during the four weeks thereafter. The truth is that, when I awoke the following morning, I could dismiss those troublesome images as if they'd been no more than a bad dream.

That isn't to say that I didn't think about it at all, but I contented myself with the thought that, if anything serious had happened, I would certainly hear something soon. I kept half an eye on the local newspapers but, I must confess; that is as far as my enquiries extended.

But, as if in vindication of my nonchalance, when I arrived at this evening's meeting, I found GJ already happily ensconced in the turret room, enjoying a glass of champagne and seemingly none the worse for wear. I hoped there might be an opportunity to take him to one side to find out if my impression of previous events had been correct, but it never presented itself.

Beyond that, there is little to report about this gathering without risk of repeating myself. I had already decided that I would play along for the time-being. To be truthful, I still rather suspected that I'd been rumbled by EH last time and I wanted to put paid to any lingering suspicions. Anyway, I knew that the 30th October meeting would be the much-vaunted celebration of the rare second new moon in a lunar month, the Black Moon, and I had set my sights on that (for now at least, comfortably far distant) date on which to forego the mystery potion and see for myself what was going on - provided my resolve held out of course.

We drank more superb champagne; our host talked about the new moon again (he was relatively prosaic this time); EH dispensed the sugar cubes and we submitted to that strange dreamlike state which, despite its indescribable vibrancy and clarity, is, now, almost familiar territory. There were the same watery images; the looming swan's head and the impression of someone being immersed (though I have no idea who it was this time). Throughout it all I was aware of a murmuring voice, like a distant incantation.

Arriving home, I had none of the misgivings I experienced on the last occasion and now, as I bring this entry to a close, I am more at peace about my involvement in the Black Moon Society than I have been at any time since I embarked on this adventure.

It has only been three months but, somehow, it feels much longer.

The train had now drawn to a halt at Colwall Station. Dennis looked up and peered out of the window at the empty, dimly lit platform. No-one joined the train, and no-one alighted from it either. A gentle exhalation of steam from the resting engine, two coaches in front of him, somehow made the place seem emptier than if there had been no sound at all. He returned his attention to the journal, scanning the next five entries to see if anything of note stood out. They were all short – no more than two or three brief paragraphs – and he had a strong sense that Harry would to be treading water until the 30th October entry, the one that promised to be the most intriguing of all.

Generally, his feeling proved to be right: the June, July, September and the first of the October entries were largely innocuous repetitions of a well-established pattern. But the entry for Wednesday 3rd August was unusual because it began with an account of an afternoon business meeting Harry had had with the occupants of Symbiosis House.

Wednesday 3rd August 1921

Our host has installed new weathervanes on the roof of his house. I noticed them glinting in the afternoon sunshine as my Oxford bullnose struggled up the steep drive. It was three o'clock in the afternoon and I was on my way to discuss a small business matter at the request of our host and his associate, EH. This was the first of two visits today because I was due to return for a meeting of the Black Moon Society this evening. I remember the old weathervanes as being functional and rather dull affairs, but their replacements are very striking indeed. They are the brightest gold in appearance and are crowned by an abstract symbol, best described as a large, inverted equilateral triangle.

Both EH and our host came out of the front door to greet me as I brought the Bullnose to a squeaky halt. Their manner was subtly different from usual in that they were cordial but plainly focused on the matter in hand and not inclined to refer in any way to our other association. They seemed rather unexceptional for a change: just two well-heeled professional men attending to the maintenance of their property. Consequently, I felt myself relax and immediately realised how keyed up I must have been about meeting them like this. Of course, I have met them under similar circumstances before (when I took on the drainage project for them) but that seems to belong to another age; the time before I joined their strange, and seemingly life-changing, little group. It did strike me, however, that the singular design of new weathervanes was intended to make a symbolic statement of some kind; one that echoed the arcane imagery our host often referred to during his lengthy and spellbinding discourses. In fact, now I come to think of it, I'm almost certain that an inverted triangle is one of the alchemy symbols representing water – I must remember to look this up later in my encyclopaedia. Today though, as I said before, the brisk manner of the two men, left one in no doubt that we were here to discuss practicalities and nothing else. Even when I praised the aesthetic qualities of the new weathervanes, our host made no reference to their significance or what they might represent but simply remarked on the technical challenges that mounting them on the high roofs had presented.

Indeed, it was these very issues that had prompted our host to summon me this afternoon. It seems that the men who positioned them had reported a large crack running down one of the turret walls. On further investigation, it had become clear that the same crack extended down the front wall of the house; all the way to ground level. Naturally our host and EH were concerned that this might indicate major structural problems – possibly subsidence attributable to the drainage problems they'd had before. Apparently, the weathervane contractors had readily confessed to having little in the way of expertise regarding this sort of thing, hence the decision to call me in.

I followed EH and our host across the gravel to a position where they could show me a distinct crack descending from the eastern turret. They stood before me, pointing up at various sections of the wall to show the extent of the damage. As they did so, I was able to observe them more carefully than I have ever done before. Our host is a fair-haired, clean-shaven man of medium height, in his mid-forties. Although his English is impeccable, I can detect a faint Germanic undertone which betrays his origins. It is generally known locally (although he has never spoken about himself in my presence) that he was born in Austria and that he attended the same seat of learning as Sigmund Freud – though not, I think, at the same time. Indeed, I am aware (and GJ has confirmed this) that, like Freud, he is a psychiatrist by profession and was previously employed as such at Powick, our local mental asylum.

EH is a fine-boned, acetic-looking man with very short, brown hair. He wears a pair of tiny, gold-rimmed spectacles with thick lenses that have the effect of magnifying his remarkable pale blue eyes. I would estimate that he is around the same age as our host, but it is difficult to be sure because his smooth complexion gives him a boyish appearance – albeit a rather earnest and severe type of boy. His speech matches his appearance in that he tends to restrict himself to the briefest of utterances delivered in clipped, monotonous phrases.

I examined the wall carefully, noting that the crack did indeed appear to reach down into the foundations. I told them that I would have to bring in some men and equipment to reach a more considered verdict, but that damage to the structure of the house, caused by subsidence, was certainly a distinct possibility. I qualified my verdict by saying that I thought it highly unlikely that the problem had anything to do with the issue I'd worked on before. He raised his eyebrows slightly at this point, no doubt suspecting I was only saying that to protect my reputation.

Nevertheless, he stated that he was happy to accept my professional opinion and asked if I had any other theories about what might have caused the problem. I said there were two possible explanations: quarrying and tunnelling. All around the Malvern Hills there is evidence of quarrying: much of it the result of Victorian builders extracting stone to satisfy the huge demand for construction materials when the town became a centre for the water cure. I said that I would need to consult my map to see if there had ever been quarries close by where blasting might have caused damage to the surrounding bedrock and thus affected the foundations of the house. Similar disturbances might be a long-term legacy from when the Victorian railway tunnel was cut through the hills. Although it does not pass directly beneath the house, it is sufficiently close to be a possible culprit. Another (and possibly even more likely) cause could be test drillings for the proposed new tunnel. The original one has become rather unstable and is long overdue for replacement.

Our host questioned me further about the properties of Malvern stone and the locations of the various quarries in the area. He was particularly fascinated to hear about the deep lakes that had formed in some of the abandoned Victorian workings. He confessed to knowing little about the local geography and said he was keen to plan some walks so that he could familiarise himself with some of the places that illustrated Malvern's more recent history. I told him a little of what I knew about the old quarry workings in the area and said that I would be very happy to look out some detailed maps if they were of interest to him.

He went on to ask me if I knew anything about a spring – once used for bottling the water – inside the Victorian railway tunnel. I confirmed that I did know of this feature and told him that it had been discovered back in 1853 during construction. I said it was my understanding that there was a small pumping station in the tunnel that contained a boiler and steam engine that pumped water from the spring into a tank above. He nodded and said that the reason he'd mentioned it was because he'd already had some tentative discussions with CP (a fellow Black Moon Society member who is in the wines and spirits trade) about the possibility of reviving it as a commercial enterprise.

I should point out (though I am sure it will be eminently clear from what I have written) that this long and involved conversation was conducted solely between me and our host. Although EH was always present, he was utterly silent throughout: his expression blank; his pale blue eyes cool and impassive.

Finally, returning to the business that had brought me there, I said that I would bring two of my most reliable men over within the week so that we could take a closer look at the damage and recommend some possible remedies. After that, apart from exchanging brief courtesies (including the lightest possible handshake from EH), we concluded our meeting and I walked back to my car. When I glanced back, our host and EH had already gone back into the house and I heard a click as the front door closed softly behind them.

There was a shrill whistle blast from back down the platform as an unseen guard signalled that they were ready to proceed and then the carriages began to creak and groan as the train edged forward. Billows of steam tumbled past the window and, after a few slow, laborious thrusts from the pistons; the engine began to find its rhythm. Ominously, the lamps in the compartment briefly flickered and dimmed before becoming steady again. It reminded Dennis that they were about to enter the tunnel and he realised that he was holding his breath, convinced that the electricity was going to cut out. Then, just as he'd started to relax again the train braked sharply and squeaked to a halt.

The engine hissed and wheezed and an image came into his mind of a wild animal coming to rest on the threshold of danger: an immense yet benign creature taking stock of its surroundings and listening warily for sounds of any potential predators that might be lurking out in the darkness.

The lamps flickered again, and he appreciated fully, for the first time, how the prospect of being plunged into total darkness, in the middle of the tunnel, would have filled Harry Parsons – a man who was prone to nervous, and evidently life-threatening, palpitations – with dread.

Rather than start on the next part of the journal, he sat back and reflected on some of what he'd learnt so far. Firstly, despite Harry's coy use of the phrase "our host" and the initials he had used for everyone else, the identities of all the key players were obvious: CP was Charles Powell; GJ was Greville Jobson; EH was Emery Harcourt and "our host" was obviously Mathias Friedman himself. Secondly, it was fascinating to learn of Greville Jobson's disdain for Friedman's oratory - what he'd described as his "spurious pontificating" and it begged the question; why the need for long speeches and all the other pseudo ritual elements, culminating in the forced immersion of one of the members? What hidden motive lay behind it all? The thought made him shiver and, despite the warmth of the compartment, he pulled his jacket more tightly around him.

The carriages creaked and then, as abruptly as it had stopped, the train lurched forward, quickly gathering speed; the noise level increasing to a roar as they entered the tunnel under the hills.

As the train rattled on, Dennis started reading the next entry in Harry's journal, but he was barely halfway through the first paragraph when the lights started flickering again. And then they went out completely.

CHAPTER 22

Pivotal Revelations

Friday 29th March 1957

9.10 p.m.

After what had seemed like an eternity, the train emerged from the tunnel again. The noise was now more bearable and through the window he could see the lights of houses strung out along the lower slopes of the hills.

They began to slow for Malvern Wells and then, after a few tentative flickers, the lamps in the compartment came back on again. Dennis gave a sigh of relief and sank back into his seat as the train pulled into the station. A solitary passenger - a tall man, wearing a trilby and a long overcoat - alighted onto the platform, slamming the door behind him. After taking a few steps towards the exit, he turned on his heels and marched back towards the rear of the train. Moments later, Dennis heard raised voices above the hiss of the resting locomotive. He couldn't make out what was being said but guessed that the guard was being taken to task for the electrical failure. After a few seconds the man appeared again and went out through the station with a renewed spring in his step. Dennis smiled as he watched him go, thinking how much Harry Parsons would have approved of what had just happened.

It was a quarter past nine by the station clock as Dennis made his way across the footbridge at Great Malvern. As he descended the stairs to the other platform, he realised he was still clutching Harry's journal. He dropped it into the tartan shopping bag he was holding with his other hand and made his way down the platform and out into the car park to retrieve the Triumph Tiger.

There was a damp mist in the air, some of which seemed to have seeped into the old motorbike's temperamental engine and made it reluctant to fire up. It took about ten kicks on the starter pedal and more than twice as many curses and expletives before the Tiger finally spluttered into life. Dennis rode off along Manby Road. He was planning to make one of his rare, unannounced, visits to Margaret's house and he was hoping against hope that this wouldn't turn out to be one of the times she'd gone off to bed early with a cup of cocoa and a good book. She hated being disturbed if she'd decided to do that.

But, as he wheeled the Tiger up the front path of 23, St James' Road, he was relieved to see that the light in the lounge was on and the curtains were still open. He considered knocking on the window as he passed but stopped himself just in time: an unexpected figure, looming up out of the darkness was the last thing Margaret needed at this time of night. He propped his motorbike up next to the dustbin at the side of the house and retrieved the tartan bag from the pannier before knocking cautiously on the front door. He could hear that Margaret had the wireless on and going by the urgency of the voices it sounded as if she was listening to a particularly stirring radio drama. He waited for about thirty seconds and when there was no response he knocked again, more loudly. The wireless went silent and then he heard the flip and flop of slipper-clad feet as Margaret made her way along the hall's parquet floor.

'It's only me,' he called out.

There was a double clatter as two bolts were slid back, followed by the click of a latch and then the door opened. He couldn't see the expression on her face because she was silhouetted against the glare of the hallway light behind her but something in her demeanour suggested that she wasn't particularly pleased to see him.

'Sorry,' he said, to pre-empt the barbed greeting he sensed he was going to receive. 'Were you in the middle of listening to something?'

'Only the concluding episode of a detective series I've been following for the last three weeks, that's all.' She stood aside to let him in.

'Sorry,' he said again as he closed the front door behind him and followed her through to the front room.

'Don't keep apologising Dennis,' she said, gesturing him towards the settee on which he could tell, from the indented cushions at one end, she'd just been reclining. 'You don't really mean it.'

'I do,' he said as he sat down. 'I'd have left it until tomorrow if I'd known what you were doing.'

She smiled suddenly and said, 'That's all right, it wasn't that important really. I'd already worked out who'd done it by the end of the first episode. I had a feeling you'd turn up tonight anyway. In fact, to be honest, I'd have been rather disappointed if you hadn't. I've got a feeling what you've come to tell me is going to be a lot more interesting than some corny old radio play. Do you want a drink by the way or is that a stupid question?'

'It's a stupid question: I'll have whisky please.'

'Let me draw the curtains first. I was looking out at something earlier and I forgot to close them.'

She got up and went over to the bay window.

'Looking out at what?'

'There was an unusual looking car parked across the road, under the lamppost. It looked like something out of an American film: it was painted in two colours; dark at the top and light at the bottom and it had a big, shiny grille at the front. I waited to see if anyone got out because I was curious to see which of my neighbours had visitors with a car like that but, after a few seconds, the engine started, and it drove away.'

'Did you see who was inside?'

'No, of course not, it was dark. I could tell by the glow from their cigarettes that there were at least two of them though.'

'Interesting.'

'Why?' said Margaret, as she fiddled with the closed curtains to make sure she hadn't left a gap. 'Have you seen it somewhere too? I wouldn't be surprised if you had, it's pretty distinctive.'

'*I* haven't, but both Judith and Julian have mentioned seeing something very similar, a Standard Vanguard, in two-tone silver and grey. Apparently, it belongs to a man called Clarry Franklin; brother of Percy Franklin, James' assistant.'

'That's odd, isn't it?' she said, turning to look at him again. 'Given what's been going on recently with James and everything.'

'It's food for thought, certainly. And speaking of James, the good news is that he's turned up at last. I saw him at Hereford Police Station, earlier this evening.'

'Good grief. How was he?'

'All right physically I think, but mentally he was in a

terrible state: withdrawn and completely uncommunicative. Apparently, he was dumped out of a Land Rover at the main entrance and had to be lifted up and helped inside.'

'Just hold it there a minute Dennis,' said Margaret, raising her hand in a "stop" gesture. 'I think we need that drink before you go any further.'

She went over to the sideboard and poured two large tumblers of whisky. She brought them back and sat down next to him. 'Cheers,' she said as they clinked their glasses together. 'Now you can continue.'

'There's not a great deal more to say. They called in a doctor to try and get some sense out of him and when he didn't get anywhere, I suggested they contact Dr Gajak at Powick.'

'What did they think about that?'

'The doctor thought it was an excellent idea. He said he'd telephone Dr Gajak straightaway to make the arrangements. I wouldn't be surprised if James is on his way to Powick as we speak.'

'What about Susan? Has anyone let her know?'

'Susan wasn't even aware he'd disappeared, so maybe it's better for her to stay in blissful ignorance while he's being sorted out. Anyway, we haven't got any contact details for her, just a vague reference to a friend in Droitwich.'

'I suppose you're right,' said Margaret, sipping her drink. 'So, what other momentous revelations have you got for me? I thought you'd gone over to Hereford to see this Harry Parsons character; how was it that you ended up in the police station?'

She listened with rapt attention as he told her everything that had happened since he'd set off that morning, only stopping him once so that she could go and top up their glasses.

'It's incredible,' she exclaimed, after he'd finished.

'I know,' said Dennis. 'And I haven't even got on to Harry Parsons' journal yet.'

'It's almost too much to take in.'

'That's why I came straight here after I got off the train. I knew if there was anyone who could help me see the wood for the trees, it would be you.'

'And you were missing me as well, I expect' she said with a chuckle.

'Of course,' said Dennis, shuffling uncomfortably.

She laughed again as she kicked off her slippers and reclined into the cushions at the end of the settee, putting her feet up so that they were now resting against his thigh. 'It doesn't take much to embarrass you, does it?' she said, prodding him with her toe.

'After a couple of whiskies, you'd be an embarrassment to anyone.'

'But at least I can see the wood for the trees. That's what you said, wasn't it?'

'I did, so prove it, what do you see?'

'A litany of deception.'

'Meaning what exactly?'

'We've got a drug den masquerading as an astronomy club; an old man hiding his guilty secrets in a locked drawer; a senior policeman at the centre of a web of corruption; an estate agent and a detective inspector trying to escape from their pasts. Need I go on?'

'No, that's a good summary.'

'I'm not sure where it gets us though.'

'Maybe we should take one of your examples and try teasing out a bit more detail.'

'All right, which one do you want to go for?'

'What about Goodall's web of corruption and the way he's using it to pressurise people and distort the truth about the body at Symbiosis House? I think he's known about Morel being buried there all along. In fact, I wouldn't be surprised if was responsible for putting him there in the first place.'

'You think he murdered him?'

'Not personally, but he could easily have arranged for someone else to do it.'

'But why for goodness sake?'

'Because he saw him as a degenerate.'

'That's hardly grounds for murder though, is it?'

'It might be for someone like Goodall.'

'No, it would have to have been something more specific than that.'

'Perhaps he was worried about Morel exposing him, like he was with Dan Yeats.'

'Who was Dan Yeats?'

'He worked at Hereford with Sergeant Bowen; he was a police sergeant too. He'd transferred there from Malvern to escape Goodall's clutches. Apparently, he used to rant on all the time about how Goodall had got everyone under his thumb, including the top brass, so he could do whatever he liked, without fear of retribution. He was particularly annoyed about the way the Laurent Morel business had been handled; he couldn't understand how something as potentially serious as that could be closed down locally without any intervention from on high. He concluded that Goodall must be part of a big conspiracy.'

'Did he say what sort of conspiracy?'

'He might have done but it seems that everyone had stopped paying attention by then because they thought he was becoming obsessive. It was only later that Bowen started thinking there might be something in it but, by then, Dan Yeats was dead.'

'Good grief, what happened?'

'He was doing point duty one day and he was knocked over and killed by a car.'

'You mean a hit and run?' she said, staring at him wide-eyed. 'The same way Dad was killed.'

'Yes,' said Dennis, shocked to see that all the colour had drained from her face. 'Sorry, I probably shouldn't have told you that.'

'Don't be ridiculous, I'm not a child. Obviously, you had to tell me if that's what happened.'

'I could have been a bit more tactful about it though. Anyway, I'm sure it's just a coincidence.'

'No, you're not. I can tell by the look on your face that you think Goodall had Dan Yates knocked over on purpose to silence him, and you think what happened to Dad was the same sort of thing. That's the truth, isn't it?'

'All right it is, but I haven't got an ounce of evidence to prove any of it.'

'You still should have said though.'

'And risk upsetting you for the sake of a crazy theory? There wouldn't be much sense in that, would there?'

'Crazy or not, you have to tell me these things so that I can make up my own mind about them. I'm a lot tougher than you think and I certainly don't need *you* to act as my protector.'

She held his gaze for a few seconds, before continuing.

'So, assuming you're right about all this, who do you think was behind Dad's, so-called, accident? It couldn't have been Goodall because he'd have been too young."

'I'm guessing it was Mathias Friedman. I think your father had either broken, or was planning to break, the vow of secrecy all Black Moon Society members had been made to swear.'

'And you think this is what Charles' note was about?'

'Yes, I think that Greville was planning to speak out about something he'd witnessed at a meeting and my father was warning him against it. The only thing is though, the warning never reached him. My father obviously changed his mind and locked the note away in his desk.'

'Why would he do that?'

'Maybe Greville spoke out before he could send it. Either that or Friedman had worked out what Greville was up to and had already taken steps to stop him.

'Arranged the hit and run, you mean?'

'That's what it looks like to me.'

'So, have you got any other evidence for this, apart from your father's note?'

'There are some interesting sections in Harry Parsons' journal that shed more light on things.'

'Why haven't I seen them then?' exclaimed Margaret. 'Is this another of your misguided attempts to protect me?'

'Not at all. I haven't finished them myself yet either. I was only about halfway through when the lights on the train conked out.'

'In which case, we need to pick up where you left off,

don't we?'

He nodded and reached for the tartan shopping bag which he'd dropped onto the floor, next to the settee, when he'd first sat down. He pulled out the slim blue notebook and handed it to her.

'You can read as far as I got on your own - that's up to and including the third of August. After that, we'll read it together, is that all right?

She nodded.

'Just up to the third of August remember,' he said, wagging his finger. 'No looking ahead without me.'

'We'll have to see about that,' she said, winking at him as she opened the journal at the first page.

While she was reading, he tested himself to see how much of it he could recall from memory. It turned out to be quite a lot and he found himself anticipating when she'd emit a little gasp or shake her head because of a particularly striking revelation. He guessed that the section that would have the greatest effect on her would be where Harry described his conversation he'd had with her father. He was right because, when she reached it, her eyes moistened, and she pulled a hanky from the sleeve of her cardigan. She glanced at him before proceeding but said nothing.

As she read on, he found his mind racing back to the first entry in the journal and realised that there was something there he needed to check.

'It's made me feel quite strange,' said Margaret, when she'd finished reading. 'Especially the references to Dad. They ought to make me feel closer to him, but they have completely the opposite effect because the world he's immersed in is so alien to me.'

'I know, it feels alien to me as well.'

'Shall we see what happened next then?'

'There's something I'd like to check first. Can you find that paragraph at the beginning of the first entry, where Harry lists the men in attendance?'

'Where he uses their initials, you mean?' She turned back through the notebook and ran her finger down the page. 'Yes, here we are, shall I read it out?'

'Go on.'

"There were eight guests including myself: AF, a dealer in antiques; AG and NC, two police officers; GJ, a schoolmaster; JM who runs a fleet of lorries and charabancs; HF, his business partner and CP who is in the wine and spirits trade."

'All right,' said Dennis, 'we know that GJ is Greville Jobson and CP is Charles Powell. I don't know who JM and HF are, but I reckon AF is Alfie Franklin; father of Percy and Clarry Franklin.'

'So, what about AG and NC, the two police officers?'

'I'm not sure about NC but I'm wondering if the G in AG stands for Goodall. It could be Superintendent Goodall's father.'

'It's certainly worth checking. It shouldn't be too hard to find out if there was an A Goodall serving with Malvern Police, during the early 1920s.'

'And while we're at it, we might be able to find NC as well.'

'Maybe it's the father of that nasty Sergeant Collins you spoke to.'

'Of course, C for Collins. You could be right.'

'Different generation, same affiliation.'

She yawned and glanced at her watch.

'Have you had enough?' said Dennis. 'Do you want to go to bed?'

'Without reading the rest of this, you mean?' she said, holding up the journal. 'Don't be ridiculous, how could you even suggest such a thing?'

'I just thought…'

'Thought what? That I'd obligingly toddle off to bed so that you could read it on your own?'

'Sorry. The thing is, I'm used to doing this sort of thing on my own: it's a hard habit to break.'

'Well, the more you try, the easier it will become.'

Without further ado, she turned to where she'd previously left off and started to read aloud.

Monday 31 October 1921

It is half past one in the morning, and I am at my wits end about what to do. Logically, I suppose I should telephone the police and explain what has happened, but I'm afraid that they would either arrest me straightaway or dismiss me as a madman. And maybe they'd be right; maybe I really have gone mad. I suppose I should just note down the facts, as accurately as possible, try to get some sleep and reappraise the situation in the cold light of dawn. As matters stand, I can't think of any other option.

Initially, tonight's (or now I suppose I should say last night's) meeting was the same as all the others and certainly gave no indication of turning into the "special celebration" we'd been promised. All the same, I was determined to complete the mission I'd attempted once before, certain that, this time, my resolve wouldn't fail me.

When the time came, I accepted my dose and - as on the previous occasion – I positioned it between my teeth and the side of my mouth before taking the customary gulp of champagne. I'm proud to report that my determination sustained me well because, as soon as EH's gimlet eyes met mine, I managed to contrive an expression of such innocence that he soon turned away and moved on to the next man. As the others succumbed to the potion's effects and their eyes became glazed, I gave every impression of being similarly affected.

After a while, we began to file down the winding staircase.

As we moved into a passageway beyond the entrance hall, I nearly collided with the man in front because the procession had come to an abrupt halt. I realised that the trap door entrance to the cellar room must be acting as a bottle-neck to slow our progress. Sure enough, as we shuffled forward again, I saw our host's assistant standing next to a square opening in the floor, guiding each of my befuddled associates on his first step into the void beneath.

We had ended up in a place, already somewhat familiar to me from GJ's description: an egg-shaped chamber carved out of solid rock. Light from a single bulb (perhaps twenty feet above) glinted off rough-hewn walls that were glossy with dampness. The spiral staircase we'd come down from the trap-door, ended on a mezzanine platform from which a set of wooden steps provided access to the floor of the cave where we were gathered. Oddly, our host was currently nowhere to be seen. I'd assumed that he'd led the way down here with EH, but it appeared that he must have peeled off somewhere else, en-route.

At this point, there was a hiatus in proceedings which might have felt awkward if my fellow members had been conscious enough to take any notice. It seemed as if we were waiting for something to happen and it plainly depended upon the arrival of our missing host. Sure enough, a few minutes later, he appeared on the mezzanine above us, but he wasn't alone. There was another man with him who seemed familiar, but who, for the moment, I couldn't quite place. Our host ushered him to go first, down the wooden staircase, into the body of the chamber. Once there, they both took up positions in front of the water spout, alongside our host's assistant, and then the main proceedings began.

Our host began to talk about the black moon in a strangely soporific tone which I realised I'd last heard (as though through cotton wool) in a drug-induced trance. I immediately understood what GJ had meant by "whimsical mythologizing." This was the language of a man addressing what he knew (or thought!) was a stupefied audience. Coherence of words and meaning no longer mattered; suggestion and a certain timbre were now the order of the day. A load of mumbo-jumbo would be a more prosaic way of describing it.

I stopped listening and started to study the newcomer. He was stooped, white-haired and wore a double-breasted suit that was far too big for him. His shrunken and world-weary demeanour was at odds with what I saw in his eyes. For one thing, their sheer clarity made it obvious that he had not partaken of the mystery potion, but they also spoke of a shrewd mind, trying to make sense of the bizarre situation he found himself in. I still couldn't place him though. However, I had a vague idea that, not so long ago, I'd seen a photograph of him in the newspaper, linking him to some ancient local scandal but that was as far as I got.

Our host's voice suddenly became sharper, making me pay attention to his words again. He began to speak of lifting a veil to shed light on past wrongs; of life destroyed through greed, vanity and deception; of base recrimination purified and transformed through an act of atonement. He could easily have been talking about the lunar cycle, alchemy and all his usual themes but I knew, with chilling certainty that this was different and that, contrary to my earlier doubts, the "special ceremony" was finally underway.

My fellow members stepped forward as one and, for a split second, I couldn't tell why. Then I realised that somehow, they knew that it was time to push the newcomer's head down into the brimming stone trough. I quickly joined in so as not to expose myself.

As soon as I pressed my hand down on the back of the man's head, I knew that something was dreadfully wrong. I felt his animal fear like an electric shock, as if every muscle, fibre and cell in his body was screaming in terror. I felt like screaming myself because, although every ounce of my humanity was imploring me to stop what I was doing, I was paralysed by an overwhelming desire to protect myself. I looked around, desperately searching for signs of the same distress reflected in the faces of my companions but I could only see vacant expressions.

Then, just as I thought I felt the man's body go limp; I was pushed backwards as everyone moved away from the water trough as if they were responding to yet another invisible signal. Before I knew it, I was being jostled up the steps to the mezzanine; on up the spiral staircase and through the trap door. All the time, I was trying to look back to see what was happening, but my view was always obscured by the man behind.

How I managed to endure the rest of the evening I do not know because my mind was in turmoil and I had a desperate urge to leave that place as soon as possible. Nevertheless, I somehow managed to grit my teeth and replicate the gradual return to consciousness that I observed in those around me. Our host and EH (watchful as ever) returned to the turret room with us as if nothing had happened. At midnight, I drank the customary glass of Scotch as quickly as I dared. I was not inclined to talk to anyone but, from the conversations I overheard, I could tell they were all oblivious to the hideous tableau in which we'd all played our parts.

How different everything would feel if I shared their blissful ignorance but there is nothing to be gained from going down that road. So, as I conclude my account, let me express myself without ambiguity:

I am of the firm belief that, tonight (last night), I participated in a cold-blooded murder.

There, I cannot state it more plainly that. As I said at the start, now I can only wait and see how it all looks in the cold light of dawn

CHAPTER 23

Who's Out There?

Friday 29th March 1957

10.45 p.m.

'How awful,' exclaimed Margaret. 'That has to be the most disturbing thing I've ever read.'

'I agree,' said Dennis. 'It's sent shivers down the back of my neck. But don't stop there, I want to hear what happened next.'

'But I thought you realised, there isn't any more. The rest of it's completely blank.'

She handed it over so that he could see for himself.

'How strange,' he said, flicking through the empty pages. 'I just assumed it carried on. I wonder why he gave up.'

'He was too shocked I expect.'

'But why didn't he tell me all this while we were on the train? Why insist I make the trip to Hereford to pick up the journal?'

'Because he'd only just worked out there might be a link between the body at Symbiosis House and what happened in the chamber all those years before. He wasn't sure what to say about it.'

'In case he incriminated himself?'

'Possibly.'

'What a twisted business it is.'

'But it wasn't of Harry's making was it? It was Friedman and that shadowy assistant of his, Emery Harcourt. Which begs the question, if they were so intent on murdering someone, why choose to go about it in such a convoluted way?'

'Maybe because they were trying to make a point.'

'What sort of point?'

'I'm not sure. I just get the feeling that all the ingredients: the drugs; the trickery; the dramatic setting; the pretentious speechifying are meant to tell us something.'

'*Us?*'

'Not us in particular, I just mean a wider audience.'

'But why?'

'As I said, I'm not sure yet.'

'It gets murkier and murkier.'

'You're right, it does. And the only reason we know about it at all is because of this.' He waved the notebook in the air before placing it on the floor beside him. 'Which might explain why certain people are so keen to stop it falling into the wrong hands.'

'What are you talking about?'

'The burglary at Harry's house.'

'You think that was to do with the journal?'

'Yes, one of the neighbours saw a man going in through the back door, twenty minutes before I arrived; a man with a pronounced limp. I reckon it was Percy Franklin.'

'That's a big assumption, isn't it? There are probably lots of men around who walk with a limp, especially ex-soldiers.'

'I'm sure you're right, but not every ex-soldier has a direct connection with Harry Parsons, does he?'

'I don't follow you.'

'We know from the journal that Percy's father, Superintendent Goodall's father and Harry were all members of the Black Moon Society.'

'But we're only guessing that from the initials, we don't know it for certain.'

'It still seems pretty likely though.'

'But what's it got to do with Percy breaking into Harry's house?'

'I think Goodall got wind of the fact that Harry was about to hand over the journal to me and he sent Percy over to get it before that happened.'

'Why would he do that?'

''Because he's got a reputation to protect and he's afraid that any information about the dubious activities his father was involved in could tarnish it.'

'You're only guessing that though.'

'I know, but I bet I'm not far wide of the mark.'

'So how do you reckon he found out about it?'

'From one of his informers I expect. I'm sure they're everywhere.'

'Maybe one of them overheard you and Harry talking on the train.'

'I shouldn't think so. We were in a compartment on our own, with the door shut.'

'Is there anyone else you've mentioned it to?'

'Only you… oh and Julian of course.'

'There's your answer then, Julian must have told someone.'

'No, I specifically asked him not to.'

'Ah, but can he be trusted?'

'Yes,' said Dennis firmly. 'We chat all the time; we've been doing it for years. I'm certain he'd never pass anything on if he knew it was sensitive for some reason.'

'Where were you anyway? In the office or in the pub?'

'In the office.'

'So one of the other reporters must have overheard you.'

'Impossible, the office was deserted apart from us…'

He thought for a moment.

'I did mislay the bag of notebooks for a while though – I didn't tell you, did I? It could have something to do with that I suppose.'

'No, you *didn't* tell me. When did this happen?'

He explained how, in his haste to avoid Jeff, he'd left the bag of notebooks in the library and how, later, it had mysteriously reappeared on his desk at the office.

'And it definitely wasn't Jeff who brought them back?' she asked after he'd finished.

'No, because according to Julian he was really annoyed when he saw the tartan shopping bag on my desk; he thought it made the place look untidy. He obviously hadn't got a clue what it was, or where it had come from.'

'It could have been Percy then, or another member of

Goodall's shadowy entourage. Either that or there's a perfectly innocent explanation and one of the library staff dropped it round.'

'I shouldn't think so.'

'Why not? Maybe we're imagining intrigue where there isn't any; maybe it *was* just a random burglary after all.'

'No, I'm certain it wasn't, and I know you'd be saying the same if you'd been there. It was a frenzied search for something specific: everything had been turned upside down and there were discarded books and papers everywhere. It definitely wasn't jewellery or silver candlesticks they were after - I doubt if Harry owned things like that anyway.'

'Harry obviously refused to say where the journal was.'

'Either that or his heart gave out before he succumbed to the pressure.'

'How much pressure would Percy have been prepared to apply; do you think?'

'As much as it took probably.'

Margaret shuddered.

'And now we're the ones holding onto the wretched thing.'

'You're worried he might come looking for it here?'

'Of course,' she said, shooting a nervous glance at the window. 'Aren't you? You said yourself that could have been his car parked out there earlier.'

'Even if it was, it's not there anymore.'

'Well it wasn't half an hour ago, but it might have come back for all we know.'

'Why don't you check then?'

She went over to the window, pulled the curtains open a crack and peered out.

'Are they there?' said Dennis.

'Not that I can see.' She pulled the curtains together again and came back to join him on the settee. 'It doesn't necessarily mean anything though; they might just have parked further up the road. I need to think about something else to take my mind off it: can you hand me the journal again please?'

He passed it over and she started flicking through the pages.'

'What are you looking for?' asked Dennis.

'Something Harry wrote in his final entry, where he tried to pin down where he'd seen the victim before. Here we are. She bent back the covers so that she could read the words more easily. He says, "*I had a vague idea that, not so long ago, I'd seen a photograph of him in the newspaper, linking him to some ancient local scandal but that was as far as I got…*"'

'What about it?'

'I wondered if he was referring to the death of that Austrian man at your grandfather's hotel you told me about.'

'That's a bit tenuous, isn't it?'

'I'm not so sure: how many other local scandals can you name from the last sixty years or so?'

'It depends on your definition of scandal I suppose. In my experience, it's pretty loose where newspapers are concerned.'

'The business at the St Werstan Spa keeps coming up though doesn't it? Every time the place goes up for sale there's a report in the Gazette about how people think it's cursed and ridiculous things like that. Harry probably saw one of those reports with a picture of your grandfather next to it. The picture stayed with him, but the details of the story faded to the back of his mind.'

Dennis frowned as he considered the implications of what she'd said.

'So you're suggesting that the man Harry recognised – the murder victim - could have been my grandfather, Henry Powell?'

'I suppose I am, yes.'

'I wonder…' he said thoughtfully.

'Just remind me exactly what happened,' said Margaret.

He half closed his eyes in concentration before replying.

'In 1889 my grandfather, persuaded an Austrian hotelier called Oktav Baader to come to Malvern and sign up for a regime of water cures to ease his asthma. It was basically a publicity stunt because Baader came from Gräfenberg, the birthplace of hydropathy so it was quite a coup to lure him over to Malvern. Unfortunately, Baader died during one of the treatments and the hotel was forced to close down because of the ensuing scandal.'

He fixed Margaret with an excited stare as an idea struck him.

'I think Friedman and Baader were related.'

'What makes you say that?'

'Because it would explain why Friedman had Henry in his sights: He held him responsible for the death of a member of his family.'

'You think Baader was an uncle or something?'

'He could have been I suppose, but I think for it to matter to him so much, the tie must have been much closer than that: I think Baader and Friedman were father and son.'

'But they had different surnames'

'I expect Friedman changed his name when he moved here. It would have been the obvious thing to do when you think about it: being called Baader would have been a give-away from the start.'

'So you think Friedman came to Malvern with the specific intention of avenging the death of his father?'

'Yes, I do.'

'There's a complication though.'

'What's that?'

'We're forgetting that Henry died from falling into the quarry, so he can't have been the Chamber Spout victim after all.'

'That's what it was made to look like, but there's nothing to say he couldn't have been drowned at Symbiosis House and dumped in the quarry afterwards.'

'Except the Coroner would have picked up on that, surely.'

'How though? The injuries would have looked much the same either way.'

'But even if you're right; why would Friedman make such a performance out of it? He could easily have had him bumped off quietly; why go in for all the drama and mumbo-jumbo?'

'Because he wanted to give Henry a taste of his own medicine.'

'What do you mean?'

'Henry's spurious water cure had killed his father, so he decided to invent something equally spurious as a means of exacting his revenge.'

'You think the Black Moon Society was a spoof on the water cure?'

'Yes, just as Henry persuaded clients to sign up for his quack spa treatments, Friedman recruited a group of susceptible individuals to participate in seemingly therapeutic, but ultimately worthless procedures, one of which ended in death. Now if that isn't making the punishment fit the crime, I don't know what is.'

'I must admit, the more we talk about it, the more plausible it becomes.'

She sat up with a jolt.

'How much of this is Charles aware of do you think?'

'Does he suspect he was involved in the murder of his father you mean? I suppose he might have an inkling, but how much of an inkling would depend on how well the drugs dulled his senses at the time. Whatever the case, I doubt if they blotted out everything, so I wouldn't be surprised if he's haunted by a few nasty thoughts. It would certainly explain those irascible moods of his, wouldn't it?'

'He might just have pretended to take his dose, of course, like Harry did.'

'No, I think he'll have done exactly as he was told, especially if he thought everyone else was doing the same. He might appear contrary on the surface, but underneath he's a dyed in the wool conformist: someone with a strong sense of duty, who obeys orders unquestioningly. According to Nigel, that's how he describes how he was in the army and I get the impression he's still like it at work now.'

'But I thought he was in charge. He's the warehouse

manager at Thomas Radford and Sons, isn't he?'

'Nominally he is, but it's an old established family firm so his actual power is pretty limited. He might make it sound as if he lords it over everybody, but he doesn't really.'

'So he's probably living with a constant nagging fear about what happened at the Black Moon Society. It must be like the sort of nightmare you wake up from where you know you've been scared witless, but you're not sure why.'

'That sounds about right. I don't know much about drugs, but it's pretty obvious they're going to play havoc with what you remember from when you were under their influence. Maybe you recall a few random fragments of what happened, but you never get to see the whole picture. You might even prefer *not* to see the whole picture.'

'That could be why he gets so touchy when you try getting him to talk about his past. He's frightened about what he might start to uncover if he starts delving into it too deeply. It might also explain why he was so desperate to get away from here in 1921 and why he was so resentful when your asthma problems got in the way of his plans.'

'I've been a thorn in his side for years,' said Dennis, stifling a sudden yawn. 'And now we're starting to find out why.'

'We should leave it there for now,' said Margaret, gulping down the remains of her whisky. 'It's gone midnight, so I suggest we try and get some sleep.'

'I don't suppose it'll be easy though with all this going around in our heads.'

'The whisky should help,' she said, holding up her empty glass. 'I usually sleep like a log after a couple of these.'

'Do you want me to stay?' said Dennis, as they got up, 'or would you rather I went back to the flat?'

'Stay if you like. Hopefully I'll be too comatose to notice one way or the other.' She turned off the light and led the way out into the hall and up the stairs.

She paused at the landing window and peered out.

'Goodness, what a clear night. I can see thousands of stars up there. It's not as clear as that very often.'

'It's partly because there's no moon, or at least none to speak of. It's early Saturday morning now, so tomorrow's Sunday, the thirtieth of March. According to Julian, that's when we're due for a rare second new moon of the month – a black moon.'

Margaret turned and looked back down the stairs at him. She was frowning.

'Is that your warped idea of a joke?'

'No, I'm serious. It might seem like an odd coincidence, but tomorrow night really *is* going to be a black moon.'

'I rather wish you hadn't told me that,' she said with a shiver.

'Why?'

'Because it feels like a sign.'

'A sign of what?'

The question was unnecessary because he already knew what she was going to say. He'd just had exactly the same thought himself.

'A sign that someone else is about to die.'

CHAPTER 24

An Encounter on the Hills

Saturday 30th March 1957

6.30 a.m.

Margaret was still sleeping soundly but Dennis had had a restless night and he knew there was no point staying in bed a moment longer. He gathered up his clothes in the darkness and moved as quietly as he could towards the bedroom door, intending to get dressed out on the landing. But just as he reached the point where the carpet gave way to bare boards, all his loose change fell out of his trouser pocket and clattered across the floor.

'What's happening?' cried out Margaret sitting bolt upright and turning on her bedside lamp.

'Sorry,' said Dennis. 'I was trying hard not to wake you but about ten shilling's worth of coppers has just let me down.'

'It's the second time this week your early morning wanderings have woken me up,' she protested. 'Where are you off to *now* for goodness sake?'

'I thought I'd go for a walk.'

'At this unearthly hour? What's got into you?'

'Nothing's got into me; I'm just fed up with lying there wide awake that's all.'

'For goodness sake, why don't you do the sensible thing and come back to bed for a bit longer.'

'No, I'm going out to get some fresh air and clear my head.'

'Where will you go?'

'Oh, just up the hill to St Ann's Well and back.'

'But it's still dark.'

'Not really. It's well past sunrise now, so there'll be plenty of light by the time I get outside.'

'Well I still think you're mad but as you seem so determined I won't try stopping you.'

'Why don't you come with me? You're wide awake now as well.'

'You must be joking. I'm nice and warm here so the idea of a chilly early morning walk in the damp and gloom doesn't appeal at all. I expect I'll doze for a bit and then I'll get up and make a cup of tea. If you're not back by eight, I'll take a stroll up to the College.'

'But it's Saturday, you've got the weekend off.'

'I know but I thought it would be a perfect opportunity to lock myself away in the Random Repository and take a proper look at Laurent Morel's papers.'

'Are you sure?'

'Completely sure.'

'But why don't we both go up on the Tiger later and bring the files back here.'

'Because there are at least three boxes of them - far too many to fit in your motorbike panniers – besides which, it's something I fancy doing on my own.'

'Well just be careful then.'

'Why do you say that? I'll be safely ensconced in a room at the college while you'll be roaming around the hills in semi-darkness. If anyone needs to be careful it's you.'

'Sorry, I'm feeling quite tense this morning; I didn't get much sleep.'

'Didn't you? I slept really well; so well in fact that I've woken up with a much more rational perspective on things.'

'So you think we got carried away last night, do you?'

'A bit I suppose. We also drank rather a lot of whisky which won't have helped.'

'Well nothing's changed for me.'

He glared at her defiantly.

'Don't be like that Dennis: I'm not dismissing any of what we said; I just think that, before we start jumping to conclusions, we need to nail down a few more facts.'

'But sometimes you just have to follow your instincts. That's what I do when I'm tracking down water features and it usually works pretty well.'

'I'm sure you're right, but that doesn't stop us being a bit more systematic as well, does it?'

'Systematic? How?'

'By breaking down our lines of enquiry so that we're clearer about what we're dealing with.'

'Go on then.'

'Well Mathias Friedman and the Black Moon Society is an obvious one. Then there's Harry's diary and why it might be of interest certain parties. Next, there's the body at Symbiosis House and what we think we know about that. And then there's James, but I'm not sure if he's part of this or not.'

'Oh I think he's part of it all right. There's his link to Percy Franklin for a start; that's pretty significant I'd say.'

'And didn't you say Crawford, Davies and Withers acted as agents for Symbiosis House?'

'Yes, there's another connection to add to the list.'

They fell into thoughtful silence. Then Margaret said, 'Well that gives you plenty to mull over while you're out on your walk, doesn't it? Provided you haven't changed your mind about going of course.'

'No I haven't; I'm just a bit worried about leaving you on your own, that's all.'

'Why?'

'In case we're being watched.'

'But last night you said there was nothing to worry about.'

'I know I did, but now I'm having second thoughts.'

'But even if they are, it's you they'll be after because of the journal.'

'Not if they think I've given it to you for safekeeping, to throw them off the scent.'

'Oh for goodness sake Dennis, this is exactly what happens when you lie awake, endlessly mulling over things, your imagination starts to run away with you. Just stop worrying and go for your walk. You'll feel much better after you've had some fresh air and exercise.'

'Maybe you're right.'

'I *know* I am.'

'There was one more thing though, and this isn't me worrying now, it's just another random piece of information that came back to me in the early hours of the morning. Did you know about Mathias Friedman's association with the Mitarbeit Trust; the charity that funded your father's memorial library?'

'No,' she said, looking more interested. 'What was that?'

'While I was looking through newspaper back-numbers yesterday, I came across a Gazette report, from March 1924, about that special opening ceremony you told me about. It listed all the people who were there, including you and your mother, the headmaster and various other dignitaries. Most interesting of all though, the last person on the list was Dr M. Friedman, representing the Mitarbeit Trust. According to the report, the Mitarbeit Trust was a charity dedicated to the furtherance of international understanding through science.'

'So the Greville Jobson Wing would have fitted the bill perfectly: no wonder they got involved.'

'I know, but here's the really interesting thing: what do you think the German word "mitarbeit" means in English?'

'I haven't got a clue.'

'Roughly it means co-operation or collaboration.'

'So what? A lot of charities have names like that.'

'But what does it remind you of?'

She thought for a moment.

'Symbiosis,' she said. 'That means collaboration as well, doesn't it?'

'Exactly,' said Dennis, 'Technically, it describes two organisms living closely together to mutual advantage.'

'Which *is* interesting I agree, but all it tells us is that Friedman liked the idea of co-operation: that's hardly earth-shattering news, is it?'

'I suppose not, but for some reason, while I was lying awake earlier, it seemed strangely important. While I'm at it, here's something else that popped into my head at around the same time: in the second newspaper report about Morel's disappearance there was a reference to the Greville Jobson Wing; it said that Morel worked there during his time at the TRE, but I couldn't see the relevance because it didn't fit with the rest of the report at all. I got the impression it had been added later to make a point.'

'What point?'

'I don't know. I'm not quite sure why I'm telling you any of this at all really.'

They both sat quietly for a while, listening to the steady tick from the bedside alarm clock. It was Margaret who spoke again first.

'So, are you going out or not?'

'Yes,' replied Dennis, getting up. 'I'll try and be back here for eight. If I'm any later, I'll come straight round to the College.'

He paused in the doorway, intending to gather up his scattered coins, but then thought better of it and went out onto the landing to get dressed.

***

Halfway up the winding path to St Ann's Well Dennis paused to catch his breath. The sun was well up now and was bright enough to highlight the new buds on the trees all around him. He could hear the drone of a light aircraft overhead and sporadic traffic noise rose from the town below. The Priory was just visible through the screen of trees, its purplish tower dominating the haphazard mosaic of rooftops all around it. After five more minutes of climbing, he reached his destination. The well house itself was attached to a distinctive octagonal extension that had been built to greet the thousands of visitors who came to take the waters in the nineteenth century. Dennis' shoes clicked on the tiled floor inside the entrance; there was no-one else around. On the wall in front of him was a shell-shaped basin supported by a plinth. Water gushed into the basin from a stone spout in the shape of a dolphin's head. On the wall above the basin was a plaque proclaiming the message,

"Drink of this crystal fountain

And praise the loving Lord

Who from the rocky mountain

This living stream out-poured

Fit emblem of the holy fount

That flows from God's eternal

Mount

There was a chair in the corner, and he sat down and listened to the sound of water ringing on marble.

He'd been intending to reflect quietly on everything that had happened over the last two days, but instead he immediately fell into a deep sleep.

He was woken by the heavy clump of approaching footsteps. The thought that it might be someone coming after the journal set his heart racing. Seconds later a tall man in mud-caked clothing made his entrance, but it wasn't one of Goodall's henchmen as he'd feared, it was Andrew Morrigan.

Dennis looked up at him in bewilderment.

'Have you been following me?'

'Not following you exactly,' replied Morrigan. 'Our paths happened to cross, that's all, so I thought I'd come and have a word.'

He casually pulled a long knife from his overcoat pocket and held it at arm's length, turning it one way and then the other so that the light glinted on its blade. Then, without warning, he swung round and thrust it into the door-post where it stayed; embedded in the wood, quivering from the impact.

Turning back to look at Dennis, he said, 'you've been busy lately, haven't you?'

'What do you mean?'

'Oh, I think you know exactly what I mean: turning over stones; asking questions; generally getting up people's noses. As a man of the outdoors, I notice these things, and a lot more besides.'

He bowed his head to look at the front of his overcoat and brushed ineffectually at a patch of dried mud.

'The trouble with the outdoor life though,' he continued, 'is that you get covered in shit.' He cocked an eye at Dennis. 'I bet you can smell me from here, can't you?' Without waiting for an answer, he turned around and ducked his head under the water spout. When he stood up again his thick hair was slicked over his scalp like a hood. 'That's better,' he said. 'This is what all those Victorians used to pay good money for isn't it, the bloody water cure?'

With remarkable grace for such a big man, he sat down on the floor 'Best to be comfortable,' he said. 'I've got quite a tale to tell, so we'll be here some time. Let's start with our old friend James Crawford and see where we go from there...

Suddenly, the peace of the well house was shattered by the scream of a jet aircraft passing low over the hills and to Dennis' amazement, Morrigan instantly rolled over into a foetal position with his hands clasped protectively around the back of his neck.

After the noise had subsided he sat up again and leaned back against the marble plinth, breathing heavily as he struggled to regain his composure.

'Sorry,' he said eventually. 'For a minute there I could have sworn I was back in Burma, being strafed by a Kawanishi.'

He fixed his gaze on Dennis again. 'So, where was I? Oh yes, I was about to tell you about our mutual friend James Crawford. You found his Rover wrapped around a tree at Wynds Point, didn't you?'

Dennis nodded.

'Fortunately, I was nearby at the time and I heard the crash. I rushed there to find him slumped over the steering wheel, covered in blood. After I'd dragged him out and taken him somewhere safe, I went back to check the damage. At first, I thought I might be able to get the car started or, failing that, tow it out with my Land Rover and move it under cover but the bastard wasn't going anywhere.'

'You've got a Land Rover?' said Dennis.

'You needn't sound so surprised. Just because I look like this doesn't mean I haven't got the wherewithal to keep a vehicle on the road. Anyway, as I say, it didn't do me any good because the bonnet of James' Rover was embedded in the tree trunk and the engine was all mangled up. The only reason he wasn't killed by the impact is because those things are built like tanks, so the front end took all the punishment rather than him. Also, he had his briefcase on his lap, so that'll have acted like a cushion between him and the steering wheel. It wedged him in and stopped him flying through the windscreen as well.'

'He was lucky then.'

'That's how we see it, but I doubt if he'd agree.'

'Why not?'

'It's obvious, isn't it? He wanted to kill himself. That's why I dropped him off at the police station. I thought he'd be safer with the cops – well, the ones at Hereford anyway.'

'You thought he'd try again?'

'I knew he would. I did think about looking after him

myself but, as you might guess, I'm a bit limited on the hospitality front. The best I could come up with was a disused ice cream kiosk. There's quite a few of them dotted around the hills, all belonging to Thomas Radford and Sons. A few years ago, old Radford decided to diversify into the ice cream trade, but it turned out to be a bit of a flash in the pan and his new enterprise only lasted a couple of seasons. You'd think he'd have sold the kiosks or rented them out after that, but he just left them lying empty. The locks are a piece of cake, so I can get in whenever I like. The trouble is, I didn't think being cooped up in a wooden box was going to do much for James' mood, so rather than risk having it on my conscience that he'd topped himself, I decided to pass him on to the boys in blue. I knew he needed protecting from the others as well, of course, that was a big consideration.'

'Which others?' said Dennis, staring at him aghast.

'It's complicated,' replied Morrigan. 'It'll only make sense if I go back to the beginning.'

He shuffled backwards across the floor until he was leaning against the wall with his long legs pulled up against his chest.

'It all started in early 1940 when James enlisted in the Gloucestershire Regiment. He liked organising things, so he was put in charge of supplies. He's wasn't much good with people but that didn't matter because he was very efficient and as long as everyone got what they needed they didn't worry about him being a bit odd. In 1942 the Glosters got posted out to Burma and James found himself in an extremely uncomfortable place. For one thing the climate was foul, and for another, the Japanese soldiers were complete and utter bastards. It's wasn't where James wanted to be at all, but he had to put up with it like everyone else. And to be honest, compared to a lot of other people, he didn't have a lot to worry about because he was safely tucked up inside the fence most of the time. Unless a bomb landed on his tent or the Japs came storming through the gates, he wasn't in much danger at all – not physically anyway. His psychological wellbeing was a different matter altogether though. I don't know if you're aware of this, but James is particularly susceptible to the charms of good-looking young men and soon after he arrived in Burma he started having an intimate relationship with a particularly handsome Burmese government official. They tried to keep it discreet, but that's easier said than done when you're crammed together with a lot of other soldiers, in the middle of the jungle, as James soon found out to his cost.

'Now, there was a sergeant in the platoon called Leonard Robards who was a really nasty piece of work; the sort of bloke who makes it his mission to find someone else's weakness and then exploit it for all its worth. He saw what James was up to and he decided to make his life a misery. It soon got to the point where James couldn't do anything or go anywhere without Robards or one of his cronies being there to taunt him about his little peccadillo.

'James was desperate to get the man out of his hair but, at first, he couldn't think how? Then It occurred to him that out here in the jungle soldiers sometimes just went missing. Whenever it happened everyone assumed that it was just another poor devil who'd got separated from his platoon and been dragged off by the enemy, never to be seen again. James realised it was an assumption he might be able to use to his advantage. As I said, he was desperate and desperate times call for desperate measures.'

'How do you know all this?'

'Because I was there when he shot Robards in the side of the head. When the deed was done, we pushed the body over the side of a ravine and left the scavenging wildlife of the Burmese jungle to take care of the rest.'

'But why were you there?'

'Because James doesn't have the strongest of constitutions and it was obvious needed a bit of moral support.'

'So you're an accessory to murder.'

'I suppose I am, but Robards was an evil bastard, he got

what was coming to him, we were all agreed on that.'

'*All?*' Are you saying others were involved?'

'Just the one, a man called Percy Franklin: I expect you know him.'

'The man with the limp? James' assistant at Crawford, Davies and Withers?'

'The very same.'

'So, how did he come to be involved? How did either of you come to be involved for that matter? Did James ask you?'

'He didn't *need* to ask us: we could see what was happening with our own eyes. We just went to him and offered our services; it was as simple as that.'

'But why shoot him? Couldn't you have simply warned him off instead?'

'You can't warn off someone like Robards, he'd just laugh in your face and carry on as before. Anyway, different rules apply in a shithole like Burma because you know that everything outside the perimeter fence, is ready to kill you: the enemy; the climate; the wild animals; all the nasty diseases. The last thing you need is someone on the inside - someone who's supposed to be your comrade - turning the only refuge you've got into a living hell. You're in a situation where you need to be absolutely certain you're amongst friends and if anyone threatens that, you've got to act quickly and decisively to stop them. It might be rough justice but, in the end, it's a question of survival.'

'So, you and Percy saw what was going on and offered to help.'

'That's right, but we were both acting on our own volition: we approached him separately. I barely knew Percy before that. I hadn't had much contact with James either, apart from going to fetch supplies from the stores and coming away thinking what an odd bugger he was. It was only discovering that we came from the same town that made me notice them at all really. Percy and James obviously had history though because ever since we'd arrived in Burma they'd seemed to be joined at the hip. I assumed they were old pals from school or something, even though it was hard to imagine James being pals with anyone. As time went on though, I began to notice that they didn't really get on at all; it was just that, for some obscure reason of his own, Percy had decided to stay close. Then I noticed Percy was forever saying stupid things to James, just to goad him. Most of the time it didn't work, but occasionally he'd provoke him into shouting back or banging his fist on the table, which always got a laugh from the other men because it was so out of character. Percy was quite a gambler, so I wouldn't be surprised if he'd been having a sneaky bet with them about how James would react.

'Anyway, the long and the short of it is that Percy got to him first and had somehow managed to come up with a Nambu pistol, salvaged from a dead Jap soldier, and some spare ammunition. He hadn't got much of a plan beyond that, so I think he was quite glad when I came along to fill in the details. To be honest, I don't think he was particularly bothered about the practical side of things, he was more interested in seeing how James would respond to the challenge. That's what he's like you see, a schemer through and through.'

'So, how *did* James respond to the challenge?'

'Pretty well as it turned out. I'd come up with the idea of telling Robards that a few of the men had got hold of some crates of beer and were planning an impromptu party at a safe, but discreet, location somewhere along the road between the compound and the town. I hinted that a few local women might be involved as well, so there was no stopping him after that. I offered to take him to the rendezvous point on the back of a motorbike I'd acquired for the evening. Of course, the only people waiting when we got there were Percy and James. Robards smelt a rat immediately but Percy and I had him pinned to the ground and we were screaming at James to do the business with the pistol. I thought he was going to chicken out at the last minute, but then there was a bang and Robards was a goner. The rest I've already told you.

'A few months later though, James got malaria so badly that he was very nearly a goner as well. Eventually he was shipped back here. When he got better he went back to work at Crawford, Davies and Withers and got married to your sister. I expect you remember that bit, don't you?'

'Vividly,' replied Dennis. 'I also remember Percy gracing us with his presence.'

'With a leg full of shrapnel. He was sent back on the boat, a few months after James, only to turn up at the wedding like a bad penny. But you'd know more about that than I do, you were there, whereas I was still languishing out in that shitty jungle.'

'James certainly didn't look very pleased to see him from where I was sitting.'

'Not surprising really, is it? The man who knows all your darkest secrets, walking back into your life again on the very day you're trying to put the past behind you by getting married.'

'You think James saw him as a threat?'

'Of course he did: James might be many things, but he's not stupid. He knows full well that Percy could blow the gaff at any time; that's one of the reasons he's teetering on the brink as we speak.'

'Surely, by revealing what happened, Percy would have as much to lose as James.'

'No,' said Morrigan, shaking his head, 'not by a long chalk. Killing Robards wouldn't have troubled him one little bit. He's a gambler remember, so he'll have calculated that the chances of it coming back to haunt him are very low indeed. It's all about attitude in the end: Percy's a rough diamond who couldn't care less who knows it, while James is a walking deception. He plays the part of a strait-laced, model citizen, while underneath he's anything but.'

'So, what's Percy's real game then? He's not just out for

amusement, is he?'

Morrigan got up without answering and went to the entrance. He gripped each side of the door frame and leaned out, peering one way and then the other.

'I need to be moving on soon,' he said, turning back to look at Dennis.

'You think the police will track you down here and arrest you?'

'Being arrested is the least of my worries,' replied Morrigan, slumping down on the floor again.

'Why, what else would they do?'

'Don't pretend you're that naïve. You know exactly what they'd do.'

'You think they're planning to harm you?'

'Give me strength,' exclaimed Morrigan. 'Do I actually have to spell it out? I think they're planning to *kill* me.'

CHAPTER 25

A Higher Vantage Point

Saturday 30th March 1957

7.30 a.m.

'How's it looking?' asked Dennis.

'There's no-one out there at the moment,' replied Morrigan. 'I reckon I'll be safe enough for a little while yet.'

'You can't possibly be sure though; we're surrounded by trees.'

'Oh I'm sure all right. You get a second sense about that sort of thing when you live the way I do. Anyway, I can't go yet; I haven't finished telling you about James.'

'There's more is there?'

'There's lots more.'

Morrigan leaned back against the marble plinth before continuing.

'Basically,' he said, 'after the wedding was over, James had to face up to the fact that he had a big problem. His old partner in crime had come back to haunt him and was obviously here to stay, so what was he to do? After a bit of thought he decided to make Percy his assistant, which was quite clever in a way because at least it meant he could keep an eye on him. Of course, it meant that Percy could keep an eye on him too, but James probably tried not to think about that.

'He set about establishing himself as the reliable husband and pillar of the community. He bought a big, black Rover that he drove around the area, showing people expensive houses and doing inventories of country estates that were coming up for auction. He looked after some swanky rental properties as well: letting them out when he could and organising their upkeep when they were lying empty. One of them was Symbiosis House.

'Crawford, Davies and Withers had been agents for the place for three years, so once James had settled back into work again, it was somewhere he'd drive out to from time to time to check that the lawns had been mowed and the paintwork was being kept in good order. Then, halfway through 1943, the Ministry got in touch and said they were requisitioning it as a technical training centre.

'Once Symbiosis House had been taken over there was less need for him to visit because the military had their own ways of doing things and they didn't really want him poking around unless something serious needed attending to. Being James though, he couldn't keep away. At first, it was simply because he thought the place would go to rack and ruin if he didn't show his face at least once a week, but later it was all because of Laurent Morel.'

'James knew Laurent Morel?' exclaimed Dennis, staring at him aghast.

'He certainly did,' said Morrigan, smiling with obvious satisfaction at the reaction he'd triggered. 'He knew him very well indeed.'

'Do you mean...?'

'Do I mean he knew him in the romantic sense?' Morrigan interrupted. 'If you'll just bear with me for a moment, I'll get on to that.

Morel's main job was up at the TRE, but like a few of the other scientists there, he spent part of his time teaching the wireless techs at Symbiosis House. It just so happens that I was there when he and James first met because I'd been called in to sort out a problem with the plumbing. As I rolled up in my Land Rover I saw James standing outside the front door, deep in conversation with a tall man in an expensive looking overcoat. Something about him – the style of his coat I think – told me he was one of the émigré French scientists I'd heard about. I could also tell that this was no ordinary encounter because of the way James was standing; head to one side, peering up at his new friend as if he was the most interesting person he'd ever met.

'And so, in answer to your previous question, within weeks of their first meeting, James and Morel were having a fully-fledged affair. This time though, there was no Sergeant Robards around to make their lives a misery and James must have learned a trick or two about discretion since he'd got back from Burma because, as far as I'm aware, no-one, apart from me and Percy Franklin, knew what was going on.

'And so it continued, through to the end of the war, and beyond. The training centre closed down in 1947, but James was still agent for the place, of course, so it provided a convenient hideaway for them. I'd see them together from time to time when I went up there to do odd jobs, and as far as I could tell they were getting on very well indeed. Unfortunately though, in the Autumn of 1948, everything changed.'

Morrigan paused, plainly expecting a response.

'What happened?' asked Dennis, obligingly.

'James got jealous.'

'Presumably because Morel had started seeing someone else.'

'You'd have thought so from the way he reacted, but, as it happens, it was a professional dalliance rather than a romantic one. Morel was spending most of his time working on a particularly absorbing project and James felt neglected.'

'What sort of project?'

'A miniaturised signalling system, designed to transmit and receive messages over long distances, using apparatus that could be carried in a briefcase.'

'Astrred,' said Dennis, under his breath.

'What was that?'

'Astrred,' he repeated. 'My friend Margaret found some of Morel's papers in a storeroom attached to the College library and they describe the same sort of thing. There was a single code word on every page: Astrred, spelt A-S-T-R-R-E-D.'

'It's an anagram of red star.'

Dennis mentally shuffled the letters around.

'So it is,' he said. 'Why didn't I see that before?'

'Not many people would.'

'How come you saw it then?'

'Partly because I do a lot of crosswords and partly because of what James did next.'

'What was that?'

'In order to get back at Morel for his so-called neglect, James accused him of plotting to sell secrets to the Soviet Union. The red star is a Soviet symbol of course.'

'Good grief, how did he come up with that?'

'I expect Percy suggested it to him.'

'Why?'

'Presumably because it suited his purpose – or somebody's purpose anyway. Tell me what else was in those papers you found?'

'Papers?' said Dennis, momentarily thrown by the change of tack. 'Oh yes, I was telling you about Astrred wasn't I? Well, they were hard to understand really, but there were a lot of diagrams that made it look as if Morel's apparatus was designed to beam signals up into space. It sounds like science fiction, but…'

He suddenly remembered something. He reached into the pocket of his jacket and pulled out the folded copy of the Daily Express he'd written notes on during his train journey to Ledbury. He spread it out on the floor and pointed at the headline.

"Red Peril! Are the Soviets preparing to launch their first satellite into space?"

'What do you make of that?'

Morrigan shuffled forward to take a closer look.

'Interesting,' he said when he'd finished reading.

'I wondered if there might be a connection between this and what Morel was working on, but maybe I'm barking up the wrong tree.'

'I don't think you are,' said Morrigan, leaning back against the plinth. 'In fact, I'm sure you aren't. But you'll need to hear the rest of the story before you see why. Where had I got to?'

'You told me James had accused Morel of selling secrets to the Soviets.'

'That's right. Well after that, all hell let loose. Morel decided to fight fire with fire. He said he was going spill the beans about their relationship and make sure James' carefully cultivated, upright reputation was well and truly blown to smithereens.'

'The same thing he was worried about in Burma.'

'Yes, except James had no-one to blame but himself this time and he knew it. He'd just about managed to keep himself together with Robards, but with Morel he crumbled straightaway. He'd been seriously ill of course, so he had no resilience left at all. The next thing I knew, Percy Franklin had tracked me down to discuss what needed to be done. Not that there was much discussion really because he'd had already worked most of it out. He said James was well beyond being able to make any decisions for himself, so we'd have to steer him forward as best we could. It was Friday the 27th of November when he came to see me. He said Morel needed to be disposed of as quickly as possible and he suggested we did it three days later, on the night of Monday the 30th. He reckoned there'd be a new moon then, so we'd have the cover of darkness. We'd use Percy's twin brother Clarry's car, which Clarry would drive. He'd also be there to provide extra muscle if we needed it. Percy's plan was to intercept Morel after he'd left the

TRE and was on his way back to his digs in Barnards Green. Over the weekend, I was to go and dig a pit in the garden of Symbiosis House. He'd identified a good secluded spot inside a hedged off area to the front of the property, where he knew I'd done some gardening work before. He said not to worry about the weapon because he'd managed to acquire just the right tool for the job: a Nagant revolver, complete with silencer.'

'So you *did* kill Morel,' said Dennis, staring at him aghast.

'I played my part in killing him yes, just like I did with Robards. It was nothing like the newspaper's saying though: there weren't any drunken fisticuffs; thanks to Percy, it was a lot more efficient than that.'

He glanced towards the door before continuing.

'Anyway, on the 30th of November, at around 10.30 in the evening, we were parked in Clarry's flash Standard Vanguard, halfway along Barnards Green Road and waiting for Morel to appear. Percy knew he always worked late, and he'd followed him home a few times to check his route. Sure enough, he came past at twenty-five to eleven and Percy rolled down his window to ask him for a light. He fumbled in his pocket and found some matches and Percy offered him a swig from his hip flask in return, which he gladly took. Percy said we could take him the rest of the way if he wanted, but Morel said it wasn't that far, so there was no need. Then he started yawning because of the Mickey Finn Percy had slipped in the whisky and said, on second thoughts, perhaps he'd accept that lift after all. He got in the back of the car and we drove off straightaway. It was only then that he realised James had been there, next to me, all the time. He started to protest and made a half-hearted attempt to open the door, but by then it was too late. He keeled over as the drug finally took effect and the next thing we knew; he was sleeping like a baby.

'Once we'd pulled up at the front of Symbiosis House, Percy, Clarry and I got out and dragged Morel out of the car. Percy slipped some sort of hood over his head and then we frog-marched him over to the hedged off section of the front lawn with James following behind. As soon as we got there, Percy went and lit a paraffin lamp I'd left there before on his instructions, while Clarry and I kept hold of Morel next to the pit. He'd flopped down into a kneeling position and he'd have slumped over completely if I hadn't been clinging onto his arm. Percy gave James a nudge which was the signal for him to pull the revolver from his belt. He didn't respond at first and I heard Percy hissing at him impatiently. Seconds later, there was a muffled shot and Morel folded up on himself and rolled straight into the pit.'

'That's awful.' exclaimed Dennis. 'Pitiless and cold-blooded, like an execution.'

'It's no different from what happened in Burma.'

'Not in practical terms maybe, but it *feels* completely different: far crueller somehow.

'Actually,' said Morrigan with a sigh, 'I agree.'

'But I thought…'

'You thought I took it in my stride, the way I did with Robards, but no. As soon as we started shovelling soil back into the grave, I realised I'd made a terrible mistake.'

'How?'

'By assuming that the two killings were equally justified when they obviously weren't: Robards was pure evil and got his just desserts, but Morel was different. All Morel had done was come out fighting because he'd been backed into corner, the same as anyone would. He didn't deserve to die for that.'

'So why go along with it in the first place then?'

'Because I was duped. I was drinking heavily then, so everything was a blur. Percy knew that, and he used it to his advantage. He made me think we were protecting James, the same way we had in Burma. I just went along with him because he seemed to have worked everything out and I was too befuddled to question any of it.'

'But now that's changed?'

'Completely. That's why I dug up the body and raised the

alarm. I decided it was about time people learned the truth about why Morel was killed.'

'And why *was* he killed.'

'I think it was to do with the signalling device. He gave it James to look after to stop it falling into the wrong hands - this was before things went sour between them obviously. He must have known by then what a poisonous commodity it had become. It was in the briefcase James had with him when he crashed the car. He was pretty agitated about carrying it around, so later I went and hid it under the floor of the ice cream kiosk at the top of the Beacon.'

'What does it look like?'

'It's made up of two halves: two metal cylinders screwed together to make a single unit, about three feet long. There's a glass lens at one end and some electrical connectors at the other that must be for linking it up to a power supply; a car battery probably. He said, before that, he'd been keeping it hidden inside the long case clock in his office.'

'That'll be the one Miss Collingford, his secretary, told me about. She reckoned he always made sure he came in and wound it up, by noon each Thursday, at the latest. Except this week he didn't.'

'Because he'd already been in, early on Wednesday morning to pick up the device. He said he was worried that news about the body would stir up old memories

'Whose memories? Did he say?'

'No, he just kept rambling on about needing to keep it close so that it didn't fall into the wrong hands.'

'Why not leave it where it was? No-one would think of looking inside a clock.'

'Percy would though; he watches James like a hawk."

'If that's the case, why hadn't he already taken it.'

'Why bother? He assumed it would still be there when the

time came. Unfortunately, he hadn't reckoned on James panicking before it did.'

'When the time came for what?'

'For the device to prove its worth.'

'And when would that be?'

'When the man in charge said so.'

'Who's that?'

'Who do *you* think it is?'

'Superintendent Goodall. It's clear from everything I've seen that he's been running a corrupt operation for years now. And he seems to have a whole network of crooks, including Percy and various police officers, working with him. Presumably that's why you're in fear of your life now: Goodall knows you've got information that could blow his set-up wide open, so he's got his henchmen on your tail, with instructions to silence you once and for all. Am I right?'

'Up to a point you are. Goodall's important all right, but nothing like as important as he'd like to make you think.'

'So you're saying he gets his orders from someone else? Someone higher up the tree?'

'Yes, and funnily enough it's the same person you get your orders from - Jeff Stephenson.'

'No,' said Dennis, shaking his head in protest. 'You must have got that wrong, it can't be.'

'I'm telling you for a fact, it is.'

'But Jeff's the editor of a local newspaper, not some criminal mastermind.'

'He hasn't always been in newspapers though, has he?'

'No, he used to run the technical training centre at Symbiosis House, I'm well aware of that.'

'The same technical training centre that Morel taught at.'

'But that was during the war: people did all sorts of things then. As soon as it was over, they just went back to their normal lives.'

'And so did Jeff,' said Morrigan. 'Except his idea of a normal life was a bit more colourful than most. Take the society he set up at Cambridge for example.'

'What society?'

'IMPACT, International Movement of Physicists Acting in Comradeship and Trust. I'm sure I don't need to tell you what that was all about.'

'Physicists from different countries sharing ideas presumably.'

'That's right, but the country Jeff Stephenson was *most* interested in sharing ideas with was the Soviet Union. A lot of people wondered about how far his idea of sharing went, especially as he was also a leading light in the university Communist Society.'

'How do you know all this?'

'Because I've spoken to people who were there; who were at Cambridge with him.'

'Which people?'

'People I was at school with; other Old Malvernians.'

'You went to Malvern College? exclaimed Dennis.

'You needn't sound so surprised.'

'Sorry, it's just that...'

'Just that you're wondering how an Old Malvernian could have ended up as a drunken odd-job man, of no fixed abode.'

'I suppose so yes, but then you're probably wondering how someone as diffident as me ever ended up as a local newspaper reporter.'

'Never judge a book by its cover,' said Morrigan. 'That seems to be an appropriate adage all round, doesn't it? Anyway, as I was saying, a couple of people I was at school with were at Cambridge with Jeff Stephenson and they both remember him being a committed communist who was always getting on his soap box to say how scientific advancement should never be constrained by ideological differences.'

'Was he like that at school as well?

'I couldn't tell you. He was two years above me, so I didn't see that much of him. He was a big one for the horses though, I do remember that much. He organised illicit sweepstakes in the dorms, which nearly got him expelled. He also spent a lot of time at the races. I don't know how he got away with it, but somehow, he did. And it was through going to all those race meetings he got involved with Percy Franklin.'

'I heard about that a couple of days ago. Percy still acts as his personal bookie, apparently.'

'There you are then, now you see what I mean by a colourful life. There's a lot more to Jeff Stephenson than meets the eye.'

'I always saw him as a bit of a dark horse, but it never occurred to me that he could be involved in anything as serious as this.'

'He's more than *involved*; he's running the whole show.'

'So you're saying he collaborated with Morel to build the Astrred signalling device?

'Yes, he'd been wanting to develop something like it for a while. He needed it to be compatible with the satellite system his chums in the USSR were working on, but he didn't have quite enough technical know-how to pull it off on his own. Then Morel came along with all the scientific brilliance he could ever have wished for and lo, Astrred was born. Unfortunately though, he and Morel were about ten years ahead of the game, so the device had to be mothballed until the Soviet scientists had caught up with them. In the meantime Morel got cold feet so he gave the prototype to James for safekeeping. He also threatened to blow the gaff on the whole enterprise which would explain why he had to be killed. Jeff didn't mind James holding onto the device because, thanks to Percy, he knew he'd always be able to lay his hands on it when the time came. But then, three days ago, James decided to remove it from its hiding place, just as news started coming through that the USSR was finally about to launch a satellite. From that point onwards, he was a marked man.'

'Like you.'

'Exactly,' said Morrigan, getting to his feet. 'But only because I was reckless enough to dig up Morel's body. Before that I think they just saw me as an eccentric itinerant with a drink problem. They knew that I'd been involved around the margins, but they probably thought I was too far gone to be threat to them anymore. Digging up the body changed all that though and now, just like James, I'm a marked man. Frankly, it's a wonder they haven't picked me off already.'

He went to the door and peered out again.

'Still no-one around as far as I can see,' he said, looking back into the room. 'So now I've told you everything, I might as well be off.'

'And what are you expecting me to do now?'

'I'm not expecting you to do anything. I just wanted you to know what I know; in case anything happens to me.'

'Where are you heading for?'

'The ice cream kiosk at the top of the Beacon. I need to pick up the signalling device and find a better hiding place for it.'

'Why?'

'Because someone's bound to put two and two together at some point and work out that an abandoned ice cream kiosk is just the sort of place I'd use.'

'I'd better come with you then?'

'No, I'll be exposed enough as it is. Two of us would stand out like a sore thumb.'

'But I could help find a new hiding place. I'm freer to move around than you are so it gives me more scope to find somewhere really secure. Also, if I get involved, it might throw them off the scent for a while.'

Morrigan frowned as he weighed up the idea.

Then he said, 'You might have a point there I suppose. I'm still not happy about us going up together though. You'd better give me five minutes head start and then follow on behind. Just walk normally and try not to draw attention to yourself.'

He turned and pulled his knife out of the doorpost where he'd embedded it earlier and strode off without another word.

Dennis checked his watch: it was now ten past eight. He got up, went over to the door and gazed out. Regardless of Morrigan's talk of a "second sense", he thought it would be impossible to tell if anyone was watching and waiting, somewhere out in the surrounding woodland. Effectively, the big, dishevelled man had stepped out on a wing and a prayer - or maybe he was past caring anyway.

He looked at his watch again. It was still only twelve minutes past, but he estimated that, by now, Morrigan would have moved beyond the tree line onto the open hill and that enough of a gap would have opened up between them to make it safe to set off.

He followed the path around the side of the well house and then upwards through the woods. Leafless branches rattled overhead in the breeze and cawing birds provided a mournful chorus in the background. Soon he was out in the open too. He could see the summit of the Beacon far above and the mottled ridge of the Malverns extending to the north and the south on either side. There was no sign of Morrigan, and he assumed he must have rounded a bend in the spiralling path, taking him around to the far side of the hill. Dennis continued climbing between rocky outcrops and clumps of gorse before pausing for breath and wiping his brow with the back of his hand. He was high enough now to be able to see the town below and the chequered expanse of the Severn Plain beyond.

Then, as he started climbing again, he caught sight of Morrigan disappearing over a ridge which from this angle looked like the top of the hill, but which he knew from past experience was an optical illusion; a false summit. He reached the same point himself ten minutes later, and now he could see that the other man really was within striking distance of the Beacon's rocky pinnacle.

At last, breathless and dripping with sweat, it was Dennis' turn to scramble up the final precipitous section. As soon as he stepped up onto the highest point, he was almost blown backwards by a violent gust of wind from the south west. He steadied himself and checked his surroundings. Straight ahead he could see the squat cylindrical shape of the toposcope with its circular map showing walkers all the landmarks that might be glimpsed from this panoramic viewing point on a clear day. Over to his right, in a slight dip, he could see the grey, corrugated roof of the café and a little further on, set slightly apart, a flimsy looking timber building that he guessed was the abandoned ice cream kiosk.

Although the sun was shining, it was bitterly cold in the wind and this appeared to have deterred anyone, apart from him and Morrigan from attempting the climb to the summit today. The café was completely boarded up and presumably wouldn't open again until Easter.

Dennis clambered across the uneven rocks and along a narrow path to the rear of the café which was sheltered from the wind and consequently much quieter. He took the opportunity to call out to Morrigan, to let him know he was nearly there, but there was no answer. Reaching the other end, he was blown sideways again and just ahead he could see that the ice cream kiosk door was swinging on its hinges, crashing wildly against the side wall. He darted over and grabbed the door mid-swing so that he could look inside. As his eyes adjusted to the dimness, he saw a large, chest shaped ice cream refrigerator and a cash register on one side and a counter, running the full length of a shuttered serving hatch, on the other. Stretched out along the strip of floor in between was the body of Andrew Morrigan, with a horrific wound to the side of his head; a dark, oozing crater of blood and splintered bone.

Dennis recoiled, staggered, retching and gasping, away from the door and was promptly sick on the shingly ground between some rocks. He wiped his mouth and made his way back to the kiosk, looking nervously around him as he went. His heart was thumping and, despite the freezing wind, sweat was pouring down his face and back. He was desperately fighting an impulse to flee down the hill and seek help from the first person he found but he knew that first he had to confirm that Morrigan really was dead. Not that he believed for a moment that there was any doubt given the obvious severity of the injury.

He stepped back into the timber-scented darkness of the kiosk and sidled along the thin strip of floor between the refrigerator and the body. He choked back another surge of nausea as he took in the glistening pool of blood that had formed around Morrigan's head and he paused to steady himself, gripping the edge of the refrigerator behind him with both hands. The wind whistled through cracks in the shutters and the door continued to bang relentlessly against the side wall. He lowered himself onto his haunches and lifted Morrigan's right arm, pressing hard against the wrist to find a pulse. He couldn't feel anything at all but, just to make sure, he rested his hand on the big man's back, trying to detect a rise and fall that would show he was breathing, but again, there was nothing.

Then, above the background noise of the wind and the banging door, came what sounded like the rumble of a car engine. For a moment he thought he'd imagined it because the idea of a car being all the way up here seemed ridiculous. But then it occurred to him that they regularly used a Land Rover to bring supplies to the café. The ruts in the track he'd followed from St Ann's Well were testament to that. Naturally, Morrigan's assailants would have brought a vehicle too; otherwise how would they have been able to remove the body?

He suddenly realised he only had seconds to make his escape, but where could he go? He took hold of the clattering door and cautiously peered out. The only option he could think of was to take refuge behind the café in the hope that that Morrigan's killers would come around from the front.

He ran the short distance between the kiosk and the café,

ducked into the shadows and looked back. Seconds later, two men emerged from around the corner to his right. They were both wearing police uniforms. One had a coil of rope over his shoulder and the other was carrying what appeared to be a folded green tarpaulin. Under normal circumstances he would have found the uniforms reassuring, but logic told him that, far from being the friendly face of the law, these were Superintendent Goodall's henchmen, Sergeant Collins and Inspector Bates.

Despite being buffeted by the wind, the two men proceeded purposefully over to the kiosk and went straight inside. Dennis kept his eyes fixed on the door which continued to flap wildly backwards and forwards. Minutes passed and then one of the men came out, followed closely by the other. Between them they were carrying a long, green, rope-secured bundle, resembling an Egyptian mummy, which was plainly the trussed-up corpse of Andrew Morrigan.

They disappeared around the corner of the building, the way they'd come, and it wasn't long until Dennis, once again, discerned the rumble of an engine which briefly got louder and then faded away until the roar of the wind and the clattering of the kiosk door were the only sounds remaining.

He dashed over to the kiosk again and looked inside. He wasn't sure why, but he felt the need to make sure that what he thought he'd just observed had really happened. Unsurprisingly, the only sign that Morrigan's body had ever been there was the dark patch of blood near where his bludgeoned head had lain, and even that was now starting to dry up and blend in with various other stains on the scuffed wooden floor.

There was something else though; something he couldn't have seen before because it would have been hidden by Morrigan's bulky torso: a hole where two of the floorboards had been removed and within which the briefcase containing the signalling device must once have been stowed. He knelt and reached inside, hoping against hope that the briefcase would still be there. Predictably, however, it was long gone.

Back outside, he found a slight dip from which he could take in the wider view without making his presence too obvious. For some reason he assumed they'd be driving down to St Ann's Well and would soon come into view as the track brought them round to the north east side of the hill. However, after waiting two or three minutes and seeing nothing, he realised he was wrong and that they must have gone the other way. He turned around just in time to catch a glint of sun on glass as the vehicle rounded a hairpin bend to the south east, just below Summer Hill.

He watched the olive-green Land Rover as it bounced along the track and then turned back on itself around another hairpin, onto the next level down. It performed the same manoeuvre twice more, bringing it ever closer to the point where it seemed it would join the main road, at Lower Wyche. But then, just short of what Dennis estimated was going to be its final turn, the vehicle came to an abrupt halt. For a moment he thought it must have stalled or one of its tyres had burst, but then, with a jolt, it occurred to him that it hadn't stopped there by accident at all: it had stopped there because it was just above Earnslaw Quarry and that was where they were planning to dump Andrew Morrigan's body.

Hoping the two men would be too engrossed in their task to look up, he set off down the hill. Because he was on foot he was able to take a straight diagonal line, cutting across the different levels of the winding track the Land Rover had been forced to follow and reducing the distance to the top of the quarry by two thirds at least. It was perilously steep though and twice he lost his footing; sliding two or three yards over coarse grass on the seat of his trousers. As far as possible - and without deviating too much from the direct route - he used the cover of gorse bushes and the occasional rocky outcrop to protect himself from view.

Within less than five minutes, he reached a point just above the length of track where the Land Rover was parked. He hid behind a bush and peered out. The rear section of the vehicle had a canvass canopy and plainly this was where Morrigan's body had been stowed.

Bates and Collins – he remained in little doubt about their identities – were still sitting in the cab, having an animated conversation. He listened hard but their voices, though raised, were too muffled for him to make out what they were saying.

Eventually, the heated exchange seemed to run out of steam and the two men got out and went around to the back of the vehicle. They opened the tailgate and dragged their swaddled cargo towards them. As soon as it was three quarters of the way out, one of them seized it at shoulder level while the other kept hold of the feet. They paused for a couple of seconds as if getting used to the weight and then they carried the body off through a belt of trees that separated the track from the top of the quarry.

Dennis stepped cautiously out from his hiding place, scrambled down a precipitous bank and crossed the track. Once he'd reached the trees he held back and strained to detect any tell-tail sounds that would help him work out where the men were. Then, he was shocked to hear the crack of a stick underfoot, close by and he quickly took cover behind a thick clump of gorse; squatting down low to make himself as small as possible. Seconds later, one of the men passed within feet of him, seemingly returning to the Land Rover to fetch something. Soon there was a creak as the vehicle's door was pulled open, followed closely by a bang as it was slammed shut again. The man – he guessed it was Sergeant Collins doing his Inspector's donkey work – trudged back the way he'd come, and this time he was carrying a long knife that looked suspiciously like the one Andrew Morrigan had thrust into the doorpost at St Ann's Well. After waiting a few seconds for Collins to get ahead, Dennis came out from hiding and cautiously set off in the same direction. The belt of trees was no more than twenty yards across, so it wasn't long until he saw open sky ahead which told him he was nearing the edge of the quarry. Pausing again he heard voices nearby. He crept closer, conscious that if he could hear them, they would certainly be able to hear him if he put a foot out of place. And then, suddenly, there they were, about five yards in front of him: two crouching figures partially obscured by a screen of saplings; busily unwrapping Morrigan's cocooned body. One of them was using the knife to cut through sections of rope while the other concentrated on pulling the newly loosened tarpaulin apart. Dennis kept his head down and watched as the dead man's bulky, mud and blood-stained frame was revealed.

He edged closer and took up position behind a tree stump which he was just able to peer over if he stood up on his toes. By now, Bates and Collins were on their feet, gazing down at the corpse – now standing out starkly against its green backdrop - as if contemplating a singularly perplexing work of art. The freed tarpaulin flapped in the breeze and one corner of it was lapping over the side of the quarry. Then, without further ceremony, the two policemen bent over and rolled Morrigan's body into the void.

CHAPTER 26

Closing In

Saturday 30th March 1957

8.45 a.m.

As soon as Morrigan's body had dropped away into the quarry, the two policemen started folding up the tarpaulin and gathering together the strands of rope. Dennis knew that within minutes they'd be ready to go back to the Land Rover and that he'd be in danger of being discovered if he didn't act quickly. He had two options: to stay put and hope he could keep the tree stump between him and whichever path they took through the trees; or make a run for it while they were still focused on what they were doing.

He decided to run and at first it seemed he'd made the right choice, but then as he emerged from the band of trees, he heard shouting behind him and glancing back he saw two dark figures in hot pursuit. They were still about thirty yards away but closing on him steadily. Breathless now, he turned left, down the track. He didn't know this part of the hills particularly well and he soon realised he'd underestimated how much the circuitous route around the quarry added to the distance to the main road. Then, from behind, he heard an engine roar into life, and he knew it wouldn't be long before they came speeding down the hill to run him down. He needed to get off the track and up into the woods before they spotted him.

He scrambled up the steep bank, grabbing hold of clumps of undergrowth and exposed tree roots to stop himself from slipping backwards. The roar of the engine quickly grew louder, and he just managed to take cover behind the trunk of a huge oak tree before the Land Rover reached the point where he'd left the track. It travelled on for a few yards and then there was a raucous squeak as the brakes were applied, followed by a grating of gears as the vehicle was put into reverse. He decided to make a break for it and move further up the hill before they got out and started checking the obvious hiding places - his present location certainly being one of them.

As he reached the edge of the tree line, he heard the two policemen's agitated voices down below, as they started searching for him in the woods above the track. He could tell that they were calling to each other from some distance apart which suggested they'd agreed on a form of pincer movement to increase their chances of flushing him out. Their strategy would have been a good one if he'd stayed behind the oak tree but now he'd moved on, he hoped it would play to his advantage.

Listening carefully to make sure he still knew where they were, he started to work his way around the edge of the trees which he judged would lead him close to Earnslaw car park. There he hoped he'd find a departing motorist, willing to give him a lift back towards town. It was hard going because there wasn't a proper path and he had to make frequent detours to avoid dense clusters of gorse and bramble. Eventually though, his erratic course intersected with the main walkers' path, leading down from Summer Hill and he was able to follow it the rest of the way to his destination.

As he mounted the stile into the car park, he was

alarmed to see a Land Rover entering through the road entrance on the other side. He shrank back and watched it proceed slowly around the perimeter, eventually coming to rest by another gate over to his far left. His panic subsided as it slowly dawned on him that this was a different Land Rover from the one Bates and Collins had been driving: dark green rather than olive green. Also unlike theirs, it had a shield shaped insignia on the door which identified it as an official police vehicle. Then he noticed that it had parked next to a dark, police standard issue Wolseley that must have arrived earlier. The Wolseley's door opened, and a familiar figure got out – it was Nigel.

Dennis climbed over the stile and walked cautiously over to join his brother who was now talking to the occupants of the Land Rover: two uniformed policemen who, from a distance, looked disturbingly like Bates and Collins. As he got closer though, he could see that these were younger and thinner than the pair he'd been running away from only minutes before. All three men swung round to look at him as he approached.

'Good grief,' said Nigel, managing to sound surprised and irritated at the same time. 'Where did you come from?'

'I've been up on the hills,' replied Dennis, 'Something terrible has happened. I need to tell you about it.'

'Sorry, it'll have to wait. The quarry people will be here any minute. They've got to undo the padlock on this gate so that we can take the Land Rover through.'

'Why, what's going on?'

'You know I can't tell you that, it's police business.'

'Somebody's reported a body, haven't they?'

Nigel frowned. 'Where do you get that idea from?'

'Because I know how it got there; that's why I need to

talk to you.'

There were a few seconds silence, during which Dennis noticed that the other two were watching Nigel with interest, waiting for his response.

'All right,' said Nigel irritably, 'I'll give you two minutes to explain.'

He turned to the two uniformed policemen and said, 'Make sure you keep a close eye on things. We don't want anyone sneaking in there before we're ready.'

He led the way over to the stile and leant against it, fixing Dennis with a challenging stare. 'This had better be good,' he said. 'I don't like being made to look an idiot in front of junior officers.'

'How did I make you look like an idiot?' protested Dennis. 'All I did was tell you I knew about the body. I was trying to be helpful.'

'It's not helpful when you make out you know more about what's going on than I do. I'm supposed to be the one in charge here remember.'

'But you *are* in charge. All I'm doing is giving you some extra information to help you do your job. Why are you being so sensitive about it?'

'I don't know,' said Nigel, 'Maybe it's down to all the pressure I'm under. Just tell me what happened will you?'

Dennis summarised the events on the Beacon that had culminated in Morrigan's body being rolled into Earnslaw Quarry. To keep things simple, he decided not to mention anything about the signalling device or the conversation at St Ann's Well at this stage.

'And you're sure it was Bates and Collins?' said Nigel when he'd finished.

'It was the first time I'd seen them, so I couldn't be absolutely sure, but from what you told me about them the other day, it seemed more than likely.'

'You're probably right then.'

'So who reported the body?'

'I don't know, it was an anonymous call. We traced it to a public phone box at Lower Wyche.'

'Why are *you* here though? I'd have thought you had more important things to do than respond to anonymous tip-offs?'

'I'm here because Goodall ordered me to be here. Apparently, the caller was at pains to let us know it was the body of Andrew Morrigan, so the Superintendent decided I was the most appropriate person to follow it up. He said it would give me a chance to close the case down once and for all. I didn't roll over that easily though: I told him that even if it was Morrigan's body that had turned up, I didn't consider it the end of the investigation at all and that I'd continue digging around regardless.'

'How did he react to that?'

'He was furious; angrier than I've ever seen him. He told me I'd better do as I was told, or I'd be very sorry indeed.'

'He threatened you then?'

'I'd say so, yes.'

'So, he'll have his eye on you more than ever now.'

'Yes, and it'll only be a matter of time before he decides to clamp down on me once and for all.'

'And do what, do you think?

'I won't know until it happens.'

For a moment Dennis considered mentioning Morrigan's revelation about Jeff Stephenson's place in the scheme of things but decided it was still probably best not to complicate matters.

Instead, he said, 'It's pretty obvious that Goodall's out of control.'

'I know, but as things stand, I haven't got enough to nail him. That's why l need you to keep digging around behind the scenes while I deal with all this.' He gestured in the general direction of the quarry. 'Obviously, because there's a bloody great lake in there, the only way of getting to the body is by boat. We've brought an inflatable dinghy in the back of the Land Rover, but it's too heavy to carry, that's why we need the gate open so that we can drive in there.'

They both turned as a small van came in through the car park entrance.

'The quarry people are here,' said Nigel. 'I need to go.'

'Can I come and watch,' said Dennis, as they walked back.

'No, you can't.'

'Why not? I promise I won't get in the way.'

'Because, if Goodall found out it would give him just the excuse he needed to take me off the case, or worse, and we're trying to avoid that, aren't we?'

'That's true, in which case I'd better head back to town. I'm not quite sure how though; it's a long walk from here.'

'That's easy, go and ask your friend over there to give you a lift.'

Nigel pointed towards a grey Morris Minor parked a few yards away from the Land Rover, the Wolseley and now the quarry van, but the sun's glare on the windscreen obscured the driver's face.

'Who is it?' asked Dennis.

'That soppy theatre reporter you work with, Julian whatever his name is.'

'Julian Croft. What's he doing here?'

'He's been here all along, I'm surprised you hadn't noticed. He reckons your editor sent him up to find out what's going on.'

'But why would he send Julian? He's a theatre correspondent, this isn't his sort of thing at all.'

'That's exactly what he said. Apparently, he went into the office early to pick up some tickets or something. As it's Saturday, he wasn't expecting anyone else to be around, but as soon as he walked through the door he was greeted by Jeff Stephenson who told him to get up here straightaway. I suppose he drew the short straw because he was the only reporter available. He tried asking me a few questions, but it was obvious his heart wasn't in it and he must have known I wouldn't tell him anything anyway. In the end, he just got back in his car and he's been sitting there ever since.'

'So how do you think Jeff got to hear about it?'

'He was tipped off by the same caller I suppose. That's what usually happens: they phone the police and then they phone the press, to try and get as much attention as they can.'

Dennis hesitated as he weighed up whether or not to broach the subject uppermost in his mind. He decided to take the plunge.

'What if Jeff Stephenson was in on it as well and he sent Julian here as his eyes and ears, to make sure everything was going to plan?'

Nigel looked at him aghast. 'You're not serious, are

you?'

'I am actually. I wasn't going to mention it now because you've got more than enough on your plate already but, from what I hear, there's a strong likelihood that Jeff's the one behind it all.'

'He can't be. That doesn't make any sense at all.'

'That's what I thought at first, but the more I find out about his past, the more plausible it becomes.'

'So where does Goodall fit in?'

'Goodall's his strong-arm man; his agent on the ground. He's still highly dangerous, obviously, but the real power rests with Jeff.'

'But what have you found out exactly? How on earth does Jeff Stephenson's past have anything to do with this?'

Dennis opened his mouth to reply, but Nigel immediately held up a hand to stop him.

'Forget it,' he said, 'I haven't got time for any of this now. Get Julian to drive you back to town and we'll talk about it later'

He strode off towards the others, shouting instructions to them as he went.

Dennis went over to the Morris Minor and tapped on the window. There was no response, so he tapped again. Julian slowly opened his eyes as if emerging from a trance and peered up at him.

'Hello Dennis,' he said, sliding the window down. 'Sorry, I was lost in my thoughts there for a minute.'

He reached for a packet of cigarettes on top of the dashboard, but then seemed to change his mind and rested his hand on the steering wheel instead.

'Why are you here?' he said. 'Did Jeff send you?'

'No, I was just out for an early walk and...'

He stopped himself just in time. Twenty-four hours ago he would have relished telling Julian the whole story, but suddenly that didn't seem such a good idea.

'... I strayed a bit off the beaten track. Is there any chance you could give me a lift back to Great Malvern?'

'Sorry I can't. Jeff's told me I've got to keep an eye on things here.'

'But it's a waste of time, Nigel's never going to tell you anything.'

'He's been telling you things though, hasn't he? I've been watching you. Was Jeff right, is it Morrigan's body in there?'

'I don't know. I don't think Nigel knows yet either. I honestly think you're wasting your time. Just tell Jeff you tried, but you couldn't get anything and then you can enjoy the rest of your weekend.'

'You could vouch for me, couldn't you?' said Julian, his face brightening a little. 'You could say you spoke to your brother on my behalf and there was nothing doing. That would do the trick, wouldn't it?'

'I expect so. I'm the one who's supposed to be reporting on this business anyway, so I could just tell him I've taken over from you.'

'Good, in which case I'm happy to take you wherever you need to go. I suppose the office is the obvious place; Jeff's probably still there, so it would give you a chance to make amends. I have to tell you, your name's been mud since you went off on that jaunt yesterday.'

'No, I'm not going into the office yet. I'd like you to drop me off at the College if that's all right; Margaret's gone there to do some work and I need to have a word with her.'

'But you said you'd vouch for me. Until you've cleared things with Jeff, I won't be able to settle to anything.'

'What are you so worried about?'

'I told you, I don't want Jeff thinking I fell down on the job.'

'It's more than that though, isn't it? Come on, you can tell me; what's going on?'

'Nothing apart from Jeff being in a stew about this Symbiosis House story and making the rest of us suffer as a result. You know as well as I do that when he gets like that, it's best to just play along with him until he calms down again.'

'As long as that's all it is,' said Dennis, deciding not to press the point. 'Anyway, are you going to give me a lift or not?'

'All right,' sighed Julian. 'You'd better get in.'

As they bumped across the car park towards the exit, Dennis glanced back to see the Land Rover passing through the, now unpadlocked, gate into the quarry. He decided not to mention it to Julian whose attention seemed to be fixed resolutely on the way ahead.

They travelled on in silence for a while but then, as they were passing through Lower Wyche, Julian said, 'Are you sure I can't persuade you to come back to the office?'

'Sorry,' replied Dennis, 'I'm afraid you can't. The last thing I need is another pasting from Jeff, especially when it's supposed to be my day off. Anyway, Margaret will be expecting me at the College.'

'What's she doing in there on a Saturday?"

'Sometimes she goes in for a few hours when it's quiet, just to catch up with things.'

'Maybe she'll find time to have another rummage in that store room you mentioned.'

'Store room?' said Dennis, warily.

'Yes, the one where you said she found all those old papers of Laurent Morel's. Maybe she's decided to take another look.'

'Oh, I doubt if she'll have time for that.'

'I mentioned the papers to Jeff, by the way. I hope you don't mind.'

Dennis swung round to stare at him.

'Why on earth did you do that?'

'I thought he might be interested because of the links he had with the TRE during the war.'

'I was hoping we could keep the information about Morel's papers to ourselves for now.'

'Were you?' said Julian vaguely. 'Sorry, I didn't realise.'

'How did it come up anyway?' asked Dennis, trying hard to keep his voice level, despite his increasing agitation.

'He'd been having another go at me about forgetting to open the window when I have a smoke. It was getting on my nerves to be honest, so I tried to think of a way of changing the subject and that was the first thing that popped into my head.'

'And how did he react?'

'Just as I'd hoped. He forgot about the window straightaway and asked me to tell him more.'

'What did you say?'

'Just that Margaret had found some old TRE files in her library store room and thought some of them looked as if they were Laurent Morel's. That's all I could remember really.'

They'd made the turning into College Road now and, after a few yards, Julian pulled up next to a metal gate set into a tall hedge.'

'Is it all right if I drop you here?' he said. 'It's probably quicker if you cut across the playing fields rather than having me drive you all the way round to the main entrance.'

'It's fine thanks,' said Dennis distractedly.

Before he got out of the car he said, 'What else did you tell him?'

'What do you mean?'

'I mean, after you'd told him about the papers, did you mention any of the other things we talked about?'

'I did, yes. Sorry Dennis.'

'But why?'

'One thing simply led to another. You know how persuasive Jeff can be.'

'So he knows all our theories about Morel's disappearance?'

'I'm afraid he does. I didn't mean to tell him, but he kept pumping me for more and more information.'

'Are you frightened of him?' asked Dennis.

'I'm frightened of everyone,' exclaimed Julian, his eyes blazing. 'I'm a homosexual man, living in a small, conservative English town. The slightest whiff of scandal would destroy me. Can you imagine how it feels to have to live like that?'

'Are you saying Jeff threatened to expose you if you

didn't reveal what you knew?'

'Jeff's far too sophisticated to make threats. He just leaves you to read between the lines.'

'So you *are* frightened of him.'

'Yes I am,' Julian replied, turning to gaze out through the windscreen. And, if you've got any sense, you should be too.'

***

As Dennis pushed down the latch on the metal gate, he could hear the booming note of Julian's Morris Minor heading away along College Road, towards the town. He walked through into the green open space of the College's cricket ground and sat down on a bench to gather his thoughts.

He weighed up what Julian's next steps were likely to be. Would he drive around for a while, trying to summon up the courage to confess to Jeff that he'd failed in his mission or would he bite the bullet and go straight to the office to make a grovelling apology?

He sat bolt upright as the harsh truth dawned.

Julian would undoubtedly have calculated that his best chance of placating Jeff was to go straight back with some fresh information: the news that Margaret Jobson was, at that very moment, sitting alone in the college library storeroom, leafing through Morel's lost plans. It had to be assumed that she was now in mortal danger: no mercy had been shown to Andrew Morrigan when they'd come for the signalling device, so why should any be shown to Margaret when they came for the papers associated with it.

Dennis set off at a jog across the playing field. It suddenly felt as if he was on a life or death mission to get Margaret away from the library before any harm came to her. He calculated that it would take Julian ten minutes to get to the office and park his car; another ten for him to put Jeff in the picture about what he'd found out and ten more for someone to get back to the College and then... But further speculation was pointless; he just needed to concentrate on the task at hand.

He walked around the side of the gymnasium and came out onto an asphalted area in front of the college's north wing. He turned right and followed a more familiar path towards the kitchen where clattering and clinking sounds, interspersed with the occasional shouted exchange, told him that the catering staff were still washing up after breakfast. It suddenly reminded him how hungry he was; he couldn't for the life of him remember when he'd last eaten.

He climbed the fire escape at the back of the library and tried the door. It was locked. Coming back down he heard someone calling from the direction of the kitchen. He turned to see a grey-haired woman, in an apron, waving at him from an open door.

'You're Mr Powell, aren't you?' she said as he approached.

'Yes, I am. How do you know?'

'I've seen you coming and going a few times, so I asked Miss Jobson who you were. I sometimes take her a cup of tea when she's on the fire escape having a cigarette, and we have a little chat. Anyway, I just wanted to tell you that Miss Jobson's gone out.'

'Gone out? Where?'

'I don't know. Two men turned up in a car, about twenty minutes ago, and she went off with them.'

Dennis suddenly felt sick.

'Did she say anything?' he asked.

'No, nothing at all. I doubt if she even knew I was

watching. I'd just come out to put some rubbish in the bins when I saw her coming down the fire escape with one of the men in front of her and one behind. They'd parked their car right at the bottom of the steps, and she got in the back.'

'What did the men look like?'

'Just ordinary. Quite smart I suppose. They were both wearing dark overcoats and trilby hats.'

'So they didn't look like policemen?'

'Well they weren't in uniform if that's what you mean but I suppose they could have been a couple of those plain clothes types.'

'Were they young or old?'

'In their forties maybe. I don't know, it was hard to tell from that distance. They were both small and thin though, and one of them had a nasty limp. He was a bit slower coming down the fire escape and I could see that he was dragging one of his legs as he walked round the side of the car. The other one was carrying a box.'

'A box?'

'Yes, a big cardboard box. It looked heavy because he was staggering a bit as he brought it down.'

'Did Margaret - Miss Jobson - look as if she was going with them willingly?'

'Yes,' she said, frowning at him. 'As far as I could tell anyway. Why? Do you think she might have been kidnapped or something?'

'It's possible.'

'But why would anyone want to kidnap a nice lady like Miss Jobson? And here in Malvern as well. People don't go in for that sort of thing round here, surely?'

'I'm sorry, I realise how improbable all this must sound, but I honestly think Miss Jobson could be in serious danger. Can you remember what sort of car it was?'

'I'm not sure of the make, but it was definitely unusual; a bit like one of those gangster cars you see in American films. It was grey, and silver and it had a funny sort of sloping back.'

Dennis felt his stomach tighten again.

'And could you tell which direction they went in?'

'Not really. I know they drove off quickly though because I heard the tyres squeal. I saw them go around the front of the college and then I suppose they'll have gone down to the main gates and onto the road. Sorry, I don't suppose I'm being much help.'

'It's not your fault,' said Dennis, with as much consideration as his current state of anxiety would allow, 'you can only tell me what you saw.'

'I just wanted you to know she'd gone out, that's all. I didn't expect you to be so worried about it.'

'I know,' said Dennis, wretchedly. 'But the truth is, I'm at my wit's end. I really don't know what to do next.'

'Come in and phone the police,' said the woman, gesturing over her shoulder at the kitchen door. 'That's the best thing to do, isn't it?'

'No, believe me, that wouldn't be a good idea at the moment. I can't explain why; it just wouldn't.'

The woman shook her head as if utterly bemused.

Then she said, 'I think you need to speak to Mr Sanchez.'

'Who's Mr Sanchez?'

'My boss. He came out just before they drove Miss Jobson away. He might remember a bit more about what happened. Just wait here while I go and fetch him.'

Dennis paced up and down impatiently while he waited. After a minute or so, the woman returned, accompanied by a burly, red-faced man in chef's whites. He had a shaved head and sported a bushy white moustache.

'Iris says you want to talk to me,' he said, with a strong Spanish accent.

'Yes, I understand you were out here when Miss Jobson was driven off earlier. I hoped you might be able to tell me a bit more about what you saw.'

'Why you want to know? Are you with police?'

'No I'm not with the police, I'm a friend of Miss Jobson's. I'd arranged to meet her in the library but, according to Iris here, two men picked her up in a car twenty minutes ago.'

'I remember,' said Sanchez. 'I think I give them the shock of their lives, so they drive off, as quick as they can, in a cloud of dust.'

'What did you do to give them such a shock?'

'They see me carrying this maybe,' he said holding up a mean-looking knife that was about a foot long and stained with blood.

Dennis gasped. He hadn't noticed it before, and he assumed Sanchez must have been keeping it pressed against his leg.

The chef smiled and said, 'You see? Now you feel like running too but I mean no harm. The only one that needs to fear this is hanging up in my kitchen ready for the butcher's block and he don't worry too much now.'

'So these men thought you'd come out to threaten

them?'

'I think so, but they get it wrong. I only come out to see where Iris is because I need her to fetch things for me. I happen to be carrying this blade that's all.'

'And they jumped straight into their car and drove off?'

'You've got it. They drive off so fast they forget to close their trunk… boot… What you call it?'

'They left the boot of the car open?'

'That's right my friend. They speed away with the thing flapping and banging around like crazy.'

'Sorry,' said Iris, blushing as she butted in. 'I forgot to mention that.'

'Later on,' said Sanchez, 'I come out here for a smoke and I see a sheet of paper stuck in that hedge over there. I think it has blown out of one of our dustbins, so I go and pick it up. This is what I find.'

He reached into one of his deep pockets, pulled out a foolscap sheet and handed it to Dennis.

'I know straightaway this not kitchen trash,' he said.

Dennis studied the page of closely written notes, mainly comprising strings of equations that he couldn't make any sense of at all. What did make sense to him though was the one-word inscription at the top of the page - "Astrred."

CHAPTER 27

Desperate Decisions

Saturday 30th March 1957

10.30 a.m.

'You know what this is?' asked Sanchez, as Dennis gazed at the sheet of paper.

'Yes, it's from a collection of papers that were kept up in the library store room. Do you mind if I hold onto it?'

'Why not? It's no use to me.'

Dennis folded it up and stuffed it into his pocket

'So,' said Sanchez, 'the men came here to steal these papers you think?'

Dennis nodded.

'So what does this mean for your Miss Jobson?'

'I think she could be in great danger,' said Dennis, shakily.

'But she seemed happy enough to go with them,' interjected Iris. 'I told you that didn't I? She just walked down the fire escape between them; they weren't manhandling her or anything.'

'The one behind her will have had a gun. He'll have

kept in in his pocket so that it couldn't be seen, but it will have been trained on her all the time. She must have known that if she tried to make a break for it, she'd get a bullet in the back.'

He was starting to feel breathless now and he feared that the asthma, he'd been mercifully free from for so long, was making a return.

'These men are gangsters then?' said Sanchez.

'Yes, I suppose they are.'

'In which case, we should contact the police. I'll do it now.'

'No,' shouted Dennis, causing the chef to come to a dead stop just as he reached the kitchen door.

'Please don't,' he said more calmly, as Sanchez turned to stare at him, looking just as bemused as Iris had earlier.

'Why not?'

'As I told Iris before, it's too complicated to explain at the moment. You just have to believe me when I say it would be a very bad idea.'

'What are you going to do then?'

'I'm not sure... I suppose the first thing I need to do is retrieve my motorbike.'

'Where is it?'

'Parked at Margaret's... Miss Jobson's house.'

'You saying you walked here?'

Not exactly. I *did* go for a walk earlier, up on the hills, but then someone gave me a lift to the back gate.'

'So where is Miss Jobson's house?'

'In St James Road, about a mile away.'

'You like me to give you a lift?'

'Oh yes, that would be marvellous if it's not too much trouble.'

'It's no trouble if you don't mind going in dirty old van I use to carry meat and vegetables.'

'Of course I don't, I'm just grateful for your help. Thank you very much.'

'Iris will take care of lunch preparations while I'm gone,' said Sanchez, confirming the directive with a firm nod. 'You wait here, and I come back in two minutes with van.'

He strode off around the side of the building. Dennis and Iris stood in awkward silence for a few seconds before she muttered something that sounded like, 'good luck' and disappeared back into the kitchen.

As promised, two minutes later, the chef pulled up next to him in a cream-coloured Morris van. As Dennis got in he was overwhelmed by a stench of stale cabbage and rancid meat that made him start to retch. Thankfully though, as they started off again, the breeze through the open windows soothed the impulse away.

'You OK?' asked Sanchez, as they passed through the main gates, onto College Road.

'Not really,' said Dennis, 'but at least I'll be back on my motorbike again in a few minutes and I can start doing something.'

'Do you have a plan?'

'The first thing I need to do is talk to my brother. Hopefully, he'll still be up at Earnslaw Quarry where I saw him half an hour ago.'

'You think *he* will have a plan?'

'I doubt it, but at least he knows what we're dealing

with, so that's a start.'

'What does he do, this brother of yours?'

'He's a policeman; a detective inspector.'

'But you say you're not wanting to talk to police,' exclaimed Sanchez, shooting him a sideways glance.

'It depends which ones we're talking about. Sometimes, not all police are on the same side.'

'And sometimes, not all *people* are on the same side. I know that also from La Guerra Civil. I am Bando Republicano, but people I grow up with are Bando Nacional. That is complicated: complicated and *desagradable*.'

'You understand what I mean then.

'I think I do my friend; I think I do. But now I'm needing directions. Which way we go at the end of Priory Road?'

Dennis gave him directions and five minutes later, they turned right, into St James Road.

'Thank you,' said Dennis as the van squeaked to a halt outside number 23. 'You've been very helpful.'

'You want me to come in?' asked Sanchez. 'Check there's no-one here to give you trouble?'

'No, I'll be fine now thanks,' said Dennis, getting out onto the pavement. 'I'll pick up my motorbike and go back up to Earnslaw Quarry to see if I can find my brother.'

'In which case I will leave you. But be careful my friend and let me know if I can be of further assistance. You know where to find me.'

With that, he revved the van's engine and roared off.

Dennis walked up the path and knocked on Margaret's front door. He knew there wouldn't be an answer, but he felt he had to try. He left it a minute before trying again. The sound of the knocker echoing around inside the empty house only added to his sense of desolation. He couldn't let himself in because he and Margaret had never exchanged keys to their respective properties. They had an agreement that neither would ever venture unbidden into the other's domain and it was just one more feature of their relationship that no-one else seemed able to understand. The poignancy of the thought made him feel even worse.

He went around the side of the house to fetch the Tiger. He wanted to go back and find Nigel as quickly as possible now because something told him that working together was the only chance they'd have of getting Margaret back alive. He'd just positioned himself on the saddle and was about to push down on the starter pedal when he noticed that the gate into the back garden was open.

He'd lost count of the times that Margaret had told him off for not closing the gate behind him whenever he'd come in or gone out that way, so it was partly habit that made him dismount in order to go and secure it. Only partly though because he was sure *he* hadn't left it open and it went without saying that Margaret couldn't have been the culprit.

It therefore came as little surprise to find back door hanging wide open, with splinters of painted wood, from where it had been forced, scattered across the flagstones. He stepped cautiously inside and passed through the kitchen; noting the sad sight of Margaret's bowl, plate and cup and saucer from breakfast lying on the draining board. He went out into the entrance hall and listened hard. The house was completely silent, which made him think that whoever had broken in was now long gone. He had no doubt what they'd come for though and sure enough, as soon as he entered the sitting room, he saw that the tartan shopping bag, he'd left next to the settee the previous evening, was no longer there. He looked around the room, turning over cushions, newspapers and magazines, just in case it had been moved, but there was no sign.

As a last resort, he decided to check Margaret's bedroom - there was a slim chance she'd have taken the bag of notebooks back up with her to read while she enjoyed her early morning cup of tea - but as he turned to go back out into the entrance hall, he found the doorway blocked by a wiry, thin-faced man pointing a revolver at him. It was Percy Franklin.

'Well, well, well,' said Percy, sneeringly, 'Look who's here. We thought we were going to have to waste a lot of valuable time chasing after you, but thankfully you made it easy for us.'

'But I thought…'

'You thought we'd scarpered and you're right, we had, but then we spotted that old van turn in at the end of the road, so we decided to come back and investigate.'

'What have you done with Margaret?'

'Taken her to a nice safe place - the same place we're taking you to as it happens.'

He took a step backwards and waggled his revolver.

'So the sooner you make a move, the sooner you'll see her.

Once he was out in the hallway, Dennis felt the jab of the revolver barrel between his shoulder blades as Percy directed him into the kitchen and out through the back door. A Standard Vanguard, in two-tone grey and silver, was parked at the road end of the alleyway with another wiry, thin-faced man - unquestionably Percy's twin brother, Clarry - leaning against it.

'Get in,' snarled Percy.

Dennis climbed into the back seat while Percy went around the other side to join him. Clarry slammed both rear doors shut, before getting in behind the wheel and starting the engine. The car lurched forward with a squeal of tyres and soon they were out on the main road, heading for Malvern Wells.

'Where are we going?' asked Dennis, even though he was pretty sure he already knew the answer.

'You'll find out soon enough,' replied Percy.

Minutes later Clarry braked and made a sharp right turn into the driveway leading up to Symbiosis House.

Clarry changed down through the gears as the Vanguard climbed the steep hill. The dense laurel hedges lining the way blotted out most of the light until they rounded a bend and emerged onto a gravel concourse in front of the house. Apart from a glimpse of pinnacled turrets through the trees, this was the first time Dennis had come face to face with Symbiosis House and the sight of its melancholy gothic façade only served to deepen his sense of foreboding. The Vanguard came to a halt outside the front door and Clarry immediately came around to open the rear door, gesturing for Dennis to get out while Percy gave him a poke with the barrel of the revolver to emphasise the point.

Clarry took up what seemed to be his habitual position; leaning nonchalantly against the car, while Percy jabbed the revolver into Dennis' back again, propelling him towards the front door.

The door was ajar, and they passed through into a cavernous entrance hall with a central staircase leading to a balcony.

At the top of the stairs, they turned right along the balcony and into a gloomy corridor with a series of closed doors along each side. A dim lamp at the end marked the foot of a spiral staircase, up which Dennis was now directed with yet another jab of the revolver barrel. A door at the top creaked open as he pushed against it and he found himself in a space that was so dazzlingly bright after the murky corridor and stairway he'd just come from, that it took a moment for his eyes to adjust.

Then he saw that he was inside one of the turrets he'd observed from outside. One half of the circular room was dominated by four arched windows, through which spring sunshine poured. A line of wooden chairs formed a crescent against the opposite wall, and right in the centre of the floor, stood a tall brass tripod, minus the telescope it must have once supported. Next to it; arms folded uncompromisingly across his chest, loomed Superintendent Goodall. Since Dennis' last encounter with him, he'd swapped his police uniform for a dark suit, but even without the epaulettes and silver insignia he still exuded steely power.

'You can go now,' Goodall barked at Percy. 'I'm sure there are plenty of other things that require your attention.'

There was no audible reply, just the creak of the door opening and closing, followed by a scrape of boots on the spiral staircase.

Goodall grabbed one of the chairs and placed it with its back to the windows.

'Sit down,' he said.

Dennis lowered himself into the chair as instructed and looked up at the Superintendent's big, pugilistic face.

'You ignored my warning,' said Goodall. 'I told you that if you deviated from the line you'd been instructed to follow, you'd regret it. I told Brian Fairclough the same, but he stupidly chose to ignore me as well.'

'It won't make any difference to him now though, will

it? He's gone away to a new job in Fleet Street.'

Goodall gave a twisted smile.

'Ah, but you obviously haven't heard: The Whippet never made it. He set off for London, full of hope and enthusiasm, but his car skidded into a wall, halfway between Powick and Worcester. I understand he was killed instantly.'

'That's terrible,' said Dennis, with a shudder.

'Yes, it was most unfortunate. 'But then fatal motor accidents happen here in Worcestershire, just like everywhere else. The Whippet was just another of those sad statistics I'm afraid.

The glib response made Dennis see red.

'What sort of fool do you take me for?' he retorted. 'That was never an accident, it was down to you. And, from what I hear, it won't have been the first time you've had blood on your hands either.'

Goodall glared down at him.

'Casting wild aspersions like that isn't going to help your situation. And it won't do that lady friend of yours any favours either.'

'Where is she?' shouted Dennis, leaping to his feet. 'If you've harmed her I'll…'

Goodall stepped forward and pushed him back into his chair.

'You'll what?'

'I don't know,' sighed Dennis, blinking back tears of frustration.

'You're starting to see what a sticky situation you're in now, aren't you? But you've only yourself to blame: life would have carried on normally if you'd only seen sense and done as you were told.'

A clump of footsteps coming up the stairs made them both turn towards the door.

'And now for the grand entrance,' said Goodall. 'Because, if the pleasure of seeing me wasn't enough for you, here's someone who's *really* going to make your day.'

The door creaked open and Jeff Stephenson entered the room. He blinked a couple of times as his eyes adjusted to the glare and then he focused his gaze on Dennis.

'How disappointing,' he said, 'I thought this was going to be a big surprise, but, going by the expression on your face, it seems you were expecting me.'

'I was.'

'Presumably Julian told you, is that right?'

'No it isn't; Julian hasn't breathed a word.'

'I'm amazed; usually he's a dreadful old blabbermouth: he can't keep quiet about anything. He gave me chapter and verse on his conversations with you for example. So if it wasn't Julian, it must have been Andrew Morrigan.'

Dennis didn't answer.

'Your silence speaks volumes,' said Jeff, smiling. 'I should have known it was him really. Once he'd dug up that body, he'll have been on a mission to cause as much mischief as possible in the short amount of time left to him.'

'Until your thugs caught up with him and shut him up forever, you mean.'

'Something like that.'

He shook his head with apparent pity.

'Oh Dennis, if only you'd kept on minding your own business, life would have been so much easier for you.'

'Why make me take over the Symbiosis House story then? You must have known I wouldn't just churn out what I was told.'

'But the thing is, I *did.* I weighed up the risks and concluded that, in order to get back to normal as quickly as possible, you'd choose the path of least resistance.'

'You underestimated me then, didn't you? It wouldn't be the first time.'

'And I admit I made the same mistake about your meeting with Harry Parsons: I thought you'd be so obsessed with the Chamber Spout that you'd overlook anything else that might come up. I was cautioned against it on both occasions, but the gambler in me chose to make a different call.'

'Why?'

'*Why?*' repeated Jeff. 'It's clear you don't know much about gambling if you have to ask me that. The answer is, I thought I had enough inside knowledge about you to predict which way you'd swing, but I got it wrong. Backing the wrong horse has to be a possibility though, otherwise there'd be no risk, and for a hardened gambler, risk is what it's all about. Having said that, whenever the odds seem resolutely stacked against me, I don't have any qualms about giving them a little nudge in the right direction.'

'You're happy to fix them, in other words.'

'Why not? This is gambling we're talking about, not religion; there aren't any high moral principles involved. Not that I'd be bothered if there were, because I don't have a principled bone in my body. I think it's one reason why Julian likes talking to me: my barefaced lack of scruples gives him a vicarious buzz.

'So Julian's part of this as well, is he?'

'Julian's not really part of anything, he's just one of

life's outsiders. There are quite a few like that in Malvern I've noticed: I'm not sure why; maybe it's something to do with the water.'

'But he's sympathetic to your way of thinking?'

'Not particularly; he's just drawn to me, like a moth to a flame. And I hardly need to tell you that Julian's a hopeless gossip: he swears blind what you tell him won't go any further, but like all gossips, he can't resist passing on any snippets of information that have come his way. I've heard him chatting away to you about this, that and the other; soaking up everything you tell him and giving you a few colourful insights into Malvern life in return. The next minute he'll be doing exactly the same with someone else. Quite often, that'll be me.'

'So, that's how you've been able to keep tabs on what I've been up to.'

'One way certainly, but the truth is Julian's take on things can be a bit hit and miss, so I prefer to rely on other sources for most of my information.'

'Like him, you mean?' said Dennis, pointing at Goodall.

'Less of the *him* I think,' said Jeff. 'This is a senior police officer you're talking about, so a bit more respect would be in order if you don't mind.'

'I don't think someone as dodgy as him *deserves* any respect.'

Goodall lunged at Dennis, fist raised, but Jeff reacted quickly and seized his forearm before he could land a blow. The two men stood facing each other for a few seconds, then Goodall backed off and took up his menacing stance, next to the brass tripod again.

'Superintendent Goodall *does* keep me informed,' said Jeff, returning his attention to Dennis as if nothing had happened. 'But it's his little band of watchers and listeners - men like Percy and Clarry and a few select police officers – who do the real donkey work.'

'And presumably the information they've collected about me suggests I've become a threat.'

'Exactly, along with Margaret, Nigel and that oddball brother-in-law of yours, James Crawford: hence the need to curtail your activities and bring you all here.'

'Nigel and James are here as well?' exclaimed Dennis.

'Of course.'

'Where are they then?'

'In a special place you're really going to appreciate – I expect you've already guessed where I mean, haven't you? But first, I want to show you something.'

He extended a hand towards the brass tripod as if introducing a silent guest. Dennis saw now that it was far more elaborate than he'd first thought. It was a fine piece of Victorian engineering, standing about five feet high, with a string of embossed stars and moons cascading in a spiral down each of its legs.

'What happened to the telescope?' asked Dennis.

'We - that is Laurent Morel and I - put it into storage. It had done noble service, but the time had come for it to make way for its technological successor. We'd built a microwave device that was destined to revolutionise telecommunication. It also had the advantage of being compact and therefore easily portable. Ironically though, its small size presented quite a challenge when we tried to fix it onto this beauty.'

He indicated the tripod again.

'The original screw-head was far too big for the delicate apparatus we'd created. Obviously, we could have used a purpose-built tripod instead, but, for various reasons, I was very keen on the idea of merging the old with the new. Morel thought I was mad, but he went along with me all the same. In the end we got a factory over in the Black Country to make us a precision-milled adapter so that the two objects would fit together. It was ridiculously expensive, but, to me, worth every penny.

'The trouble was, even though we knew it worked, there was nothing for it to work *with*. What we needed now was a satellite in geocentric orbit around the earth: an object we could bounce a signal off, but such a thing was just theoretical at that stage and neither of us could predict, with any certainty, when it would become scientifically feasible.'

'Until now,' said Dennis.

'Exactly. You'll have seen the headlines speculating about an imminent Russian satellite launch just like everyone else. Naturally, because of my well-placed contacts, I knew about it long before the press did. I also happen to know that the launch is still months away and nothing like as soon as all the newspaper reports are making out. So, if it hadn't been for Andrew Morrigan deciding to put a spanner in the works, I'd have been perfectly happy to leave the device in James' safekeeping for the time being and, quite possibly, none of this unpleasantness would have been necessary.'

He glanced at his watch.

'But we are where we are and now it's time for me to go and see how all the arrangements are progressing. Percy will be back in a minute to escort you downstairs.'

He turned abruptly and left the room. His shoes pattered on the stone steps before fading away along the corridor.

Now they were alone, Dennis fully expected Goodall

to take the opportunity to follow through with the blow Jeff had stopped him from landing earlier. He braced himself for a punch in the face, but nothing happened: the big superintendent just stood there, staring down at him malevolently.

A few tense seconds later, the door swung open and Percy appeared. He hesitated for a moment as if gauging the situation he'd walked into, then he met Dennis's eye and jiggled the revolver, as he'd done before, to signal that it was time to move. Dennis got up and walked to the door. Percy moved into position behind him and, with another jab between the shoulder blades, ushered him down the spiral staircase.

Dennis now knew perfectly well where they were going and, as the all too recognisable pressure of Percy's revolver against his back drove him onwards, he found himself replaying Greville Jobson's experience of the same short journey, as related in Harry Parsons' journal,

... down the winding staircase from the turret room.

... we descended the main staircase, along a passageway

... down another, even narrower spiral staircase, accessed via a trap-door.

... a cave- like cellar

The space they'd entered, though utterly recognisable from the journal description of *an egg-shaped chamber carved out of solid rock*. It was far smaller than he'd been expecting.

What also surprised him was the deafening noise: the roar of a torrent of water, gushing from a stone spout and plummeting into the swirling pool beneath, reverberated around the chamber. He was now standing on a mezzanine and the light from a single bulb, dangling overhead, cast sulphurous, vein-like reflections on the damp rocks and refracted off the water droplets in the air so that everything seemed to be shrouded in a yellowish mist.

More words came back to him from Harry's journal,

... a stone trough

... water flowed from a spout shaped like the head and neck of a swan

A set of steep wooden stairs led on down from the mezzanine into the chamber and standing at the top of them, as if on guard, were two uniformed policemen. Dennis could only see their backs, but he'd spent long enough observing them earlier to know that it was Inspector Bates and Sergeant Collins. It seemed that his narrow escape from them at Earnslaw Quarry had counted for nothing.

His heart sank even more as his eyes adjusted to the dim light and he saw, for the first time, Margaret and Nigel standing side by side, down on the floor of the chamber. They were both staring straight ahead; plainly oblivious to his and Percy's arrival. Nearby, James was sprawled on the ground leaning against the side of the water trough; his head drooping pitifully.

Percy went over and tapped Bates, then Collins, on the shoulder. Both policemen swung round, gave nods of acknowledgement, then pushed past Dennis to exit the chamber via the spiral staircase.

Once they'd gone, another poke in the back from Percy's revolver told Dennis it was time for him to make his way down to join the others.

CHAPTER 28

The Chamber Spout

Saturday 30th March 1957

9.00 p.m.

Just as Dennis reached the bottom of the stairway, the roar of gushing water stopped. The silence that followed was almost as disorienting as the cacophony that had preceded it and he froze for a moment to collect his thoughts.

Noticing his arrival for the first time, Margaret rushed over and flung her arms around him. Nigel gave a grim-faced nod of greeting from behind her. Dennis was shocked to see a deep gash on his brother's forehead and thick strands of dried blood down one side of his face.

Before they could speak, they were distracted by a flurry of movement on the mezzanine. Jeff, Goodall and a third figure - currently obscured by shadow - were standing there, looking down at them. Apparently, their arrival meant that Percy was now relieved of his guard duties because he immediately handed his revolver to Goodall and proceeded to haul himself up the spiral staircase - his bad leg dragging behind him - and exited through the trap door. Once he'd disappeared Jeff took a step forward to address them.

'You see how easy it was to shut off the flow,' he said, his voice echoing in the rocky space. 'I trust you're suitably impressed.'

There was no reaction, so he continued.

'There's an array of stop cocks and gauges in a little room next to the kitchen that gives us complete control over the whole system. As you might guess, there's a secondary channel which can be brought into service to stop the chamber from flooding when water volumes are particularly high or when, as now, a bit of peace and quiet is called for. Thanks to the wonders of hydraulic engineering thousands of gallons of water are, at this very moment, being diverted away from this chamber via the overflow outlet. Rest assured though; everything will be returned to normal later so that you can experience the Chamber Spout in its full glory again.'

'And then what?' asked Dennis.

'Oh, that's for later. In the meantime, there are a few things I need to tell you about.

'In other words, we have to stand here in serious discomfort and listen to you pontificating,' growled Nigel. 'Why don't you just get on with whatever you've got planned for us, and stop wasting our time?'

'I couldn't possibly do that,' replied Jeff, shaking his head. 'It wouldn't be appropriate at all. This place might not look much to you, but as Dennis well knows it has already been the scene of one momentous drama and now it falls to me to stage a worthy sequel. Such things can't be rushed I'm afraid.

He held Nigel's gaze for a few seconds and then he broke into a smile.

'Good,' he said. 'I think we understand each other, so maybe now you'll allow me to carry on. I'd like to start with a special introduction.'

He turned and beckoned the man behind him to step

forward.

Dr Gajak,' exclaimed Dennis, staring up at the, now fully visible, figure in amazement.

'But is it?' said Jeff. 'Are you absolutely sure that this is who you think it is?'

'What an absurd question; of course I am.'

'Well you're wrong. This isn't Dr Gajak and it never has been; this is Mathias Friedman.'

'I don't believe you.'

'But you should,' interjected the other man. 'Because he's right, I really am Mathias Friedman. Dr Gajak was just an invention born out of necessity: a charming and plausible one certainly, but an invention all the same.'

The accent was heavily Germanic and nothing like Gajak's at all. It was as if a disembodied voice had taken up residence inside him and transformed his identity completely. The effect was chilling.

'I don't understand.'

'I deceived you, it's as simple as that. Please don't take it personally though: over the years I've used my impersonation skills to fool lots of people.'

'But why?'

'I'll explain in a while, after you've heard a little more from Jeff. As a consummate newspaper editor, he's very clear about the order in which this multi-faceted tale should be told and he thinks everything will make a lot more sense if you hear some of his side of things before I start regaling you with mine. I'm not entirely sure what difference it makes, but that's his view and I've agreed to go along with it.'

He gave a small, possibly ironic, bow, before withdrawing into the shadows again.

'Thank you,' said Jeff, taking a step forward to peruse his reluctant audience. I'm going to begin with a brief account of my formative years. You might question the relevance of this at first, but please bear with me and all will soon become crystal clear.

He cleared his throat before continuing.

'I was born in the county of Norfolk where, for the first few years of my life, I lived perfectly happily with my parents in a cottage on the large country estate where my father was gamekeeper. However, soon after my fourth birthday, this blissful existence ended abruptly when a faulty shotgun exploded in his face, killing him outright.

'The cottage came with my father's job, so we could easily have been evicted. Fortunately though, the lord of the manor, Lionel Harcourt, took pity on us. No doubt he felt guilty because the accident had happened on his land, but whatever the reason he let us stay on. He gave my mother a job as housekeeper up at the manor and, on the face of it at least, our lives slowly returned to normal.

'Lionel Harcourt was a widower with an only son, Emery, who was nine years older than me and a boarder two hundred miles away at Malvern College during term times, so I only saw him during the holidays. We got on well enough whenever he came back, but we weren't really friends at that stage because of the age difference.

'My mother's relationship with Lionel quickly moved beyond that of employee and employer. Within a year they were married, and the family name was formally changed to Harcourt-Stephenson, presumably so that we could all feel included in their glorious union. Emery seemed happy enough about the change, but I didn't like it at all. Despite my lack of years, I resented the way Lionel seemed to think his position gave him the right to change the name I'd been known by since birth without any reference to me whatsoever. Obviously, I was too young to express it in quite those terms at the time, but deep down I'm sure that's how I felt. Rightly or wrongly I began to loathe him for his arrogance and as I got older this feeling took on a more political complexion. I started to see Lionel Harcourt as the embodiment of upper-class entitlement: something I've railed against, passionately, ever since.

'In the summer of 1907, Lionel, my mother, Emery and I went on a day trip to Hunstanton. The weather had been pleasant enough when we set off, but by the time we got there, a storm was setting in. It's a mark of Lionel's arrogance that, despite the raging gale that was churning the sea up into a fury, he insisted on going for a swim. My mother pleaded with him not to, but he wouldn't be dissuaded. To cut a long story short, he was swept away by a huge wave and, despite desperate efforts by some brave bystanders to rescue him, he drowned.

'My mother was devastated of course. In fact, within three years, she was dead herself. I, on the other hand, was just glad to see the back of him; especially when I discovered that the terms of his will meant I'd continue to be well provided for without having to put up with him lording it over me all the time. It was the best of both worlds as far as I was concerned.

But it's Emery's singular reaction I really want to tell you about. After the funeral was over, he started acquiring weather charts and tide tables for the date and time of the storm and spent hours poring over them to the exclusion of everything else. At the time I assumed he'd just taken up a new hobby to take his mind off things, but as he explained to me, years later, it was a lot more involved than that. He said he'd been consumed with anger about the ease with which the forces of nature had snuffed out his father's life and he felt honour bound to strike back. To me it sounded completely mad, but I didn't say anything. He thought that, if he could discover more about how nature worked, he'd be able to start playing it at its own game. That's why he started collecting all the charts and tables.

'Predictably though, he soon realised he was wasting his time. Being able to tell when to keep out of the sea because a storm was brewing was one thing, but it was never going to give him the total control over the elements he was looking for. However, he wasn't downcast for long because a few days later, while looking through a microscope in the school lab, he happened to witness, for the first time, the activity of enzymes attacking and breaking down protein molecules. It was suddenly apparent to him that, by setting up the reaction, he'd single-handedly triggered an irresistible force, capable of destroying everything in its path. He knew at that moment that not only had he found a means of exercising the power over nature he wanted, he'd also found his vocation.

'To cut a long story short, after leaving Malvern College, he qualified as a pharmacist and then worked in various hospitals before securing a post at Powick Mental Asylum in January 1919. It was there, a few months later, that he first came across Mathias Friedman.'

He glanced over his left shoulder, which appeared to be a cue for the older man to pick up the story.

'And what a momentous encounter it turned out to be,' said Friedman, coming forward and resting his hands on the rail that ran along the front of the mezzanine. 'But before we get on to that, I'm going to follow my friend's example and take you right back to the beginning.

I was brought up in a small hotel in the town of Gräfenberg; in what was then Austrian Silesia but is now Czechoslovakia. It was run by my parents, Karina and Oktav Baader. During the early nineteenth century, Gräfenberg was the home town of Vincent Priessnitz. As you know Dennis, Priessnitz is generally considered to be the pioneer of modern hydropathy and he founded a spa in the town which became famous throughout Europe and beyond. Consequently, our little family hotel played host to people from far and wide who had come to avail themselves of the water cure.

'Those guests, with their multifarious accents and mannerisms, were a source of endless fascination to me. I was an only child, so I would amuse myself by imitating them in front of the mirror and I quickly became an expert mimic. Someone very like Dr Gajak may well have stayed at our establishment at some point, though it's more likely that he was an amalgamation of any number of the well-educated, central European gentlemen who graced us with their presence – but more about that later.

'One day in the spring of 1889, when I was eight years of age, an Englishman, from Malvern, came to stay. His name was Henry Powell. We naturally assumed that, just like all the other visitors, he'd be spending his time sampling the various treatments available in the town. However, it soon became clear that the real purpose of his visit was to drum up business for his own hydropathy establishment back in Great Malvern; The St Werstan Spa Hotel. Malvern was past its prime as a spa town by then, but he hoped that the testimonials of any clients he managed to entice from the reputed home of the modern water cure would help to increase future custom.

'Every night after dinner, he'd sit at the bar with my father, drinking brandy and talking enthusiastically about his dream of a mutually beneficial link between our hotel in Gräfenberg and his own establishment back in Malvern. During one of these conversations, my father mentioned that he periodically suffered from a debilitating respiratory condition and that he was in the habit of using the local water treatments to relieve the worst of his symptoms. He explained that this was what had drawn him to Gräfenberg in the first place. He and my mother had previously owned a hotel in the town of Troppau, about fifty miles away, but they'd sold up so as to be closer to the hydropathy expertise that had proved so helpful to him and which he sometimes thought was the only reason he was still alive.

'It wasn't long before Henry suggested that my father come to the St Werstan Spa Hotel and try out the wide range of therapies available there. He promised that he would bear all expenses and that all he asked in return was that my father should write a short, and hopefully complimentary, account of his experience, making it clear that he had gladly travelled all the way from Gräfenberg, birthplace of Vincent Priessnitz, the father of modern hydropathy, to take advantage of all that Malvern had to offer. My father gladly agreed and in the autumn of that same year, he travelled to Malvern and checked in at The St Werstan Spa Hotel.

'He immediately began an intensive regime of treatment: a typical round of sweating, plunging baths, head baths, half baths, sitting baths and douche baths; along with a strict diet and early morning walks to the top of the Beacon and back. Apparently, all went well at first, but on the third day of his visit, my father started to experience some mild breathing difficulties and naturally he reported these to his host. Henry's recommendation was that, rather than indulge his condition, they should intensify the hydropathy regime and augment it with a selection of organic remedies, as recommended by some of the more go-ahead practitioners in the field. Despite feeling increasingly unwell, my father bowed to Henry's superior knowledge and embarked on an even more rigorous routine of dousing and plunging, interspersed with regular herbal preparations in both tablet and liquid form.

'By the fourth day my father's condition was even worse, but by all accounts, Henry insisted that he trust the process because he would soon reach a point of catharsis when his illness would break and then disappear completely. That same afternoon, whilst taking his second douche bath of the day, my father had a massive heart attack and died.

'To say that the news of his death turned my life upside down is an understatement. It didn't help that my mother's way of dealing with it was to immerse herself in the running of the hotel, so that I became lonelier and more self-absorbed than ever. I'd turn the reports of what had happened over and over in my head for hours, building up an ever more vivid picture of Henry Powell reigning supreme over his domain of cruel water rituals and toxic concoctions while my father convulsed and grimaced in his death throes.

'As the years passed, I learned to compartmentalise my feelings, primarily by concentrating on my studies. I was a bright boy and learning came easily to me. I've already mentioned my interest in mimicking the accents and mannerisms of the hotel guests, but as I got older I found that I was starting to observe people more deeply than that. I started speculating about what had happened in their lives to cause a certain nervous tick, a tendency to laugh too much, an inability to make eye-contact, or any other notable trait they might display. This, although I didn't know it at the time, was the first stirring of my interest in psychiatry and explains why, later, I was drawn to that particular branch of medicine at the University of Vienna and later at Vienna General Hospital.

I won't dwell on my Vienna years because there was little about me then that would have set me apart from any of my contemporaries: I was a young man, immersed in my studies and in gaining the necessary experience to qualify as a psychiatrist. In retrospect, it was a blissful time because I was far too busy and focused on the task in hand to think about the troubles of my childhood. The only point of note is that, just before I left home for university, I decided to change my name from Baader to my mother's maiden name, Friedman, as a way of separating myself from the past and embarking on a new life, unencumbered by old preoccupations. And, for a few years, it worked, but as my professional training should have told me, the dark things we try to bury have a nasty habit of rearing their ugly heads again.

'And so it was that, once I was established in my profession, I found my thoughts returning more and more to what had happened to my father. Although I enjoyed my work, I was no longer able to displace the nagging sense of injustice as easily as I'd done before. I kept recalling that the inquest had described my father's death as an unfortunate accident which, as far as I was concerned, had let Henry Powell off the hook completely. Not only that, the long and arduous nature of my own recent medical training reminded me just how bogus his credentials were and how, by rights, he should never have been delivering such dangerous and unproven treatments in the first place. These sorts of thoughts began to obsess me and the more they churned and festered in my mind, the more I realised that the only way I was ever going to silence them was to go to England and deal with this dangerous charlatan once and for all.

'I did some research and discovered that there was an institution near Malvern, Powick Mental Asylum, that I knew would be ready snap up a psychiatrist with my exemplary background and where I felt sure I'd be able to fade into the background while I decided on my next move. I also contacted estate agents in the area and - without ever laying eyes on the place before I moved in - purchased Symbiosis House. I had no specific plan at that stage, but I was confident that, once I'd established myself there, everything would start falling into place.

'It was spring 1919 when I arrived at Powick. I was thirty years of age and starting work in what my colleagues back in Vienna had disparagingly referred to as a professional backwater; an institution that was completely unworthy of my talents. However, it turned out to be nothing of the sort. Powick Mental Asylum was suddenly the centre of attention for the whole psychiatric world because it had recently inherited a group of highly distressed shell-shock patients which no previous institution had been able to help. This had put immense pressure on my new colleagues, so naturally they were hoping I'd bring some inspiration with me from the land of Freud and Jung. Part of me was flattered of course, but in truth I was no more equipped to deal with these difficult patients than they were. Anyway, the last thing I really wanted was a lot of attention from the wider profession when what I'd come here for was a chance to bide my time in relative anonymity - but then I met Emery Harcourt and, as I said a few minutes ago, that changed everything.

'It should be said that Emery was, and is to this day, a cold, unsociable man. He'd been at Powick for nearly four months before I arrived, but most of my colleagues had barely registered his existence. They knew he was there to make up any prescriptions they needed in the course of their work, but they didn't have any direct contact with him because it was the nurses' responsibility to collect drugs from the pharmacy and Harcourt rarely emerged from there at all. He'd arrive at half past seven in the morning and leave at six at night. He never used the canteen or any of the common rooms; he resolutely kept himself to himself.

'The only reason *I* came across him was because I got lost wandering around the corridors during my first week and happened to find myself outside the pharmacy. Harcourt was in there on his own; sitting at a bench, looking through a microscope. Hearing the scrape of my shoes on the stone floor, he looked up and appraised me for a few seconds without saying a word. He intrigued me straightaway, if only because of his remarkably penetrating pale blue eyes, magnified by thick spectacles. Then he asked if he could be of assistance, but with such obvious indifference that normally I'd have taken the hint and moved on. However, as I said, I found him strangely intriguing, so I explained about losing my way and, merely as a ploy to extend our conversation, asked if he'd mind telling me what he'd been studying under his microscope.

'This seemed to make him a little less frosty and, after we'd shaken hands and introduced ourselves, he led me over to his bench and let me peer through the lens at the slide he'd been examining. After a minute or two, he asked me if I recognised the substance in question. He obviously didn't think I would because he seemed quite taken aback when I identified it straightaway as an ergot alkaloid. I explained that, during my studies, I'd made a special study of psychoactive compounds and that, consequently, the structures of ergopeptines had become etched on my memory. I asked what his interest was and, after a lengthy account of the various processes he'd been experimenting with, he announced that he'd come up with a revolutionary formulation of lysergic acid that he thought could be of benefit to my shell-shock victims. He said the drug was designed to unblock connections within the brain, thus enabling patients to gain new, and potentially liberating, perspectives on their deep-rooted fears and troublesome memories.

'I was sceptical to begin with because, while my previous research had indicated that these compounds might have some theoretical potential, it had seemed to me that they were likely to be something of a blunt instrument when treating an organ as delicate and finely balanced as a human brain. But my initial doubts were assuaged by a combination of Emery's intense certainty and an awareness that my own work on the subject was nearly ten years old by then and had never been a specialism anyway. There was more to it than that though: a jolt of recognition had passed between us while he was speaking, and I'd suddenly felt a singular connection with him, as if we were kindred spirits. It sounds strange, but I knew, from that moment on, that by working together we'd be many times stronger than either of us could ever be on his own.

'A week later, I administered the drug for the first time. To make it as easy as possible, Emery had infused sugar lumps with what he'd calculated to be the minimum effective dose. He'd packed them into an empty biscuit tin so that I could transport them discreetly from the pharmacy to my consulting room. Neither of us wanted to draw attention to our enterprise at this early stage. There were nine shell-shock patients in total and they were all there waiting for me: slumped in armchairs; hollow-eyed and lifeless as usual. I didn't bother with any preamble; I simply offered the tin around and each of them took a sugar lump and swallowed it automatically. That's how they were, so utterly drained of will that they never questioned anything. I then sat down and waited for the reaction.

'A long time passed and very little happened. If anything, they seemed to become even more withdrawn and languid than ever. But then I noticed that one or two had shifted position and appeared to be fixated on the movements of something which only they could see. Slowly, they all started to exhibit similar behaviour as if, somewhere behind their eyes, a wondrous entertainment was taking place. Some of them even began to point in various directions, seeming to draw attention to whatever spectacle was unfolding before them. The desolate stares that I'd observed before were now transformed into expressions of rapture. I was tempted to ask them what was happening, but I knew that, from a scientific point of view, it was important to allow the experiment to proceed uninterrupted.

'After an hour or so, it became apparent that the effects were starting to wear off: the darting eye movements subsided, and their hands became still. What remained, however, was the air of blissfulness that had settled over them. Even though they were slumped back in their armchairs again, they now looked like men at peace with themselves, rather than the victims of perpetual mental torture they'd so obviously been before.

'Gradually, one by one, they began to talk about their experiences. They were all remarkably consistent: they mentioned feeling completely at one with their surroundings; so much so that their bodies and minds seemed to have physically blended with the walls, ceiling, floor and the very chairs they were sitting on. They recalled constantly shifting, fluid shapes and colours that were brighter and more vibrant than any they'd ever seen before. They said that colours and sounds were often the same thing and that distinctions between the senses seemed irrelevant. Most notably of all though, they spoke of a separation from their memories; a sense that the terrible battlefield images that had plagued them for so long, had floated off into a place where they could be examined objectively and without fear because they now seemed to belong to someone else.

'This was music to my ears because, if I'd bothered to write down my ideal outcome in advance, this is exactly what I would have described. The goal in dealing with such patients is always to try and induce a state of detachment, so that they might start rationalising their fears rather than continuing to be oppressed by them. I went straight back to Emery to tell him what had happened and to congratulate him on his achievement. Naturally he was pleased, but he didn't want to dwell on it. He was far more interested in my thoughts on what should happen next, as if this stage had been a foregone conclusion and the more interesting part was yet to come. He wasn't interested in giving the drug a name either, despite my insistence that continuing to define it by its formula was unnecessarily cumbersome and dull. He greeted my suggestion that we call it Ergophantasos with a noncommittal shrug of the shoulders.

'A few days later, I administered the drug for the second time. The effects of the first dose had completely subsided by then and the patients were back to being as disturbed as ever. Nevertheless, during the intervening period I'd managed to organise individual consultations and found, to a man, that they were far more prepared to describe the terrors that assailed them than they had been on previous occasions. They were still just as distraught, but at least their fears now had shapes we could start talking about. I felt sure that another round of Ergophantasos would draw them out even further, and so it proved – though not in quite the way I'd expected.

'Unfortunately, there'd been a nasty incident as they'd come in: two patients had been having an argument out in the corridor, which one of my colleagues had been trying to calm down. It was a common enough occurrence at Powick as it is at any mental institution, but I could tell the group had been badly affected. After a while, the eye movements and pointing began as before, but this time, whatever was playing out in their minds was making them recoil and become agitated. A few of them started to call out in alarm and plead for it to stop. It was extremely uncomfortable to observe, but once again, on professional grounds, I resisted the temptation to intervene.

'Afterwards, they were angry. They all agreed that it had been a terrible experience and demanded to know why I'd given them a different drug when the previous one had worked so well. When I assured them that it had been exactly the same formulation, they made it clear they didn't believe me and became angrier still. There was little point in arguing with them, especially as, despite their suffering, I secretly thought this phase of the experiment had been even more encouraging than the first. I believed it had taken us a step closer to the core of their fears and increased our chances of triggering a catharsis.

'But this was uncharted territory and much as everyone was desperate for a breakthrough, I knew I was gambling with the health of these patients and that most of my colleagues would take a very dim view of such a reckless approach. However, Emery was dismissive of my concerns: he said the men were suffering anyway, so there was nothing to be lost by pressing ahead, whatever the risks. As someone who showed an alarmingly low level of human empathy, his judgement in such matters was far from reliable, but I went along with him anyway and agreed to proceed with another course of treatment and see how the land lay after that.

'But, as I should have predicted, my colleagues had already guessed something was going on. They'd all seen a change in the shell-shock patients since I'd started working with them and they were keen to know what I'd done to bring this about. I tried to keep it vague at first, but they were relentless in their questioning, so in the end I gave in and told them about the Ergophantasos. To say their reaction was conflicted is to put it mildly. On one level, they were excited because, by any standards, this was a radical form of treatment and they were intrigued to see where it would lead. And they wouldn't have been averse to the glory it could bring them either - anything that boosted Powick's reputation was bound to boost theirs' too. But, on an ethical level, they had significant concerns, just as I'd predicted they would.

'In the end, they grudgingly agreed to let me continue on condition that as soon as I became aware of any serious complications, I was to stop the treatment and alert them to what was happening.

'Two days later, I administered the third dose. Understandably, the patients weren't at all happy about taking it, but their powers of resistance were low and after some gently persuasive words from me, they all succumbed. To my relief, their reaction was as positive as it had been the first time and when the session ended, I decided to let them enjoy their brief respite of peace and leave further questioning for another time.

'We gathered again at ten o'clock the following morning, but I could tell straightaway, from the sullen faces that confronted me, that something was wrong. I asked what the problem was and one of them, a particularly articulate, ex-cavalry officer, responded on behalf of the group. He told me that they'd all woken up with the same terrifying feeling: one of detachment from their own memories; as if everything they recalled belonged to someone else's life rather than their own and that their very identities were now under threat. He said the worst of it had passed now, but, to a man, they were agreed that - even considering the horrors of the trenches and the shell-shock they'd suffered since - they'd never been more frightened. He concluded by saying that the cause of their anguish could only be the drug they'd been made to take, and he begged me to guarantee that this latest adverse reaction was the last they'd have to suffer.

'But realistically I couldn't guarantee anything of the sort, and it was suddenly obvious to me that continuing to test this drug on such a damaged and irretrievably disaffected, group could only end in disaster. By the time I reported back to Emery, I was all for giving up on Ergophantasos completely, but, typically, he took a more pragmatic view: he thought we should test it on a new batch of less vulnerable subjects and do it somewhere away from Powick, where we'd be free from oversight and interference. I was sceptical at first because I thought we were just storing up trouble for ourselves, but then it occurred to me that by turning his suggestion on its head and concentrating on the failings of the drug rather than the benefits, the plan might serve my purpose – the one that had brought me here in the first place - very well. I now realised that Ergophantasos could be seen as a modern-day equivalent of hydropathy: a quack remedy, masquerading as a legitimate cure. My father had been the victim of one such travesty, so maybe I could arrange for his killer to be the victim of another. Of course, all this assumed that Emery had no inkling of my true motivation and that his plans for Ergophantasos and mine were running along parallel, but very different, tracks. However, as will become clear later, I badly underestimated him.

'The following day, we both resigned from Powick and, soon afterwards, Emery moved out of his lodgings in the village to come and live with me at Symbiosis House. I didn't cut my links with Powick completely though. For one thing, we still needed a source of pharmaceutical supplies, and, for another, I was reluctant to withdraw from a profession I'd been successful in and which, despite everything, still meant a lot to me. Hence, I grew a neat beard, reminiscent of Sigmund Freud, donned a pair of gold-rimmed spectacles and acquired a set of forged diplomas. These, combined with my well-honed impersonation skills enabled me to secure a part-time post there in the guise of respected Polish psychiatrist, Dr Tomas Gajak.'

CHAPTER 29
Full Flow

Saturday 30th March 1957

10.00 pm

Friedman stared into space, seemingly lost in his own thoughts. In the ensuing silence, stray plops of water, falling from the spout into the trough, echoed around the chamber like random xylophone notes. Jeff stood to one side, apparently in no hurry to interject and Goodall continued to hover at the top of the staircase; his revolver trained on the assemblage below.

'I need to describe Emery Harcourt to you,' said Friedman eventually. 'He's a pivotal figure in all this – perhaps *the* pivotal figure – so it's essential that I do him justice. I want you to try and picture a rather intense and aloof pharmacist, sitting at a bench in his laboratory where he's just placed a slide, coated with a film of biochemical compound, under the lens of a microscope. He's holding a pipette in his right hand which contains another compound; a reagent that, once introduced to the slide, will trigger a series of chemical reactions. He releases a droplet and then watches with fascination as synthesis occurs - innumerable metabolic pathways developing at lightning speed before his eyes. Some of them he has predicted, and this pleases him. Some, however, are unexpected, but this pleases him too because the real satisfaction is knowing that neither would have occurred without his intervention.

'Now, instead of chemical compounds, imagine I'd just described a carefully selected group of people being subjected to certain stimuli. Once again, many complex reactions are likely to occur, but this time psychological rather than biochemical.'

He looked directly at Dennis. 'What does that sound like to you?'

'The Black Moon Society.'

'Exactly, the Black Moon Society was the embodiment of everything that excited Emery about science, but on a human scale. So, do you see what I meant earlier when I said I'd underestimated him?'

'Yes, it sounds as if he'd been ahead of you all the time.'

'You're right, he had, but it didn't worry me because I knew that the benefits cut both ways. At Emery's suggestion, I started to contact certain men in the town, inviting them to join a small astronomical society. There was a fine telescope in the north turret room that had been installed there by one of the house's previous owners and we agreed that this would be the perfect prop for the little charade we were planning. Despite his aloofness – or perhaps *because* of it - Emery was a great observer of people, so he'd already drawn up a list of suitable candidates; men he thought had the right blend of battle trauma, self-doubt, petty ambition, and suggestibility to meet our purpose. His idea of including your father in the group was so obvious I'm amazed I didn't think of it myself. He thought an unwitting act of patricide would add an extra frisson to proceedings, and, of course, he turned out to be right.

'The final group consisted of eight men: Charles Powell, Greville Jobson, Harry Parsons, Jack Masters, Herbert Faulkner, Alfred Franklin, Alex Goodall and Norman Collins - and so the Black Moon Society was born.

'By the time we met for the eighth, and last, time on the thirtieth of October 1921, I was exhausted. It was my own fault really for making an idiosyncrasy of the lunar cycle our raison d'être, but once we'd set out on that course it was too difficult to go back. Also, Emery was so fixated on the idea, it would have been impossible to deter him.

'As you might have gathered, the idea of a Black Moon Society was completely arbitrary – it could just as easily have been the Golden Cockerel Society for all it really mattered. The thing is, I wanted a concept that I could embellish and embroider until it started to look like a genuine philosophy with precious truths at its heart, as opposed to the empty concoction it actually was. In other words, it had to be as useless as hydropathy had been to the poor fools in the nineteenth century who'd believed it would lead to better health, when, at best, it made no difference at all and, at worse, made their conditions even more serious.

'It was the telescope up in the turret room that first sparked the idea and then it just took on a life of its own. It's surprisingly easy to create a plausible creed because as soon as you've started, one thing just leads to another. A hidden yet ever-present moon is a satisfyingly potent symbol in its own right, but then there's the matter of its constant influence on the tides which in turn suggests a link to the gallons of water that flow through this chamber. The spout itself - shaped like the head and neck of a swan – provides the perfect opportunity to insert a few references to a dichotomy between the grace and purity of the swan paddling on the surface of the water and the darkness and detritus lurking below. As you see the potential for making entirely meaningless connections becomes endless.

'And, just as I'd expected, the men hung on to every word of the gibberish I fed them until, with the additional help of some Ergophantasos, a few glasses of champagne and my well-honed hypnosis skills, they were like putty in my hands.

'At each meeting I stressed that we were moving ever closer to a climactic event – the occurrence of a rare black moon. I then led them through a ritual, during which they were required to immerse one of their number – a different member each time - in the trough. I told them that, regardless of any unease they felt, they must only let him come up for air when I gave the signal. After eight monthly sessions of this it became routine for them – a text-book case of conditioning - which was, of course, exactly what I'd been aiming for.

'Now all I had to do was make sure that Henry Powell appeared at Symbiosis House at the appointed time, on the night of the thirtieth of October 1921. At Emery's suggestion I wrote to him saying that I was working with a private consortium of businessmen on a plan to turn Symbiosis House into a luxury hotel and, being mindful of his estimable entrepreneurial reputation, we would appreciate any advice he could give us on how we might proceed. I said that, because we were still at an early stage, my associates would prefer it if the details of our proposed meeting were kept confidential. I invited him to join us, and hopefully address us with a few words of wisdom, at nine-thirty p.m. on the thirtieth of October. I concluded by saying that, in his honour, we had decided to use Symbiosis House's magnificent, and rarely seen, subterranean chamber as the venue for our meeting.

'I thought I might have raised his suspicions by piling on the flattery so much, but I needn't have worried because, when I phoned him a few days later to confirm that he'd be coming, he couldn't have sounded more eager if he'd tried.

That was when I knew the trap was set.

'And sure enough, when the big night came, he turned up at nine-thirty on the dot. Five minutes earlier I'd detached myself from the procession down to the chamber and lingered in the entrance hall to await his arrival. Although I'd previously been in the same room as him at various social functions I'd attended, I'd never seen him at close quarters until now and I must admit it came as quite a shock. He was stooped and shrunken, and his face was so comprehensively etched with lines that it resembled an ancient map drawn on parchment. His rheumy eyes were deep set in their sockets and seemed to be peering out at me from a very dark place. It was obvious that I was in the presence of an extremely troubled man and I suppose I ought to have felt some sympathy for him, but the harsh truth is he revolted me more than ever.

'I shook him by the hand, uttered a few welcoming platitudes and then led him across the hall, along the scullery corridor until we reached the trap door opening onto the ladder that leads down to this place. Throughout that short walk I'd been wondering what to do if he proved too frail to tackle the steep spiral staircase. To my relief though, once I'd indicated the way down, he proceeded enthusiastically and with surprising ease.

'However, I was pretty sure that once he was on the mezzanine and saw the vacant stares of those gathered below, he'd realise that something was amiss. And indeed, as soon I came down to join him, the mixture of confusion and fear I saw written across his face was a joy to behold. I gently tugged his arm to usher him down the stairway and into the body of the chamber. As we advanced, the group members backed away to clear a path, just as I'd trained them to do every time a new victim was about to be dowsed. Henry stopped at the side of the trough where Emery was already standing and then turned around to survey the strange assembly before him, obviously wondering what on earth was going to happen next. I went to stand next to him and immediately launched into my well-worn spiel about the black moon; hidden forces; tidal shifts; light and dark; and so on and so forth. At first it was just the usual meaningless incantation, designed to stir recognition in eight befuddled men that the high point of the evening was approaching, but gradually I realised that, tonight, my words were coming from a different place altogether and that I was finally giving voice to the rage I'd been bottling up for nearly three decades. The previously hackneyed phrases seemed imbued with a new significance and for the first time, I found myself speaking straight from the heart. And, despite their drug-addled brains, the members of the group had noticed a difference too. I could tell that they were galvanised and ready to do my bidding. My change of tone seemed to have alerted them to the fact that something unprecedented was about to happen.

'I announced that the time to atone for a terrible injustice had finally come; the cathartic act they were about to carry out was the zenith of the process they'd all been part of for the duration of eight consecutive lunar cycles. It was, I proclaimed, an act of redemption; an act of resolution; an act of release. I nodded to Emery who immediately seized Henry Powell's elbow and turned him around so that he was facing the trough. The group had been conditioned to see this action as a sign that it was time for the immersion ritual to begin. The men surged forward and before Henry could object, they all pressed down on his back and neck and forced his head under the water. Normally, after a very short length of time, Emery would have touched one of them on the shoulder to indicate that he should let go - as soon as one released the pressure; all would automatically follow. But this wasn't normal of course, so he just let the seconds tick on.

'I watched as Henry flailed and twisted in a vain effort

to resist until, within what seemed to me to be a remarkably short time, he stopped moving and I knew he was dead. Emery belatedly gave his signal and the men all straightened up. Then, before they had a chance to register that anything was amiss, he herded them off up the staircase and out of the chamber.'

'Leaving you to gloat alone,' said Dennis.

Friedman shook his head. 'It wasn't like that at all. I'd done what had to be done and now he was an irrelevance. It was as if he'd never existed.'

'You still had to dispose of his remains though.'

'True, but we already had a plan for that. We knew that Henry liked going for lone nocturnal walks on the hills - an eccentric and potentially hazardous pursuit by anyone's standards – so we knew that if it were made to appear that he'd missed his footing one night and tumbled into the quarry lake it would generally be regarded as an accident that had been waiting to happen.'

'And by the time he was found, the combined effects of the fall and twenty-four hours in the water, any signs of the real cause of death would have been obliterated anyway.'

'Exactly.'

'So how was it then, that despite all your diligent planning, you failed to foresee that someone might avoid taking the drug in order to witness everything that happened?'

'That's a good question,' said Friedman, 'And I wish I had a good answer, but I don't. The embarrassing truth is that I probably overestimated the extent of my influence over the group, or some of the group anyway. Actually, Harry Parsons wasn't the only inquisitive member to do such a thing.'

'I know, the other one was Greville Jobson.'

He sensed Margaret flinch at the mention of her

father's name, and he took hold of her hand.

'Greville Jobson,' echoed Friedman, suddenly sounding wistful. 'He was an intelligent man, I liked him a lot.'

'But you were still prepared to have him silenced.'

'That was down to Emery, it had nothing to do with me.'

'You must have known about it though.'

'I knew it was something he considered necessary, but I thought I'd talked him out of it. It was only later, after the deed had been done, that I found out I hadn't.'

'So much for being kindred spirits then.'

'It isn't as simple as that. Just because we had a symbiotic relationship doesn't mean our expectations were perfectly aligned. Yes, we shared a desire for retribution, but my need was specific and finite, whereas his was boundless and therefore insatiable.

'He'd been suspicious of Greville and Harry from the start and he was convinced that, sooner or later, they were both going to step out of line. The only question was, which would go first? It turned out to be Greville. At our inaugural meeting he left the room, soon after the Ergophantasos had been administered, and despite returning ten minutes later, still seeming as dazed as the other men, Emery became suspicious. So suspicious in fact that early the next morning he went out to scour the garden for evidence of what Emery had been doing, only to discover traces of vomit underneath one of the laurel hedges. He concluded from this that Greville had purposely brought up his dose of Ergophantasos in order to ensure he was in a fit state to spy on us. I countered that it was probably just a case of him drinking more champagne than he was used to and politely going outside to be sick in the undergrowth, but I could tell my words were falling on stony ground.

'From then on Emery followed Greville's every move. It was hard to see why because as far as I could tell the man never put a foot out of place. In fact, I would have described him as one of our most committed acolytes. What *did* interest me though was how close Greville and Harry had become since their first encounter and I wondered what Emery was making of that.

'We didn't discuss the matter again until a week after that final meeting. We were on our way back to Symbiosis House after attending the inquest into Henry's death and I was in excellent spirits because the coroner had arrived at exactly the verdict we'd hoped for. Emery, on the other hand, was unaccountably gloomy, so I asked him what was wrong. He said that, although he was pleased about the accidental death judgement, he wouldn't be able to relax until two potential loose ends had been tied up. I knew straightaway that he was referring to Greville Jobson and Harry Parsons. I restated my opinion that he was reading too much into Greville's – unproven – transgression and furthermore, allowing it to poison his interpretation of a perfectly innocent friendship between two men. It was then he told me he was convinced that Harry had also avoided taking his dose of Ergophantasos the week before and had witnessed, with full lucidity, everything that had happened in the chamber.'

A moan came from the direction of the trough and Dennis turned to see that James was stirring. He'd raised his head and if it hadn't been for the blankness of his gaze, he might have been assimilating his surroundings after waking from a deep sleep. He squirmed a few times and then his head lolled forward, and he became still again. Despite the lack of movement, however, he continued to emit moans that reverberated around the rocky space. Nigel went and sat on the side of the trough next to him and rested a hand on the back of his neck. The contact seemed to have a soothing effect and after a while the noise ceased.

'What have you done to him?' exclaimed Dennis, staring up at Friedman again.

'He was overwrought, so we had to sedate him.'

'But why was he moaning like that? What sort of sedative have you given him?'

'Just something Emery prescribed.'

'Emery's still around then?'

'Of course, where else would he be?

'I just assumed he'd died or moved away somewhere.'

'No, I can assure you, he's still very much with us. Indeed, yours and his paths have probably crossed numerous times over the years, without your ever realising it. Emery's a master of invisibility, until, that is, he fixes you with those piercing pale-blue eyes and then, just as if you'd looked into the eyes of the Gorgon Medusa, something inside you will turn to stone.'

'So, this drug he prescribed for James: was it Ergophantasos?'

'It would have been normally, but tonight it became necessary to give him something to counteract one of its undesirable side-effects. Just now, when I described him as overwrought, blind rage would probably have been a better description. And that's what Ergophantasos induces unfortunately: it's a problem that's hounded us all along, which is a great shame because, in every other way, it's a highly effective preparation.'

'Why give it him in the first place then?'

'The same reason we gave it to all the others: to scramble his memory and thus render him an unreliable witness if he ever felt inclined to reveal anything that might embarrass us. The trouble is, the frustration induced by these gaps in recall quickly turns to anger, hence the need for a strong sedative.'

He glanced back at James before continuing.

'But enough of that. I was telling you about the conversation I had with Emery after the inquest. In a nutshell, he was convinced that Greville and Harry had seen things they shouldn't and reckoned we ought to take steps to silence them before they caused us any trouble. I disagreed and expressed my longstanding, but previously unstated, view that he had a pathological attraction to chaos which made him seek out trouble where it didn't really exist. As you might expect, he didn't like that at all, and we spent the rest of our journey home in total silence.

'We didn't speak about it again until one evening in February 1923, more than a year later. During the intervening months I'd noticed that he'd become thick as thieves with three members of the, now lapsed, Black Moon Society: Alfred Franklin, Alex Goodall and Norman Collins. Alfred was an antique dealer and Alex Goodall and Norman Collins were both police officers: Inspector and Sergeant respectively. They'd always struck me as men with a penchant for subterfuge, so it came as no surprise that, to compensate for my disinterest, Emery had engaged them in his pursuit of Greville and Harry.

'On the February evening I mentioned, Emery entered my study where I was working and placed a single sheet of paper – what appeared to be a handwritten note – on the desk in front of me. Obviously, I was meant to read it, so I did. Although no names were mentioned, it was plainly a communication between two Black Moon Society members, in which the author was begging the recipient not to speak out about an incident he'd witnessed and reminding him of the price they'd all been warned they'd pay if they ever broke their code of silence.'

Friedman peered at Dennis.

'Didn't you tell me you'd found a similar note amongst your father's possessions?'

For a split-second Dennis was confused: it still felt as if it had been Dr Gajak he'd told, not this man who seemed like an imposter.

'Yes.'

'And you assumed it had never been sent.'

'Of course.'

'So it didn't occur to you that what you'd found might have been a first draft or a copy of a note that *was* sent?'

'No.'

'Well, whatever the case, Emery saw it as the final proof that Greville was about to spill the beans about The Black Moon Society and once again I told him I didn't agree. I said that, in my view, someone – at the time we both assumed it was Harry, but now it seems it was your father – had misconstrued Greville's intentions. Maybe he *had* sounded off about things, but I couldn't imagine it going any further than that. I explained that I saw Greville Jobson as someone who, when faced with the choice between a quiet life and causing trouble, would always opt for a quiet life. Over a year had passed since the Society's final meeting and there hadn't been a squeak from him. I felt the risk of that changing now was very low indeed.

'Throughout this soliloquy, Emery gave every appearance of hearing what I had to say, but really I knew it was just going in one ear and out the other. And the truth is, I didn't really care because, as I've already said, I was finished with intrigue and I just wanted to concentrate on something more positive. So, as soon as he'd gone – taking his, supposedly, incriminating, piece of paper with him – I just pushed the whole business to the back of my mind.

'A month later I read in The Gazette that Greville had been killed in a hit and run road accident. Emery hadn't said a word, so I went and asked him what he knew about it. He didn't beat about the bush, he simply stated that Alex, Norman and Alfred had acted on his instructions to have Greville run down. He could have been describing a shopping trip he'd sent them on for all the effect it seemed to have had on him. He even went into a lot of unnecessary detail about how they'd acquired a car especially for the job and then had it scrapped to destroy any evidence of what had happened. I was used to him favouring the mechanics of a situation over any human elements – it was part and parcel of his peculiar psychological makeup - but this time it was particularly infuriating because I'd liked Greville and I didn't think he deserved having his death – a completely unnecessary one as I saw it - described in such matter-of-fact terms. But I couldn't undo what had already happened, my only option now was to try and impress upon him, in the practical terms he plainly understood, why pursuing anyone else – Harry for example - carried a far greater risk than just leaving well alone.

'And he seemed to take it on board because, after that, he confined himself to his laboratory and, as far as I could tell, his contact with Alex, Norman and Alfred ended completely. Meanwhile, I thought about how I might be able to make amends.

'One of the positive steps I'd taken, since concluding my business with Henry. was to set up a charitable organisation The Mitarbeit Trust, and over the past year I'd hosted a series of exclusive dinners and other high-class social events to raise money. It occurred to me that the Trust would provide a perfect means of funding a permanent memorial to

Greville, and what could be more appropriate than a new science library named after him, in the institution where he'd taught Physics and Chemistry for so many years?'

'So you used charitable funds to try and salve your conscience,' said Dennis, scathingly.

'I suppose I did, yes.'

'And did it work?'

'No,' he replied, slowly shaking his head, 'I'm sorry to say it didn't.'

For a moment it seemed as if he was going to elaborate, but then he backed into the shadows without another word.

'As you can tell,' said Jeff, as if on cue. 'That's a sensitive issue for him; so sensitive, in fact, that it always renders him speechless. Fortunately though, it's time for you to hear a bit more from me.

He glanced fleetingly at Friedman before continuing.

'After I left Malvern College, I went up to Cambridge, where; after initially gaining a degree in Physics, I was awarded a PhD for my work on advanced wireless communication systems. Eventually, my research activities came to the attention of some senior military people and, towards the end of 1938, I was invited to set up an advanced field communications training centre. The people who approached me were seasoned strategists who knew that war was coming and were understandably keen for us to steal a march on the enemy. By the time war was finally declared a year later my team was up and running and, purely by coincidence, based locally, at an army barracks on the outskirts of Worcester.

'I hadn't laid eyes on Emery since he'd left Malvern College, twenty years before. However, through our occasional exchange of letters, I knew that he'd previously been employed as a pharmacist at Powick Mental Asylum and that he was now sharing a house in Malvern Wells with a psychiatrist who'd worked there as well. As I was now living nearby, I took advantage of my first free weekend and drove over here to see him.

'Naturally I'd phoned in advance and by chance had ended up speaking to Friedman rather than Emery. I was pleased actually because, unlike my stepbrother, he sounded like a most agreeable fellow, and so he turned out to be. We bonded so quickly in fact that, within five minutes of my arrival, he told me in confidence that he and Emery were planning to disappear. He explained that, because of the worsening political situation in Europe, his life as an Austrian living in England was becoming harder every day. There were people who thought that, because he had a German-sounding name, he must be a Nazi sympathiser and he feared he would soon become such a figure of hate that it would become impossible for him to go about his business. He also feared that, because of their close association, Emery was likely to become a target as well, which was why they'd decided to vanish at the same time.

'Of course I nodded with due sympathy while he was telling me all this and when he'd finished, I asked him where they were planning to go. His face broke into a smile and he replied that they weren't going anywhere, they were just going to make it appear that they had. He explained that he was planning to stage their eviction at the hands of a German hating mob, after which he would transform himself into Polish psychiatrist called Dr Gajak, while Emery would do what came naturally to him and simply fade into the background. He said there was a garden flat, to the rear of Symbiosis House, where they could both live in comfort, well out of the public eye. He asked if I'd be interested in helping them to put their plan into action and naturally, I agreed straightaway.

'It turned out that Emery had already come up with a list of suitably xenophobic locals and the pubs they frequented. My job was to sidle up to them, buy them a drink or two and see if they'd be interested in dishing out a bit of rough justice in a patriotic cause and I'd soon got fifteen men on board who were all raring to go. I'd told them to rendezvous outside the gateway to Symbiosis House, at nine o'clock, the following Saturday night. They were each to bring a heavy stick and something metallic, like a dustbin lid, to bang and create as much noise as possible. Naturally, Emery had already made sure that his friendly contacts in the local constabulary were primed to appear at the right time and make an elaborate show of breaking things up. He'd also seen to it that a pet reporter from the Gazette would be on hand to faithfully record everything that happened.

'In the event, it went perfectly. On my signal, the mob stormed up the drive, shouting at the tops of their voices and banging their dustbin lids as they went. Once they reached the house, they just had time to smash a few windows before three police cars roared up the hill in a blaze of headlights and a clamour of bells. The climax came as two shadowy figures burst out of the front door and ran across the garden and off into the woods, pursued by a few of the sharper-eyed vigilantes. Meanwhile, throughout this drama, Emery and Friedman had been comfortably ensconced in their new accommodation, confident that, from now on, it would be generally assumed that they'd left Malvern forever.

And so, seeing as, to all intents and purposes, Symbiosis House was now a vacant property, it seemed sensible to move my communications training centre here: it was certainly a lot more salubrious than the premises we'd been using over in Worcester. By pulling strings behind the scenes, Emery had arranged for Crawford, Davies and Withers to be appointed as letting agents and it was through them, I made all the arrangements for our relocation a few weeks later.'

'Which is presumably how James got involved?'

'That's right, but only briefly at that point because, within weeks, he'd been called up and shipped off to foreign parts with the Gloucestershire Regiment.'

'Along with Andrew Morrigan and Percy Franklin.'

'Correct.'

'Who'd both been primed by Emery to keep a watchful eye on him.'

'Also correct. I take it these insights come courtesy of your encounter with Morrigan earlier on.'

'Before you had him killed and dumped in the quarry you mean?'

Jeff gave a thin smile.

'He suddenly became a liability I'm afraid. We'd been giving him the benefit of the doubt for a long time, but then he had a crisis of conscience and decided to, quite literally, dig up something from the past he should have left well alone. Then he compounded his mistake by spilling the beans and, in so-doing, not only signed his own death-warrant, but yours as well.

CHAPTER 30

Diminishing Returns

Saturday 30th March 1957

11.00 p.m.

With Jeff's chilling words still hanging in the air, Friedman moved to the foot of the spiral staircase. He climbed carefully, but sure-footedly, before making his exit through the trapdoor.

'It seems he's finally had enough,' said Jeff, making fleeting eye-contact with Superintendent Goodall who continued to stand guard with the barrel of his revolver pointing down into the chamber. 'So now it's left me to relate the final chapter.'

Dennis put his arm around Margaret's waist and found that she was shivering violently. He wasn't shivering himself – not yet anyway - but he did have a tight knot in his stomach accompanied by a rising tide of nausea. Nigel looked pale but resolute while James seemed to have toppled sideways and was now lying in a foetal position on the rocky floor.

'What are you going to do with us?' said Dennis, conscious of the fear in his voice.

'*We* won't be doing anything,' said Jeff. 'We're just

going to let the world-renowned Malvern water do its work.'

'What's that supposed to mean?'

'Do I have to spell it out for you? Just try to recall how strong the flow was before we turned off the valve. Then imagine how quickly this chamber would fill up if, for some reason, the water was unable to escape.'

'You're going to leave us here to drown?'

He felt Margaret flinch as he said it.

'That's the harsh truth of the matter,' said Jeff. 'But, as far as the public is concerned, it will just seem like the regrettable consequence of an utterly plausible series of events. You've made no secret of your fascination with the elusive Chamber Spout, to the extent of mentioning it, virtually every month, in your column in the Gazette. Therefore, few will be surprised to learn that, after your precious chamber came to light during a major police investigation here, you begged your brother - the detective inspector in charge - to let you and a few of your nearest and dearest take a look. But, of course, the chamber is very old and probably hasn't been entered at all, let alone been maintained, for decades. While you're down there, a blockage occurs in the drainage system, filling the escape channel with debris. Meanwhile, a diligent police constable, on a routine patrol of the house, notices water gathering around the area of the trap door. Naturally he opens it up to see what's going on, sees that the chamber is flooded and calls for help because it looks as if the whole of the ground floor is about to be inundated. Do you get my drift?'

'Presumably this is the outline for the report you'll get one of your minions to write up for the front page of the Gazette.'

'That's the general idea, in fact I'll probably ask Julian Croft to do it. It'll make a refreshing change from all those hammy productions he usually writes about.'

'He knows too much, he'll see through the story straightaway.'

'You could be right, but he won't say anything. Believe me, despite being a consummate gossip, he knows when keeping quiet or speaking out can mean the difference between life or death.'

'That doesn't apply to everyone though.'

'People like your family you mean?'

'Yes.'

'Well, let's hope, for their sake, you're right.'

'Is that meant to be some kind of threat?' roared Nigel, breaking into the conversation for the first time.

'Well, well, well,' said Jeff, leaning over the rail as if verifying the source of the interruption. 'The brother finds his tongue again. I was starting to think you'd taken some of that drug James is so partial to and it had rendered you speechless.'

Nigel moved to the foot of the wooden staircase and stared up at the two men on the mezzanine.

'I wouldn't come any further if I were you,' said Jeff, nodding in the direction of Goodall who was now holding the revolver in an extended, two-handed, grip and pointing it directly at Nigel's head. 'And, in answer to your question,' he continued, more temperately. 'No, it wasn't a threat; merely a reflection on the reality of the situation.'

Nigel silently held his gaze for a few seconds and then, apparently accepting defeat, backed away, head bowed, to stand with Dennis and Margaret again.

'And so, to the denouement,' continued Jeff. 'I've already told you how much I loathed my stepfather, Lionel

Harcourt, for taking control of my life after marrying my mother. I saw it as typical of how a certain type, or rather a certain *class,* of Englishman, assumes it's his God-given right to lord it over a vast swathe of humanity. He's the reason why, to this day, I see it as my mission to subvert the entire, so-called, ruling class who maintain such a grip on this septic isle of ours.

And so, during my time at Malvern College, I became something of a schoolboy anarchist. I was very subtle about it though and I managed to cause all sorts of trouble around the place without anyone having the faintest idea I'd ever been involved.

'Then, when I reached sixth form, I discovered the joys of horse racing. I came across Percy Franklin at Worcester Racecourse and with his able assistance I started to undermine the order of the racetrack by indulging in some profitable horse doping.

'I joined the Communist Party when I got to Cambridge and I was soon spending as much time talking about Marx as I was about Physics. In fact *more* about Marx probably, though, after a while, the two subjects became tied up with each other anyway. By that I mean that I began to see Physics as the means by which revolution might be achieved particularly as I was starting to build up my international scientific contacts, including quite a few in the USSR. I didn't hide my politics, mainly because, in that febrile academic environment, I didn't need to. It was de rigour to hold one radical viewpoint or another. So much so that we used to make up nick names, usually playful little anagrams, that reflected the particular philosophy each of us was seen to espouse. Mine was Astrred in honour of the red star on the Soviet flag.

'My specialism was telecommunications, which is how I gained my PhD. It helped me make quite a name for myself which is why I was approached to set up the training centre in Worcester which I subsequently moved to Symbiosis House.

'In May 1942, the Telecommunications Research Establishment moved from Dorset to Malvern. Initially they were based at Malvern College as you know. The TRE was mainly involved in the development of advanced radar systems. Because of the vital importance of its work to the war effort, it had all the very best physicists at its disposal; the crème de la crème. Amongst these was a young French émigré, a scientific phenomenon, called Laurent Morel.

'Having the TRE on my doorstep was a gift to me of course. I was able to draw in scientists of the highest calibre in the country to give lectures to my students. Naturally they had to be cagey about exactly what they were working on, but they were invaluable all the same. My kudos in military circles rose exponentially as a result of their contributions. The Malvern Wells Training Centre, or MWTC in military parlance, was widely regarded as a model of excellence and so, by association, was I.

'But it soon became clear that, despite his scientific brilliance, Laurent Morel was a hopeless teacher. The one and only time I let him loose on the students he proved to be an out and out disaster. He was arrogant, bad tempered and patronising. He had no rapport with the group whatsoever and made no attempt to hide his disdain for the subject matter he was supposed to be communicating to them.

'Nevertheless, despite his deficiencies in the classroom, I continued to invite him over to Symbiosis House because I sensed he could be a useful man to have around. I told the TRE I needed him to deliver more lectures, but really I just wanted to talk to him and find out what made him tick. Having said that, I didn't get much out of him at first because he plainly had as little time for me as he'd had for his students. Gradually though, after plying him with copious amounts of flattery and five-star brandy, he started to open up.

'He admitted that, although he was grateful for the refuge Malvern had given him and for the opportunity to continue using his skills, he was desperately bored by the monotonous tasks he was expected to perform. He said he was homesick as well. He missed Toulouse, his birthplace, badly even though he had no family left alive there to welcome him back. He revealed that, in order to distract himself from his woes, he'd taken to working on his own schemes alongside the radar development he was undertaking for the TRE. He found it easy enough to do because he'd usually complete a research report in a fraction of the time that his head of section would have allocated for it, thus leaving him ample opportunity to turn his mind to something more stimulating.

'As the brandy took effect, he began to talk animatedly about the personal project he was working on and the more he told me, the more excited I became because he was describing something I'd recently been thinking about as well: the concept of satellite communication. The big difference between us though was that while I'd done no more than chew the idea over in my idle moments, he'd already drawn up detailed plans for a long range, high intensity signalling device that was capable of beaming a stream of data up to a receiving station orbiting the earth. He hadn't actually constructed the instrument yet, but he said he was certain that it would work. What worried him however was that space and satellite technology might not develop quickly enough for him to ever be able to put it to the test. That was when I realised I had a bargaining chip up my sleeve that could buy me a stake in moving his project forward and possibly even enable me to assume control.

'To his delight – I'm sure it was the first time I'd actually seen him smile - I was able to reassure him that the technology he'd just been referring to might not be as underdeveloped as he imagined. I said that I had a number of international contacts who had already made significant advances in the fields of rocketry and extra-terrestrial electromagnetic communication. I explained that, by international contacts, I was mainly referring to my scientist friends in the Soviet Union, though I also had links with colleagues doing similar work in the USA. I slipped in the amusing snippet about my being known as Astrred when I was at Cambridge. I told him that, if he was prepared to share the drawings and specifications for his signalling device with me, I'd be more than happy to act as an intermediary with people who might one day – hopefully within the next ten to fifteen years - be able to provide the means for it to be set to use.

'As I say, he was delighted, and he agreed to my proposition immediately. He even announced that, from now on, he would be calling his project "Astrred" in my honour.

'Now I'm sure it won't surprise you to know that I'd been passing on snippets of information to my Soviet friends for years. At first it was all fairly innocent - in the spirit of open borders and all that – and not so very different from the way I would have exchanged information with anyone else. As my political viewpoint sharpened however, it quickly became a lot more serious than that. Snippets became chunks and suddenly there was method to it: I was doing it because I wanted a different type of political system – one based on egalitarianism rather than a fixed hierarchy – to take root in my home country.'

'Are you saying you wanted the Soviet Union to take us over?'

'Not at all, that's a typical Western interpretation based on the assumption that change can only be brought about when one powerful force imposes its will on another. I'm talking about something far subtler and more effective than that.'

'But you were passing them top secret scientific information. If that isn't about giving them power over us, I don't know what is.'

'That's because, like most people, you've been conditioned to see it like that, whereas, from *my* point of view, it's simply the paradigm of international scientific co-operation, whereby ideas are allowed to flow freely; unrestricted by arbitrary territorial borders.'

'But the fact remains, you were imposing your will by passing on information subversively: that's an odd sort of paradigm, I'd say.'

'Except that, in order for the paradigm to become normalised, the scales have to be rebalanced to address the unfair advantage one side happens to have over the other. Once that's been done and equilibrium has been established, ideas will start to flow freely of their own accord and change will occur naturally from within.'

'That sounds like a pretty warped concept of freedom to me.'

'I daresay it does, but quite frankly, your ethical position on the matter is of no interest to me at all. All you need to understand is that I was in the business of sending a steady stream of information to my comrades in the Soviet Union. My problem was that it usually involved passing on dense amounts of text and data and, with the best will in the world, these are quite hard to transfer without drawing attention to what you're doing. Conventional wireless or cable technology is all right up to a point but there's always a serious risk of interception. Because of the long distances involved, complex relays are necessary, thus increasing the risk of third parties tapping into information they shouldn't see.'

'So you set about the task of finding an alternative method of communication.'

'That's right, but although the exercise was highly stimulating from an intellectual point of view, for a long time, a practical way forward seemed destined to remain the stuff of science fiction.'

'That's until Laurent Morel came along and changed everything?'

'Precisely. I knew, as soon as I saw it, that his work provided the leap forward I'd been hoping for. The rocket and satellite research were already there in the background as I've explained, but it required another element; a new ingredient to bring some much-needed impetus to it all and Morel's terrestrial based signalling technology fitted the bill exactly. Not only that, he'd progressed well beyond the plans and specifications stage and come up with a fully working prototype. I don't know how he did it because he never said but he must have had access to workshop facilities somewhere and pretty advanced ones at that.'

'Presumably at the TRE?'

'He was taking quite a risk if he did it there but it's hard to think of anywhere else round here that would have been suitable, and it had to be local really because his work schedule didn't allow him enough time to go traipsing off further afield. And he certainly used, or should I say *adapted* items that came from the TRE: alloy casings, output couplers, oscillators and such like. Morel was exceptionally clever but even he didn't have the skills to produce specialist components to the microscopically precise specifications that were required. His true genius was to take aspects of existing technology and reconstitute them so that they added up to something vastly more innovative.

'As I'm sure Morrigan told you, he essentially came up with two cylinders that could be interlocked to form a single continuous unit. Of course it would have been simpler if he'd simply produced one cylinder, but he was restricted by the dimensions of the items available to him. The TRE used casings of a length and diameter that exactly suited the capacity of the radar systems they were designed for but obviously they weren't sufficient for Morel's purpose. The solution was to adapt the ends of the cylinders so that they could be screwed together.

'When I saw the prototype for the first time - the materialisation of the Astrred project - I knew exactly where to set it up. The brass Victorian telescope, that had once been the centrepiece of Black Moon Society meetings, was still up in the turret room. Detaching it from its tripod took no time at all and soon Morel's stupendous creation was fixed there in its place, pointing at a forty-five-degree angle towards the sky. We plugged everything in and went through the transmission sequence stage by stage, right up to the point where all the gauges confirmed that we were beaming a strong and consistent signal through the atmosphere. Unfortunately though, because we were so ahead of our time, there was no silver orb up there waiting to receive it so no doubt our test message is still travelling through space, completely unheard, to this day.'

'A bit of an anti-climax then?'

'I wouldn't say that. Naturally it would have been better if we'd been able to establish communication straightaway, but most scientists accept that their biggest goals will only be achieved incrementally and, on a scale of one to ten, we knew we'd probably just notched up about five increments in one go. So, from that point of view, it felt more like a triumph rather than an anti-climax. Having said that though, once I'd informed my Soviet contacts about our exciting breakthrough, all we could really do next was wait for them to make equivalent progress on the orbiting technology side of the equation.'

'Which was likely to take a very long time indeed?'

'That's how we saw it, especially as we had the additional hindrance of a world war to contend with.'

'So what did you do?'

'The only thing we *could* do. We disconnected the cylinder and put it in storage.'

'You shut it away?'

'Yes in what *I* regarded as a perfectly secure place, here at Symbiosis House, where it could be kept until we were ready to put it to proper use.'

'But it sounds as if Morel didn't agree?'

'Oh he was all right at first but then he became more jittery about it. He said he thought the TRE had got wind of his unofficial activities and that it would only be a matter of time before they were hot on the trail of his signalling device. He was convinced that, because of his links with MWTC, this was the first place they'd come looking.'

'Could he have been right?'

'No because I'm certain I'd have been one of the first to hear if someone up the line had had suspicions about any of the people working for me.'

'And you told him that?'

'Of course I did but it didn't make the slightest difference. The idea was fixed in his head and so he insisted that we make other arrangements. That was when he came up with the bright idea of involving James.'

'Who was presumably back from Burma by now?'

'Yes, he was still recovering from the nasty bout of malaria that had almost finished him off, but he was well enough by then to be working a few hours a day at Crawford, Davies and Withers. One of the duties he took up to get him back into the flow was driving around the area, keeping an eye on the leased properties the firm had on its books. One morning he turned up at Symbiosis House at the same time as Laurent Morel. Morel was there to deliver one of his fictitious training sessions, meaning he'd really come for a tête-à-tête with me. James must have asked him his business and before long they'd struck up a conversation. James can be surprisingly affable when the fancy takes him, and Morel's Gallic moodiness must have appealed to him in a big way because from then on they were virtually inseparable which made me very nervous indeed.'

'Because you knew Morel was going to spill the beans about the Astrred Project?'

'Yes, it was obvious he was besotted with James and itching to give him some token of his trust and complete devotion.'

'Like the signalling device?'

'Precisely. And sure enough it wasn't long before he started demanding that I return it to him forthwith so that he could hand it over to James for safe keeping.'

'Did you try to talk him out of it?'

'I went through the motions, but I knew he'd made up his mind, so it was obvious I was wasting my time. Eventually I decided to take Emery Harcourt's advice and let events take their natural course.'

'So Emery was in on it as well then?'

'Oh completely, I couldn't keep him away. He suddenly found me fascinating because, thanks to my new proximity, he'd belatedly discovered that we had the same anarchic view of the world. The fascination was mutual actually.'

'So you handed the device over to James. What happened next?'

'Nothing much. Not for about five years anyway. It was a blessed relief actually because once I'd conceded to his wishes, Morel was a lot calmer.'

'What about James?'

'To be honest I rarely saw him after that. He and Morel

were fairly discreet about things after the first flush of passion had passed. The only times James and I ever came into contact were when he was operating in his official capacity as agent for the property.'

'But it must have bothered you that he'd got the signalling device.'

'Not as much as you might think. I'd reconciled myself to the fact that I wouldn't be able to make proper use of it for another decade at least so I decided that James might as well be the one taking care of it as anyone else.'

'But you didn't know where he was keeping it did you?'

'I knew it would be safe, that was the main thing. When James is given a task to perform, he's diligent about it to the point of obsession.'

'Or to the point of making it impossible for anyone to find.'

'Oh that was never a worry I can assure you; I always knew I'd be able to get my hands on it when the time came.'

'Which, presumably, it now has?'

'Almost, but unfortunately not quite. Morrigan having his brainstorm and digging up Morel's body forced us to jump sooner than we wanted to. It won't be long now though, certainly within the next six months. Did you see the report in the paper by-the-way?'

'You mean the one in The Express a couple of days ago?'

'Yes. Normally I'd be inclined to take anything the British press says with a sizeable pinch of salt, but for once I suspect they're spot on.'

'But if the Soviets are about to launch a satellite, it can't be long until the USA launches one as well.'

'You could be right, but I'm still pretty confident that the USSR will get there first.'

'All the same, isn't all this impressive scientific progress likely to make your signalling device redundant? If the Soviets are capable of sending a satellite into space, they must have devised some equally advanced communications systems to go with it. I'd have thought a couple of metal cylinders botched together using fifteen-year-old spare parts would look laughably primitive to them now.'

'You might think so, but you don't realise just how ahead of his time Morel was. I'm sure both the USSR and USA will have developed the types of systems you're referring to because without them there'd be little point in building and launching a satellite at all. They might even be better than Morel's device in some ways, but they'll have one significant disadvantage – their sheer size and consequent lack of portability. The communications equipment the USSR and the Americans have designed is so massive that it has to be mounted on steel gantries. It's just about possible to move everything around on specially built lorries but just compare that with a device small enough to mount on a conventional telescope tripod yet still capable of beaming a signal to a satellite, two hundred and fifty miles above the earth's atmosphere and much, much further if required.'

'I see.'

'That's why I've been so keen to get my hands on it again. Can you imagine how much certain people would be prepared to pay for such a thing, especially now I'm on the brink of being able to demonstrate its full potential?'

'So it's about money now is it? I thought your motivation was purely ideological.'

'My motivation has never been *pure* in any way; I can assure you of that.'

He glanced at his wristwatch which Dennis took as a clear sign that their discourse was coming to an end. Suddenly, more than at any stage during the hour or so before, it seemed essential – literally a matter of life and death – to keep Jeff engaged in conversation as long as possible. He had absolutely no idea what advantage buying extra time would bring. No-one had a clue where they were so there was little chance of rescue but if nothing else, he wanted to delay the moment when Jeff disappeared through the hatch at the top of the spiral staircase, bolting the trapdoor behind him; the point at which they would all be left there, huddled together, waiting for the inexorable torrent of water to start flowing from the Chamber Spout. Seeming to sense the dark turn his thoughts had taken, Margaret pressed hard against him. When he spoke again, it was hard to keep the quiver of emotion out of his voice.

'You said Morel calmed down after you handed the cylinders over so why did it suddenly become necessary to silence him in 1948?'

'Because he finally cracked. It was inevitable he would at some point, so it's a miracle he lasted as long as he did.'

'Why was it inevitable?'

'I've already told you how moody and paranoid he was. He was basically a wreck of a human-being who, despite his obvious genius, was riddled with self-doubt. Various things could have been at the root of it I suppose: childhood trauma; estrangement from his family and his country of birth; guilt about his sexual inclinations; a combination of all those factors or something else entirely, who can tell?'

'And when you say he cracked, what actually happened?'

'He decided to expose everyone as the liars, cheats and traitors he thought they really were.'

'*Everyone?*'

'Me, Friedman, Emery, Percy, Andrew Morrigan, Superintendent Goodall and his band of followers – oh and James of course.'

'So his relationship with James had fizzled out?'

'Oh, it had fizzled out all right, but rather than walk away and accept it, Morel decided that vengeance was required.'

'What had James done to deserve that?'

'Nothing at all as far as I know, apart from seducing him perhaps, and exploiting what he saw as a flaw in his make-up.'

'So he was issuing threats all round was he?'

'Stupidly, yes. He said he'd been complicit in their scurrilous activities for too long now and that he was going to come clean before it all caught up with him.'

'Meaning he intended to blow the whistle about Astrred?'

'About Astrred and about everything else: my political allegiances; corruption in the Malvern Constabulary; James' marital infidelity; the whole works.'

'Why get involved with him in the first place if you knew he was like this?'

'It was a gamble, pure and simple: I took the risk that the benefits of working with him would outweigh the disadvantages.'

'But, in the end, he had to be eliminated?'

'Yes. The alternative was a huge scandal and I simply couldn't allow that to happen. Eliminating him was a crude, but necessary solution.'

'But not as crude as having to kill him yourself.'

'That's true I suppose. Despite the urgency of the situation, I still managed to ensure it was managed with a certain finesse.'

'By framing James you mean?'

'Exactly. All we had to do was remind him about his little showdown with Sergeant Robards out in Burma and he was putty in our hands. He sensibly concluded that removing Morel was as much in his interest as it was in ours.'

'So you enlisted Percy Franklin and Andrew Morrigan to help him re-enact the scene in the Burmese jungle a few years before, only this time in the garden of Symbiosis House.

'That's about the size of it yes. I happened to have a Russian revolver, a Nagant, equipped with a silencing device which was perfect for the job.'

'And then Morel was buried in a shallow grave, in the garden of a house that James Crawford was the agent for.'

Jeff nodded.

'Perfect, wasn't it? No-one could come near the place without asking his permission.'

'And thanks to your cosy arrangement with Superintendent Goodall, he wasn't likely to be asked anyway.'

'As I say, it was perfect – or perhaps I should say, *almost* perfect. The one slight problem was the way my friend Friedman reacted: he had the same response to Morel's death as he'd had to Greville Jobson's in that he saw it as totally unjustified. And just like Greville's demise, it was a fait accompli by the time he got to hear about it which meant that the only option left to him was to try and dignify his memory in some way. You'll have seen the disdain with which Morel was treated in the press: almost as if he was a piece of rubbish we should be glad to be rid of. Naturally, Friedman took great exception to this and he insisted that I put some pressure on the temporary editor, Don Blackmore, to moderate the tone of the reports and add a few details that might paint Morel in a more human light. He was particularly keen for it to be made known that Morel spent some of his time looking after the Greville Jobson Science Library which of course Friedman had established through his Mitarbeit Trust. It so happens that I was already pulling strings to become the Gazette's full-time editor at that point - I felt the time had come for me to take on a respectable civilian role - so it wasn't hard for me to get the changes he wanted. Everything was plain sailing after that.'

'Until Andrew Morrigan hadn't had a change of heart.'

'Yes, it seems I underestimated him which is hard for me to accept because normally I pride myself on reading people pretty well.'

'So, when he dug Morel's body up the other day, it was a complete bolt out of the blue?'

'It was, and obviously it could have been disastrous for us if we hadn't leaped into action straightaway and brought everything back under control.'

He looked at his watch again.

'And now, barring any misguided interference from the rest of your family, you four are the only loose ends left for us to worry about.'

Dennis opened his mouth to reply, but Jeff shook his head discouragingly.

'That's it I'm afraid,' he said, a note of impatience suddenly entering his voice. 'We've spun it out long enough. There's nothing else I can usefully tell you now.

He nodded to Goodall who made straight for the spiral staircase and climbed it in three easy bounds before squeezing out through the hatch.

Jeff turned to follow, but then swung back around with a thin smile on his face as if something droll had just occurred to him.

'Just to let you know,' he said. 'We've tested everything thoroughly and I can assure you that, once all the valves have been closed, everything will be completely watertight. It takes just over an hour for the chamber to fill, so that should give you ample time to reflect on your lives and utter your fond farewells to each other.'

He started to climb the staircase, but then stopped to look down at them again.

'Oh, and one last thing Dennis,' he added. 'Just in case you were still thinking this is the long-lost Chamber Spout you've been searching for all these years, I'm sorry to have to tell you that you're wrong. The plain fact is, it's just a folly: the extravagant indulgence of a long-forgotten, Victorian tycoon. Harry Parsons knew that from the start, but he allowed his imagination to take over and by the time he finished renovating it he'd convinced himself it was the real thing. He even started to believe his own illusory drawings. He was a complete fantasist I'm afraid, which makes this place a perfect monument to his delusions – and sad to say, yours as well.'

With that he continued up the stairs and disappeared

through the hatch.

They heard a heavy thump as the trap door fell shut behind him; followed by the rasp of metal against metal as two bolts were slid into place… and then there was silence.

CHAPTER 31

Black Moon

Sunday 31st March 1957

12.01 a.m.

For a few moments they stood there in dazed silence. Then Nigel rushed forward and cleared the stairway to the mezzanine in two leaps. He bounded up the spiral staircase and used the impetus to ram the trap door with his shoulder, but it didn't budge. He cursed then tried again, but to no avail.

'Solid as a rock,' he shouted. 'The panel's been reinforced with riveted steel bands and they've obviously fitted a good strong bolt - or more likely two or three. Not surprising really. They were hardly going to stint on securing the only way out, given the rest of trouble they've gone to. Our only hope is a good old-fashioned jemmy. I don't suppose anybody's seen one of those lying around, have they?'

'No such luck,' said Dennis.

It struck him that, despite the bleakness of their situation, Nigel seemed strangely elated. He went over to the trough to see how James was.

'He's breathing all right,' he said, meeting Margaret's anxious gaze. 'But he's obviously in a bad way.'

'Should we sit him up, do you think?'

'He'll only topple over again if we do. It's not worth it.'

'We'll have to move him upstairs when they start flooding the chamber though,' said Nigel, coming back down the steps. 'And it's not going to be easy shifting a dead weight like that.

'Maybe they won't flood the chamber after all,' said Margaret. 'Maybe they were just trying to frighten us.'

'No, they intend to flood it all right,' said Dennis, grimly. 'The only reason there might be a delay is because they've got to close off the drainage channel first to stop the water escaping. They won't redirect the inflow until they've done that.'

'How would they close off the drainage channel? asked Nigel.

'From what I remember of Harry's plans there's a sliding plate built into the exit pipe, controlled by screw mechanism. I doubt if it's been used that often, so chances are it'll be a bit stiff, which is obviously good news from our point of view because it buys us more time.'

'But if this is a fake chamber, maybe the plans are fake as well,' said Margaret.

'No, I'm sure the plans are genuine enough. They were drawn up to guide the men carrying out the construction work; they weren't intended to deceive anybody.'

'Anyway,' said Nigel. 'What if that swine Stephenson was lying about it being a fake because he fancied a last twist of the knife before he went. I wouldn't put it past him, would you?'

'No I wouldn't, but in this instance, I think he was telling the truth. To be honest, he just confirmed what I already suspected.'

'How do you mean?' said Margaret.

'Something about it didn't feel right, that's all.'

'What exactly?'

'I'm not sure. I need to give it a bit more thought.'

'It's still bad news though, isn't it?'

'I'll get over it. I've had so many setbacks over the years, one more isn't going to make any difference. Anyway, all I'm bothered about now is getting out of here.'

'I'm with you on that,' said Nigel. 'But the big question is how?'

'I haven't got a clue. The only obvious escape route is via the trap door but, as you've already pointed out, we haven't got anything to force it open with.'

'What about the uprights supporting the rail at the front of the mezzanine,' said Margaret. 'Would one of those be any good?'

Dennis and Nigel craned their necks to see.

'It's possible,' said Nigel, making for the steps again. 'Let's just take a look.'

'Well spotted,' he called back from the top. 'I'd assumed they were made of wood, the same as the rail, but it turns out they're wrought iron or something like that.'

'How are they fixed?' asked Dennis.

'There are three screws, top and bottom.'

He produced a penknife from his trouser pocket.

'I'll try undoing them with this,' he said as Dennis and Margaret came up the steps to join him.

He tried turning the first screw, but the knife immediately slipped out and skittered away across the wooden floor. Cursing loudly, he retrieved it and tried again. It took him three attempts before the screw finally gave way. After numerous turns and further slippages, he finally pulled it free and started on the next one.

It took nearly fifteen minutes to withdraw the remaining five screws. He brandished the metal upright triumphantly and ran up the spiral staircase to the trap door.

Calling down he said, 'There's a slight gap between the panel and the frame; let's see if I can get some purchase.'

He pushed one end of the bar into the narrow space and pulled down hard with both hands. There was a rasp of splintering wood and, for a moment, it seemed as if the trap door might give, but then it became apparent that the bar was bending under the strain.

'Turn it round and try again,' said Dennis.

'It's too pliable,' said Nigel. 'It isn't going to work.'

'Just try anyway. Your first effort might have weakened the bolt a bit, you never know.'

Nigel made a second attempt, but this time the badly misshapen implement slipped out of position and dropped to the floor.

His cry of frustration rang out briefly before being blasted into insignificance by an explosive roar as a torrent of water started gushing from the spout. The revitalised deluge plummeted into the trough and became a maelstrom that spilt over the rim in ever increasing waves. The resulting overspill spread out across the floor in dark tentacles that wrapped themselves around James' prone body and began to form a pool that would shortly become a lake.

'Look what's happening,' shouted Dennis, pointing down into the chamber. 'We need to move him.'

He clattered down the steps with Margaret and Nigel close behind. The water was two inches deep by now and it was obvious to all of them that their only option was to carry James up to the mezzanine as quickly as possible. Nigel seized him under the armpits, Dennis grabbed his legs and Margaret took hold of the sodden clothing around his torso. On a nodded count of three from Nigel, they lifted James off the floor and staggered towards the staircase.

By the time they'd lowered him onto the mezzanine floor the flood had reached the third step with only another nine to go before it would start encroaching on them again. Out of breath after their efforts, they leant against the balustrade and listened to the water as it gushed raucously into the trough.

After a while though, the noise became less insistent and they turned around to see that the inundation was now almost level with the spout and about to engulf it completely. Seconds later, the previously thunderous roar was no more than a gentle background gurgle.

'At least we can hear ourselves think again,' said Nigel.

'Just as well,' said Dennis. 'Because if there was ever a time for clear heads, this is it.'

'How high do you reckon this place is from floor to ceiling?' asked Margaret.

'Somewhere between eighteen and twenty feet,' said Dennis.

'The water's only been flowing for ten minutes it's risen about six already. That just leaves half an hour before it fills up completely.'

'It should slow down a bit now,' said Dennis. 'It's an egg-shaped chamber, so the middle section will take slightly longer to fill. That might gain us another ten.'

'So around forty minutes,' said Nigel.

'If we're lucky, yes.'

'Surely someone will have missed us and called for help by now?' said Margaret.

'Who though? There's no-one waiting for you, Dennis or James to come home and I usually get back so late these days that Judith's stopped worrying about it. She usually goes to bed at around eleven, whether I'm there or not, and sleeps right through.'

'And who would she contact anyway?' said Dennis.

'The police of course,' said Margaret.

'But they all report to Goodall, so she'd just be wasting her breath.'

'I can't believe they're all as corrupt as he is though.'

'It's hard to tell,' said Nigel. 'To be honest, apart from Ronnie Clarke, my sergeant, I wouldn't trust any of the blighters further than I could throw them.'

'Well what about him then? said Margaret. 'Won't *he* be wondering what's happened to you?'

'I doubt it. As I explained to Dennis a few days ago, I'm a bit of a lone wolf, so Ronnie and I don't work together as much as we should. It's entirely my fault, nothing to do with him, but the truth is he'll be at home tucked up in bed by now and he won't be thinking about me at all.'

'So we really are on our own then,' said Margaret.

'I'm afraid so.'

They stood in dejected silence, gazing down at the point above the spout where the water churned as it continued to flow into the chamber. The level had now risen above the fifth step.

'I know,' said Margaret suddenly. 'What about the plans Harry Parsons gave you? Is there anything you remember from them that might help us find a way out of here?'

'Like a convenient escape hatch you mean?'

'This isn't the time to be flippant Dennis, it's a serious question.'

He thought for a moment.

'Well, there is one thing,' he said. 'But I'm not sure how useful it is. As I said a few minutes ago, I'd felt all along that something about this chamber wasn't quite right and now I realise why:

it's because, going by the plans, it's in the wrong place.'

'Why, where should it be?'

'Directly underneath the house. All my research described it as being integral to the building's foundations. But in Harry's father's plans it's shown under what's obviously a later extension.'

'How do you know it's an extension?'

'All these grand, early Victorian houses have a similar floor plan. The core of the building is basically a rectangle with stylish embellishments around the edges: bay windows, turrets and that sort of thing. As a rule, anything that extends beyond that will have been added as an afterthought, some years later. The corridor directly above us leads to a scullery that was probably built on as a laundry room or an overflow kitchen to cope with the growing needs of whoever was living there.'

'So you think the chamber was excavated when the scullery was added?'

'I'm sure it was; probably ten to fifteen years after the original house was built.'

'Meaning it really is a folly, just like Stephenson said.'

'Yes, but a very good one in that it's a remarkably accurate imitation of the real thing. I can only assume that whoever designed it had seen the same documents as me.'

'How does knowing all this help us though?'

'Not at all probably. It certainly doesn't mean it'll be any easier to escape from. After digging it out, I daresay they'll have reinforced it with concrete and then faced it with stone. It might not be as resilient as solid rock, but you'd need some pretty hefty tools to make a hole in it. Even then, breaking through layers of stone, concrete and compacted earth would probably take days.'

'So presumably this isn't a real spring either?' said Margaret.

'No, I imagine they diverted the course of a stream so that it fed into here along a culvert or pipe.'

'And they built in those valves and gauges that Jeff mentioned, to control the flow.'

'Exactly. In fact that's another reason I was sceptical about the place: it didn't seem natural enough. Even allowing for the legendary ingenuity of Victorians, I couldn't see how anyone could exercise so much control over a spring that was meant to emerge straight from Precambrian granite.'

'It's a shame we can't control it from in here then.'

'I agree, but unfortunately all the regulators are up in that little room, beyond the trap door.'

Another silence descended, broken only by the sounds of churning water from below. The water was now level with the seventh step.

Then Dennis jolted to attention as a thought came to him.

'There is one thing we might be able to reach though,' he said.

'What?' said Margaret and Nigel simultaneously.

'I'm fairly sure one of the drawings showed an overflow pipe, level with the spout. It will have been there to prevent the house from flooding if the main outlet ever got blocked.'

'But when they shut off the main outlet, they'll have shut the overflow off as well,' said Nigel. 'Otherwise the water would have stopped rising ages ago.'

'I know, but my point is they'll have found overflow pipe a lot trickier to shut off than the main drainage pipe.'

'Why?'

'Because no-one in their right mind would fit an overflow with a control-valve, would they? It's meant to stay open all the time, otherwise there'd be no point in it. Therefore, in order to seal it off, they'll have been forced to improvise.'

'By blocking it with cement or something? Is that what you mean?'

'Yes, except I doubt if they'll have used cement because it won't have had time to set properly.'

'Why not?'

'Things have been happening quickly for them since Morrigan dug up Morel's body, so they won't have thought about bringing us here until fairly recently. Rather than use cement they've probably plugged the pipe with an old blanket or something like that. Any sort of material that expands as it gets wet. With luck they'll have pushed it in from this end rather than the other so that, with a bit of brute force, we might be able to pull it out and let the overflow get back to doing what it's supposed to do.'

'It sounds like a hell of a long-shot to me.'

'Have you got a better idea?'

'No,' said Nigel, with a sigh. 'I haven't.'

He gestured at the swirling water which, by now, was only four steps below the top of the stairway.

'I suppose it means one of us is going to have to dive in there doesn't it?'

'It'll have to be you I'm afraid,' said Dennis. 'I can't swim remember.'

'Of course, they wouldn't let you learn because of your weak chest. Can *you* swim?' he added, turning to look at Margaret.

'Yes, I've even got badges to prove it. Why, would you rather I went in?'

'No, it's all right,' he said, glancing back at the ever-rising water. 'But if I don't come up again within three minutes you'll have to come and rescue me.'

Margaret smiled at him. 'Be careful, it's going to be dreadfully cold in there.'

'After the initial shock I expect I'll be too numb to notice.'

He stripped down to his underpants and placed his clothes

on a step, hallway up the spiral staircase.

'All right,' he said, already shivering. 'Where do you reckon this pipe's going to be?'

Dennis pointed at a point on the wall, just above the turbulence caused by the submerged spout.

'Can you see that slightly darker patch of rock?'

'Yes.'

'The outlet should be about three or four feet down from there.

'Right,' said Nigel, 'let's give it a try.'

He descended the four steps of the wooden staircase that were still visible, hesitated for a moment and then took the plunge crying out as the freezing water engulfed his upper body. For a moment he seemed paralysed by the shock, but then he kicked out and swam to the spot Dennis had indicated.

'Is this it?' he called back.

'I'm pretty sure it is, yes.'

He took a deep breath, arched his back and dived under. Dennis, Margaret leaned on the rail and watched his ghost-like form flexing and turning, just below the surface.

After about a minute, he re-emerged in a cascade of spray.

'No good I'm afraid,' he said, gulping for air. 'I've looked all around, but I can't find it anywhere.'

'Blast,' exclaimed Dennis. 'I could have sworn that was the right spot?'

He closed his eyes and tried to concentrate.

Then he said, 'Are you up to giving it another try?'

'Yes, but what's the point? I'll only come back with the same answer.'

'Not if you widen your search slightly.'

'But you said it would be there.'

'I must have got it wrong. I only saw the drawing a couple of times, so it's amazing I remember anything really.'

'You seemed pretty sure to me.'

'I was, and I still think that's what it showed, but maybe I was interpreting it too literally. I doubt if anyone gave two hoots about where the overflow went really; just a mundane consideration that would have been left to the site foreman decide.'

'So it could be anywhere then?'

'No, it'll definitely be on the outer side of the chamber, furthest from the house, where the water can easily drain away. Putting it anywhere else would require installing a pipe under the floor, which no-one in their right mind would do if they could avoid it. That means it's got to be somewhere in the vicinity of the spout, so you just need to extend your search a couple of yards further in each direction.'

'All right,' said Nigel. 'Here goes.'

He took a deep breath, only to release it again straightaway.

'What's the matter?' said Dennis

'Look where the water's got to.'

Dennis and Margaret turned to see that it had now reached the top step and was about to spill over onto the mezzanine itself.

'We need to move James back a few feet and lean him against the wall,' said Dennis. 'If we leave him lying where he is, he'll drown in seconds.'

'Sorry, but you'll have to do it by yourselves,' said Nigel. 'I need to concentrate on finding that outlet before the place fills up completely.'

Without further ado, he took a deep breath and dived.

Dennis and Margaret immediately seized James under the armpits and dragged him across the platform. The water was already an inch deep all around them and the floorboards were slippery underfoot, making progress even harder.

They'd just managed to prop him up against the wall when Nigel reappeared in a burst of foam. He swam to the gap in the balustrade at the top of the, now submerged, stairway and climbed, dripping, onto the platform. His skin had a bluish tinge and he was shivering violently.

'I've found the outlet,' he said. 'You were right, it was just a few feet away from where I was looking before. Whatever they used to block it has been wedged into the narrow space like a cork in a bottle. I could just touch it with the tip of my finger, but I need that iron bar I was using earlier to reach in a bit further. Can you remember where it went?'

'It landed down here somewhere,' replied Dennis, feeling around in the icy water at the foot of the spiral staircase. 'Yes, here it is.' He retrieved the makeshift tool and handed it over. 'But look how bent it is. Will it be any good?'

'It's going to have to be.'

He turned and launched himself off again, paddling with his left hand and holding the iron bar above his head with his right. Then, for the third time, he took a gulp of air and ducked under.

Looking round, Dennis was horrified to see that the water was now level with James' chin and Margaret was straining to raise him into a more upright position before it reached his mouth.

'He keeps sliding under,' she called out. 'I desperately need some help here.'

Dennis waded over and took hold of James' other arm.

'All right,' he said. 'Let's try and haul him up together.'

They both pulled hard, but it barely made any difference.

'He seems heavier,' exclaimed Margaret. 'It must be because of the water that's soaked into his clothes.'

'We're also running out of energy.'

At that moment, Nigel burst to the surface and swam to the gap in the half-submerged balustrade. He waded over to them through waist deep water. He was no longer carrying the iron bar.

'What are you doing?' he said.

'Trying to stop James drowning,' replied Dennis.

'He's still not responding then?'

'Not at all.'

'Have you checked his pulse recently?'

'No.'

'Well before you strain yourselves any further I think you should because he looks like a goner from where I'm standing.'

They both stared at him, aghast.

'You think he's dead?' said Margaret.

'I do, yes.'

Nigel reached down and pressed two fingers against the side of James' neck. He held them there for a few seconds, then he looked at Dennis and Margaret, shaking his head.

'Nothing there,' he said. 'I was right.'

'But how?' cried Dennis. 'He was definitely breathing earlier.'

'He was in a bad way, you said so yourself.'

'I didn't think he was *that* bad.'

'Well he obviously was.'

'No pulse at all?' said Margaret, tears streaming down her cheeks. 'You're sure about that?'

'Completely sure, but by all means feel for yourself if it helps put your mind at rest.'

She shook her head and looked down at James as the water started to lap around his mouth.

'It's so sad,' she said. 'Whatever he'd done, he didn't deserve to die like this.'

'Maybe not,' said Nigel. 'But at the risk of sounding callous we need to put it behind us and move on to more pressing matters. The main one being that, despite my strenuous efforts, that overflow is still blocked.'

'So the iron bar was no help?' said Dennis.

'None at all,' said Nigel, his teeth starting to chatter violently. 'It was too bent to be of any use, especially in such a narrow pipe.'

'You're freezing,' exclaimed Margaret. 'You need to put something on before you catch your death.'

She grabbed his jacket and passed it to him.

'Interestingly though,' he added as he pulled it on with shaking hands. 'I've discovered that his place is even more phoney than you thought.'

'How's that?' asked Dennis.

'On closer inspection these supposedly rock-faced walls are actually just rough cement, painted a sort of granite grey. And the cement isn't particularly resilient either: it's already been washed away in a few places to reveal the bricks behind. It's like a stage set at the Festival Theatre: real enough on the face of it but go behind the scenes and you see it for what it really is.'

'A complete illusion.'

'Exactly.'

'But still pretty solid,' said Margaret. 'Too solid for *us* to break through anyway.'

'Unless...' said Dennis distractedly.

'Unless what?'

'I found a photograph of the chamber in one of the notebooks which, at first glance, appeared to confirm everything I'd already seen in Harry's father's drawings. Looking more closely though, I realised there was one essential difference: in the drawings, the trough was shown to the right of where we are now, but in the photograph, it was over to the left. At the time I assumed it was because the photo had been printed in reverse by mistake, but what if it wasn't a mistake and it was actually showed a different chamber altogether? What if it was a photograph of the *real* chamber?

'That sounds like wishful thinking to me,' said Nigel. 'But even if it isn't and you're right, how could it possibly help us now?'

'Because of something else I've remembered: in the photograph there was a ladder fixed to the wall opposite the trough. I presumed it had been put there temporarily, to help the men carrying out the renovation to reach the upper part of the chamber, but that was when I still thought I was looking at the structure depicted in the drawings.'

'And what do you think now?'

'I think it might have been there to provide access to the fake chamber from the real chamber and vice-versa.'

'Are you seriously suggesting the real chamber's next to this one?'

'Yes.'

'So why bother building a replica then?'

'I don't know. Maybe the real chamber became unstable, or the natural spring dried up, or rising damp started causing problems in the main house. There could be any number of reasons. My guess is that Matthew Parsons, Harry's father, was contracted to seal off the old chamber and replace it with the new version. The fact that none of this has come to light until now suggests that he was under strict instructions to keep quiet about what he was doing in order to preserve the mystique surrounding the place. The thing is though, I suspect Matthew didn't feel happy about sealing the place off *too* securely, so he built a secret connection between the two chambers in order to preserve the possibility of opening it up again at a later date. That'll be why he installed the ladder.'

'You think the ladder led up to a doorway of some sort?'

'Yes.'

'But why not put it at floor level and save himself a lot of trouble?'

'Who knows? Maybe the structure was weaker higher up and easier to break through.'

'So what you're saying is, if we could locate the doorway on this side, it might turn out to be the convenient escape hatch you were so scornful about earlier?'

'That's the theory.'

'And what if that's all this is – a theory?'

'We won't know until we've tried, will we?'

'In which case we'd better get a move on,' interjected Margaret, who, by now, had backed halfway up the spiral staircase to avoid the rising flood. Just in case you hadn't noticed, the water's now up to your shoulders. I suggest you join me up here while we decide exactly what we're going to do.'

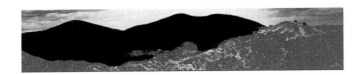

CHAPTER 32
Last Resorts
Sunday 31 March 1957
12.50 a.m.

Dennis and Nigel hauled themselves onto the staircase while Margaret moved further up to give them space. Her head was now barely two feet below the ceiling of the chamber.

'Margaret's right,' said Nigel. He was shivering so hard that the words came out in breathless spurts. 'We're running out of time. This passageway is our last hope; we need to find it straightaway.'

'That might be easier said than done though.'

'But surely you can work out roughly where it is.'

'Well, as I said, in the photo the ladder was against the wall of the chamber opposite the trough which, because everything in the original chamber is the reverse of what we've got in here, means the entrance to the passageway should be over to our left; slightly above the balustrade rail and a bit further out.'

'How *much* further out?' asked Margaret.

'A couple of feet maybe; certainly no more than a yard.'

He indicated a point on the wall that was only seconds away from being covered by the rising water.

A sudden fizzing noise from behind made them all turn around. Simultaneously, the light in the chamber dimmed and then brightened again and Dennis was reminded of his train journey under the hills; appreciating properly, for the first time, the terror Harry must have felt at the prospect of being stranded, deep underground, in total darkness.

'It looks as if the water's got into the electrics,' said Dennis. 'Chances are they'll conk out completely in a minute.'

Amidst more fizzing, the bulb faded and recovered itself twice in quick succession.

'I think I just saw something,' proclaimed Margaret.

'Where?' said Dennis and Nigel together.

'I was concentrating on that section of the wall again. I thought it might be the last chance to look before the light went out completely. There's definitely some sort of irregularity in it.'

'I can't see anything,' said Dennis, peering at the same spot.

'Watch carefully the next time the bulb falters – provided it comes back on again of course – and then you'll see. It must be the sudden contrast between dark and light that makes it more noticeable.'

Dennis and Nigel stood shivering while they waited. Dennis thought he now knew exactly what people meant by the phrase, "frozen to the core". The relentless chill of the water was working its way through his body, breaking down its resistance layer by layer and fast approaching the point at which, like the glow from the ailing light bulb, it would extinguish the last flickering spark of life forever.

As if responding to his thoughts, the bulb dimmed again. The near darkness lasted much longer this time and it seemed as if the electrics had finally failed, but then, like the houselights coming on in a theatre auditorium, the glow slowly returned. Moments before it reached full strength, he saw the irregularity Margaret had been referring to: a vaguely arch-shaped outline, about a yard wide and three or four inches above the surface of the water; a slight darkening, on the concrete's surface where paint had recently been washed away by the encroaching ripples.

'Yes, now I see what you mean,' he called out.'

'I don't,' exclaimed Nigel. 'It just looks like a blank wall to me.'

'I didn't see it that time either,' said Margaret.

'It looked like the top of a doorway,' said Dennis. 'But it was gone in a second, so I'm not surprised you missed it.'

'And you really think it could be the entrance to the passageway?'

'I certainly hope so. The only thing is though, there's still the small matter of breaking through whatever it was they used to seal it up.'

'But it'll only be a thin layer, won't it?'

'Not thin enough for us to shift it with just our bare hands.'

'What if we use this,' said Nigel, reaching down to retrieve something from the flooded step he was standing on. He straightened up again, brandishing the iron bar they'd salvaged earlier.

'You kept it then,' exclaimed Margaret.

'Of course I did. I know it hasn't been much use so far, but it's the only thing resembling a tool we've got. In fact the bend in it might work in our favour this time because we'll be able to swing it like an axe to chip away at the mortar.'

'You could be right,' said Dennis. 'Let's give it a try.'

'That's my cue to dive into the murky depths again I suppose,' said Nigel

'I might be able to help you this time actually. The doorway is right next to the end of the balustrade. The rail will only be a few inches below the surface, so I should be able to grab hold of it fairly easily if you tow me over there.'

'But I've just had a terrible thought,' said Margaret, 'Even if you do manage to open up the passageway, the water's just going to flow through into the other chamber, and before we know it the level's going to be just as high in there as it is in here.'

Dennis shook his head. 'You're forgetting that the other chamber will have an overflow drainage channel just like this one. Provided it's clear, which hopefully it will be, the water will be able to escape through that. It might back up a bit at first because of the sheer volume but it should work its way through after a while.'

'Let's just hope you're right,' said Nigel, wriggling out of his dripping jacket as he lowered himself into the water. He looked back at Dennis and said, 'You might as well ditch yours as well. You'll find it a lot easier to move around without all that heavy tweed weighing you down.'

Dennis shed his jacket and let it fall onto the surface alongside Nigel's. Spread out there together the abandoned garments resembled two drowned men, floating face down. Dismissing the unwelcome image from his mind, he stepped down into the water and seized Nigel's left arm.

'Here we go,' said Nigel as he propelled them in the general direction of the submerged balustrade with Dennis letting his free hand drag below the surface, ready to grab hold of the rail as soon as they reached it.

'Got it,' he called out after they'd travelled a few feet through the water.

He let go of Nigel and gripped the top of the balustrade with both hands. Nigel took hold of it as well and they both moved sideways, using the rail to guide them over to the wall.

'Look,' said Nigel, 'the outline's quite clear when you get up close.'

'It is,' agreed Dennis, 'If you give me the bar, I'll make a start and then you can take over.'

But before Nigel could respond, the light faded again and then went out completely.

'I think the electricity's finally packed up.' Margaret called out quaveringly.

'We'll just have to carry on in the dark then,' said Nigel.

'Not necessarily,' said Dennis. 'I've got a small torch in

my trouser pocket for when I'm peering into dark crevices for hidden springs. Let me just try and grab hold of it.'

Retaining his grip on the rail with one hand he twisted and turned until he'd found what he was looking for. He flicked a switch and a bright white beam shone out across the water.

'Thank goodness for that,' exclaimed Nigel. 'I'm amazed it still works.'

'It's made of rubber, so it's meant to be waterproof,' replied Dennis. 'Even so, I'm just as amazed you are.'

'If you pass it to me I'll give you the iron bar so that you can make a start.'

'After they'd made the exchange, Dennis turned to face the wall with the makeshift tool in his spare hand. He raised it and made a lunge with all the force he could muster, but only managed to graze the surface. He tried again but the result was little better.'

'It's hopeless,' he said. 'I'm hardly making any impression at all.'

'It's because you're not attacking it from the right angle,' said Nigel. 'You need to be striking from above, so that you've got gravity on your side and you can use the full force of your upper body.'

'But how can I do that without letting go of the rail?'

'If I moved closer, I could probably hook my feet around the balustrade supports. Then, if I grabbed you around the knees, you'd be able stand up on the rail and take advantage of the extra height it gives you.'

'I'm frightened I'll go under.'

'No you won't. Just let me get into position and then I'll be able to support you.'

He swam alongside and then, having kicked his legs a few times to locate the balustrade, gave a confirmatory nod.

'Are you sure this is going to work?' asked Dennis, nervously.

'Of course. Just pass me the iron bar for a second, then

you'll have both hands free to press down on my shoulders and lift yourself up.'

Much to his relief, Dennis soon had both feet firmly planted on the rail. He took possession of the tool again while Nigel seized him around the knees. He took a swing at the wall and was delighted to see a large chunk of concrete immediately break away and drop into the water with splash.

'You were right,' he cried out triumphantly. 'Coming at it from higher up makes all the difference.'

He repeated the action and this time an even bigger chunk broke off. After five further blows, a new layer, beneath the concrete, started to become visible.

He paused while Nigel shone the torch into a jagged-edged hole in the wall, approximately two feet in diameter.

'Wooden boards,' said Nigel. 'If you could prise a couple of those apart it would *really* speed things up.'

'They're fixed too tightly though. There's nothing to latch onto.'

'Try making a hole between them and then you can hook the bar through it to apply some pressure. A few more solid blows should do it.'

Dennis raised the tool above his head again. This time he aimed directly at the groove between two intersecting planks and managed to detach a wedge-shaped lump of wood which ricocheted away and landed on the water where it bobbed around on the surface like a toy boat.

'Nearly,' said Nigel. 'Go for the same spot again and see if it gives way.'

Dennis took aim and struck. This time one of the boards split apart. The resulting crack was two inches wide and stretched upwards for about a foot and a half. More importantly though, it plainly extended below the water line as well because a strong eddy was flowing sinuously through the opening and into the space beyond.

'I think we're finally getting somewhere,' he shouted to Margaret. 'The boards have given way and it looks as if the water's started spilling over from here into the other chamber. It's only a trickle at the moment but it's a good start.'

'You need to keep going though,' said Nigel. 'Try and make a bigger hole.'

Dennis nodded and pushed the end of the bar through the gap he'd created. Using it as a lever he pushed forward as hard as he could, so as to apply pressure to the front and back of the barrier simultaneously. Almost immediately there was a loud crack followed by a tearing sound and both boards fell away, taking a lot of the surrounding concrete with them. The sudden lack of resistance made Dennis lose his balance and he would have toppled into the water if Nigel hadn't tightened his grip just in time to stop him. Once they'd steadied themselves they saw that what had previously only been a trickle through the opening was now a swirling rush and that a much bigger area of woodwork had been exposed.

'Well done,' said Nigel. 'I'll take over now, if you like.'

'You'd better have this then,' said Dennis, offering him the iron bar.

'No, I want to give something else a try before I use that. Let's lower you back into the water and then I'll explain.'

Once he'd got a tight hold on the rail again, Dennis tucked the iron bar under his left arm and took the torch from his brother with his free hand.

'All right,' he said, 'What's your plan?'

'Actually,' replied Nigel, 'Rather than waste time explaining, I think I'll just show you.'

With one kick, he propelled himself over to the long thin hole that Dennis had made in the woodwork and seized the rough edge of boards on its left with both hands. Then, after gathering his strength for a moment, he rammed his shoulder against the boards on the other side. The result was instant and devastating: a huge area of panelling caved in to reveal one half of the arched entrance. The water coursed through in a torrent and, within seconds, the level in the chamber had dropped sufficiently to reveal a brick ledge at the opening's base on which Nigel was now able to stand. He immediately reached up and used the top of the arch to steady himself while he kicked the remaining boards out of the way with two solid, sideways kicks.

The rate of flow through to the other chamber gradually slowed as the depth on their side began to draw level with the bottom of the archway. Now that the whole opening had been exposed, they could see that it was about five feet high, from base to apex, and approximately four feet wide.

Hearing Margaret splashing towards him through the inch or so of water still covering the platform, Dennis swung the torch round to light her way. She stopped in her tracks as the beam picked out a dark hump-like shape on the floor in front of her.

'It's James,' she said, stifling a sob. 'What are we going to do with him? We can't just leave him here.'

'We haven't got much choice I'm afraid,' said Dennis.

'He's right,' said Nigel, 'We'll worry about James later, when we're out of here. But, for now, we need to concentrate on getting you two over here, so that we can move into the other chamber. Are you all right to swim across Margaret?'

'Yes,' she murmured distractedly, still staring at James' body. Then, apparently regaining her composure, she looked up and said, 'But I'd better take my skirt off first, so that it doesn't weigh me down.'

After removing it, she bundled it up and threw it over to Nigel.

'No time for modesty in an emergency,' she said, matter-of-factly as she went to the gap in the balustrade. She stepped down into the water, gasping as the coldness hit her, then swam the short distance along the front of the mezzanine, passing Dennis on the way, and climbed onto the ledge to join Nigel.

'That was easy,' she said, pulling her skirt on again.

'What about me?' said Dennis.

He was still holding onto the rail but perched on the

outside of the balustrade with the retreating flood lapping around his feet.

'You're close enough for us to haul you across,' said Nigel. 'Just pass me the iron bar and the torch, then you can lower yourself into the water and we'll reach out and grab your hands.'

Seconds later, the three of them were huddled together on the ledge, looking back at the inundated chamber from which they'd had such a narrow escape.

'I'm surprised the water's still so high,' said Margaret. 'Look, it's flowing over our feet even now.'

'That's because it's being topped up by the inflow,' said Dennis. 'Water's continuing to pour into the fake chamber at the same rate as it's going out.'

He took the torch from Nigel.

'So let's take a look at what's on the other side, shall we?' he said, swinging around.

'What can you see?' said Nigel.

'Almost a mirror image of where we've just been, but far more worn and natural-looking. You can tell straight-away that you're looking at the real thing rather than a pale imitation. It's truly remarkable.'

'Is there a way down?' asked Margaret.

'Yes, there's a ladder fixed to the wall, just as it was in the photo. I'll start down it now, then you'll be able to move forward and see for yourselves. By the way, you'll need to be prepared to start paddling again when you get down into the chamber. Although the overflow outlet's doing its best, there's obviously a bit of a backlog. Anyway, here I go.'

'Mind what you're doing,' said Margaret. 'Make sure the ladder's secure before you put your full weight on it.'

'It seems solid enough,' said Dennis as he tested one of the rungs with his foot. 'Yes, I'm sure it's all right.'

Holding on with his right hand and clutching the torch in his left, he climbed halfway down and then called to Margaret.

'I'll wait here, just below, in case you lose your footing.'

'I'll be fine thanks; I've always been pretty good on ladders. Some of the upper shelves in the college library are just as high as this I can tell you.'

'It's not the height that bothers me; I'm more concerned about how slippery the rungs are after the dousing they've just had.'

'All right,' said Margaret as she eased herself over the edge. 'I'll be careful.'

Soon they were both standing on the floor of the chamber, up to their knees in water again. Dennis kept the torch shining on the ladder while Nigel made his way down to join them.

'I take it there's a platform in here just like next door,' said Nigel, peering past Dennis, into the gloom.

'Yes, look,' said Dennis, turning to face the same way and pointing the torch beam upwards. 'As you can see, it's lower than the other one; a couple of feet lower than the entrance we've just come through in fact, and rather than being made of wood, this one's formed from a natural ledge in the rock with stone steps leading up to it.'

'Very impressive,' said Nigel, 'so can we get up there now please? I've had as much wading around in icy water as I can take.'

'Just let me take a quick look at the spout first, I want to check …'

'No Dennis,' snapped Margaret, simultaneously gripping his arm to restrain him. 'You're not doing anything of the sort; we're going to do exactly as Nigel says.'

She took the torch from him and, without a further word, set off across the chamber. Dennis and Nigel followed meekly behind as she led them through the knee-deep water, then up the uneven steps and onto the ledge. The rock platform was about three yards from end to end but its uneven shape meant that it ranged from six feet wide at some points along its length to as little as three at others. But, just as in the replica chamber, a spiral staircase at the rear of the ledge provided access to a trap door, set into the ceiling, above.

'It's a bit crude compared with where we've just been isn't it,' said Nigel as he took in their surroundings.

'Precisely. That's because whoever first discovered it was content to utilise its natural features without feeling the need to enhance them in any way. The only embellishments that I can see are the stone trough and the swan's neck spout.'

'Which look exactly the same as next door,' said Margaret, pointing the torch downwards to illuminate the centrepiece of the chamber.

'I'd still like a closer look though. Just give me the torch will you, it'll only take a minute.'

'No,' snapped Nigel. 'Leave it for another time. We need to try and get this trap door open before we all finally freeze to death.'

He started up the ladder, brandishing the iron bar.

'I hate to sound defeatist,' Dennis shouted after him. 'But I can't imagine this is going to work any better than it did last time. Also, I've got a nasty feeling that there might be more to contend with here than just a trap door.'

'Oh no,' exclaimed Margaret. 'You think a floor's been laid over it don't you?'

'I'm afraid so, yes. After all, if you'd gone to all the trouble of having the old chamber closed off, why would you draw attention to its existence by leaving the original trap door in place?'

'Well let's not give up quite yet,' said Nigel, calling down from the top of the ladder. 'There's a nice gap here to slot into so I should be able to get some leverage on it, here goes.'

At that moment, there was a loud rumbling from the other side of the chamber. They all swung round to see what was happening, including Nigel who let go of the steel bar in the process, so that it fell onto the ledge below with a clank. Margaret swept the torch beam across the opposite wall and around the opening they'd recently come through, trying to identify the source of the disturbance.

'I can't see anything,' she said. 'It must have come from next door.'

'You could be right,' said Dennis, 'noise travels easily along that passageway and it probably gets amplified in there as well. I don't like it though; it sounded structural; as if a wall was shifting or something.'

'A wall shifting?' said Nigel. 'I shouldn't think so; everything looks pretty solid down here to me.'

'I'm not sure it's as solid as it appears to be,' said Dennis. 'The other chamber isn't much more than a brick shell. It wasn't designed to bear the weight of all that water pressing against it.'

'That won't be a problem in here though will it?' said Margaret. 'I thought you said this place was carved out of solid rock?'

'I'm sure most of it is but that doesn't mean there won't be weak points in it, especially if it was damaged when they dug out the cellar, prior to installing the fake chamber.'

'Do you think that's what happened?' said Nigel.

'It's a possibility isn't it? Let's just hope I'm wrong.'

He bent down to retrieve the steel bar.

'You'd better give it another go,' he said as he passed it back up to Nigel.

Nigel repositioned the end of the tool and pulled down hard with both hands.

'This isn't getting us anywhere,' he cried out exasperatedly. 'All I've managed to do is straighten the bar again.'

'Give it another try,' said Dennis, with far more conviction than he felt. 'Maybe you've weakened it and it'll give way next time.'

'I doubt it,' said Nigel, pushing the tool into the gap again, 'but, in the absence of any other options, let's see what happens.'

He braced himself before pulling down on the bar with

all his strength. As before, his efforts had no effect at all from returning the metal to its previous misshapen state.

'What now?' said Nigel in a tone of utter defeat as he looked down at them.

'How about using it like an axe,' said Dennis, 'the same way we did on the wooden partition?'

'You have a go,' said Nigel, coming down the staircase. 'I'm completely whacked.'

Dennis took the bar from him and had just put his foot on the first step when another burst of rumbling made him freeze. The noise was much louder this time.

'Oh my goodness, look what's happening,' Margaret exclaimed as she focused the torch on the opposite side of the chamber, 'I think it's starting to break open.'

They all watched as she moved it around an area, just below and slightly to the left of the opening. A jagged line had appeared in the rock and water was seeping through all along its length.

'You were right,' said Nigel, 'the weight of the water must have caused the structure on the other side to collapse and now the wall in here is giving way as well.'

'There was probably a weakness in it already,' said Dennis. 'In some places the rock will just be held together by compounded earth which the water can easily soak through. The more it gets dissolved, the more unstable the chamber's going to become.'

'Do you think it's going to fall in?' said Margaret.

'I don't know but I certainly don't intend to stay here to find out.'

He ran to the top of the spiral staircase and swung the metal bar at the centre of the trap door. A few splinters of wood broke away but when Margaret shone the torch on the area of impact, it was depressingly clear that the damage had only been superficial. He immediately aimed another swing at the same spot but, once again, with minimal effect.

'It's hopeless,' he cried out.

'Have a rest for a minute,' said Margaret. 'Take some deep breaths and then try again.'

He shook his head. 'It won't make any difference. I might as well be flailing at it with a bendy twig for all the good I'm doing.'

'Just try anyway.'

He paused for a moment before smashing the bar against the trap door for a third time, then a fourth and then again and again repeatedly until, on finally running out of steam and seeing that he'd achieved little apart from scarring the surface of the wood, simply gave up and retreated down the staircase.

He'd just reached the bottom when the rumbling started again. This time it was loud enough to make the whole chamber vibrate. He dropped the iron bar in alarm and, as he did so, the whole of the opposite wall burst open and, as if in slow motion, a swirling black tidal wave came rolling towards them.

CHAPTER 33
Chain Reactions
Sunday 31 March 1957
1.50 a.m.

'Watch out,' yelled Dennis, just before the deluge hit him full in the face, sweeping him off his feet and tossing him backwards. For a few seconds he couldn't tell where he was and then, with a bruising jolt, his right shoulder collided with the chamber wall. He reached out wildly for the staircase banister and felt what seemed like many other hands, trying to do the same. Locating it at last, he held on tightly, trying to ignore the searing pain in his shoulder and then, as suddenly as it had arrived, the tidal wave subsided.

After taking in a deep draught of air, he looked around frantically, trying to work out where the other two were. Then he realised that the only reason he could still see anything was because Margaret had somehow managed to keep hold of the torch and she and Nigel were clinging to the staircase next to him; their strained expressions reflecting his own dismay at what had just happened.

'I thought that was it for a minute,' exclaimed Nigel. 'Where's all the water gone?'

'Nowhere, it's just found its level again,' replied Dennis. 'The initial surge hit us as it breached the wall, but it's settled in the bottom of the chamber now. In effect, the flood we were contending with before has now got twice the volume of space to occupy, so fortunately it's only going to be half as deep.'

Margaret pointed the torch over the edge of the platform and the beam glinted on the dark water just below. Then she raised it so that they could see the damage to the chamber wall. The narrow opening they'd passed through only minutes before had been displaced by a jagged fissure that extended six or seven feet either side of where the little archway had once been and well below the surface too, so that the two chambers were now linked by a narrow channel of inky water. The ladder had been torn away by the force of the wave and was now bobbing around like an abandoned rowing boat on the newly enlarged subterranean lake.

'The trouble is,' continued Dennis, 'I think the rock fall has probably blocked the escape channel on this side which means the level is likely to keep rising. It'll obviously be slower than before, but it still doesn't leave us much time to get out of here.'

'So, what are we going to do?' asked Nigel.

'I honestly don't know. It seems to me we've run out of options, unless either of you have got any bright ideas.'

They stood in gloomy silence, watching the ellipse of light from the torch playing on the opposite wall.

Then a trundling sound overhead, made them all look up.

'What was that?' exclaimed Margaret.

There was more trundling accompanied by the clump of heavy footsteps.

'There's someone up there.'

'You're right, there is,' said Dennis.

'In which case, we need to attract their attention,' said Nigel. 'You're in better shape than us two, Margaret, so why don't you go up and knock on the trap door as hard as you can? Better still,' he added, handing her the iron bar, 'Use this.'

'But what if it's Jeff and the rest of them?'

'No, I'm sure they'll be long gone by now. Anyway, even if it is them, the worst they can do is turn a deaf ear.'

'That's true. All right I'll give it a try.'

She turned and made her way up the spiral staircase. As soon as she reached the top, she raised the bar above her head and banged it against the trap door repeatedly. For over a minute a series of sharp raps ricocheted around the chamber like gunshots, then she took a short rest before starting again. After three further bouts she stopped completely.

'They aren't taking any notice,' she called down, her voice breathless from exertion. 'Maybe the thickness of the floor is preventing the sound from getting through.'

'But we could hear *them* remember,' said Dennis, 'So I'm sure more sound's getting through than you think. Just keep trying.'

She raised the iron bar, ready to continue, but then she froze.

'Did you hear that? It was a sort of grating sound, directly overhead. Listen, there it is again.'

'That sounds like heavy stones being moved to me,' said Dennis.

'Stones?' said Nigel.

'Big flagstones.'

'You think they're lifting the floor?'

'Probably.'

There was more grating, followed by a series of substantial thumps.

'It sounds as if they're dropping them down somewhere else or leaning them against the wall,' said Dennis. 'Hopefully that means they'll be able to get to work on the trap door.'

No sooner had he said it than they heard the crack of metal on wood, directly overhead.

'I reckon they're using a pickaxe,' said Nigel.

'That should make short work of it,' said Dennis.

'As long as they don't bring the whole chamber down

on our heads in the process,' said Margaret.

A small crack appeared, through which they could see light. It grew wider and wider as the pickaxe came down repeatedly on the surrounding area, breaking through the trap door and showering the staircase with chunks of wood. Margaret withdrew to re-join Dennis and Nigel on the platform. The three of them watched as even larger pieces of wood started to rain down and then the panel disintegrated completely. There was a clatter as the pickaxe fell to the floor and then a pair of silhouettes appeared in the rectangular opening.

'Are you all right down there?' a man's voice called to them.

Margaret shone the torch upwards and in the split second before both figures recoiled from the glare, Dennis was able to identify them as the two policemen he'd last seen - seemingly a lifetime ago - in Hereford.

'Inspector Gwilliam and Sergeant Bowen,' he exclaimed.

'At your service,' replied Gwilliam, 'And it looks as if we've arrived in the nick of time.'

***

'Look at you all, you're completely drenched,' exclaimed Bowen as, one by one, they emerged into the light of three paraffin lamps that had been arranged on the floor behind him.

'And half frozen to death as well I should think,' said Gwilliam. 'Take one of the lamps and go and find something for them to wrap up in, will you Sergeant?

'There were some old coats hanging on the stand, just inside the front door,' said Bowen. 'I'll go and grab a few. Back in a jiffy.'

He dashed off and returned, seconds later, with an assortment of mackintoshes and overcoats.

As he pulled on a musty-smelling, double-breasted overcoat, Dennis saw that they were in a corner of the main entrance hall. He had a side-on view of the grand staircase and the entrance to the scullery corridor was over to his left. Four large flagstones lay haphazardly on the floor, along with the pickaxe that had been used to dislodge them.

'Where's James Crawford?' said Gwilliam. 'We thought he'd be down there with you, but we must have got that wrong.'

'He was,' said Dennis, 'But unfortunately he died. He was in a bad way from the start, so he never really stood a chance.'

'Sorry to hear that.'

Yes, it's a real shame,' said Bowen. 'Once we've finished here, we'll arrange to have his body brought up.'

'There'd have been three more bodies to bring up if you hadn't arrived when you did,' said Margaret. 'How on earth did you work out where we were?'

'Because they've got a talent for it,' said Nigel.

'What do you mean?'

'This isn't the first time they've come to my rescue. We served together in northern France at the end of the war. It was an extremely nasty situation and it all got a bit much for me. I hate to think how I'd have ended up if they hadn't turned up when they did.'

'Don't worry,' said Gwilliam. 'You'd have done the same for us if the situation had been reversed.'

'Probably, but it doesn't make up for the fact that I behaved abominably after you helped *me* out. I'm not trying to excuse myself, but the truth is I hated the fact that I'd shown weakness, so I just tried to pretend it had never happened.'

'That's why you've been avoiding us all these years, isn't it?' said Bowen. 'And why you ignored all our letters and phone calls about the Regiment reunions.'

'It is and I can't begin to tell you how sorry I am for having been such a vain, pig-headed idiot.'

'That's all right,' said Gwilliam. 'It's all in the past now.'

'Not quite, I need to say a proper thank you first. Thank

you for everything you did for me twelve years ago and thank you for what you've done for the three of us tonight. Words can't begin to express our gratitude.'

He went to shake Gwilliam's hand, then changed his mind and embraced him instead. After a few seconds he turned to Bowen and did the same.

'Well,' said Gwilliam, looking askance at Dennis and Margaret. 'What a touching scene? How can we possibly follow that?'

'By answering a few questions hopefully,' said Dennis.

'No problem at all, but wouldn't you rather leave it until you've had a chance to take a hot bath and put on some dry clothes?'

'No, I'd rather talk now, provided that's all right with Margaret and Nigel.'

They both nodded.

'Fair enough, but we can't do it standing here. Let's go somewhere a bit more comfortable.'

Gwilliam led the way across the hallway and into the dining room. He and Bowen pulled dustsheets off the table and chairs and then they all sat down.

'Right,' he said, 'What do you want to know?'

'Lots of things,' replied Dennis, 'But let's start with the men responsible for all this: do you know what's happened to them?'

'I understand a number of them have been apprehended. As I'll explain properly in a minute, we had a couple of back-up cars with us when we came over from Hereford and the officers in those concentrated on rounding up anyone making a break for it while Sergeant Bowen and I came in search of you.'

'Do you know any names? Were they able to arrest the ringleaders for instance?'

'I take it you mean Goodall and Co.'

Dennis nodded.

'No, it's too early for that sort of detail I'm afraid. All I know is what I heard over the police car radio about twenty minutes ago: a brief message saying that they'd detained a number of men attempting to leave the property and that more information would follow.'

'And when will that be, do you think?'

'I don't know. It depends how talkative these characters are under pressure. I'll get on the radio again later and see how it's going.'

'You still haven't told us how you knew where we were,' said Nigel. 'In fact, I'm not even clear what prompted you to come looking for us in the first place.'

'Let's go back to the beginning then,' said Gwilliam. It all started about forty minutes after we packed your late brother-in law, James Crawford, off to see that psychiatrist friend of Dennis' at Powick Hospital, Dr Gajak.'

'Who, it turns out, might not have been quite the pillar of the medical establishment you thought he was,' interjected Bowen

'Yes, sorry about that,' said Dennis. 'He completely took me in I'm afraid. When did *you* start to suspect him?'

'When we received a report saying that the car carrying James Crawford had been intercepted at Wynds Point, at around nine-twenty p.m. and James had been forcibly transferred to another vehicle and driven away.'

'Of course, we didn't know for certain that Gajak had had anything to do with it,' said Gwilliam, 'But later, when we questioned Dr Crowther, who'd been looking after James at the police station and had accompanied him in the car, he told us that the only person he'd spoken to about bringing James over was Gajak himself.'

'That'll be because I gave him a direct number to avoid having to go through the hospital switchboard.'

'I expect so, yes. It also seems that, during the same telephone conversation, Gajak stressed that he was only taking James on as a personal favour to you and he wouldn't be saying anything to the hospital authorities because it would just complicate matters.'

'Meaning he wouldn't want Dr Crowther to say anything either.'

'Exactly,' said Bowen. 'He's a cunning chap your Dr Gajak.'

'Except he *isn't* Dr Gajak,' said Dennis. He's Mathias Friedman. He's one of the men responsible for all this'

'What are you talking about? Friedman died years ago.'

'But he didn't, that's the point. He just switched identities and successfully fooled everyone, including me.'

'Why, for goodness sake?'

'It's too complicated to explain at the moment. 'You were in the middle of telling us about the business at Wynds Point.'

'That's right, we'd had a call from Malvern saying they'd received a report of an incident up there, during which a middle-aged man, thought to be James Crawford, had been abducted: one of our vehicles had been badly damaged; and the two remaining occupants, Dr Crowther and PC Bentley, had been left stranded at the scene. By Malvern's standards it was quite a detailed message, so we assumed they were going to be co-operative for a change. However, when we got to Wynds Point, the two local PCs who met us there turned out to be about as talkative as a couple of Trappist monks.'

'We knew what had happened straightaway,' said Bowen, 'Our old foe, Superintendent "Bad'n" Goodall, had stepped in and instructed all his officers to keep schtum.'

'That's the problem with Malvern you see,' said Gwilliam. 'They'll be perfectly helpful one minute and then, for no apparent reason, they'll shut you out.'

'Except *we* know the real reason is that Goodall's put the fear of God into them,' said Bowen. 'You remember me telling you about Dan Yates, don't you?' he added, turning to Dennis.

'The sergeant who transferred to Hereford after falling out with Goodall.'

'That's him.'

'I remember Yates,' said Nigel. 'He died soon after he moved, didn't he?'

'Yes, he was out on point duty and got killed in a hit and run.'

'Strange isn't it?' said Gwilliam. 'That someone who'd openly crossed Goodall and seemingly got away with it should then die in unexplained circumstances, shortly afterwards.'

'Put like that, I suppose it is.'

'You'd think twice about speaking out of turn if you knew his reach extended that far, wouldn't you?' said Bowen.

'You're right,' said Nigel. 'It explains a lot.'

'So, we sent the two PCs packing,' said Gwilliam. 'We knew they weren't going to be any use to us, and they were obviously itching to go anyway.'

'They didn't mind leaving you in charge of the scene then?'

'Not at all. The way they saw things, it had been *our* car and *our* people involved and now we'd turned up to sort it out. It wasn't their problem anymore.'

'But there'd been a kidnapping on their patch; they couldn't just ignore that surely?'

'Oh, they made all the right noises about finding the people responsible, but we knew they didn't mean any of it.'

'Anyway, once they'd made themselves scarce, we finally had a chance to talk to PC Bentley and Dr Crowther,' said Bowen. 'They both remembered a black saloon coming alongside as if about to overtake and then swing closer to try and force them off the road. Bentley said he'd desperately tried to keep a straight course, but within seconds they'd been shunted sideways into a ditch and the car had slid to a halt on its belly. Almost immediately, two men had appeared. They'd dragged James out through the rear door, frog-marched him over to their waiting vehicle, and then driven off towards Malvern at top speed.'

'I don't suppose they caught sight of either of the men's faces, did they?' asked Nigel.

'No, they said it all happened too quickly; everything was just a blur.'

'So, what did you do next?'

'We radioed for a pick-up lorry to come and tow the damaged police car away, then we drove Crowther and Bentley back to Hereford.'

'By the time we got back, it was the end of our shift,' said Gwilliam. 'But the incident at Wynds Point was still preying on our minds and we knew we wouldn't be able to let it lie. After pacing around for ten minutes, we decided to go ask our boss, Superintendent Morris, if we could go back over to Malvern to sniff around a bit.'

'He wasn't keen at first,' said Bowen. 'He said it was none of our business and we'd just end up causing trouble. But after we'd explained our concerns and jogged his memory about Dan Yates and the other shady things Goodall's been associated with over the years, he started to warm to the idea.'

'The fact is, he's always detested the man,' said Gwilliam. 'He thinks he's a disgrace to the Force. He doesn't broadcast it, especially at work, but we happen to be cousins, so he's a lot more forthcoming where I'm concerned.'

'Anyway,' continued Bowen, 'Once he'd come around, he asked us what our plan was, which immediately put us on the spot because we hadn't really thought it through. Seeing we were a bit flummoxed, he suggested that the best course of action might be to drive over Malvern, park on the outskirts and listen in to the radio communications between the mobile patrols. He said we all knew how much gossip took place over the airwaves during a quiet shift, so what better way of finding out what was really going on than to earwig on all that? As it was a quiet night, he offered to deploy a couple of additional cars to set up in different locations and do the same. That way, we'd be able to monitor all the short-wave traffic and alert each other on a prearranged channel if anything significant came up.'

'So that's what we did,' said Gwilliam. 'We set off for Malvern in convoy at a quarter to midnight. As we were driving down the hill towards Little Malvern, I tuned in to a new frequency, and suddenly, instead of the wall of static we'd been picking up before, we heard the stentorian tones of Superintendent "Bad'n" Goodall. We'd only met him once before, but he must have made a big impression on us because we recognised his voice straightaway.'

'There happened to be a pull-in just ahead,' said Bowen, 'So, I stopped there before we lost the signal. As you can imagine, it's a bit hit and miss around here because of the hills.

'We wound down the window,' continued Gwilliam, 'And the four men who'd stopped behind us in the other cars gathered around to listen in. Goodall sounded furious. He mentioned Symbiosis House a few times and we managed to ascertain that he was sitting in a car outside, talking to a man parked nearby, but out of view. It became apparent that they were waiting for a signal or message of some sort and getting more and more impatient because it hadn't come.'

'Having established their whereabouts,' said Bowen, 'We decided to carry on and regroup once we'd got nearer. We kept listening as we drove along, still trying to get a sense of what they might be up to. And then, after carrying on in the same vein for a bit, Goodall lost his cool completely and yelled, "How long does it take to drown four people for heaven's sake? It's over an hour now since they started filling that bloody chamber, so what the hell's keeping them?" The shock of it nearly made me swerve off the road.'

'We were amazed he'd be so indiscreet over the radio, but I suppose that's a mark of his arrogance,' said Gwilliam. 'He's had things sewn up in Malvern for such a long time, he thinks he's untouchable.'

'By now, we were approaching Malvern Wells,' continued Bowen, 'So we pulled in again at the first opportunity and briefed the others on what we'd just heard. We assumed that one of the four he was talking about must be James Crawford, but at that point it didn't occur to us that you three might be involved. All we knew was that we had to act quickly: there was still a chance we could save the people being drowned and even if we couldn't, it was vital that we round up Goodall and the other perpetrators before they got away. Ideally, of course, we hoped to do both.'

'We checked the map,' said Gwilliam, 'And saw that Symbiosis House was substantial enough to be named and that it was located about a quarter of a mile further down the road, on the left.'

'We set off again,' said Bowen, 'And then, just short of what looked like the gateway, we switched off our engines and headlights and coasted to a stop. I got out for a quick recce and saw the glow of a cigarette, fifty yards or so up the drive. Now I knew where the second bloke – the one Goodall had been ranting on to – must be parked. Then, the flash of a match, followed by the glow of another cigarette, told me that a second person was waiting there as well. I went straight back to discuss tactics with the others, but while we were talking, events suddenly took their own course. First one car and then a second came roaring down the drive with headlamps blazing. They both took a sharp left at the bottom and sped off along the road towards Great Malvern. Inspector Gwilliam immediately sent our backup men off in hot pursuit while we drove up here to face the sorry scene, we feared would be waiting for us.'

'The front door was open, so we went straight in,' said Gwilliam, 'And after a bit of toing and froing, we finally managed to locate the trap door in the corridor beyond the entrance hall. But it was double padlocked and as solid as a rock and we knew straightaway that we'd never be able to open it with our bare hands. Then it occurred to us that there must be a tool shed, somewhere on the premises. We rushed back outside and, sure enough, around to the rear of the house, we found a workshop stuffed full of hand tools and garden implements. We gathered all the bits and pieces we needed, loaded them into an old wheelbarrow and trundled back through the house to start work.

'We'd just grabbed a couple of crowbars to try and break open the padlocks,' continued Bowen, 'When we heard a loud rapping noise coming from the entrance hall. It turned out the noise was coming from underneath the floor, near the main staircase, so we immediately started using the crowbars to prise up the flagstones. Once we'd revealed the other trap door, underneath, we used pickaxes to smash through - and the rest you know.'

'Well, all we can do is thank you again,' said Margaret. 'I dread to think what would have happened if you hadn't got to us when you did.'

She shivered and pulled the overcoat more tightly around her.

'This is ridiculous,' said Gwilliam. 'You're all completely frozen. We need to get you somewhere warmer right away.'

'Only after you've radioed for an update from your other men,' said Dennis. 'I need to be sure that everyone responsible has been rounded up.'

'All right,' sighed the Inspector, 'I'll do it now. But after that, I'm going to insist on taking you all home.'

After he'd left the room, they heard the front door creak open and slam shut and then the muffled crunch of his footsteps as he made his way across the gravel to the car.

'Right,' said Bowen, as if keen to avoid what might turn into an awkward silence. 'Ever since we came in here, I've had a funny feeling that one of these dustsheets might be hiding a handy drinks cabinet. I think it's time I had a shufty, don't you?'

He got up and pulled sheets off various items of furniture around the room. After uncovering a sideboard, three small tables and a bookshelf, he gave a whoop of satisfaction as he found what he was looking for.

'Just what the doctor ordered,' he exclaimed, holding a bottle of brandy aloft, like a trophy.

He placed it on the table while he located four glasses and then he poured them all a generous measure.

'Warms the cockles of the heart, doesn't it?' he said as they took their first sips.

'I'm amazed it's still here,' said Nigel.

'I'm not,' said Dennis. 'It was probably on one of James' inventories when he took over as agent for the house, so woe betide anyone who interfered with it. You know how pernickety he was.'

'Poor James,' said Margaret, sadly.

They all nodded as they drank their brandy and listened to the urgent sounding but unintelligible radio exchange that was taking place outside.

A few minutes later, it stopped and then they heard the crunch of Gwilliam's boots on the gravel as he came back to the house.

'So, what's the news?' Dennis asked anxiously as the Inspector sat down at the table again and took the glass of brandy that Bowen had just poured for him.

'Very good, I think,' said Gwilliam. 'They managed to catch up with them pretty quickly, and then gave them a taste of their own medicine by forcing them off the road at a place where buses pull in, just before you get to Great Malvern.'

'And have you got the names of the men they arrested?'

'Yes, they knew three of them straightaway – that's Superintendent Goodall and a couple of his dodgy colleagues, Bates and Collins – simply because they're from a neighbouring force and, inevitably, there'd been previous occasions when their paths had crossed. There were two more they didn't know, but they *did* recognise their car - a Standard Vanguard in two-tone silver and grey – because they'd stopped it once before, in Hereford. Apparently, that was because a similar vehicle had been stolen in the area and the patrols had been told to keep an eye open for it. It hadn't been the one they were looking for, but they remembered it because it had a police radio console on the dashboard, which the occupants had explained away as being just a replica they'd fitted for a bit of fun.'

'They're Percy and Clarry Franklin,' said Dennis distractedly.

'Who?'

'Percy was James' assistant at Crawford, Davies and Withers, but they both work for Goodall. There were three others though; have you got any information about them?'

'Which three others?'

'We've already talked about one of them: Mathias Friedman; alias Dr Gajak. The other two are Jeff Stephenson and Emery Harcourt.'

'Sorry,' said Gwilliam. 'None of those names came up.'

'But they must have done, they're the ones behind it all,' said Dennis, banging the table in exasperation.

'I thought Goodall was behind it all.'

'No, Goodall's just part of it.'

'Well, that's news to me. Why didn't you mention any of this earlier?'

'I told you about Friedman, didn't I?'

'Only that he'd been fooling everyone by pretending to be someone else. I realised he was mixed up in the abduction business at Wynds Point, but I assumed he was just another cog in the wheel of Goodall's shady outfit.'

'So,' said Bowen, 'Apart from Friedman; Gajak or whatever his name is, who are these people?'

'Jeff Stephenson's my editor on the Malvern Gazette but years ago, during the war; he was in charge of a communications training centre here at Symbiosis House. He's a dedicated communist and he used this place as a cover for developing a highly advanced signalling device which he now intends to pass on to the Soviet Union. Emery Harcourt was a friend of Mathias Friedman, the original owner of Symbiosis House and...'

He sighed and slumped back in his chair.

'Sorry, I just don't have the energy to explain.'

'But if you'd told us all this yesterday, when we were over in Hereford, we'd have known what we were dealing with and there might have been a different outcome.'

'Except I *couldn't* tell you yesterday because I didn't know. The only reason it's come to light now is because Jeff Stephenson felt a sadistic need to put the record straight before he left us to drown in the chamber. That's what was taking so long earlier, and why Goodall was getting so impatient. I expect Jeff, Friedman and Harcourt had another vehicle tucked away somewhere; a Land Rover maybe, so that they could drive out through the woods to the side of the property and make their way down to the road without being seen.'

'They can't have got far though, can they?' said Gwilliam. 'Just give me their descriptions and I'll get on the radio straightaway.'

'There's no point,' said Dennis, shaking his head despondently. 'They've done this sort of thing before; it's just a case of history repeating itself. Believe me, they'll be long gone by now.'

EPILOGUE

Saturday 12th October 1957

11.45 a.m.

Dennis and Margaret walked up the path through the woods that led to St Ann's Well. Dennis was pushing his father in the wheelchair so their progress was much slower than usual. Charles Powell sat erect in the chair and was apparently alert, but stared ahead, saying nothing.

'Do you want me to take over for a while?' said Margaret as they rounded a sharp bend.

'No, it's all right,' said Dennis, 'I'm sure the exercise is doing me good and it's not far now anyway is it?'

They paused for breath by an ancient oak; its trunk was gnarled and scarred, and it had deep hollows where a mouth and eyes might be. They always called it the Green Man.

'How are you doing Mr Powell?' said Margaret. 'It isn't too bumpy for you is it?'

There was no reply.

When they got to St Ann's Well, Dennis went into the café while Margaret positioned the wheelchair next to one of the outdoor tables.

Dennis brought their drinks out on a tray. He set down a cup of tea and a packet of digestive biscuits in front of Charles and then he and Margaret adjourned to a table on the terrace, higher up the slope, with their coffees.

'This doesn't seem right,' said Margaret, as she took a first sip from her cup. 'Shouldn't we be sitting with him?'

'I don't see why. He obviously doesn't want to talk to us, and I feel as if I've already gone beyond the call of duty by bringing him up here at all.'

'Maybe the stroke has made it more difficult for him to talk than we think.'

'Nonsense, he's forever having cosy tête-à-têtes with Nigel, so his speech doesn't seem to be much of a problem for him then. He assumes nobody hears him, but Mum and I do. She gets quite upset about it actually because, these days, he doesn't talk to her any more than he does to me. No, the silence is just an act. Maybe this wheelchair business is as well. For all we know, he's running up and down the stairs and doing handstands and cartwheels in the garden whenever he thinks our heads are turned.'

'You're being cruel now,' she said, wagging her finger at him.

'No crueller than he's been to me for most of my life. I know it seems petty, but I don't feel I owe him much. I don't mind wheeling him out from time to time, to give Mum a break, but that's about it really. Anyway, I've just bought him tea and digestive biscuits, haven't I? What more do you want?'

'What about Nigel? How are you getting on with him these days?'

'Not too bad I suppose, but he's busier than ever since he was promoted to Superintendent, so I hardly ever see him anyway, and neither do Judith and the girls.'

'Putting a stop to Goodall changed everything didn't it.'

'Yes, they went through Malvern Constabulary like a dose of salts and Nigel's come out of it smelling like roses.'

'You're mixing your metaphors there Dennis.'

'No, I'm mixing my *similes* actually.'

'All right Mr Pedantic, your similes then. Talking of pedants, how's Julian getting on? Have his editorial skills improved at all recently?'

'He's a lot more decisive these days, so going to press isn't quite the race against time as it was when he first took over. But he's only acting editor at the moment of course, so there's no guarantee it'll be a permanent appointment.'

'I still think it should have been you Dennis.'

'I know you do,' he said, giving her hand a squeeze.

'And it isn't too late is it? If they don't appoint Julian, they might offer it to you instead.'

'No, they won't. They're more likely to bring in some young hot shot; someone like the late, lamented Whippet. I don't want it anyway. I'm quite happy as a roving reporter and one good thing about Julian is that he gives me a lot more leeway than I used to have.'

'That's because he needs you there to lean on.'

'Perhaps he does, but it's always good to be needed isn't it?'

He paused to take a sip of coffee and then he said, 'actually Julian gave me something interesting yesterday. Something very interesting indeed. It's the reason I wanted us to come up here, so that I could show you, away from prying eyes.'

He produced a large, rolled-up envelope from his overcoat pocket and pulled out its contents: a folded newspaper and two separate sheets of foolscap. He spread the newspaper out on the table. Margaret gasped as soon as she saw what it was.

'Pravda,' she said.

'That's right, the official newspaper of the Communist Party of The Soviet Union. It's dated 5th October and the front page is devoted to covering the launch of Sputnik, the first satellite to go into space.'

'The same as it was with all our newspapers, a week ago.'

'Exactly, but the language Pravda uses to mark the event is slightly more celebratory than the way most of our papers described it. There's something in there about it showing how "the freed and conscientious labour of the people of the new socialist society makes the most daring dreams of mankind a reality". I don't recall the Daily Express putting it quite like that do you?'

'So, where did this come from? How did Julian get hold of it?'

'For goodness sake,' he retorted. 'Isn't it obvious?'

'Oh, of course, I see,' she said, nodding her head as the penny dropped. 'Jeff Stephenson sent it didn't he.'

'Yes, all the way from Moscow I assume.'

'And how did it get here? Surely it didn't just come in the post?'

'I don't know, Julian didn't say. To be honest, he was pretty cagey about the whole business. He just handed it to me and said, "You might be interested in this when you've got a minute to spare. I suggest you take it down to your unofficial desk in the cellar to open it though, don't do it in the main office".'

Margaret leaned forward to look at the front page more closely.

'I can just about make out the word Sputnik, 'she said, 'but the rest of it doesn't make any sense to me. How do *you* know what it says? You don't speak Russian, do you?'

'There's a very helpful, typewritten translation with it,' he said, sliding one of the separate sheets over to her. 'But even more interesting than that, there's this.'

He passed her the second sheet.'

Margaret perused it, shaking her head in amazement.

'" Greetings from the USSR,"' she read aloud. 'And there's a little drawing underneath: a stick man, standing on the earth pointing something that looks like a torch at a sphere overhead. The beam is reflecting off the sphere down to another stick man on the opposite side of the earth.'

She looked up at Dennis again.

'So, the signalling device he and Morel designed all those years ago, is finally up and running. That's what he's telling us isn't it?

'He's gloating. He's pulled off his big plan against the odds and there's nothing any of us can do about it.'

They sat in thoughtful silence as Margaret studied the typewritten translation and Dennis flicked through the smudgy pages of the newspaper.

After a while Margaret looked up and peered down the slope towards the table where Charles was sitting.

'Someone's talking to your father,' she said.

Dennis followed her gaze and saw that an elderly man wearing a trilby and a dark overcoat was leaning over the wheelchair, speaking into his father's ear.

'What's going on do you think?' asked Margaret.

'I'm not sure,' said Dennis. 'We'd better go and see.'

They gathered up their papers and stood up. By now, the man was moving away down the path that led back to town. Then he stopped to look back and they were momentarily transfixed by the gaze from his pale, cornflower blue eyes before he turned and moved on again.

Charles twisted round in his seat to look up at them as they approached. His face was ashen, and his eyes seemed to be burning with fear.

'Good grief, you look as if you've just seen a ghost,' said Dennis. 'Who on earth was it?'

'Emery Harcourt.' The words came out as a gurgling exhalation.

'And what did he say?'

'"Beware, your time is near, the black moon is calling you."' He slumped back in his chair, staring wretchedly into space.

Dennis and Margaret looked down the hill just in time to see the elderly man in the trilby and dark overcoat turn and give them a valedictory wave before melting away into the trees.

FOR FURTHER INFORMATION...

Black Moon Over Malvern is also available as a Kindle ebook:

https://amzn.to/3gWl3zI

For further information about Rob Kail-Dyke and for news about the forthcoming sequel to this book, Hell At High Water, please go to black-moons.com

Twitter @robkdyke_author

Printed in Great Britain
by Amazon